Testing the Heart

Testing the Heart

Melva Michaelian
and Lorene Morin

Writing as
Isabel Barry

Library of Congress Control Number: 2010909885
ISBN: Hardcover   978-1-4535-3302-4
                 Softcover   978-1-4535-3301-7
                 E-book   978-1-4535-3303-1

To order additional copies of this book, contact:
Xlibris Corporation
1-888-795-4274
www.Xlibris.com
Orders@Xlibris.com
74502

DEDICATION

We'd like to dedicate this book to all the teachers out there who may not realize the important role they play in the lives of others. What they say and do today ripples into tomorrow's promise for countless individuals. We also want to pay tribute to the many talented students who have given us the desire to fight for their right to learn in ways that make sense to them.

We also want to dedicate this to the memory of Richard Morin, who encouraged us to finish this work and promote its message.

ACKNOWLEDGEMENTS

W e wish to thank all who helped to make this book possible. Several very important people helped in the process of gathering information and editing various sections of the story. The appreciation we extend to Michele Barker, Anna Bowling, Carol Munro, Mary Ellen O'Connor, and especially Phyllis Desilets, is immeasurable. We also would like to give credit to Mary Anne O'Connor and Bernie Hamilton for contributing their artistic talents.

We owe a heartfelt debt of gratitude to our families and friends as well for their patience and understanding while we worked on this story.

PROLOGUE

June

"Shit," he muttered as he pressed his hand to his belly.

He attempted to staunch the ooze of red that dripped onto the cobbled pavement in the dark space between the two vacant apartment buildings. His shoulder leaned heavily against the grimy brick of the Stanford Arms, a fancy name for a structure on the verge of collapse. No one had lived in the "Arms" in five years. No one could help him. At first he had not felt the pain as the knife had slid into his gut. He had stood there astonished as the weapon had been retracted, and his body had jerked with the invasion and retreat of the sharp object. He should have expected the assault, but he had become too cocky, too negligent.

He chided himself for his stupidity as his knees gave out, and he began his descent to the garbage littered pathway. The stench became more pronounced the closer he got to the ground. He slid by fractions of inches and realized with certainty that he would probably die here, alone, terrified. Well, he had chosen to be by himself, and here he was. The pain began to push its way into his consciousness.

"Son of a bitch," he spewed through gritted teeth. He struggled to get up and take a few steps out of the shadows and into the main street, now deserted. His feet would not advance under the pressure of his weakened knees and throbbing body.

He emitted a gurgling half laugh when his ass landed with a painful bump onto the waiting walkway. He knew he would never be able to get up again. He heard a distant string of melodies wending through the dark recesses of the ally as he grasped the edge of an overturned trashcan so that he could hold his upper body above the rank compost. Where was the music coming from? He heard it more and more clearly now. He raised his head to listen more intently to the strains as dark shutters began to close on his vision. Abruptly, the music stopped.

CHAPTER 1

The previous September

Four uniformed police officers lined the back wall of the cafeteria like sentinels in a war zone. Penelope Parsons felt a foreboding overcome her as she arrived at the opening teachers' meeting. The dawn of a headache began to throb behind her eyes as she contemplated the possible reasons for the presence of these burly men in a school that was not even in session yet. *They must have chosen these specimens for their breadth and muscle tone*, she thought. The ordinary pre-meeting sounds distracted her from the police presence, however. All around her she heard the normal grumblings and conversation of the day before school opening.

"Where are the damn doughnuts? There used to be doughnuts," croaked a husky fifty-something, balding gentleman near her in tan Bermuda shorts and a turquoise and white striped polo.

"What's the matter? Didn't you hear about the budget cuts?" a less mature man with a crew cut asked as he hefted a waxed bag with a single sugared donut nestled in the bottom. "You bring your own now," he stated, shaking the little white bag in front of the complainer.

Penelope had heard it all before. After ten years, she had an extreme case of déjà vu. She widened her enormous, alert gray eyes and perused the room, nodding to colleagues she had not seen since the beginning of summer. Her chestnut hair was pulled into a ponytail as a concession to the heat. She blushed under her light makeup when she noticed some of the male members of the faculty stealing glances at the casually sensual image she unintentionally projected. Her denim capris and white tee emphasized her well proportioned figure. These, plus her classic features, were more than enough to make the opposite gender take a second, and even third, look in her direction. She always felt uncomfortable under their scrutinizing gazes.

I've got other things to think about, she thought as she lifted the brown envelope with her name on the front.

The noise in the room started with a hum, escalated to a thrum, and culminated in a throb of voices. Summer garbed men and women of all shapes and ages swarmed around the tall chrome coffeepot although the temperature of the room was a semi-tropical eighty-five degrees. Penelope could not even contemplate coffee as she fanned herself with the envelope. The long, picnic type tables were lined up in precision across the wide cafeteria, and the mostly middle-aged men and women carefully bore their cardboard cups to the tables, wrestling with the manila envelopes they also carried. The conversation consisted of polite inquiries about how the summer had fared, casual commentaries about the humid weather, and complaining about the new schedules and lack of pastries to accompany the swill-like coffee.

Penelope neatly extracted the sheaf of paper and scanned through the printed sheets to determine if there was anything new. It appeared to be the same packet of papers she had received for the last ten Septembers. The only thing that seemed different was the date on the cover sheet. She mentally readied herself for the annual gospel reading. She knew that the principal would be reciting these pages to his faculty once more as if to make certain they had not forgotten any of the rules and regulations that were spottily enforced throughout the year.

The papers almost dropped to the floor when she read the new rules and addendums that had been tacked on to the back of the old list. Courses had been dropped, extra teacher duties were scheduled and additional math and English courses had been added over the summer. Scripted lesson plans geared to the state test were also included in the parcel. She exhaled indignantly as she surmised that these were to ensure that every core subject instructor would be on the same page at the same time, disregarding student ability and learning style. These changes were adopted as an attempt to appease state demands and the federal mission to leave no child behind. Of course, success of the program would only be measured by boosting the sagging state test scores. "Teach to the test," seemed the new mantra.

She breathed out a long, discouraged sigh and pondered the impact on students who were already struggling with the present curriculum. She could already see their eyes glaze over and the corners of their mouths start to drool. These new courses had replaced such popular offerings as photo studio, industrial arts, and home economics. Thank God chorus and art had not been touched. They seemed to be the last arts left standing.

She caught a glimpse of the sun reflected off the bit of metal that peeked beneath the holsters at one of the patrolmen's belts, a reminder that there were probably more important agendas today. Other faculty busied themselves looking over the materials in their packets, but she could see that they, too, frequently glanced up to the steadfast policemen at the front of the room.

As she examined the supplementary pages, she discovered that all math and English teachers would be teaching at least one extra remedial class on top of their regular schedules. Thirty more students a day would definitely affect her teaching style. How would all the individual attention she showered on each student be impacted? She couldn't continue reading the damning document.

Penelope uncharacteristically slammed the packet on the table. She thought, *as usual, they put these changes in over the summer and without any input from the teachers.* Once again, teachers were only the soldiers in the war against ignorance. Unfortunately, some of the officers in the battle had never even been in the classroom.

She looked around the stuffy cafeteria again and noticed that the teachers had once more clumped themselves into cliques. The chatter seemed to be instigated by the police presence and the new regulations, and nobody was happy about the changes.

School would be officially in session tomorrow, and the faculty seemed even less eager to begin than the students. Her face reddened, her eyes narrowed, Penelope was pondering the issue of how she would adjust to the dictates as Marci Wickers, the administrative assistant to the principal, lunged through the throng with a smiling woman in her early twenties. Marci was a petite woman with a bubble of light hair that made her look several inches taller.

"Your intern, Miss Parsons," she intoned breathlessly, as she deposited the young woman at the table.

Penelope signaled the practice teacher to a chair beside her. "Why don't you sit down? The meeting will begin in a few minutes, and then I'll show you around and answer any questions you might have."

"Do you know where Claire is?" Marci asked. "I've got two more student teachers to drop off, one English and one history."

She shook her head abruptly, as if to clear her mind of the complication that had arisen. She looked to a point several yards away at a table surrounded by English Department members.

"There's Claire now. See you later." She departed in the same cloud of energy in which she had arrived, chugging toward a woman in her sixties. The two hapless novices, one male and one female, trudged along in her wake.

Penelope watched from across several tables as Claire Harvey's gray and black head was bent over her packet as if she had never seen any of the text before. She scanned the words diligently. If there was a rule or policy change, Penelope knew Claire wanted to be aware of it. Claire felt that ignorance of the law was no excuse. A regulation watchdog from the old school, she had been taught that education was a disciplined profession that worked well when everyone obeyed authority and all were respectful of each other's individuality and talent.

Penelope contemplated how the changes inserted in this year's packet would be greeted by Claire. She respected this teacher who had once taught her and inspired her to enter teaching. As if on cue, the older woman's head popped up, wide eyed, in shock. Penelope caught her attention, shrugged her shoulders, and shook her head in empathy.

*   *   *

Marci materialized at Claire's elbow with an ethereal lass whose long, gauzy skirt floated breezily around her well-shaped, braceleted ankles. Claire gasped, almost inaudibly. This facsimile of a flower child of the sixties oddly reminded her of her own youthful, carefree days, filled with optimism and new teaching ideas. Over the years, she had changed her style and outlook, adopted the lessons that worked, and became a disciplined force in the classroom. She felt she was an effective and respected instructor after all her years of experience. This young woman, however, seemed to be a ghost of her youth.

Her reverie lifted as Claire remembered that the student teachers were to arrive today. She had hoped their grand entrance would be tomorrow, postponing the inevitable awkward first moments. Claire simply was not certain what to say to someone who was just beginning a career in education, especially in light of the new and unyielding requirements. Her first reaction was to shout, "Turn back. Save yourself while you still can."

She still loved teaching, she reminded herself. The guidance counselors and the administration kept telling her she was a successful educator and a valuable resource.

Secretly she had always felt that the profession had limited her chances for a fulfilling private life as an author. Writing was a demanding job, and the preparation of lessons and the endless correcting of papers had sapped the energy she needed to finish the several manuscripts she had already started on her summers off. This year's additional classes and new demands would now destroy any chance she thought she had for completing those unedited romance novels piling up in her closet.

*   *   *

Penelope gazed at her practice teacher, a young woman with large brown Bambi eyes that glance away as her future mentor looked up at her. Some of her sand colored hair drooped over one shoulder, and the rest splattered over her upper back in a nondescript style that did little to enhance her very standard facial features. Her nose was straight, but small, and her mouth seemed a slight slash of some neutral lipstick that might have been clear gloss.

"I'm Christie Edwards. We talked on the phone in the spring," she said in a barely audible murmur.

"Of course. Sit down."

She was saved from having to create a "welcome to teaching" speech when Principal Benjamin Bradford, a formidable man in a gray suit, blue shirt, and pin-striped tie, tentatively tapped the microphone with his index finger. The gesture was partly to test the sound system and partly to catch the attention of his audience. It failed on both levels when the light tap sent the mic flying to the floor. Bradford, beads of nervous sweat trickling down his face, looked helplessly toward the custodian standing by the door. George, the head maintenance man, jumped to the rescue, turning the amplifier off before scooping the mic from the floor. Efficiently replacing the apparatus securely and revving the amps, he gave the principal a ceremonious "thumbs up." Taking a small bow, he assumed his position next to the door. Principal Bradford, dubbed B. B. the King by his detractors, wiped his face with a handkerchief and coughed roughly into the mic. The audience, including Penelope, responded by giving him their undivided attention.

"I want to welcome you all back to Skinner High, where each graduation is a success story. This year will be the best yet, and with your help, we will again navigate our educational vessel to home port. As we say, we don't wait for our ship to come in, we take the wheel and steer it right up to the dock because we value our cargo, those young minds waiting to be cultivated." No one dared to groan or snicker, but there was a concerted effort to stem the tide of derision. Penelope had to give the man credit for saying something that dramatic in front of a large audience of educators. The man had guts.

Bradford cleared his throat again, a hoarse and grating sound that brought side conversations to a halt. He did a sweep of the audience with his eyes and put his lips a mere inch from the microphone.

"Before we begin our business for the day, I would like to introduce a guest speaker."

Penelope's curiosity rose quickly to the surface. There was never a guest speaker at the opening meetings. She glanced again at the four uniforms against the wall, and then watched intently as the chief of police approached the podium from the doorway where he had evidently been waiting for his cue. Everyone knew him from the newspapers. His picture had been featured in several articles above the fold of page one because of his stepped up efforts to thwart a recent upswing in violent crimes.

There were some murmurings as Bradford continued, "Chief Franklin asked if he could have a few minutes of our morning to address a rather serious issue that affects us as we deal with the school opening. Chief?"

He gestured to the man standing near him to the right of the microphone. The chief appeared calm, his posture erect and commanding. He was a slim, African American whose face was serious and honest. He placed a wrinkled piece of yellow legal paper in front of him and began to speak.

"I wish it wasn't necessary to be here today, but I'm afraid we need your help as well as that of every other citizen who lives in this city." He took a deep breath and continued. "The gangs are more active than ever before, and we must be watchful. There have been drug related assaults, and we know that some aggressive initiations are happening in this very area. We caught a sixteen year old the other day when he stalked an elderly woman and beat her to get her purse as proof he had done the job. We also had a shooting just last night a couple of hundred yards from the high school."

He paused to let the last bit of information be absorbed by his audience. One of the Spanish teachers gasped at the news, and history teacher Sidney Polep slammed his fist on the surface of the table, startling several of the others seated near him.

"I knew it," he snarled. "We're not as safe as we thought."

Franklin proceeded. "We need you to watch for suspicious behavior among the students."

"Student behavior is always suspicious," Harry Feinstein, the math department head, stated. "How are we supposed to tell the difference?"

The chief's mouth quirked only slightly. "You know the kids better than most. What's unusual for them? Watch for the gang colors and tattoos. Be aware of the secret handshakes and guarded conversations. Be aware if any of the students seem afraid of others. Observe the cocky ones, the ones that flaunt some degree of power. Be on the lookout for any strange activities. These gangs are as dangerous as a nest of rattlesnakes awakened from a nap. Don't try to intervene when something comes up. Just call us."

There was an outburst of chatter and comments, some fearful, some skeptical. Penelope wondered where all of this would lead. What the police chief had just outlined as suspicious behavior was a typical day in the life of the high school anyway. It would be difficult to differentiate between regular activity and that which would indicate gang goings on. The year would be even worse than a few extra duties and an additional class. Penelope felt a prickling sensation roar down her spine.

"Look, I'm not trying to scare you, but the problem does exist, and we have to enlist your aid to get it under control. Please help us, and we will be there for you if you need us, as we always are." Franklin gave a little salute, nodded to Bradford and left through the same door from which he had so suddenly appeared a few minutes before. The four officers followed him like body guards at a presidential press conference.

The tone of the meeting turned more neutral when Bradford came back to the podium. Penelope wondered what these strong words of caution would mean to the young interns who were listening to these warnings.

With the dignity and pomp he always felt the subject deserved, Bradford announced the reading of the papers from the brown packet as if he had the Dead Sea Scrolls before him.

"We will now review the opening day literature," he stated gravely as he waved his thick copy in his fisted hand. He then lapsed into a drone that the assembly recognized as his usual low, business monotone. Penelope let out another sigh.

After an hour and fifteen minutes, emphasizing the new obligations and duties, as well as the altered curriculum, Bradford signaled the end of his presentation by wishing everyone a good year.

"Yes, we have a few challenges to meet, but working together, we can make this a memorable time for our students."

Penelope marveled that he did not take a bow like the maintenance man had earlier. He merely removed his wire-rimmed glasses and smiled benignly.

Teachers had begun collecting their bags, packets, and used coffee cups, when a shrill voice rose above the shuffling.

"Stop! Stop! Stop!" The second and third commands were pronounced more boldly than the first.

Everyone turned to locate the source of the interruption. A general gasp emanated from the large group when they spotted the very proper Claire Harvey shrieking and waving her arms.

"Dr. Bradford, we are not done yet." The gasps turned to moans. "How can all of you sit here and say nothing?" she scolded, looking around at the assemblage. "Don't you understand what's going on here? We have more to worry about than the gangs. The state is ganging up on us. It is being suggested that we have not done a good job. We are professionals. These changes," she sputtered, brandishing the papers from the superintendent's office, "were implemented without our input and now it is without our protest. This is our school. These are our students. We know what they need and how to meet those needs. We don't need a script to tell us how to teach."

"Make an appointment with my administrative assistant and we'll talk this over," Bradford suggested, his smile still broadcasting confidence.

"Not good enough," Claire retorted. The faculty was stunned. What had happened to the staid Miss Harvey over the summer?

"Claire, I really think . . ." Bradford began.

Drawing on the phantoms of protests past, Claire forged ahead. "Educators, unite! We are being subjugated by those who don't know the real story. Let's take our profession back. We are the experts here."

Amidst the stares and gawks of her coworkers, Penelope approached her once venerated and now venting former mentor. She saw the child of the sixties emerging, and she needed to call back the woman of reason and decorum.

"Claire, now's not the time" she whispered. "We'll get together later and discuss this. Maybe I can help."

Claire appeared dazed, but quietly sat down as the cafeteria emptied. The two bewildered student teachers followed their mentors when Penelope and Claire finally exited behind the others.

CHAPTER 2

Penelope stepped outside the building to clear her head from the long meeting. She had always loved this school. She had been a student here, and now a teacher. Skinner High was named after a local World War I flying ace, Daniel J. Skinner. The school held a little over fifteen hundred students, most from poor homes in this once thriving city near Boston.

The mills that kept the city booming had moved south, leaving empty buildings and squandered dreams. Property values had plummeted, and cheap housing was plentiful. Impoverished families had flooded the city, knowing that they would have affordable housing and services. Sometimes school was not a priority when money was scarce. Some students looked to gangs as a way to survive. Maybe the demographics and issues had changed, but Penelope felt the school still provided a good education for those who wanted it or could be made to want it. Stonefield was still a great place to live, but she was having her doubts about the new direction of education in this city.

Penelope, needing to get into the fresh air for a few minutes, had asked Christie to gather the mail from her slot in the office and meet her in the main hall. As she breathed in the motionless air just outside the front door, she saw smoky plumes curling around the corner of the building. Fearing a fire or some other hazardous condition, she approached the corner of the building with a modicum of trepidation. She had helped to put out a suspicious trash can fire just last year. These small incidents happened fairly often, so she was not fearful, just cautious. She was on familiar ground and help was just a holler away. Curiosity pulled her forward.

She peeked around the weathered brick that formed the corner. There, leaning lazily against the brick and mortar lounged a tall, well-tanned figure, his right leg supporting the weight of his taut frame. The jacket of his dark brown suit drooped over one arm where the sleeves of his pristine white shirt had been rolled to reveal his muscled forearm. He gazed skyward at the murky and turbulent clouds that had begun to creep their way across the sky. He took another drag on his cigarette and exhaled.

"Are you going to bust me, Teacher? Smoking on public property?" His raised eyebrow challenged her.

She moved closer. "Not this time," she responded with a smile.

He gazed at her with his heavy brown eyes, and she felt a shiver travel the length of her body.

"Don't you realize smoking can kill you?" she asked, not able to think of anything more profound.

He took another pull and closed his eyes as the orange light traveled closer to the filter and again let out a stream of smoke. His nose was straight and his mouth sensual. His dark, thick hair had a slight wave to it.

"Technically speaking, I'm not a smoker anymore. I quit." He looked longingly at the stub between his thumb and forefinger. "I allow myself one a week, for old time's sake. Today was my day."

He dropped the stub and crushed it beneath his shoe, picked it up, and tossed it into a nearby trash barrel.

"It's a dirty habit. Don't start." His smile did not soften his face. His teeth were almost perfectly white against his darkened skin. She wondered who he was and tried to look away from him, but her interest nudged away her discomfiture.

"Actually, it's too late for your advice. I took it up when I was eighteen and a college freshman, but I quit, too," she responded too quickly.

"How old were you when you quit?"

"Eighteen," she answered, the spirit of a smile beginning to play at her mouth although she still felt the tension in her neck and the tingle in her stomach.

"You started at eighteen and you stopped at eighteen?" He put a finger to his lips as if pondering the issue. "For how long did you smoke?"

"About four hours. It was really easy to give them up since I choked and sputtered for three of those four hours." She laughed lightly at the memory, her apprehension easing. "I didn't even have time to acquire a favorite brand. Well, I have to go in. There's someone waiting for me."

She felt his eyes follow her as she headed back toward the front door.

*   *   *

Jonathan reached into his pocket and felt for his cigarettes. It would be another seven days before he could pull another one out of the pack. That was all right. He believed in control. He was in control, always. It surprised him that he reacted so strongly when that intriguing lady had come around the corner. He was used to people sneaking, stalking, creeping around him, but she had made more than his brain go on alert.

He had become comfortable in suits instead of camouflage, but he could not condition his senses to turn off their highly attentive habits. He gazed back up at the threatening clouds and almost laughed. Here he was working at a school, the last place he could ever have envisioned himself. He was contracted for the first semester, and now he thought perhaps the time might go by quickly if he could cozy up to that one-pack-per-lifetime woman he had just encountered, but that would go against his own distance rules. He had spent his first career learning to trust the men he had to work with, but women were still an ambiguity to him, and he hadn't met one yet that was worth the time to explore the mystery.

*　　*　　*

Penelope sauntered back into the cool building to reconnect with her intern. She found the young woman standing by the mailboxes in the main office where she had told her she would meet her. She noticed Christie's gaze ripple over her, the one who would be her constant companion for the next few months. She seemed to be assessing the differences between them.

Penelope put her slender hand on Christie's shoulder. "Come on. Let's enter your new kingdom."

She smiled companionably at the student teacher and led her into the hall, down the long corridor and up the stairs to the math rooms. The building was relatively quiet except for the movements of teachers readying their classrooms for the next day of business.

"A lot of us come in during the summer to straighten the files, put up bulletin boards and get supplies in place. I've got most of the work done, so we just have to clear out our mental cobwebs and gather our books. The department head won't allow us to take them out of the supply closet until the day before school starts because there were some people hoarding the texts. Can you imagine?" Penelope inquired with a hint of a smile.

Christie stood at the threshold of the room, barely moving, as if holding her breath. Her drab attire almost caused her to blend in with the beige walls that had not yet been completely decorated. There was a sheen of moisture that made her eyes appear much brighter than before.

Penelope immediately sensed her hesitance to come into the room. "What's the matter, Christie?" she asked with concern. She went to the motionless woman and pulled her into the classroom gently by the hand, guiding her to a chair by the massive desk in the front of the room. When Penelope had seated herself as well, she leaned toward Christie.

"Is there a problem?" she asked softly, keeping her voice low.

Christie shook her head as the tears spilled over the rims of her eyes, looked at Penelope, and then changed to a nodding motion.

"I don't think I can do this. I don't know what I was thinking. Both of my parents are accountants, and I inherited that whole number thing, but I didn't want to do what they do. It seemed so boring, so I went into education in college." She swiped at her eyes with the back of her hand. "I guess I didn't think this all the way through. When I went on my observations last semester, all those kids seemed so big, so intimidating, and so smart. I doubt that I can teach them anything."

Penelope handed her a tissue from her desk drawer. She still had a few left in the box from last year.

"I'm not going to tell you right now that it will be easy or that your experience here will be rich and rewarding. It might be and it might not, but a lot depends on you, on your approach, your attitude." She pulled the rest of the tissues out of the drawer and put the box on the desk since Christie had wadded the first one into a wet ball in the palm of her hand. "I was beyond scared when I did my internship. I was sure that I would have a mental breakdown before my first sets of quizzes were corrected, but it got better. Now I can honestly say that I love what I do. Time will tell if this is the profession for you, but why not give it a chance since you're here?"

She saw the doubtful expression on Christie's face begin to ebb. "I'll be the first to tell you, though, that if it isn't for you, don't do it," Penelope continued. "You'd be making a mistake that will affect your life as well as your students. Right now, though, this is our plan. You can watch me for a week or two and when we think you're ready, you can take on a class, then maybe another when you get the feel for it. Let's pace this well so that you're comfortable."

Christie looked uncertain, but then straightened her posture and leveled her eyes with Penelope's. "I'm sorry. I must have made a really bad first impression." She paused as if considering her options. "You said you were nervous at first, too?"

"Absolutely," Penelope affirmed.

"I guess I owe it to myself to at least try."

"Don't just give it a try. Put your whole effort into it, and I will help you in any way I can. That's why I'm listed as your mentor on the paperwork. Now let's get started on that part of the bulletin board that still needs some work. There's only a little bit left to do, so it won't take long."

"Now *that* I know I can do."

"I'll bet you can do a whole lot more," Penelope assured her and went to the closet to get the materials.

CHAPTER 3

The next day

The sun was subdued, shyly peeking from behind gray puffs parked over the city as if waiting for permission to move on. The front of the building pulsed with life as cars slipped into slots on the asphalt or lingered in the outer regions of the extensive grassy property as they released bubbling, bouncing, anxious youths. A towering blond crew-cut topped teen, fresh from his morning treatment of acne cream, loped along the concrete path toward the double doors of the school. He jabbed at acquaintances with a loosely clenched fist, a friendly greeting which maintained his machismo.

Three girls, polished toes brightly displayed in almost identical high heeled sandals, checked their blush and eye shadow in hand held mirrors, flinging fluid phrases at each other in rapid and diluted Spanish.

Another tangle of male teens reclined on the cement steps, mutely ogling the leggy blond and the buxom brunette who had recently debarked from a minivan.

Heavy metal and rap, emanating from laptops, iPods, and car radios, did battle for air space, clashing one minute, synchronizing the next. Knee length denim skirts, tube tops, tee shirts, camper shorts, and bared navels moved languidly around the parking lot and front lawn.

Penelope surveyed the scene as she braked her old Mitsubishi, extracted the Styrofoam cup from the holder built into the console. She took a long breath over the steaming brew, appreciating the aroma of the rich coffee she had bought at the gas station ten minutes earlier. Fortified from the one whiff, she opened her car door and pulled out the black leather bag that housed what soon would be the contents of the left drawer of her desk—bandage strips, hand cream, throat lozenges, her special advanced function calculator, a fresh box of tissues, and a package of jumbo paper clips she considered essential even though the school refused to supply them. She also brought her own stapler without staples. *One of these days the school will supply both the staplers and the staples,* she thought. Every budget cut over the last several years had led to the elimination of certain supplies. This year protractors joined the staplers on the endangered species list. *What next—textbooks?*

Another beginning, another opportunity for the students, another chance for teachers to get across their material. Her heart always felt hopeful in September. Penelope smoothed a stray strand of her shoulder length hair back behind her left ear, which usually kept it captive for only three class periods. She nodded acknowledgements to several former students, allowing a sedate smile to accompany the occasional head bobbing. She also raised her coffee in salute to a six foot eleventh grader who had taken her Algebra I class for three consecutive years. Since he had failed once more to navigate the mathematical waters last June, she wondered if his name would again appear on her class list. His guidance counselor last spring had attempted to persuade him to forget about algebra and go for a remedial course called "applied practical math" that broke down most concepts to the lowest common denominator, but he had bonded with Penelope, as had happened so many times with other students. She wasn't sure he was yet willing to desert her for another teacher. She was vaguely confident that he would retake this course until he passed it, with any luck before his twenty-first birthday.

She proceeded to the entrance of the sprawling building. The black bag hung heavily from her slim shoulders as she pulled open the cumbersome metal and glass door with her free hand. It was a difficult task made easier when Wally Winslow, a small framed, bespectacled man held the door. He was passionate about his subject matter and assumed all other math teachers were as scholarly. Penelope admired him for his dedication to the subject matter and to the students, but his life always seemed so wrapped up in the numbers that were his livelihood.

"Thanks, Wally," she said breathily as she slipped inside the main corridor.

"Any time. Hey, weren't we supposed to sign up for the Math in the New Age conference together in July? I was there, and I was looking for you."

Penelope had never intended to go. In fact, she wasn't sure how Wally had gotten the impression that she had been truly interested in attending. He had talked incessantly about it in June and had asked if she wanted to go. She had merely replied with "It seems interesting," and he had evidently taken it as a commitment. She liked Wally, but she was never available when he asked her out to concerts, seminars, or lectures. In fact, she had made certain these days that she was unavailable to any male who asked for her company.

"I'm sorry. I didn't mean to mislead you, Wally. I bought my uncle's place on Pineacre Street, and it needed a lot of updating, so I was really busy." She gave an apologetic smile. "I'm sure it was very informative."

Turning toward the inner hall, Penelope spied Hector Cortez, a student, enter the building. He stood about five feet ten inches with soft, wavy black hair gelled slickly away from his face and pulled into a tight pony tail at the nape of the neck. She had known him for three years, and she had worried about him for three years, and now as she looked at him, a wave of apprehension swept over her. She recognized the signs. Something was wrong, definitely wrong with Hector. The signs were there—the slumped shoulders, the shuffling gait, the defiant stride that defined "attitude."

She started walking over to him. "Hector, can I speak to you? It will only take a moment."

Hector ignored the request and turned away to the unsavory group standing in close proximity to him. Penelope chewed her bottom lip anxiously. She and others had spent years trying to save this young man from himself. He was worth it, or at least she thought he was. If she were honest, she'd have to say that she believed all of her students were worth it, and that was a philosophy she had once debated very strongly with ex-fiancé Walter.

She knew that Hector's home life was in shambles even though he seldom talked about it. In fact, during his freshman year he hardly talked at all. Her constant concern, however, had eventually led to a trust that was rare among the students who had been part of a gang, as Hector had been.

She had first become aware of his affiliation when she saw the Monks' tattoo on his forearm the day he helped her deliver books to the storage closet. She also knew that Hector had pulled away from the Monks, but at a price. The first Monday of last October, he had come to school looking as if he had been hit by an out of control bulldozer. His face was bruised and scraped, his eyes puffy, the lids scabbed. Even though he favored his right leg, he had marched into her homeroom and muttered, "Don't ask. I'm fine." It took all her inner stamina not to express her shock at his appearance. "By the way, I ain't no gang member no more," he had asserted.

When kids pulled away from a gang, there was always the question of whether or not they would survive the leaving. The exit ritual was often brutal. She had, of course, discreetly reported his condition to his counselor as mandated.

He didn't look a lot better today. There were no bruises as there had been that other time, but he looked tired, angry, and very intense. Penelope couldn't help but wonder what had happened to make him ignore her.

Penelope tried to get his attention again as she sipped the last dregs of cold coffee from her Styrofoam cup. Maybe he didn't see her, she reasoned, as he turned away from the group he had been talking to and tramped down the corridor. He headed toward the choral room, clutching a handful of dirty denim in order to hold his droopy jeans on his slender hips. The bottom edge of his gray sweatshirt fell half way between his navel and his knees. She wanted to stop him because all of the seniors were supposed to gather in the auditorium for the opening day speech by the vice principals, and he was heading in the opposite direction. She didn't call to him, however, knowing he was probably going to see Ted Tottman. Hector had also become very tight with the vocal music teacher ever since Tottman had discovered his unusually mellow baritone that had gained him awards as a district chorus member.

Claire came up behind her.

"There you are, dear. We are launching another school year." She patted Penelope lightly on the back. "I don't know how I'm going to cope with all these new things we have to do—extra corridor duties, cafeteria watch for everybody, new responsibilities. It makes my head spin."

As Claire was expounding, Penelope noticed her friend's distraction as she stared at a student sporting a sparse goatee.

"There goes Sammy Johnson. I know a lot of the teachers are afraid of him, but I tutored him after school for his term papers, and he really is a very intelligent young man." Claire tsked and shook her head. "I know he has been in a bit of trouble, but he's a gifted artist, and you know how temperamental those people can be. He showed me some of his artwork the last day of school in June. None of the other students in his class came to school that day. Maybe this year he'll grow into himself."

Sammy was of average height, thin and carried a large artist's pad under his arm. Maybe that artist's talent that Claire admired so much added to his cocky persona, Penelope thought. The street could easily claim this one if he didn't tone down his attitude.

Claire turned back to her companion. "I may need some advice. As you know, I have this student teacher. Between us, I don't know what to . . . ."

A blast of student voices erupted, ending their conversation. "Claire, watch my things."

Penelope dropped her bag and hurried toward the clamor, trying to see beyond the swarm of student bodies that had formed so quickly by the water fountain. She hated getting into the midst of a crowd, not knowing exactly what she might find at the center. She recalled all too well the time she had been punched by a very focused seventeen-year-old hell-bent on connecting his fist to the sophomore who had allegedly stolen his backpack. Unfortunately, his hand missed the mark, and he landed a blow to Penelope's upper arm. Since then she always had a mental hesitation before attempting to get in the middle of a student battle.

"Move on, move on," she commanded, raising her voice several decibels so that she could be heard above the rising staccato of shouts.

"Go, go, go," the crowd chanted as she finally pushed her way past the intoning teens. Two male bodies were locked in combat on the newly polished tiles of the hallway. They writhed and rolled, alternately gaining advantage. Penelope realized with horror that one of the combatants was Hector, and the other was Sammy Johnson.

"Step back . . . now!" she ordered, and the excited audience did so, but only by a few feet. She leaned over the fountain and quickly filled her now empty cup with water, turned, and doused the heads of the dueling duo with the cold liquid. The shock of the water in their faces brought the battle to a sudden halt, both boys turning to look at her in surprise. Penelope took advantage of the moment of astonishment.

"All right, the two of you, get up."

They slowly moved to comply. They started to disentangle arms and legs, and Penelope thought that the worst was over just before Hector's opponent slammed his shoulder into Hector's ribs, bashing him against the unyielding bank of lockers.

A harrowing crunch silenced the clamoring crowd of watchers. Hector groaned, eyes welling with unshed tears as he fought to stay upright.

A shadow loomed over Penelope and Hector, and she looked up to see the urbane stranger she had encountered the day before. His presence seemed to fill all the space around her. He reached down and laid a hand on Hector's shoulder.

"Are you all right, son?" he inquired gently.

Hector nodded unsteadily, but grasped his arm, holding it against his body.

"Let me take a look," directed the tall man with the visitor's pass clipped to his belt.

Hector obeyed. Penelope gasped softly as the arm the stranger was clutching was given up for inspection. Deep blue and purple welts were already rising around the injured wrist.

"We'd better bring him to the nurse," Penelope proposed immediately. She included this interloper out of courtesy, but there was a bothersome feeling of apprehension. He wasn't a teacher and could easily be held liable if something went awry. Nothing mattered right now except getting the boy help, she told herself.

Penelope turned her attention to Sammy who still had his fist raised in anticipation of another opportunity to strike a blow. She raised her hands, palms out, and pushed lightly against the air in front of the teen as she calmly warned, "Sammy, it's over. Are you hurt?"

"S'all right." Sammy said as he slowly let his arm drop to his side.

As he turned to leave, Vice Principal Colon, alerted by the noise in the corridor, approached Sammy.

"Let's take a walk," he said to Sammy before turning to face Penelope. "Do you two have everything under control here?" He nodded toward the stranger.

"We need to take Hector to the nurse. His arm is pretty banged up from falling into the lockers," Penelope informed him.

Colon waved Sammy toward the administrative offices, and the youth headed that way, but not before smiling at Hector's misery.

"That's enough," Colon commanded. "Let's move."

The crowd began to disperse, and the man who had appeared out of nowhere helped Hector to his feet and accompanied Penelope as they walked down the long corridor to the nurse's office. It was located right outside the cafeteria, a wise placement given the quality of the food and the short period of time allowed for digestion.

Freida Hash, the school nurse for the last twenty-five years, was busy stocking her cabinets with aspirin she was not allowed to distribute and various lotions, ointments, and bandages. She barely noticed the threesome as they entered her sanctuary. Hector still held his arm gingerly and was beginning to grow more unsteady with each step.

"We seem to have a bit of an emergency here, Mrs. Hash," Penelope stated calmly. She looked to see that the helpful stranger was still standing close behind her, and she realized that although he seemed to emanate confidence, he had let her take charge of the situation. She warmed slightly, wondering why she was thinking about him while her mind should be focused on Hector. He was alternately watching her and the boy, she noticed, seeming to dismiss Frieda as a person of little interest.

The nurse turned around and glanced at her young patient who began to weave.

"Sit down and put your head between your knees," she instructed as she reached for a pre-packaged cold compress.

Hector dropped his head between his denim clad legs and breathed deeply as Nurse Hash applied the compress to the back of his neck.

"Can I sit up now? I feel better."

"I'll tell you when you feel better," the nurse responded in a matter-of-fact tone. "Let me see that arm."

"How can I show you my arm when I'm all bent over?"

"Stick it out to the side," she said as she grabbed his elbow, steered the arm competently in her direction, and examined the swollen wrist.

Penelope noticed that it had doubled in size since the incident. She knew he would have to have it x-rayed. Her throat constricted at the sight, but she kept her gaze steady and her voice calm.

"Do you want me to call the principal's office, Frieda? I'll ask if I can take him to the hospital."

"I have to contact his parents," Frieda told her in a professional manner.

"I got nobody at home. I'm eighteen, so it don't matter."

"Then I'll contact the principal. You wait here while I ask if you can accompany him. The parents still have to be contacted because it happened on school property, and he is still a student. This shouldn't take long." She dashed off to her desk to use the phone.

She picked up the receiver and pressed one key that would immediately connect her to the principal's office. She spoke briskly and briefly, summarizing the situation. She held the receiver to her ear, waiting for a response. The brief phone conversation ended with an "Okay." She turned to the group.

"The only address they have on the computer is Hector's, and there is no phone number listed. The principal said to go ahead and take him since the emergency room is just up the street."

Penelope crouched down to face Hector. "Everything will be all right. You'll see."

The stranger, who had until this moment remained silent, drew closer.

"I'm Jonathan Perez. I'm here for a while as a computer consultant." He paused a few seconds to let the introduction sink in. "Could I offer to drive you to the hospital? That way you could be with him on the way over." He had offered so bluntly that it seemed the most natural course of action.

"Hector, what do you think?" asked Penelope.

"Okay." Hector seemed anxious to get out of Frieda's office. He kept looking at the door as if plotting a getaway from a major heist.

"Mr. Perez, you have a deal," Penelope affirmed. She was relieved she didn't have to go alone with the injured boy, but she still felt uneasy about Jonathan Perez being their escort to the hospital. She knew nothing about him except that he knew computers and indulged in an occasional cigarette. *Thank heaven the hospital was only a few minutes away.*

Jonathan Perez's black SUV smoothly navigated the morning traffic that barred their speedy progress to the hospital. Penelope and Hector sat together on the cool leather of the back seat, Hector stifling the occasional groan of pain.

"Are you all right? Is there anything I can do to make things better?" Penelope asked.

"Nope. I bet I'm going to get suspended for fighting."

"It depends on the circumstances. What happened?"

"I was tired and in no mood for his shit. Sammy bumped me and I lost it," he explained unapologetically.

She knew better than to press for details and rode in silence for the remainder of the ride.

*   *   *

Hector thought back to the night before. It had been one screwed up night. He hadn't fallen asleep until three in the morning. Living alone in his apartment since he was seventeen, he sometimes felt that he was an orphan. His mother had died when he was thirteen. God, he missed her. She had been the one soft spot in his life. He still remembered how she had thought everything would be much better for them when his father was released from jail. Yeah, right. The old man had gone back to dealing while he was still on parole, and after his mother was gone, Papa had found himself a new senorita twenty years younger. She hadn't wanted any teenagers hanging around, so his father finally set Hector up across the street so he could keep an occasional eye on him. His younger brother was taken in by his grandmother who only had room for Emilio. Hector loved his abuela, but he knew he wasn't her first concern. The living arrangements were far from perfect, especially when his neighbors got out of hand.

He had gone to bed at ten thirty last night, trying to beat the heat with an old, clunky fan moving the hot air over his body. His place was sparsely furnished, but it was clean and neat. As he began to drowse, he was suddenly jarred by the screaming coming from the apartment next door.

"You stupid bitch, I'll beat the crap out of ya." The words were followed by choked protests.

The raucous argument intensified, and Hector jumped to his feet and screamed against the wall. "Lay off. I'll call the cops!"

The fighting stopped long enough for a gruff voice yelling back, "You little shit, I'll beat your ass after I'm done here."

Hector wondered how far his neighbor would go on his threat, but that didn't stop him from picking up the cell phone his father had given him during a guilt trip and making the call to nine-one-one.

The sirens blared and the cops stomped up the stairs and crashed through the neighbor's door. Amid the hollering and profanity, Hector concluded that an arrest had been made. He finally fell asleep to the sobs coming from the other side of the wall.

He shook his head, trying to dislodge memories of the night before. Now he had a whole new set of problems, as the pain throbbed up his arm from his swollen wrist.

The car came to a halt at the emergency room door. His math teacher eased him out of the back seat. "Mr. Perez, you can go back to school. I'll stay here with Hector and when we're done, I'll call the school for a ride."

"You go back with him, Miss Parsons. I'm eighteen and I've been here and done this before."

"But Hector . . . ."

"I can do this myself. Go."

Jonathan came around and opened the front passenger door. "I think it's best for us to leave."

"But I have a responsibility to see that he gets in there and gets help," his teacher protested.

Jonathan looked at Hector, and it was as if the man could read his thoughts. He understood he didn't want Miss Parsons to see any more of his humiliation.

"Then why don't you see him to the triage station and get him registered. Then come back. I'll wait here for you."

Hector was relieved when his teacher agreed.

*   *   *

Penelope saw that all of the student teachers sat together on the hard slats of the bottom row of the bleachers. Penelope looked at the familiar scene and let her concern about Hector slide to the back chamber of her mind. She couldn't dismiss him from her thoughts, but she would try to concentrate on the job at hand. She had made it back to the school just after the official starting bell, Jonathan a silent companion on the short trip.

After being given a copy of the school handbook at the entrance to the gym, the ninth, tenth, and eleventh grade students sat for the annual reading of the rules by the principal after which they would be escorted to their new homerooms. The administrator ducked his head closer to the microphone and commanded, "Let's settle down. Settle down, please." Each repetition of the request grew louder, stronger, more intense.

The band started to play the school song, drowning out Principal Bradford's attempts at crowd control. At the end of the musical piece, he repeated the chant of "settle down" until the collective conversations became a mere annoying undercurrent.

"Now we will recite the Pledge of Allegiance, followed by the playing of the national anthem." The audience stood and calm finally prevailed.

Bradford urged everyone to sit once more and began, "We will reacquaint ourselves with the policies and programs of Skinner High School, and then we will ask teachers to accompany students to their new homeroom assignments."

Penelope watched as Christie, Stephanie, Claire's student teacher, and Jeffrey, the history intern, huddled near each other on the bottom seats. She knew what they were thinking. She recalled being there herself just ten years ago, feeling the tidal wave of students seething behind her. She remembered wondering if the teens decided all at once to leave, would she be swept away in the tsunami, never to be seen again? She never had those thoughts anymore. In fact, she seldom thought of any danger connected to the school. It just didn't enter her mind because there was too much to do, too many other issues to worry about. In the education classes at some of the colleges, students were often discussed in the abstract—how to motivate them, how to hold their interest, and how to become close, but not too close. That last point seemed to be moot as she saw the interns with the students' denim-covered knees nudging into their backs, probably thinking that things were already too up close and personal.

The rules rattled on. No smoking, no swearing, no leaving campus, no food fights, no public displays of affection. At the last point, puckered "smooch" sounds resounded from the eleventh grade section. Several sophomores hugged their neighbors in a unified public acclamation of brotherly affection. Penelope hoped the senior meeting in the auditorium with Vice Principal Pike was going better.

Principal Bradford's tanned complexion flushed to a burnished red as he tried to suppress his ire. "Teachers, if students are acting inappropriately, take them from the stands and escort them to the office where I will deal with them later."

Penelope saw Jeffrey turn and face the throng behind him. His expression told her that there wasn't a single student whom he would have dared to pluck from the audience. Vice Principal Colon made his way from his position by the wall to a prominent place in front of the right section of the bleachers, arms crossed against his chest, eyebrows knit in intimidation. The students who were testing the system reacted immediately. They turned their attention reluctantly to the speaker as a hush descended on the room.

Christie looked so small and frightened to Penelope, like a kitten among lions. Stephanie sat serenely next to her.

Finally, the rule recitation was over, and the band prepared to play an exit tune.

"While we must keep in mind what we *must* not do, also remember what we *ought* to do. Have a great year. We are most pleased to have you all back," Bradford stated although he didn't appear quite as excited to have them return as he had claimed. The first strains of "Forever, Skinner High School" signaled it would soon be time for the masses to move on to this year's homerooms. Penelope knew that most of the students did not know the lyrics to Whitman's sacred song, so they stood up, waiting to be called without adding voice to the music. Penelope waived to Claire from where she stood by the door. Claire waived back. There was always a certain exhilaration to opening day, but after the incident with Hector, the excitement had begun to wane.

CHAPTER 4

Claire signaled Stephanie to follow her, and they exited the gym. "We have only a few minutes before they dismiss the students to the classrooms, so we better get a head start."

Claire knew it was wise to get a jump start on the throng. If the elevator had not been broken, she would have used that to get to her classroom one floor down.

"How do you know there are only minutes left?" Stephanie queried.

"Well, the band plays the school song again, and the principal gives the students one final pep talk before disbursing them, asking the teachers without homerooms to escort them to class. I think the routine is written down somewhere. This is my fourth principal in the last thirty-five years, and they all do it the same way."

Claire opened the door to her room and hustled to her desk, locking her shoulder bag in the right bottom drawer where she kept her spare supply of composition paper.

Stephanie looked up with pride to the back bulletin board Claire had suggested she decorate yesterday. It was gone. Claire coughed nervously. She knew that Stephanie had spent considerable time stapling interesting images to the board, accompanied by poems from Charles Baudelaire. The poster that had taken center stage on the cork board was most noticeably missing, replaced by the dour face of a rather pessimistic female, Emily Dickinson. The rest of the board was covered by autumn photos and grammar rules.

"Miss Harvey, what happened to the picture and poems in the back?"

Claire said nothing for a full minute and then emitted a rather helpless exhalation of breath. She glared at Stephanie. The humidity had permeated the younger woman's wheaten locks and coiled them at various angles around her fresh scrubbed face.

"I'm sorry, Stephanie, but it was, shall we say, 'inappropriate'."

Stephanie's mouth gaped incredulously.

"That was a print of a famous painting, and the poems I posted were considered revolutionary in their time period." Her hand flew to her throat as if deeply wounded by their absence.

"I know, my dear, but we can't get around the fact that the subject of the picture was naked. All the boys would have been panting around the painting. We can't have that in English class. I also don't think sophomores are ready for Baudelaire."

Stephanie's mouth pressed in an impending pout. *Now what am I supposed to do?* thought Claire. "Why don't you take another look at the textbook we'll be using, and that will remind you of the curriculum contents." The mentor teachers had sent the unit outlines and book names to all the potential student teachers in the spring.

The younger woman's eyes remained glued to the back wall. "Over the spring and summer I did see the course descriptions and a copy of the anthologies you use. I thought maybe we could add to the normal order of things." She turned toward Claire. "You know, think outside the box?"

Claire stared at the lovely Stephanie. "I kind of like the box. Maybe you should try to get a feel for it before jumping out of it. There are a lot of innovative approaches I use to present the material. We can work on those."

Stephanie narrowed her eyes as if she could not believe that the woman in front of her could be innovative.

Claire's back stiffened. "We keep a lot of the literature because it's good. We work with what works. I like to make sure that no student is left clueless when someone mentions Shakespeare or Shelley. It's our job to make sure these people live again in the classroom."

The intern's face softened. "You mean a literary resurrection?"

Claire was taken a bit aback by the phrasing, but she sensed she might be starting to connect with the girl. "Exactly so."

CHAPTER 5

Monday, second week of September

As usual, the first week of school had passed in commotion and confusion, but now in the second week, students, faculty, and administration had settled into a fairly familiar routine.

Penelope snatched her purse out of the desk drawer and hurried to the cafeteria for her customary twenty minute "leisurely" lunch. It was an inconvenience to run all the way down to the cafeteria, but it was the only time she got to see her friend Samantha Treadwell, even though their classrooms were adjacent.

Penelope had not been able to spend as much time with Sam this past summer because of the house remodeling and because Sam was busy making up for lost time with her two little girls. They had managed to sneak in a couple of lunches, but they were both looking forward to their time together at Skinner High. Penelope had never had a friend as close as Sam, and as she rushed to lunch, she couldn't help but think of how opposite they really were. Samantha was short with thick auburn hair that was cut in a bouncy bob which reflected her personality.

Their lifestyles were also different. Sam was truly committed to her husband, her children, and family life. Penelope had to admit she could be called a "commitment-phobe" since her broken engagement with Walter. She had given her heart once, and it had been trampled to such an extent that she had just about dismissed any relationships of a romantic nature for the immediate future. Sam was always trying to fix her up, all the while espousing the virtues of a strong bond with a loving partner. Penelope knew that was a price she would have to pay for having such a great friend.

She had also not had time to reconnect with Claire. Christie, Penelope's intern, had already gone to lunch with her fellow practice teacher, Stephanie, Claire's protégé. Penelope spotted Samantha immediately upon entering the teacher's dining hall and headed toward the table by the window. The two student teachers were still waiting in line. They would soon learn the benefits of bringing their own food. She placed her purse on the table and extracted her yogurt.

"Why does my life seem like a washing machine?" Samantha muttered as she slid her fingers through her hair. She rested her chin on the platforms of her palms.

Penelope paused, her plastic spoon half way to her mouth. "A washing machine?" she echoed, not certain she had heard her friend clearly. This was certainly a change in attitude for the usually cheerful Samantha.

"Yes." Sam sighed dramatically. "I feel that everyone is throwing their dirty laundry at me, and they expect me to clean it. Students confess to me. Faculty members are always giving me their dirty little secrets. Who am I supposed to be—Dear Abby? Well, now I'm the one in the spin cycle."

Penelope smiled indulgently. "Well, don't worry. I don't have any problems to lay on you. I do my own laundry." She licked the underside of the spoon where a blob of pink yogurt still clung.

"Oh, you have problems. You just fail to acknowledge them," Samantha retorted, pushing her warped brown tray toward the middle of the wobbly oblong table.

Penelope's left brow lifted in surprise.

"No, I don't," she stated emphatically and planted the plastic spoon in her nearly full yogurt container as an astronaut might stake a flag in a moon crater.

Samantha lowered her voice somewhat conspiratorially. "Really? Who stays home on Friday nights with a dog the size of a tractor? Who meets with a local Audubon Society chapter Saturday morning and then spends Saturday night sketching what she saw Saturday morning?"

"What's wrong with that?" Penelope defended. "Besides, I date on weekends quite often. I also have to work on my dissertation."

"A trip to Wendy's and a rented movie with Horatio Bitterman is hardly a date. He's family for heaven's sake. And why do you need a doctorate to teach high school?"

"Horatio is a fourth cousin twice removed. That's not family. He's good company. And as far as the doctorate goes, I just love learning."

"He's good company if you like forty-two year old librarians who still live with their mamas. That relationship is a dead end."

"Which is precisely why I go out with him. I don't want a relationship that goes anywhere. I like things the way they are. Besides, he finds really great books for my research."

Samantha's head sank onto her folded arms. The scattered strands of hair fell at strange angles around her ears. She turned her head to glance at her friend.

"Wouldn't you just once like to meet someone who puts spice in your life, who knocks your socks off and who puts your head in a tailspin?"

"No," Penelope answered flatly, slamming her empty yogurt container on the table. "My relationship with Walter made me wary of all those ridiculous, romantic notions."

Samantha hesitated and with renewed spirit, suggested, "How about a nice safe relationship with one of our esteemed colleagues? Look over there at Darius Zantopoulas. He's single."

"He's dated almost every single woman in town, but never more than twice. What does that tell you?"

"That he's just like you. He's not looking for something permanent."

"Please," she pleaded. "Don't ruin my lunch." She stared at Samantha's rejected food. A circle of ketchup had formed a watery ring around the remainder of the fish patty and limp fries on the paper plate.

Observing the focus of Penelope's attention, Samantha asked, "Do you want me to wrap up the rest of that fish for Spartacus?"

"No, thank you, that dog still has some pride left."

As they gathered the remnants of their disappointing meals, another tray was placed next to Penelope's spot. She reached out to grab a stray wrapper to make room, and her hand brushed that of the newcomer.

"Thank you. May I join you?" asked Jonathan Perez, straightening his red power tie with his palm and holding it in place as he sat down and smiled at the two women.

Penelope felt her heart halt for a fraction of a second before she finally became articulate enough to speak. *How did that happen?* She wondered.

"Hi," she managed after clearing her throat. "I never got a chance to thank you for your help last week. Oh, Samantha, this is Jonathan Perez, the new computer consultant. He was there when Hector and Sammy got into a scuffle. He drove us to the hospital."

She was prattling on and she knew it, but Jonathan took it all in stride with a hint of a smile.

"It's a pleasure to meet you, Samantha," he said gallantly and bowed his head slightly in greeting.

Just as Samantha opened her mouth to speak, Claire hustled into the cafeteria and honed in on Penelope's table.

"There you are, Penelope. I've been looking for you," she pronounced emphatically. "We have to talk."

"What's the matter, Claire? Is something wrong?"

"Something is most certainly wrong. We can't operate under these new circumstances, as I told you. We have to do something before the whole curriculum falls apart. We have to take action now!" Her hands were slicing the air dramatically.

Penelope gaped in amazement at Claire's ardent appeal. She had never seen her so animated either as her teacher or as her colleague. She was even more agitated than she has been at the teachers' meeting. Claire had once told her she had been a rebel in her youth, but she never really believed it until now.

The bell reverberated through the room, ending lunch and the chance to continue the conversation. Penelope stood, gathered her belongings, and headed toward the door, but not before she addressed Claire's call to action.

"You're right, Claire. We'll set up a time to talk more discreetly. I've got to go. That fifth period class can't be left to their own devices even for a few minutes."

"It's got to be soon. This can't go on without someone taking a stand. I'm forming a committee. We'll meet for the first time Tuesday afternoon at three."

Penelope nodded and scurried toward the exit. "Nice to see you again, Jonathan," she called over her shoulder as she left the room.

*   *   *

The way she had said "Jonathan" was breathy and hurried. She was always in a rush, it seemed. He picked up his fork and started to eat. He had learned to eat quickly years ago. It was a habit he was still trying to break. There was a lot going on here, he thought, but that couldn't be his concern now. He was through worrying about what could happen to others. He had to be.

CHAPTER 6

It had bothered Hector to be out of school for the first week. He had languished in boredom enough in the summer months and was ready to have a place to be, something to do, someone to be around. Dealing with a broken wrist and bruised arm made matters worse.

He had been on his way to the choral room when the fight had broken out. Tottman always had something for Hector to do. That man could be a real hard nose when he wanted to be, making his students do music numbers over and over again until they sounded right, but at least they were better than the numbers that he had to deal with in math class. Those completely baffled him. As far as Hector was concerned, the only good thing about math class was Miss Parsons. He liked her even though she had picked a really stupid subject to teach.

He walked along the pavement two streets from the school, his head down, his free hand in the pocket of his sagging, loose-fitting jeans. There was a tune spinning around in his head. If he were smarter, maybe he could get it down on some paper.

"If you don't look like a dumb duck with a broken wing."

The words came to him from somewhere behind him. He didn't turn around, but his spine stiffened and his senses became more alert. His days in the Monks, the toughest gang in the city, came back to him.

Never show fear, he mentally cautioned himself.

Sammy Johnson came from the narrow alleyway between an old apartment building and an abandoned storefront. Hector could hear the friction of Sammy's denim pants as he approached. The voice had been unmistakable.

"What you want?" Hector breathed slowly, patiently, as he asked.

"What do I want? You got me suspended, you dumb ass. I could do that myself if I wanted to. Got enough practice. I don't need you to get me thrown out of school first day back."

"I didn't ask you to break something in me."

"Oh yeah? Tell me you weren't asking for it. You get on my case over a simple bump in the hall. If you had been watching where you was going, I wouldn't have suckered you. You know what you are? You're just plain thick in the head. You and your baby brother. He ain't no better than you are."

Hector felt the tension seep through his relative calm. The fact that Sammy even knew about Emilio was alarming. He had tried to keep his brother under the radar of all of the losers like Sammy.

Hector turned around and glared into Sammy's dark features. An over-sized, backwards cap covered most of the top half of his head, the edge of the cap skimming dark brows that highlighted sharp, coffee colored eyes. The ever-present headphones ringed a throat with a prominent Adam's apple, and loud strains of rap reverberated from the set.

Sammy's affection for music almost matched his intense love for art, mostly his own. If the two had not had an almost instinctual distaste for each other, Hector guessed that they might have had a lot in common. It didn't matter, though, since that mutual revulsion did exist.

"Go away, Sammy. I don't need you to fuck-up an already bad day."

Sammy's right hand abruptly fisted in Hector's white cotton tee shirt near the neck.

"You got balls. You fucked up a whole week for me."

His other hand came in a roundhouse to Hector's nose. Blood streamed into Hector's mouth and down his chin, but that didn't stop him from grabbing the collar of Sammy's thin jacket and yanking the garment downward, hindering any arm movement. Hector took advantage by bringing up his knee to ram it between the other boy's legs. Sammy seethed with agony and fury.

Hector turned and walked defiantly down the street; he could still beat him with one arm. He was suddenly caught from behind. A fuming Sammy hauled him by his hair down to a crouched and vulnerable position. A powerful blow to the abdomen followed. A black SUV screeched to a stop beside them, the right front tire climbing the curb and the driver's door thrusting open.

Jonathan Perez bounded in resolute speed toward the two combatants. In seconds his towering form brought a halt to the struggle, though neither of the boys fled. Both looked toward the intruder resentfully, but somewhat respectfully, then at each other with barely controlled wrath.

"Cut the crap. Don't you ever learn? You both got the boot from school for this very thing. Let it go," Jonathan admonished.

The two street warriors continued to stare fiercely at each other, their breathing beginning to ease perceptibly.

"You're not on school turf now. This is the real world. Now you're talking assault and battery. The cops aren't into feeling sorry for street punks. If you two don't go opposite ways within the next thirty seconds, we'll see what they'll do with you. I'll be keeping an eye on you guys. If this happens again, you'll answer to me."

Sammy jerked his jacket back into place, adjusted the headphones over his ears and turned belligerently to leave. He walked slowly and haughtily away from the scene.

"Why did you break us up? I can handle him," Hector complained as he adjusted his sling and straitened his shirt.

"Could you? I'll believe that when you learn to handle yourself better."

*   *   *

Jonathan watched Hector turn on his heel, looking over his shoulder for a possible sneak attack. Suddenly, Jonathan remembered himself crawling from behind a rocky knoll on a covert reconnaissance mission when he came face to face with two local Iraqi insurgents. Before he could react, one of them jumped on him, grabbed him by the neck and flipped him on his back while the other held a knife to his neck. "You are dead." Without hesitation, Jonathan had arched his back, broken the hold, and kneed the other attacker. He had quickly retrieved the knife and ended the lives of the two assailants. He grew cold at the thought of his near death experience and violent response.

It's a different kind of war here, he thought, and the general public doesn't seem aware or they don't care. These teachers are the only line of defense, and they're not even trained for the battle. He had sworn that he was finished with combat the last time he crawled out of that desert.

CHAPTER 7

Last week of September

Jonathan navigated the crammed and noisy corridors. It was as if anything could erupt at any moment, be waiting around the next corner. It had been four years and yet even now he tensed when he saw an area that was shadowed or sheltered by obstacles. This was a school, he reminded himself, as he strode the corridors from one technological trouble spot to the next. He liked the work. He especially liked not having to answer to anyone but his clients.

He spotted Hector as the boy came swaggering down the hall. Jonathan stopped and waited until he approached. He let an assessing eye rove over the young man.

"You don't look any the worse for wear. How are you feeling today?"

"All right," Hector said lazily, pulling up to his full five feet, ten inches from his customary slouch. "That street rat can't do me no permanent damage. I'm back here today, but so is Sammy. I gotta watch it because of that stupid fighting rule here. I don't want to get bounced again."

"That's a good rule. Fighting is only good if the cause is right, and I'm not sure it's a good thing then either," Jonathan said. "How's the wrist?"

"S'okay, I guess," Hector replied, fiddling with the strap that held his arm in place. "I gotta go to my guidance counselor. I got the summons in homeroom."

"Then don't let me keep you. Good luck, Hector." He watched him head down the hall and hoped the kid's fighting days were over. Probably not, he thought, as the past tugged once more at his consciousness. The battles were never really over. He headed in the direction of the library where there was allegedly an uncooperative computer.

*   *   *

44

Dr. Benjamin Bradford mopped his beaded brow with a blank piece of white copier paper. It was school issue and pliant enough for the job. A glance at the pile of folders splayed in front of him made the perspiration rise anew to slick his balding head. He rose from behind the desk and strode to his door which had been open a crack. Its position was enough to invite those who needed to speak to him, but it was closed enough to discourage those who might be tempted to just chat. Marci, his administrative assistant, sat in her windowless annex directly across from his office. The enclosed cube, however, did have a large framed pastoral picture she had purchased from a discount store's extensive collection.

Marci Wickers was a middle aged woman who was a curious blend of current trends and seventies flashback. Her light brown hair was a sleek helmet with strands of gray attempting to hide in the sprayed bubble atop her head. Her pale eggshell blouse was a manufactured silky froth with intricate lace at the collar and cuffs, the like of which had been seen in *Vogue* and *Mademoiselle* years ago. Her skirt, an abbreviated faux leather piece of material, ended several inches above her naked knees. Her feet were encased in black boots that zipped closely around her ankles. It was almost as if she had made a leap into seventies contemporary fashion and never returned.

Principal Bradford relied on her for everything. He thought up a policy, and she put it into memo form and distributed it. He made promises and she kept them. He got angry and she left him alone, plied him with coffee, or listened silently, whichever the situation required. She reminded him of appointments, supplied forgotten names, and organized the graduations, Honor Society inductions, and special occasion assemblies. He was the star and she was the director. Everyone knew it, and everyone pretended they didn't. There had once been talk that when Marci went on an emergency three day leave the year before to help when her niece had twins, Bradford had thought of petitioning the superintendent to close down the school for the trio of days. Rumor had it that he was going to use a bomb threat to the pool area as an excuse. When it did not happen, the physical education teachers referred to the alleged endeavor as the "water bomb."

"Marci, the state test score analyses have just arrived."

"I know," she said and continued to let her fingers tap at the keyboard in front of her. She squinted slightly at the seventeen inch monitor. "We have to upgrade some of this stuff," she stated matter-of-factly.

"We will. I wish we could upgrade these scores as easily. They were very disappointing."

"I know," she responded again.

"Call a faculty meeting. We have to do something about this." He began to pound his meaty fist on the door frame. "We could get taken over by the state if we don't improve. We could have the Department of Education further down our necks on the basis of these tests alone."

"I know," Marci reiterated. She pressed the backspace key and watched her last two lines disappear letter by letter.

"We need a list of things I want to address. The meeting will be next Monday at three in the auditorium."

"I'll have the list ready for you by this afternoon, but I'll need a couple of days to revise it and put it in sub-categories."

"I know," muttered Bradford and closed the door of his office.

CHAPTER 8

Hector's sling weighed heavily around his neck, something like that albatross his English teacher tried to tell him about. Even though the fracture now had no actual pain, he kept the sling because it gave him a wounded warrior image that was appealing to several of the hottest girls in his math class. Before the accident his dirty high tops and silky shorts peeking out of his droopy jeans had only turned them off. Ordinarily, he would be ripping if someone had dared to pity him, but he was willing to relent if it attracted the attention of girls like Luz Rivera. His brown, round eyes gave him a basset hound look that deepened the sorrowful, injured persona.

As he walked to the guidance wing, he patted his new cottony corn rows and scratched the tuft of chin hair that blossomed on the bottom of his face. Unbelievably, he had received an appointment with his guidance councilor on his second day back to school. He was irritated that his unsolicited meeting was scheduled part way into his lunch period. It was ravioli day in the cafeteria. This had better be good, he thought.

Hector knocked his knuckles once on the plywood door leading to the counselor's cubicle and entered without invitation. Mrs. Ruckmeyer sat with half glasses midway between nose tip and brow, his cumulative folder in her hands. Like the school secretary, she had no windows in her office, and all but one of her plants had shriveled to stringy heaps in their green plastic pots.

"You wanna see me," he said. It was not a question, but an annoyed statement.

"Yes, I am glad to see you are back from that terrible incident on the first day of school." It was a necessary prelude for a guidance counselor, to acknowledge student problems. "You're not thinking along the lines of suing the school are you?" She asked as she glared over the top of her glasses.

"Well . . . I wasn't thinking about it until now," he said, with a sly smirk on his face. "We'll see."

Mrs. Ruckmeyer cleared her throat apprehensively, pointed to some numbers in the file with the eraser end of her pencil and asked, "Do you see these test results?"

Actually, Hector couldn't see much of anything at that distance, but he nodded his head in the direction of her side of the desk. He just wanted to get out and head to the cafeteria.

"According to these preliminary scores, you have failed the state test in math by two points. It has been my experience that these raw scores are pretty accurate. You will probably have to retake it in November, so I'm going to place you into a STAR class as of tomorrow, and that will help you prepare for the next round."

Hector knew the State Test and Remediation class was comprised of those students targeted as likely to fail on the upcoming test, those who had just entered the school system and had to take it, and those like himself who had failed it on their first, second or third try. Even Hector recognized the irony of having to fail to become a STAR.

"What do I gotta drop?" he asked.

"Choir," she shot back, already deleting his beloved choir class from his computerized schedule. He saw the course disappear and fought the urge to reach for the keyboard to type it back in. It was the only class that kept him coming back to school. When he was in the choir, blending his voice with the thirty-five others, he felt like a real "star".

"Can't you get rid of the history?"

Mrs. Ruckmeyer smiled benevolently. "I'm afraid not. You might need that to get into college."

Hector blew out a disgruntled snort. "I ain't going to college. I really want to keep choir."

The counselor was squinting at the computer screen as she keyed in the code number of his new class, but spared him an indulgent glance.

Hector felt sick—school with no choir, the lowest rung of hell. As he felt his belt start to slip below his butt, he hoisted his oversized jeans up a few notches. He had to do something. He left the office without a word to the counselor.

*   *   *

With shuffling feet and slouched shoulders, Hector headed toward the small amphitheater. He slowly opened the door and ambled past the graded cement rows. He usually stood on the third step, three singers in on the left. He remembered when he was first assigned to the class. It had merely appeared on his schedule freshman year, and he had protested loudly to a fretful Mrs. Ruckmeyer. She had explained that the cooking class he had elected was full and the computer had dropped him into the first open class in its memory bank. "Choir, of all the sissy, pissy classes the computer could spit out," he had grumbled as visions of sweet girls and chocolate chip cookies began to fade into music notes and geeks.

He couldn't believe that on the very first day, three years ago, he had actually had to sing solo in front of the nerds who sat as if in anticipation of his failure. As they giggled softly, Hector was called to the piano where Mr. Tottman played the scales and then asked Hector to mimic the notes. He reluctantly opened his mouth and an almost inaudible sound emerged from the reluctant student's throat. Much to Mr. Tottman's astonishment and Hector's surprise, it didn't sound bad. Mr. "T" encouraged him to sing a little louder. The notes were sung in a rich baritone, and they were all, more or less, on key. The class quieted as Hector continued the tryout. For the first time he realized his unknown talent and the power that came with it.

He still became excited when he and the rest of the choir found themselves, at a moment's notice, being summoned to change into their formal garb and then being whisked to political gatherings or to sporting events. His instant response to requests had earned the choir director the nickname "Do-it Ted." The students loved him. He always wore a dress shirt and tie and showed genuine interest in his charges. He was the only teacher besides Miss Parsons that Hector could tolerate.

If it hadn't been for the computer blunder in freshman year, he would not have been a senior. He would have quit long ago. Tottman and the choir had been his salvation. Hector had confided in his mentor, who knew Hector's family life was beyond intolerable. He and his teacher had bonded not just at school, but on the road when they performed at competitions. Maybe Mr. Tottman could speak to Ruckmeyer, the Rottweiler, for him.

With his right hand Tottman was fiddling with the keys of an ancient piano that took center stage in the room; his eyes focused on the complicated piece of music in front of him, his chin resting on his other fisted hand, his elbow on the sheet music shelf.

Hector dug his hands deeply into the low pockets of his pants and approached him.

"Mr. Tottman." He addressed him with as much respect as he could muster since he was going to ask a favor.

The music teacher did not look up but responded with a drawled "Yes . . ."

"They say I gotta drop the choir."

Tottman's hand dropped from where it supported his head. "What!"

"I gotta take the STAR class cuz I failed the stupid test, and they won't let me drop anything else to take it."

"Who said this?"

"Rotty Ruckmeyer," he responded curtly.

"I'll see what I can do. How many points?"

"Two," Hector shot back, "in math."

"Who's your math teacher?"

"Miss Parsons, same as last year."

Tottman laced his fingers together and stretched until his knuckles cracked. "Did you do the best you could on the test?"

"I got bored an hour into it. I fell asleep, and I wasn't the only one. It was a boring test and it was hot in the room."

Tottman sighed, "Listen, the makeup is in November. If you pass it, you're home free, and I think I can get Miss Parsons to tutor you, but if I'm going up close and personal with Mrs. Ruckmeyer, you'd better make it worth my while. You show up at tutoring sessions and you pass that test on the first retake even if you break both arms and legs. You understand?" His voice took on the quality of a war general on first attack.

"Yeah, yeah, I get it."

Hector nodded once, a code he knew Tottman understood for what it was, a gesture of commitment and gratitude. He left the choral room using the right-sided dip in his gait that oozed attitude.

CHAPTER 9

The first Monday in October

Penelope hitched a hip onto the radiator, which was lined with outdated books. She wondered why the builders had placed the radiators beneath the mega-sized windows, where the heat and cold did battle for control. The heaters had two modes, "off" and "on", and "on" meant eighty degrees or better. To compensate, Penelope usually opened a window, which had only two modes, "completely closed" and "open all the way" since the lower pane swung straight out, and the hinges refused to hold them in any other position. She usually turned on the heat and used older editions of *Calculus Plus* to smother some portions of the vent, limiting the rush of warmth.

The tattered edge of *Calculus Plus* number 103-92 nudged her upper thigh as she perched on the partially rusted unit and watched some of the leaves from the maples and oaks sail down toward the parking lot. It was the fate of a good percentage of them to be crushed beneath the tires of the midsized cars that littered the asphalt.

Her headache, brought on by the tension surrounding the upcoming meeting about the test scores, had begun to subside. It had been so severe that she had gone to the school nurse for a couple of aspirin. Freida Hash had wrapped two tablets in a paper towel, looked cautiously toward the door, and pressed the package into Penelope's palm with a wink and a pat on the shoulder. All Penelope had wanted was a couple of pain relievers, not a major drug deal.

She watched from her window as Jonathan Perez, in a navy blue blazer and gray trousers, walked to his SUV and extracted a myriad of tools, cables, and keyboards. The wind lightly lifted his thick, dark hair. He paused as he untangled a thin, gray cable and seemed to sense that he was being scrutinized. He looked up and locked gazes with Penelope as she sat with her arms folded, mesmerized by the scene. A strange sensation of tingling, absent recently, but remembered from the past, overwhelmed her.

When his eyes rose to meet hers, Penelope's sudden withdrawal dislodged the *Calculus Plus*, number 103-92, sending it tumbling to the floor. She didn't know what startled her more, Jonathan's gaze or the sound of the math book dropping.

Hector entered the room, his left hand clutching a green notebook, his droopy pants worn under his oversized sweatshirt. A visored cap worn sideways completed the look.

"You okay, Miss?" he queried from the door.

Penelope turned to face him all the way, knocking her ankle on a metal bar of a nearby desk.

Damn. She always seemed to be caught off guard lately. As a matter of principle, she never allowed her students to see her discomfort, physical or emotional.

Hector stood just inside the entrance to the room. She bit hard on her lower lip to refrain from uttering a startled cry.

"Yes, yes, of course," she gasped as she gave a tremulous smile that helped her to ignore the pain that shot up toward her knee. It had traveled a direct, vertical path that had her wondering how she could reach her desk without limping.

"Tottman said you'd help me get ready for the retest. You know I failed the math?"

Penelope gathered her wits and responded. "I spoke with Mr. Tottman, and I agreed to help his star protégé. You're right on time."

Hector smiled, acknowledging the compliment.

"I knew you wouldn't let me down, Miss."

Christie tumbled into the classroom with a box of calculators that rattled in the container as she bumped into Hector upon entry. Penelope smiled. She could not help but think perhaps she and Christie had more in common than she had at first thought.

"Excuse me," the student teacher murmured as she placed the bulky box on a student desk. "Oh, Hector, there you are. We were expecting you. Miss Parsons, I know you have a meeting. I'll help Hector."

"I want a real teacher," Hector protested.

"There's nothing artificial about Miss Edwards," Penelope retorted, holding her foot off the floor to relieve the pressure. "I'd love to be with you, but I have a faculty meeting so Miss Edwards will start your tutoring." She had reservations about Christie's comfort level in a one on one situation.

"Great, I get a sub," Hector complained.

"I'm not a sub. I'm a student teacher."

"Well, if you're half a student and only half a teacher, how you goin' to help me?"

"If you're willing to be a whole student, I can help you," Christie stated.

Well, Penelope thought. That was definite progress. The corners of her mouth lifted in surprise and satisfaction. Still, she didn't want to leave the two by themselves. She saw Jonathan just outside the door as she was pondering how to handle the situation.

She called out as the thought struck her that he didn't have to attend the meeting.

"Jonathan," she called out to him, her stomach becoming jittery at the sound of her own voice speaking his name.

He stopped and turned to face her, his eyes asking her what she wanted. They seemed to be asking even more than that, she thought.

"Could you possibly stay in the area for a little while so that Hector here can be tutored by my intern? It's a rule that they can't be left alone."

"Of course," he said, the words coming softly and easily. "I'll be working next door anyway."

"Thanks," Penelope said and gathered her notebook and a pen. She couldn't look back at him. There was something that riveted her attention when she glanced his way. She had other things to think about. She left the room trying not to favor her injured ankle.

*   *   *

Penelope figured the entire faculty knew the reason for the meeting. They had anticipated that the test scores taken the previous May were finally in. The state had promised that the initial results would be ready in September. The teachers knew, however, that they had to wait another month for the final analysis from the state. That data would determine which school systems deserved accolades and which ones needed a reprimand. For the last two years Skinner had been deemed underperforming according to the state standards.

The faculty pipeline worked efficiently and therefore teachers were aware that B. B. the King was fuming over the raw scores, and they would receive the brunt of his rage and despair. They expected that he would suggest they were not doing all they could to cram the necessary knowledge into the craniums of their students. Yet here they were, coming to the auditorium like beasts to the sacrifice.

Bradford stood at the podium on the stage. The backdrop of the New York skyline hung behind him in preparation for the school production of *West Side*

Story. He placed in front of him the papers that Marci had probably put in order this morning. He was ready.

"Good afternoon," he boomed into the microphone, and the sound system whined piercingly in the wake of his full bodied voice. "I do not believe it is a secret why I asked you to gather today."

He waited while several late-comers trundled down the two parallel aisles, found empty chairs, and squeaked onto the seats. He tried to focus an annoyed glare at the tardies, but the poor lighting and his impaired distance vision did not allow him to identify the offenders. The vice principals were sitting in the back, taking attendance and writing down the names of those who had wandered in after the speech began. When the rustle of bodies subsided, he continued.

"I have received the initial scores from the state test, and forty percent of our students have failed math or English or both. Rather, you have failed them."

With that pronouncement the tone for the rest of the meeting was set.

*   *   *

The meeting had been blessedly brief and Penelope returned to her classroom within twenty minutes. She had been outraged at the accusations of the principal. In fact, she had said so.

She had stood up from her position five rows from the front. "Dr. King, we understand your frustration. We, too, are upset at the outcome. However, we cannot, will not, accept sole responsibility for what happened here."

She heard a round of clapping behind her.

"We have to consider the whole picture," she continued. "We all know our students face challenges a lot of students in other communities don't. Almost seventy percent of our students come from families whose first language is not English. We are one of the poorest cities in the state, and we have the highest teen pregnancy rate. Transient and dropout rates have soared. In many households here, education is just not deemed important. This is not just our failure."

She saw Claire rise beside her and realized she, too, was about to speak out. "Has anyone taken a look at the test itself? Is it practical for judging students' accomplishments? We don't want any child left behind either, but not all students are going to college as the state seems to think."

The audience gasped at the comment. One by one, they stood in support of the two teachers who had dared to speak.

Penelope wasn't sure anything would come of their efforts, but at least she and Claire felt some satisfaction that they had spoken up. She went back to her room. Jonathan left after she had thanked him for staying. Sitting at her desk, she resumed checking the stack of quiz papers she had left on her blotter. Her attention, however, was on the duo in the first two seats of row three. Christie's head was bent over the yellow legal pad that she was using to demonstrate the math problem solutions. Hector seemed to have changed his mind about his present math coach. Penelope couldn't help thinking that it promised to be a winning combination.

The boy stared at the math examples with exasperation and then let out a frustrated sigh. Penelope left her desk, wandered over to Christie and Hector, and then casually looked over the student's shoulder as he perused the paper.

"Remember what I said in class. Read through the problem a couple of times before you begin your calculations. Have a road map in your mind of how you're going to get from the start to the finish." She didn't want to interfere, but she wanted Hector to realize that she was there for him, too.

Hector had stuck a pencil between his teeth, nibbled on the eraser end, and read the words of the next item.

"I sure know why they call these problems," he had muttered before attacking the facts and figures.

Penelope smiled. At least he had not thrown the paper to the floor as he had the first time he was in her class his freshman year. In the last three years she had seen him improve his math skills and get better grades. She still thought it a puzzle that he could not quite pass the state test. His frustration was beginning to rise to the surface once more. She observed him as he underlined the actions he was asked to take and the important information in the question. He scribbled in the upper right hand corner and then began to line up numbers on the answer sheet.

"Good start," Penelope prodded. "Christie, would you like to leave now?"

"I'd like to stay and help Hector some more if you both don't mind."

"That's okay, Miss. I don't mind." He turned to Penelope. "She promised to help me anyway. It'll give her more practice." Penelope was surprised at this, especially after his initial reaction to the prospect of spending tutoring time with "half a teacher," but she felt that perhaps he was right.

Penelope then settled at her desk once more and pulled the pile of quizzes in front of her. She watched the two of them, their heads bowed over the word problems. She was so intent on the two that she didn't see Jonathan until his shadow overcast the paper she held in her hand. He had returned from whatever project he had left to do.

Her head lifted, startled at his presence. His broad shoulders obliterated the light from the doorway, and her mind became as murky as Hector's perception of math. His presence seemed to have a momentary muddling effect on her. She shook off the mental jumble, gathered her wits, and turned toward Jonathan.

"Hi, my computer is running smoothly after you fixed it yesterday. You were right. It must have been a corrupt version of software that one of the students sneaked onto the drive."

"I'm glad the problem is solved, but that's not why I came. It's after school hours, and I need a caffeine rush before setting up a new program on the main frame." His voice lowered considerably. "It occurred to me that you might need some coffee with the long hours you seem to keep." He smiled, but for some reason his smile seemed to have a tinge of melancholy.

Penelope's heart palpitated so strongly that it pounded in her ears. She scratched the back of her neck with the lead end of the pencil as she contemplated the situation. Within a second she realized that she was probably making gray lines where she was pushing the pencil. She stopped immediately. Feeling the heat rise to her cheeks, she responded in a voice louder than intended, "Actually, Hector is still here working. It would be an awkward time to leave."

Christie's head rose.

"Don't worry. We're doing fine, and Mrs. Treadwell is right next door. Please, feel free to go ahead,"

"It seems the fates have conspired to set you free. Come on, let's go," Jonathan said softly. He extended his hand toward Penelope, and she stared down at it as if bewildered about what to do next. She ignored the gesture, and he dropped his hand to his side.

"It's only coffee," he clarified at her hesitation.

She didn't want to go. Who was she kidding? Of course she wanted to go. It seemed epochs before she put her mind and body in alignment and reached into her desk drawer for her purse.

It occurred to her that she never really had responded verbally.

"Christie, will you shut off the lights and . . . ."

". . . lock the door. Don't worry," Christie added.

Hector was so intent on solving the problem he did not seem to notice what was happening. Penelope sighed with relief. The last thing she needed was a rumor of romance.

Penelope opened the door between hers and Samantha's rooms to be sure that Christie and Hector would not be alone.

"Samantha, I have to go now. Christie's still here with Hector. Would you mind?"

Samantha gave her a "thumbs up" sign. She rose from her chair and came to the door just as Jonathan left the room. She gave her friend a quick wink, and Penelope glared at her. Sam giggled.

"How are we doing these days?" Samantha asked, knowing that her friend understood the reference to her student teacher.

Penelope nodded. "I think we're on track. Thanks. I'll see you tomorrow."

"Usual time. Thank heaven tomorrow is Friday. It is Friday, isn't it? If not, I will really be disappointed," Samantha responded.

As Penelope moved toward the door, she passed her desk computer, which was winking in its screensaver mode, a starlit sky with scintillating pinpricks of light and several heavenly bodies revolving around an artist's rendering of the high school. She pushed a key to bring back the text and saw her last report dissolve before her. The words of the document faded slightly and then flashed out of existence.

Horrified, she put her hand to her mouth. "No!"

Her brows scrunched and her eyes widened in dismay even as Jonathan leaned into the room.

"What's the matter?"

"I just obliterated my five page report to the district on a new experimental math course," she snapped back at him.

Jonathan walked leisurely to the offending machine and gazed at the blank screen. He pressed a few keys and the vanished text reappeared instantly. Penelope exhaled a sigh of relief.

"See? Nothing is ever truly lost." His fingers flew over the keyboard for a few more maneuvers, and the document was saved and stored. The screen then went dark.

"Now, let's get that coffee. You look as if you really need it. Your work is safe," he assured her, "and so are you."

Penelope looked at him, unsure of what to make of the last part of his statement. Then, she decided, yes, she was safe . . . at least for the time being.

CHAPTER 10

Ten minutes later

Penelope pushed the glass and steel door of the Class A Café that was nestled beyond the copse of trees near the border of the Skinner High campus. Jonathan's arm reached over her head and held the door open for the time it took for them to pass through into the aromatic atmosphere of the café. Even though the tiny establishment's close proximity to the school should have invited student customers, in actuality very few teenagers stopped there, preferring instead to continue down the sidewalk a few blocks to the golden arches. There were times, however, that some of the seniors would take a side trip into the small eatery to buy a Styrofoam cup of coffee to fortify them for the first class of the day.

Penelope headed toward a front booth with a great view of the sidewalk and the late afternoon traffic. The sun had diffused to a golden blond hazy disk, lowering on the horizon.

The vinyl of the booth squeaked as she slid across the smooth surface to the middle of the seat. She laced her hands into a prayer-like position, resting her chin along the edge of her knotted knuckles. She was still shaken from the meeting. She had so much more to say. Even Claire's impassioned pleas had been cut short by Bradford's abrupt conclusion.

Jonathan slipped into a spot opposite her and reached for the plastic, accordion-folded menu that was supported by a rather heavy ceramic set of salt and pepper shakers. He held the extensive list of selections in front of him, but his gaze never left Penelope.

"Relax. I said you were safe with me, Nell. Why do I sometimes get the feeling that you're afraid of me?"

Penelope smiled. No one had ever called her Nell before, but coming from Jonathan it didn't seem offensive, so she decided not to correct him. Still, the nickname seemed a bit too intimate for their fledging friendship.

"I'm fine, actually. I'm just concerned about leaving Hector with Christie."

"Well, now. That would imply that you don't trust Hector to stay with the task of improving his math skills, you don't trust Christie to give him what he needs, or you don't trust your good friend Samantha to supervise the process. Which would it be?" He drew his dark brows together in mock concentration and rubbed his chin with his long, strong fingers as if he were contemplating an elusive conundrum.

Penelope sat silently for a few seconds while a five foot two, middle-aged waitress with a hard, wrinkle ravaged face pushed two glasses of water in front of them. She decided not to tell him about the meeting and her bold response. After all, he really wasn't a faculty member.

"What'll it be?" the server asked them in a hoarse, smoky voice. Penelope knew Sal from the many times she stopped after work for a cup of "closure coffee," as she called it.

Although she had heard Sal's approach in spite of the muffled tread of her rubber-soled shoes, the question startled her.

"Just coffee, please," she responded.

"Regular, decaf, hazelnut, or French vanilla?" Sal snapped back in her usual curt manner.

"Regular, please." She often varied the flavor according to her mood, but today she didn't want to think about such trivial choices.

Jonathan scanned his options.

"I hope you don't mind if I order some actual food. I never got to eat lunch today. Maybe you could have an early dinner?"

"No, thanks. I'm not really hungry, but you go ahead."

He focused once more on the plastic tri-fold bill of fare in front of him.

"I'll have the ham and cheese and a regular coffee." He collapsed the menu and replaced it between the shakers.

"White, rye, wheat, or oatmeal bread?" Sal listed crisply.

"Wheat," he answered leisurely.

Sal coughed into her fist twice and nodded before taking the order ticket to the cook.

Penelope watched an eighteen wheeler whiz by.

"None of the above," she stated.

"Excuse me?"

"It's none of those things you mentioned. I trust Hector, Christie, and Samantha. I just always feel I should be part of the process. I've perfected teacher guilt, I guess. I try hard not to feel that it's my fault if a student fails to achieve, especially if it's someone like Hector." She half smiled as if to apologize for the admission.

Jonathan sat watching her for a moment before Sal returned with their coffees and a handful of creamer cups, which she placed by the edge of the table. One of the small, ridged containers rolled around in circles before coming to a slow stop beside its mates. Sal pivoted and half ran back behind the extensive counter where she topped off a coffee for a gray suited man reading a paper.

Jonathan lifted his mug and studied the steamy contents.

"I know a bit about guilt. It can be very debilitating. Are you working at incorporating it as an integral part of the education program? I hope not. Guilt often means that you don't trust yourself to do the right thing." He paused and then took a small slug of his coffee.

Penelope raised her eyes from her own mug and looked at him directly. She thought she detected a disengaged look come over his face. In spite of that, he looked ruggedly handsome in an aloof sort of way.

"Maybe I don't. I always thought I did, but maybe I've been delusional. All of the pressures of the state tests and the demands of the federal government programs often make it difficult for students and teachers to know what the right thing is."

"I think you know. It's just that the issues have become muddied, and the students are fighting different battles than you did. I'm sure you'll make it through the mire." He gave a little salute with his coffee mug.

"Yes. I'm sure I will. I just hope that the kids can."

Jonathan considered the statement.

"Let's hope so."

Sal sauntered over, balancing a platter on her left palm and two plates on her right hand and wrist. She placed Jonathan's order in front of him and continued to the next booth to deliver the remaining items. She placed the green, grainy textured check face down on their table when she passed them on her return to the counter area.

"Wouldn't it be nice if schooling were that simple? You just order an educated kid, you get one, and you pay the price," Jonathan mused.

Penelope lifted her lips in a semi-smile.

"The way we do it now, there is definitely a price, but sometimes the price is too high and the wrong people are paying it."

She stopped with that statement because she realized that she was actually talking about her passions and doubts to this sexy stranger. The thought made her blush. She mused that she must stop thinking like this.

CHAPTER 11

Tuesday, second week of October

Being the consummate English teacher Claire couldn't stop herself from thinking of that famous opening line: "It was the best of times. It was the worst of times." This was going to be a most peculiar year, she thought as she eased out of her Taurus and closed the door behind her after she had gathered her handbag, briefcase and satchel full of corrected papers. She reflected on the opening meeting with some sense of embarrassment. She had made a fool of herself, but she felt vindicated after the principal's latest gathering. It was worth it. Penelope and some of the other teachers had rallied behind her cry and now they were a committee focused on taking their school back. In a short period of time they had managed to inform a good number of parents of the changes affecting their children. The first meeting with a handful of faculty had been disappointing, but their initial efforts were emerging into a mini-movement. She was thrilled. It was like the old days when she had marched against the Vietnam War in her braids and flowing skirts.

Her memories were interrupted as she crossed the median strip of grass. Hundreds of students were standing in front of the entry to the school building. Usually they would already have been inside making their way to homerooms or to the cafeteria for a nourishing breakfast of Danish, sugar coated cereal and chocolate milk. Her spirits soared at the possible protest. Had the students finally been motivated to action? Had she been responsible for lighting the spark that had long been dead in these teens. Elated, her thoughts turned to the practical about how she was going to navigate this human barricade. She spotted Penelope heading from the opposite direction. She called, "Penelope, wait for me and we'll tackle the crowd together."

Penelope paused on the asphalt strip in front of the building, and together she and Claire pushed toward the tide of students. Claire's eyes danced with excitement.

"Isn't this wonderful? All these young faces experiencing for the first time the thrill of peaceful protest. They have found a cause."

Penelope tried to interrupt. "Claire!"

"This is so exhilarating. We have motivated them. They are supporting their teachers and each other in a way no students have ever done here before. Should I call the news station? Do you think this was impromptu or is there a student leader?" She craned her neck to see the center of the teaming mass. "Maybe the parents are behind this. Oh, Penelope, I can't believe how much we have accomplished since that horrible episode on our first day."

Quoting a familiar song lyric from the seventies she murmured, "We've only just begun."

*   *   *

Penelope had to stop Claire before she made a spectacle of herself. While Claire caught her breath, Penelope jumped right in with a forceful, "Please, stop!" Penelope felt remorse for yelling at her, especially when she stared at the disbelief in Claire's eyes.

Subdued and somewhat shocked, she uttered, "Why?" Penelope gently guided her friend away from the crowd.

"Claire, it's not what you think. I wish it were, but it's not. Over the summer the School Committee decided to take precautions against the wave of violence that is occurring throughout the city. Remember, the chief told us about the gangs? The warning signs of increased activity?" Penelope looked over at the restless throng of students in front of the main door. "Random searches of backpacks and lockers were approved. This is the first search."

"How do you know that's what's happening?" Claire asked, disappointment clouding her eyes.

"I was here late yesterday, and Bradford told me before I left. It looks like the administration isn't letting the students in yet. They're probably getting organized and letting the arriving faculty know. He said the teachers will be assigned duties to assist the process and keep order."

Claire looked dejected. She managed to recoup and whispered, "I guess it was too good to be true." The two teachers just shook their heads in silent acknowledgement.

"Excuse me. Excuse me. Please make room. Let us through, please," Penelope and Claire exclaimed as they worked their way through the crowd. They made it to the main office where Christie and Stephanie stood waiting for them.

Vice principals Jorge Colon and Annette Pike, as well as several faculty members were setting up tables in the foyer across from the office. Colon left to enter the office.

"What's going on?" Stephanie asked Claire, her confusion evidenced in the high pitch of her voice.

A wide-eyed Christie stood mesmerized by the scene. "How often does this happen?"

"Extreme measures are necessary when the gangs start creating problems," Penelope told her.

Just as Penelope and Claire turned to leave for their rooms, Principal Bradford called, "Can you two do search duty? I'll get your homerooms covered."

"Our two practice teachers will take care of the homerooms," Claire responded.

The two interns nodded. Probably glad to remove themselves from the confusion, Penelope thought.

Slouching, Wally Winslow tentatively walked into the office and was promptly commandeered to work with one of the two police officers who were already dictating procedures for the search. Hesitantly, he complied and joined Penelope and Claire at the tables set up for examining book bags and purses.

As Penelope, Claire, and Wally positioned themselves at their assigned stations, the crowd outside was building, and they heard a crescendo of protests in the entrance hall even through the closed, heavy doors. This was not going to be easy, Penelope thought. The teachers waited for Colon, a tall Latino with close cropped, black wavy hair and a well trimmed mustache. He was to give the command to open the doors and line the students up in an orderly fashion. Penelope knew if anyone could make it work, it would be the VP, who was well respected by both faculty and students.

The trio behind the table turned, surprised to hear the usually soft spoken Colon's voice come from the direction of the glass enclosed office. "Where's my metal detector wand? I can't find it. I had it yesterday. We can't start without the wand."

Penelope watched through the glass wall as a full scale flurry of activity in the office broke out. The clerks scurried to find the all important piece of equipment. Then a female voice shouted, "I forgot, Mr. Perez took it to make sure all the settings were correct. I just paged him and he'll be here shortly."

Mr. Colon countered, "It better be quicker than th . . ."

Before he could finish, Jonathan entered the office and delivered the wand to Colon. Penelope could see him pointing to various parts of the equipment as if giving last minute instructions. The vice principal shook his head in understanding and quickly strode to the door and opened it.

*   *   *

Jonathan edged closer to Penelope at the end of the table when he came into the foyer. "Sorry to crowd you, Nell, but I need to be next to Mr. Colon in case there's a technical problem."

He noticed the flush to her cheeks as he brushed against her arm. She turned from him as if to hide the color that had crept into her face. He saw her shake her hands a bit as if to compose herself for the task at hand.

"Not a problem, Mr. Perez," she stated in a voice too formal for the situation.

"It was 'Jonathan' the other day," he whispered in her ear. There was something about her that made him feel comfortable in spite of the fact that she usually appeared flustered by his presence. He would love to spend some personal time with her. He was ready for a pleasant liaison with no strings. "No strings" was a safe policy for all parties . . . He was all about "safe" these days. Closeness led to pain.

With what seemed a sigh of relief the vice principal informed Penelope and Claire that the magic number was "seventeen". "Okay, every seventeenth student—pull them out of the line and search all their bags. Tell them to empty their pockets. Then I'll pass the wand over them. Got it?"

Jonathan thought it somewhat amusing to watch the process. The word was given, and in streamed the shuffling multitudes. Soon the students figured out the count and the repositioning games began. After thirty minutes over half of the student body was still waiting to pass through the gauntlet of suspicion. Clearly something had to be done. At this rate it would take a couple of hours to complete the process.

Jonathan was well aware that Bradford had been watching from the office window, seemingly removed from the situation, but yet very present and interested.

Bradford exited the office and quietly ordered, "Claire, Penelope, change the count to thirty. Let's speed this up. First period is about to start,"

Jonathan realized that it didn't matter that the command was made in secret; the students were alert that something was about to alter, and they started to shift positions once more. They figured out the new count in short order and tried to insert themselves into the lines in places where they were immune to the search.

There was a gathering of young men sporting dark jeans and black and orange shirts. Jonathan became watchful as two of the teens ambled nonchalantly to where a lone figure was leaning against the rough tiles of the entrance hall. Hector. He started to walk toward the boy as the other two came up and bracketed the injured Hector. He saw one of the orange and black clad lads shove something into the gap of the sling.

As he approached the trio, he heard the one on the left say in a low voice, "You used to be one us. Remember, you never really get away."

"All right, guys, let's get moving through the check point." He motioned them to where Penelope, Claire, Wally, and the vice principal were processing the mass of students still waiting to get to their homerooms and lockers.

He held out his hand to Hector and looked into the youth's troubled eyes. Reluctantly, as if unsure what to do, the boy reached into the sling with his good hand and pulled out a twenty-two caliber pistol by the handle.

Jonathan stepped in front of him to shield the sight from the others in the hall. "Give it to me."

The barrel was pointed toward the floor, and Jonathan saw that the safety catch was off. Slowly, he removed the weapon from Hector's hand, and there was no resistance on the boy's part. Jonathan snapped the safety latch in place and slipped the gun surreptitiously into the waistband of his trousers under his sport coat.

The taller of the two departing students came back toward Hector. "Watch your back," he spat out and stabbed his index finger in Hector's direction.

Jonathan wedged himself between the two boys and signaled one of the police officers. The cop was of medium height, and had a bulky, but muscular build. His left arm hung down parallel to his thigh and his right hand hovered over the night stick that was belted to his side.

Jonathan inclined his head to the boy who had just made the threat, and the uniformed cop stepped in front of the retreating form. The kid was medium build, ponytailed with a black do-rag. His companion, wearing a similar head cover, but in orange, turned toward the exit, and stopped as the cop came toward them.

Pointing both of them out, Jonathan said, "These two need to be detained. I'll give details later." He could still feel the gun beneath his belt. He had to turn it over to the cops and do some explaining. From what he observed, Hector had been an unwilling participant in the exchange, but he still had to implicate him when he related the facts. He only hoped Stonefield's finest could read between the lines. Handing over the weapon to the officer, Jonathan said, "I believe this belongs to him and his buddy over there." He let his eyes indicate the co-conspirator.

The officer put his hand on the first boy's shoulder and signaled to his friend to join them. The three walked toward the office.

Jonathan turned his attention back to Hector. "You a gang member? I recognized the colors of the boys next to you. The police have been warning us about that group, among others."

Hector was quiet for a few seconds, and then lifted his head. "No, at least not anymore. Never really wanted to be."

Jonathan believed him. He nodded and walked back to the main activity in the hall. Wally was sweating, Claire was wilting, and Penelope was waving through the last of the line in her section.

He saw her turn toward Bradford who was standing at a distance, watching that all went as smoothly as possible. "I hope it is your intention to rotate this duty," Penelope said emphatically.

"It was always my hope that we wouldn't have to do it at all. I'm sorry. Yes, it will be done on a rotating basis. Thank you all." Bradford raised his hand in a salute to those who had participated.

CHAPTER 12

Jeffrey John Warren III, Sidney Polep's student teacher, was frantically trying to pull himself together to teach the government class. He couldn't believe he had actually been teaching recently after his long observation period. He had to just concentrate on the matters at hand, not the backpack search of yesterday nor the allure of Stephanie Lewis.

He was sweating, but it was a good sweat, the perspiration of one whose energy oozed from his pores. Glistening droplets formed on his furrowed forehead. His eyes grew narrow, his voice intense, as he explained the problems associated with the presidential veto. He could feel the focus of the students, who leaned forward at their hard, sand-colored plastic desks. At last, he had them, especially Hector, who had not seemed engaged until today. Jeffrey could not help but think that perhaps he was the one who was making the difference.

He looked over the crowd of students in front of him. Hector Cortez had just seated himself in the third row. The boy had been a hard sell. Nothing had seemed to penetrate the passive look and tight body language.

"Is the balance of power too great in favor of the president?" Jeffrey asked, hesitantly moving his head from side to side, looking desperately for a volunteer. Several students started speaking at once.

"The president gets the final say? Why does he have the right? He's only one man. The congress has . . . . well, lots more."

"The president's a jerk, anyway," offered a multi-pierced blond in the front row.

"What's one guy know? Besides, he's old," Hector stated under his breath, but loud enough for Jeffrey to hear. "He's at least forty."

Jeffrey smiled in satisfaction. For the first week, the room had been like a mausoleum. He had had to wake up a student or two each day at the end of class. One had not been able to awaken last Friday, and they had called the nurse, Frieda Hash, who had arrived, assessed the situation, and flicked the boy's ear hard, twice. He had responded with a snort, rubbed his face, and stumbled out of the room. Great, Jeffrey had thought, now everyone would know how boring he was.

Today was different, though. He had his rhythm. He was especially pleased to have the usually quiet Hector joining in the discussion. "Hector, you have a point. Now let's hear why you say that."

There was a noisy clearing of the throat at the back of the room. Sidney's sonic boom of a voice reverberated off the sallow green walls. "Excuse me, but shouldn't we mention here, that had it not been for the President's veto of the tax bill, we could all have been selling pencils on the pavement downtown?"

Now Jeffrey knew how he voted in the last election.

"Actually, I think that the tax bill would have helped the economy greatly," Jeffrey responded automatically, but, he thought to himself, rather stupidly.

Sidney rose from the chair and deliberately strode to the front of the room.

"Did you read that bill all the way through, *Mr.* Warren?"

"Actually, sir, I did." Jeffrey's voice faltered slightly as he adjusted his glasses more firmly on his sweat-slicked nose. "I cannot help but wonder if it would not have been more beneficial than detrimental."

Sidney boomed over his shorter student teacher like the Great Oz himself, and blustered a rather thunderous, "Really?"

Jeffrey pulled back only slightly, feeling his spectacles begin to slide back down the slippery slope on which they were perched.

"Yes, really," Jeffrey stated a little more strongly than he had in his first reply.

It only took a silent, pregnant moment before the two men were engaged in a heated debate on the merits and problems associated with the now defunct tax bill.

The twenty-eight members of the class watched, some with mouths agape, revealing the gum they had been chewing since the beginning of class, some with satisfied smirks and others with looks of confusion. They watched and listened with the same concentration they would have given to the latest blood fest video game. In the second row Marisol and Hector anteed up a dollar apiece on the outcome. "This is like watching a pit bull and a Chihuahua. My bet is on the Chihuahua," Hector stage-whispered.

Jeffrey realized he had tuned out the class and, from the look on Sidney's face, he had done the same. Simultaneously, they came to an abrupt halt in their verbal thrusts and turned toward their fascinated audience. A burst of applause broke out as the bell rang, and the crowd scrambled toward the door.

Jeffrey saw Hector lagging behind. Just a few days before, he had seemed always ready to leave at a moment's notice, as if someone would come for him and tell him he didn't belong there. The youth turned toward him as he was about to step into the hallway and gave him what seemed like a nod of approval. Jeffrey was still coming down from the rush of the lively verbal debate when he realized that maybe, just maybe, he had won the kid over, at least a bit. The teenager had a brain. It was evident in his eyes; a certain intelligent glitter emanated from them.

Now, if he could just win over the big kid in the back of the room, his time here would be a lot more pleasant.

CHAPTER 13

Next day

Penelope shivered as she closed the door of her car. The bag she constantly carried seemed especially laden with papers and books. October had chilled the air in stark comparison to the warm September. She pulled the collar of her wool blazer higher as she hoisted the bag more securely onto her shoulder.

"Penelope!" A breathless voice called from the far corner of the parking lot.

Penelope turned to see Claire hustling toward her, one arm hugging a stack of her manila folders, her free arm waving frantically. She stopped and waited for the older woman to catch up with her. When Claire reached her side, they both turned toward the entrance of the school.

"That bag search was quite an experience. I hope today is quiet and normal. This is not what I expected ten years ago when I came back here to teach." Penelope uttered quickly before entering the office.

"Not what you expected? I've never seen anything like it, and never have I been so close to a gun. I saw Mr. Perez give it to that policeman. There are things these kids are dealing with that never entered into the picture when their parents were young. Any change in our curriculum or in pedagogy will not alter the core problems these students encounter every day. It's up to us, Penelope, to do something so that the state leaves us to address the real issues."

"You're right, Claire." Penelope had been aware for some time that a confrontation with the state was brewing. "You know I'll be with you. I think a lot of the other faculty members will be, too. Even our practice teachers seem very concerned. Probably for the first time since they've chosen their careers they are finding out that not all their professors are fully in tune with the actual problems facing both students and teachers. I have met some pretty savvy instructors from the university, though." She took a breath. "Speaking of student interns, how's everything going with Stephanie?"

Claire shook her head. "I've been meaning to talk to you about that. I don't know what to do with her. She's been sitting in the back of the classroom for over a month now. What comes next?"

"My mentor is asking me for advice?" Penelope smiled.

"Well, you have had student interns before, and I haven't. I'm a novice mentor."

"No, you're really not. You mentored me my first year here. You were right there, giving me all the insider info even if we didn't teach the same subjects."

"That's different. You were already trained. I had something to work with. What do I do with someone with no experience whatsoever?"

"Well, you need to give her experience. It's time she taught her first lesson. Christie is already planning hers, and I hear Jeffrey has been teaching one of Sidney's classes for a couple of weeks now. Let her spread her wings and see what happens. You'll be there. What could possibly go wrong?"

"I did let her start the weekly writing assignment. Yesterday, I even stepped out of the room as she presented the stimulus for the essay. That partial lesson was easy enough. I gave her a picture of an idyllic scene; the students were to discuss what feelings the painting evoked and then express their thoughts in a well organized essay. I even gave her the handouts with the basic requirements."

"How did it turn out?"

"I don't know. When I came back, the class was leaving and they were all snickering. I guess I'll find out today when the assignment will be collected."

They entered the bustling office and headed toward the wooden mail slots that lined the walls. One of the clerks called to Penelope and handed her a stack of detention slips for her homeroom. Penelope turned toward Claire.

"If you want, we can talk more about this later, maybe over coffee?"

"That's a good idea. I'll let you know how things progress."

Waving the sheaf of papers she had pulled from her box, Claire strode awkwardly out of the office, off balance from her weighty files in one hand and the documents in the other.

Penelope knew that Claire would follow through; she always did. She hoped that Stephanie would measure up to the master teacher's high level of expectations.

*   *   *

Claire strode to her classroom. On the top of the notices and forms that had been in her mailbox, she noticed an envelope labeled with just her first name and written in the principal's own hand. A letter from Dr. Bradford always signaled that something was amiss.

Stephanie was already waiting for her as she entered the room. "What's the matter, Miss Harvey?" Stephanie gazed with deep concern at the older woman's contorted features. "Is something wrong?"

Claire placed the files and mail on her desk. Her face ran pale as she read the principal's letter. She looked up and daggers shot forth from her eyes.

"Other than my entire reputation going down the proverbial bathroom bowl? And you," Claire wagged her finger at the young woman beside her, "are the one who flushed it!"

She put her hand to her mouth before she spoke again. "It seems a mother called the principal and complained about yesterday's class assignment. She said she would not allow her child to write such an inappropriate paper. What did you do to my lesson?"

Stephanie inhaled in shock. "I'm not sure what you mean. We did the writing exercise just as you suggested. I gave them a slightly different stimulus, but they seemed motivated to write with the picture as a focus."

"Well," Claire wailed, "it appears it was too stimulating a stimulus. The principal is quite upset. He wants to talk to me. Why didn't you use the picture I left for you?"

"It was, um, too mundane. There isn't much to say about a field of daffodils. My picture had a human being in it, and there is a lot more you can say about people than flowers. It was just a picture of a woman surrounded by nature. It had a very down to earth theme."

"Let me see the picture," Claire demanded.

Stephanie searched through her voluminous tote bag and ceremoniously handed Claire the picture.

"Perhaps 'earthy' would be a better term than 'down to earth.' It is not suitable for sixteen-year-olds. You call a nude woman with grapes strategically placed 'appropriate'?" Claire stated, fists curled on her hips.

Stephanie cleared her throat, causing her crinkly tendrils to vibrate becomingly.

"I showed them the original photograph you gave me, and the students thought it was . . . well, boring. I happened to have the other one in my bag from an art appreciation class I took in Paris. I really didn't see the harm."

The older woman sighed softly. "I'm sorry, dear. I should have realized after the bulletin board incident that something like this could happen. It is my fault for not being there in the classroom at the time."

"I still say there was nothing really wrong with that bulletin board that I created," defended the unconsciously sultry student teacher.

Claire hoisted her darkly penciled eyebrows almost to her hairline. "I suppose you think that all the custodians gathering in my room and laughing at the display after school was a normal thing?"

Stephanie managed to appear both cute and contrite as she lowered her naturally lengthy lashes. "I'm sorry if I caused you embarrassment, but those posters were purchased at a very respectable French museum I visited. I didn't think there could be anything objectionable if an institution of high repute in France saw fit to sell prints to casual customers. They appeared to be quite mainstream."

"Only if you're a voyeur!" Claire snapped. "Look, I'm not trying to be a prude here, but you must remember the discussion we had about appropriateness. Principal Bradford is very big on appropriateness."

"Perhaps if I explained the lesson to him," Stephanie offered. "I could tell him it was all a huge misunderstanding."

Claire's eyes dropped to her own chunky black shoes. She noticed that her support hose had begun to bunch around her ankles. She thought about Penelope's advice to let her find her own way. "Maybe that's a good idea," she reasoned out loud, knowing full well that B. B. the King would make pate out of her earthy crunchy student teacher. She was at the end of her patience and her endurance, however, and maybe the principal's reprimand would get her to understand the way things should be done. Her sanity was now in as much jeopardy as her reputation at the school.

"All right," she decided. "You can keep the appointment set up for me. Meanwhile, the bell just rang. We have a class to teach."

Her class started to enter, and the two women remained silent until all were seated. Claire heaved her bag onto the gray metal desk, and two-thirds of the class creaked in their chairs as they straightened and settled into note taking positions. As Stephanie glided near her a few seconds later, the mouths of three-quarters of the class creased in silent greeting. The subtle gestures were not lost on Claire. She reasoned to herself that she commanded their respect while Stephanie cornered their amusement. She would not yield to the self-defeating idea that they were happier to see her protégé. She was their teacher; Stephanie, it seemed, was their entertainer.

When she had first agreed to take on an intern, she had thought of the possibilities. She would be giving back to the system. She would be preparing a future educator just as someone, out of the kindness of his heart, had prepared her. She herself had expected to pick up new ideas and refresh her outlook by inviting a younger person into her domain.

She then thought of the probabilities. Did her students look at her and see someone past her prime while they considered Stephanie and saw a woman primed and ready to lead them to the future? What was it Scarlet O'Hara once said? "I'll think about that tomorrow."

She told the class to open their grammar books to page sixty-two, but she smiled slightly when she thought of Stephanie's audience with B. B. the King.

CHAPTER 14

Same day

Penelope watched as Jonathan made his way across the courtyard that was formed where two of the wings of the building merged. His stride was deliberate and purposeful, and she could almost feel her pulse keep rhythm with his walk.

She turned away from the library window. She had come here to get a book, not a look at the computer consultant. She turned to the shelf on her right and dragged her finger along the titles on the shelf there. She could not lose her perspective on things. They had gone out for coffee. That's all. Why did she always find herself lurking where she could see him? It was immature and a waste of valuable time. She had classes to prepare and more research to do for her dissertation. She did not have the time nor the inclination to be interested in anyone. The time she had squandered in Walter's company could never be retrieved, and all she had to show for the year she spent as his fiancé were a few snapshots and a bad attitude toward lawyers. Walt had been a good attorney, but lousy life partner material. When she would tell an interesting tale about her day at school, he usually half listened or closed his eyes as if trying to block her frivolous chatter.

"Are you going to check out a book or do you just like to feel them?"

Penelope's jumped back at the whispered question. Her breath quickened as she turned to face Jonathan Perez.

"You turn up in the most surprising places," Penelope said as she pulled a book from the shelf and flipped through the pages.

Jonathan took the book from her hands and examined the cover. "*Starting Your Rock Garden*? Are you planning to raise a few rocks?"

"I find flowers difficult," she said, while grabbing back the book.

"Just be careful. You reap what you sow."

Penelope placed the book back on the shelf and moved to a stack of magazines and newspapers that were placed artfully on a nearby table. His masculine scent followed her.

He moved to her side and picked up a copy of *Psychology Today*. "I enjoyed our time together the other day. Is there any chance we might repeat the experience sometime?"

"I don't know. We're both so busy." She feigned interest in an article about the possibility that Shakespeare didn't exist.

"People are as busy as they want to be. There's always time for things that are really important. And . . ." He leaned closer to her ear. "This is important."

Penelope felt her heart thudding beneath her satin blouse. "Why?"

"If you're asking that, then perhaps I misread you. I thought you took some degree of pleasure in our conversation. Was I wrong?"

"No, no, of course not. It's just so difficult to get away with all the work that has to be done to get the students up to par for the state tests. We're also organizing some committees for instructional improvement and that sort of thing." Her palms began to moisten.

"Are you afraid of me?"

"No!" Her response was too loud, too emphatic. She wasn't afraid of him. She was afraid of her reaction to him.

"All right, then. I'll ask you again later. And you will say 'yes.' Not because I want you to, but because you desire it. I can wait." He walked to the large closet that now housed the main computer system.

She watched until she felt it safe to breathe again.

CHAPTER 15

Same day

Claire waited in the teachers' lounge for Stephanie to come back from her meeting. She would probably be quite distraught after being shut in with Bradford for the past half hour. She felt worms of guilt begin to crawl in her intestines. Claire should not have let her go alone. It was tantamount to sending a ten-year-old to Superior Court.

Claire thought of her thirty-five year impeccable record for decorum. She had always maintained a harmonious relationship with her colleagues and supervisors, except, of course, for Vice Principal Sweeney. He had managed to be the one person, before Stephanie, who had made her lose her temper. His funeral had been last Thursday. She stared at the clock on the wall, the hand of which had not moved in three years and eleven months. It seemed like only last year when Sweeney would march down the hall, arms swinging, green eyes ablaze behind large, Clark Kent glasses. He would bark at students to take their hats off. "What are you trying to do? Keep your brains warm?" he would snap.

If the cap was not removed within milliseconds, he would pop the offending headgear off with a flip of the bill and take possession of it until the last day of school. A good number of the hatless and hapless students forgot to reclaim them, and the caps would be on sale the first day of school in September for a dollar apiece. There were a number of students who would wind up purchasing their own hats back for a buck. The proceeds were donated to the local soup kitchen.

Still reminiscing to pass the time, she recalled Charlie Makepeace, whom she had brought to Sweeney for disrespectful behavior. He had looked at her over his hooked nose and asked, "What's the problem? Define 'disrespectful'."

"He was doing impressions of me in the hall," Claire had complained.

Sweeney had turned to the student. "Show me," he had commanded.

The young man had launched into a two minute version of Claire teaching Shakespeare. He had included hand gestures, a befuddled expression at an alleged question from the class and ended with a raspy version of Claire reciting the witches' speech from Macbeth. At that point he pulled a tissue from his back pocket and wept profusely, sniffling out, "The Bard has such a way with words."

Charlie put away his tissue, folded his hands in front of him, and waited for his sentence. Sweeney had given him a detention.

"A detention? Is that all?" Claire had protested.

"The kid is good," Sweeny had stated. "If it had been a lousy imitation, I would have suspended him."

Claire had left his office, blazing a fiery trail past the gray tiles leading to her room. It was difficult to think of bad things about a person who had just passed. It seemed rude somehow. She tried to remember a mellower time dealing with him. She couldn't.

Last Thursday Principal Bradford had thought it was the honorable thing to do, to have the entire first floor student body go to the curb in respect for the memory of former Vice Principal Sweeney. About five hundred freshmen, sophomores, juniors, and seniors had lined the road in front of the school as the black car had progressed mournfully to the church. When it was gone, the throng had receded, but Claire had heard the comment from someone in the crowd, "Nice break from class, but who was that guy?" It reminded her of how fleeting influence could be.

Her thoughts were interrupted when Wally Winslow stormed through the door. He plopped his over-laden briefcase on the scarred surface of the long table in the center of the room. Claire's head snapped upward to meet Wally's bespectacled eyes. She smiled at the sight of this frail looking man in his rumpled white shirt, a pocket protector sporting a myriad of pens and pencils. He had the clichéd absent minded professor look, but Claire knew that when he was in front of the classroom, he engaged and entertained his students. They learned to like math and did well on district tests, but not necessarily on the state test.

"Coffee, I need coffee," he whined.

"Hi, Wally. I just made a fresh pot." She returned her attention to the stack of compositions in front of her.

She was interrupted once more as Penelope pushed open the door.

"Is everything all right? I just saw Stephanie leaving Bradford's office. He seemed serious. She seemed oblivious. What's going on?"

Claire sighed. "Stephanie is a challenge. She hasn't realized that public schools are not as liberal as colleges. I'll fill you in on it later."

CHAPTER 16

Last week of October

The heating system, working overtime, only managed to produce a hot, humid atmosphere in spite of the books blocking the vents. It felt more like a day in the Caribbean than an autumn afternoon in New England. Hector settled in for the last period of the day, but the intense heat made concentrating in Miss Parson's senior math class an excruciating endeavor for even the best of students. Hector knew that he was definitely not in that category. He had always struggled in school, especially in math. Having failed Algebra I, geometry, and Algebra II, he had been forced to labor in math classes for three long summers. He attended every day and he got the credits. All the time and effort didn't matter if he couldn't pass the math part of the state test.

Hector wiped his sweaty brow as he struggled to listen to the solution of a word problem not even remotely referring to any experience he would have had. He had come a long way for a kid who could speak very little English when he had entered the fourth grade. All of his efforts had been put into learning the language.

At least I passed the other parts of the state test, he thought. Then panic crept into his soul. He'd taken that stupid test three times, and he had only one shot left before June.

Hector used his torn and dirty sleeve to mop more salty droplets from his brow.

He smiled as he gazed at his teacher with her long limbs and almost perfect figure. Her features softened with the slight curl of her lips that passed as a smile when she offered Hector help with the problem. He showed her his solution, and she nodded with approval.

He remembered that he was also staying after school this afternoon, and he could use the time on those practice questions Miss Parsons seemed to have plenty of. Hope rose to the surface as he fought to stay awake in the sultry heat.

The wall speaker crackled to life and Principal Bradford began blowing into the mic to check the status of the intercom system. Finally, he bellowed, "Code Yellow! Code Yellow!" and abruptly clicked off.

Miss Parsons hurried to her desk, quickly rummaging through a stack of papers.

She uttered, in an almost inaudible whisper, to her practice teacher, "Do you remember what a Code Yellow is? Bradford went over that at the teachers' meeting that first day because they changed the local color codes?" The young apprentice shook her head. Apparently, she didn't.

The two opposite inside doors connecting the classrooms swung open at the same time as two teachers stuck their heads into the room and in unison asked Miss Parsons, "What the heck is a Code Yellow?"

Within seconds, Miss Parsons waved a paper over her head. She replied in a very efficient manner, "Code Yellow means a lock down."

The other teachers slammed their doors, and Miss Parsons calmly spoke to the class. "This means that we will all have to sit here until an 'all clear' is issued."

Hands waved furiously as students assaulted their teacher with questions.

"How long will we be here, Miss Parsons?"

"What if the bell rings? Can we leave?"

"They can't make us stay, can they?"

"Do you think it's terrorists?"

"Miss Parsons, are we going to die?"

"Hey teacher, you want me to scope out the situation?"

"Quiet everyone. This is probably a drill. Remember the backpack search? The school is trying to protect all of us in case there is a real problem," Miss Parsons reasoned in answer to the torrent of queries.

The shouts trickled to a murmur, and Hector saw the composed way his teacher attempted to bring them back to the lesson. It seemed to be working until the loud barking started. His classmates turned their heads in one swift motion to the hall.

"It's a drug search!" Hector shouted with the authority of someone who really knew what was going on. A few students jumped to their feet and rushed to the door. It took Miss Parsons another couple of minutes to settle them down again.

"It's all right. There's nothing to worry about," Hector heard her say. "Let's stay in our seats and everything will be fine." She turned to her student teacher.

"I'll go to the English office and see if Mr. Nesbit knows what's going on. His office is a little closer to us than ours, and I can get to it by using the connecting classroom doors," Christie called from the door and was gone before her mentor had a chance to stop her.

*   *   *

Christie burst through the English office door feeling as if she were on an important undertaking. Just ahead of her two monstrous German shepherds whined as they strained against the leash, slowly dragging two police officers behind them. The dogs seemed excited, quivering in their thick fur. The cops seemed smug as they followed the two dogs, who finally sat as if by command in front of the large desk in the middle of the room. They pawed the air expectantly. The burly officers tugged and pulled, but those dogs would not budge.

Christie quickly spotted the box of donuts on Nesbit's desk. Having lived with pet dogs most of her life, she knew they wanted a treat. The policemen, embarrassed because they could not control these allegedly trained dogs, finally relented as Christie handed each animal half of a glazed cruller. This was probably strictly against the rules. Their large pink tongues lapped up every sugary morsel, and then their heads gently nudged the novice teacher for more.

Christie looked at their handlers, and they shook their heads as the department head whisked the box of fatty treats away and placed them in a file cabinet drawer marked "D". The two canines longingly stared at the closed door of the cabinet, their dreams of another confection dashed.

Nesbit put his hands on his hips. "I assume those mutts are trained to track down more than pastries. I can assure you there is nothing more of interest to you or your animals in my office. Could you please remove these beasts before they slobber all over my American literature compositions?"

At the officers' commands, the dogs reluctantly raised their haunches and lumbered back to the hall in search of contraband.

"Great, now we have to go back to the office and start the pattern over again," complained the taller officer. "What happened? I've never seen anything like this before."

"I guess they're real cops now—hooked on donuts," the other snickered.

Christie returned to the classroom, and the "Code Yellow" drill resumed without the original panic and confusion. The anxious students, waiting for the final bell of the day, were not interested in learning as Penelope tried to corral them into the lesson by standing amidst the desks and announcing that they would be playing "Math Jeopardy." The winners would be excused from homework over the weekend. Christie realized that her mentor seemed prepared for all situations.

The students erupted with a myriad of questions again.

"What are the rules?"

"Who's going to be Alex Trebeck?"

"What are the categories?"

"How many of us will get to play?"

Christie was wondering the same things herself. "Have you ever done this before?" she asked Penelope.

"I have it all worked out. Everything we need is in my 'In Case of Emergency' box," Penelope assured her.

Christie was asked to get the game cache from the closet. The class became excited at the prospect of a math match. The instructions were given and the game began.

The minutes ticked away as students became participants in the ultimate math review. They were having fun and learning, too. Christie was impressed. She would have been in a little ball of panic if she had been in charge. She began to wonder if she could ever be as fright free and self assured as Penelope seemed to be in a crisis.

*   *   *

Hector loped to the front of the room for his turn, rubbing his sweaty palms together. *If only something would happen so that I didn't have to stand in the front of the room.*

At the precise moment that Hector took his place, a loud knock disrupted the contest. Two burly policemen stepped into the room.

The shorter of the two spoke in an authoritative voice, "Jose Santos, James McNeill, and Hector Cortez, in the hall. Now!"

Hector and the other two summoned students left the room to the piercing stare of their peers. They hunched their backs and hung their heads. Once in the hall the short interrogation began.

"When did you last use your lockers, guys?" inquired the tall officer.

"Lunch," James retorted quickly. Hector and the other teen nodded in agreement.

"Does anyone else have your combinations?" asked the same interrogator.

All three young men looked at each other with smirks. Most of the school-issue combination locks had not worked for years. Students bought locks with keys or left the safety of their belongings to chance.

"No, nobody got our combinations," stated Jose with confidence.

Students, German shepherds, and uniformed police marched single file to a bank of metal units. Each student was told to stand facing his own locker.

Hector watched when James turned his head to see what was going on, and the tall officer snapped, "Face forward! Don't move!"

Jose opened his locker first as one of the large dogs sat at attention in front of it. Hector liked animals, but he wasn't sure if these hounds would prove to be friendly. They looked like they could eat him and then take a nap with no remorse.

The shorter cop affirmed that the dog had identified a suspicious odor emanating from each the three lockers. "We've got three hits." The dogs strained at their leashes a bit, then settled to high alert sitting positions as each student opened the doors of their lockers. The officers started to clear everything out of the first locker. Gym shorts, tee shirts, books and papers covered the floor.

Then, as the dogs held their poses, a signal that seemed to suggest their handlers were close to finding the contraband, one officer pulled a paper sack from Jose's locker. With a reproachful glance at Jose, he opened it with a flourish. Stifled snickers sprang from the three seniors as the bigger police officer ceremoniously pulled out a plastic baggie filled with Oreo cookies.

The bag was thrown to the floor and landed in a pile of stiff, brown-tinged white socks. With red faces and salivating dogs, the police moved to James's locker. A similar scene ensued until they found an unmarked, worn tin. Now it was the officers' turn to smirk. Again the dogs struck the stance. Now, it was the smaller policeman who did the honors. He pried the lid until it finally sprung free. Seven large breath mints rattled around the bottom of the tin. The sweet-toothed dogs and their masters had only one more chance to redeem themselves. The entourage stormed to Hector's locker.

Hector opened the narrow steel door and stood back, confident that he too would be exonerated. His belongings were scattered over the metal floor of the locker, and the dogs faced the mound of clothes and books and assumed their discovery position. Both officers started ransacking the heap, turning coats and gym shorts inside out. As the search continued, Hector saw a chocolate bar and a small, pen like object fall out of his red nylon sports jacket. It was the telescoping, blunt tipped baton that Mr. Tottman had given Hector for conducting the choir in rehearsals and for warm-ups before a show.

"What have we here?" asked the officer who was not holding the dogs' restraints. His face was grim as he hooked one thumb in his belt and held up the supposedly suspicious item.

Hector stood in silent disbelief and then relaxed. They couldn't possibly make something out of this. "It's a baton. For choir."

The officer just stared at Hector until he finally dropped his head and stared at the floor. He wasn't going to say anything that would set off an incident. Sweat began to bead on his upper lip.

"It's a potentially dangerous weapon. Having it in school is a definitive breach of the rules."

Hector couldn't believe the words. "Are you shittin' me? A teacher gave me that."

"Well, let's go down to the principal's office and see if that little tale holds water. Watch your language, too." The policeman pointed toward the end of the hall where a left turn led to the office.

As the other two boys began throwing their belongings back into their lockers, Hector shoved his hands deep into his pockets. He often did when he wanted to appear as if he wasn't concerned about anything around him. He began walking.

As the threesome, plus dogs, entered the office, several of the clerical staff began to pick up papers and open file cabinets. Hector thought that it seemed as if they were only pretending to be busy. They'd start talking about him as soon as he was out of earshot.

I don't need no more crap in my life. I just want to get out of here with a diploma.

He was rudely brought back to his circumstances with the crackle of the PA system, as the principal announced the all-clear that cancelled the Code Yellow.

Hector found himself in front of Bradford's secretary within seconds.

"We found a weapon in the guy's locker. We could take him into custody right now or we can go through the principal." The officer ended the statement with a pull on his belt and a significant sniff.

"Just a minute," Marci instructed and walked across the hall. She gave a brief knock and opened Bradford's door a crack. "We have a situation out here."

Bradford came to the door and snapped his glasses off to stare at Hector, then the two officers. "What seems to be the problem?"

"We found this in his locker," the taller officers stated, obviously the spokesman for the two.

Bradford examined the stick that was handed to him. "What's this?" He turned it over in his hand.

"It's a band wand," Hector interjected. "Tottman gave it to me because I was his assistant yesterday. He said I could take it with me and practice at home with my CD player. Ask him."

The shorter officer gave a snort of disdain, but his jaw dropped in disbelief when Bradford said, "I think we'll do that. Marci, get Mr. Tottman in here, will you?"

"Are you really going to believe there is no intent to cause harm or mischief here?"

"I simply am going to verify a story. I assume you people do that all the time," Bradford countered.

The four of them waited silently until Ted Tottman stood in the doorway with a quizzical look on his face.

"You wanted to see me?"

Bradford handed the stick to the chorus teacher. "Do you recognize this?

Tottman took the item. "Of course. It's a conductor's wand. What's this all about?"

"These two gentlemen found it in Hector's locker. Do you know anything about why he would have this in his possession?"

Tottman seemed to be annoyed with the question. "Yes, I gave this to Hector yesterday. He was to use it for practice. He's been helping me with leading the chorus while I'm arranging some of the musical presentations for the next assembly." He gave the wand back to Bradford.

"Are we satisfied?" the principal asked the officers.

The two policemen looked at Bradford as if he had just yielded to the mob. The taller one nodded curtly before they both left the office, the two dogs tagging along, tails upright and ready for more action.

"Go back to class, Hector. I don't want to see you in here again. And take this whatever it is back to the music room and keep it there."

Hector turned to leave, but hesitated as he reached the door. "Thanks," he said without turning to face Bradford. He closed the door.

*   *   *

Hector had been gone a long time, Penelope thought. He must be suspected of something if the police had come to get him. This happened all the time, she reasoned. Kids got pulled from class, they were asked to explain something that appeared amiss, and then they were sent back. Where was Hector? She was sure that he wouldn't do anything now to jeopardize his chances of graduating. He was coming to the tutoring sessions; he was excited about the possibility of working with some of the new music programs. Maybe she should find out what was going on. The class was in the last few minutes, and the students were surreptitiously packing their backpacks and watching the clock. The game had just ended, and they were still in high spirits.

She was just about to ask Christie to watch the class so she could locate Hector and help if there was a problem when he walked into the room very quietly, as if he didn't want anyone to notice. Of course, they did. The bell rang and there was a flood of bodies rushing through the door. Hector remained behind.

"What happened?" Penelope asked gently and waited.

Hector looked across the room to the half open windows and stared as a slight breeze stirred the branches of a nearby oak tree.

"They thought I had a weapon in my locker," he stated simply.

"I see. I assume that they found out otherwise?"

"Yeah." He continued to stare out the window. "Ya know, I get tired of everyone thinking the really bad stuff about me. I thought when I got out of the Monks it would be all over. I'd be like all the normal kids. I guess I never will be."

He left the room before Penelope had a chance to respond. She would have told him that he wasn't like everyone else at the school. He was above a lot of them in talent and bravery, in a lot of the things that really mattered. She would wait for the right moment and tell him. He deserved to know.

CHAPTER 17

Same week

Penelope and Claire huddled in the corner of the third floor hallway where Penelope had been assigned as monitor. The bitterness of the late October wind wended up the staircase and chilled the curve of the corridor, rendering the watch station a glacial zone. Both women, familiar with the iciness of the location, had donned thick sweaters for their time there. Claire had joined her friend to discuss the upcoming meeting of the English and math departments. True to her word, Claire had set up a full scale meeting with the entire faculty of both departments. The history and science departments were having their own meeting.

"You know, Penelope, this is our only hope for things to start changing. No matter what, I refuse to roll over and play dead because we're going to be scrutinized and prodded by some nincompoops from the state," Claire avowed emphatically, raising her frigid fist in defiance. "Teachers need to be part of the process for any educational changes."

Penelope had to suppress an unladylike chuckle at her companion's choice of the word "nincompoop." She was sure that Claire was beginning to lose her grip if she had downgraded her vocabulary to such uncharacteristic language.

"Some of the teachers have already volunteered to work on plans and objectives. This project will be infused with a solid curriculum and all the best lesson plans we know among us. In fact, I am really astounded by the ingenuity and resourcefulness they've shown so far. We need to get everyone on board, though," Penelope emphasized as she glanced at the zealous expression on the Claire's face. "Look, I'm with you all the way. Because of your experience and years here, you'd be the best person to address our colleagues at the meeting."

She looked over to the open door of the girl's bathroom. "Sorry, I don't mean to change the subject, but did you see a girl go in there a while ago?"

Claire, who had been deeply entrenched in the conversation, looked perplexed and then thoughtful. "Um, yes, I think I did."

"Did you see her come out?"

Claire again seemed to ponder the question of the girl's transit. "Come to think of it, I don't believe she did."

Penelope tipped her wrist to look at the face of her watch. It had been ten minutes since the young lady had rambled into the lavatory. It was time to check if there was a problem.

"I'm just going to take a peek to see if she's still in there." Penelope lifted herself from the hard desk seat and walked briskly to the entrance of the girls' room. She sniffed out of habit and caught the stench of smoke that had settled into the enclosed concrete room.

When she rounded the privacy wall, she could see no one in the room. One of the faucets dripped incessantly and the hum of the heaters emphasized the stillness of the atmosphere. Except for the high cloud of gray mist that circled beneath the ceiling tiles and the pervasive reek of tobacco, there was no evidence of a human presence. Odd, she thought. Too odd.

She tried unsuccessfully to turn off the dribbling faucet and then turned her attention to the stalls. She checked for feet under the elevated doors of the booths and could detect none. She then began to systematically push on the doors of the supposedly empty stalls. One by one the doors swung inward, revealing nothing but commodes and the occasional graffiti. The sixth door, however, refused to budge. She shoved again; still the door remained closed.

Now she understood and began to pound on the door with the heel of her right hand.

"Come on out. I know you're in there," she demanded.

No one answered.

"If you don't come out, I'll get the male janitor to come and remove the hinges."

The threat produced a rasp as the lock bar slid over the metal backing. A tall, russet haired girl stepped off the commode and out into the open space of the bathroom.

Claire's worried voice came from behind the privacy wall.

"What's going on? I heard the commotion." She thrust her head around the wall and then proceeded to Penelope's side in support.

The girl went to the mirror and fussed with her wispy bangs as if she had merely been there to adjust her appearance.

"Do you have a pass? What are you doing in here for so long?" Penelope inquired calmly.

The girl, who was reed slender almost to a point of appearing undernourished, opened her mouth and brushed at her teeth with her index finger as if to remove a lipstick stain, then skimmed her tongue over the same area.

"Just what do you think I was doing? Checking the toilets for leaks?"

"Actually, I would guess that you're skipping class. Where are you scheduled to be right now?" Penelope solicited.

"None of your damn business." She extracted a large pink comb from a corduroy handbag and began to rake through her lengthy locks.

"Let's see the I.D," Penelope requested simply.

"I don't seem to have one."

"Then give me your name, please." Claire remained quiet, but stood ready to help Penelope should the need arise.

The girl did not acknowledge the presence of either of the teachers and continued to adjust her makeup and hair.

"Miss Harvey, would you mind summoning the vice principal? Maybe he can identify this poor young woman who apparently has amnesia."

Claire hustled out of the room and headed toward Vice Principal Colon's office at the other end of the hall.

"While we're waiting, would you happen to recall where you are supposed to be?" Penelope ventured to break the silence.

The anonymous girl turned rapidly and confronted Penelope with a waspish glower. "I'm supposed to be in gym if you want to know. I'm not going up there and kick a ball around a smelly gym, and I absolutely will not take a shower with every loser and pervert in the building."

"That must be some class if it has all those wayward people in one place. So, let me get this straight. You much prefer to spend the hour hunched on top of a toilet seat than to attend gym class?"

The girl merely sulked angrily.

"You want to tell me your name as long as you're being so informative?"

Penelope could see the anger percolating in the teenager. Finally it erupted in a spew of invectives before she finally screeched, "You want my name? It's Amanda, Amanda Fucking Fitzwilliams."

She then clamped her mouth shut as Vice Principal Colon, with Claire in his wake, entered only as far as the edge of the privacy wall. He beckoned Amanda with a crook of his finger. "Lovely name indeed. That will look terrific on your diploma, Amanda F-ing Fitzwilliams. Has a nice ring to it."

Amanda snatched her bag and insolently twitched her way past the vice principal and into the corridor.

"You wouldn't really put that on her diploma, would you?" Claire asked incredulously.

"Of course not. Wouldn't dream of it, but mistakes do happen, don't they?" He winked and followed Amanda F-ing Fitzwilliams to his office.

*   *   *

Jonathan rounded the corner of the hall and spotted Colon following a young female to his office. Penelope was talking with Claire just outside the girls' room. She looked up quickly as he approached, and a spontaneous smile slid into place before he saw her suppress it. Maybe he was beginning to breach the ever-present guard that she always displayed when he came upon the scene.

"Is everything all right, ladies?" he asked casually.

Claire burst into a flurry of explanation about some upcoming meeting of the English and math faculty. He could only imagine what would happen when a room full of dreamers and bean counters came together.

"We're being observed by the state because of low student performance on the state tests," Penelope explained, apparently in case he didn't remember their previous exchanges. "We hope to prove that our techniques are effective and that other issues are factors in the low scores. We want to make it clear we are as concerned as they are, but they have to look beyond the test to evaluate what our students can accomplish."

"Yes, I do recall you telling me about some of the difficulties of the situation. I hope things are getting better."

"No, they aren't," Claire pronounced. "In fact, we teachers are getting more concerned by the minute, so we're going to take the bull by the horns, so to speak, and find our own solutions before the state starts making decisions for us." She slammed one hand into the palm of the other. "I plan to give a power point display, but I get a little confused. Do you think you can help me set up that day? I'm sorry I even have to ask, but when I first started here, all we needed to do a presentation was a piece of chalk and a freshly erased blackboard. How things change."

"Of course, I'd be more than happy to assist you. Just let me know what you need."

Claire grabbed his hand in both of hers and Jonathan wished that it had been Penelope who was now touching him with such fervor.

"Thank you so much. You have no idea how much I appreciate this." She then hurried down the hall toward her room.

Penelope watched her go. "I hope that something comes of all our efforts, both for her sake and for the school's. I feel all the anger she does, but she seems to be channeling it better than I am at the moment."

Jonathan wanted to say he was quite in tune with her channels, but he liked to see the spark in her gaze that the subject had ignited, and he didn't want to spoil that. There was something very formidable about Penelope when she was on a mission.

"Are you done here yet?" he asked.

She looked at her watch. "No, I still have fifteen minutes."

"I think today would be a good time to have one of those after school coffee sessions."

She seemed to hesitate for a fraction of a second. "Sure, I'd love some coffee. I'll meet you at the café at three-thirty."

He was a little surprised that she had acquiesced so easily, but he wasn't going to question his luck.

She pushed her hair back from above her eyes in one swift movement. She seemed to do everything with an economy of activity, and it was a pleasure to watch her.

"I'll see you then," he told her as he left for the library to check on the server.

CHAPTER 18

Christie glanced at the clock. It was eleven-thirty at night. She had been working diligently since six that evening, but she felt that it was well worth her time and effort. Tomorrow would her first official day as a teacher of Algebra II. She had observed Penelope for much longer than the two weeks suggested by her college, but she had been more hesitant than the other student interns. With time, the tutoring sessions, co-teaching with Penelope, and with her mentor's encouragement she now felt quite confident in her ability to plan and execute the perfect lesson.

She reflected on her first day at the school. She had wanted the urban experience, but as she had glanced around, she had been intimidated by the range of hairdos, clothing, attitudes, and yes, colors of faces. She had been very timid the first few days, but as she watched her mentor, she had overcome some of her doubts. She was ready now to attack what she thought to be an insurmountable challenge. She would do it. She would teach her first full length class.

She had wanted to bolt after the first day, but now she knew she could engage these students for fifty minutes. *My plan is perfect.* She would review the lengthy homework assignment. Then, of course, she had the new lesson to introduce with practice exercises. She was convinced that she had more than enough material to fill the allotted time.

Penelope's words echoed in her ears as she put the finishing touches on her lesson plan. "Remember, you are not experienced enough to wing it. Make sure that you have numerous activities to keep the class occupied. There is nothing worse than running out of material in front of a class."

Christie smiled. She just knew she had covered herself in all ways possible. After all, she had spent the last five and half hours anticipating every question to every assigned problem. She had even written them down with her appropriate responses. It had taken her an hour to go through her remarks, and she had practiced the entire lesson in front of her bathroom mirror. This was indeed ten minutes more than she needed, and she hadn't even included the new chapter or the homework assignment.

After she printed the lesson, she put her computer to sleep, turned off the lights, and trotted off to bed. As she lay there envisioning her first leap into real teaching, she became so enthused that she uttered aloud, "I know I've nailed it."

She fell asleep with visions of numbers, word problems, and smiling faces dancing in her head.

*   *   *

Christie stood in front of the class for the first time as their teacher. She was more nervous than she thought she would have been in light of all the confidence she exuded the night before.

"Please take out your homework and turn to page fifty-two in your books." She paused a moment and noticed that a number of students had not brought their books and a greater number produced no homework assignment. They knew she was taking over the class today. *This never happened to Miss Parsons. The students, for the most part, were always prepared for her.* She sighed. *Okay, so I'll only call on those students who have a paper in front of them.*

She called on Hector first, knowing that he usually came to class prepared.

"Hector, what was your answer to the first problem."

He answered with the right number.

"That's correct. Now can you explain how you arrived at that answer?" Christie prodded.

"Uh, I dunno. I just looked at the problem and I got the answer."

Penelope gave Christie a cautionary look from the back of the room, but Christie wasn't sure what it meant.

"Come on, surely you can tell us the process you used."

The boy dropped his pencil onto the desk.

"Hector?"

"I just don't know." He turned toward the back of the room. "Miss Parsons, can I go to the bathroom?"

Christie's mouth dropped. She had just been ignored. "I'll write you a pass," she asserted.

After Hector left the room, she tried to resume the lesson. *Now what?* She looked down at her book, then up at the class. Several of the students had their eyes on their own books, pretending that nothing had happened. Half of the class was looking at her, waiting for her to start.

She took a deep breath and plugged on. "Who can explain this problem?" There were no volunteers. She began to twirl her hair with her index finger while she held the supersized math book with her other hand.

"Miss Edwards, could you please explain the first problem on the board? I'm sure everyone is having a hard time grasping the concept." Penelope's voice was clear and calm from her spot in the last row.

Christie felt like a mannequin, frozen forever in a store window, condemned to change only clothing for eternity, but when she turned and began to write on the board, something happened. She knew what she was doing. The chalk in her hand started to pick up speed. She began to speak as she put the problems in black and white before her teenaged audience.

Tomorrow, she promised herself. *Tomorrow I will face them when I explain things.* Today, she spoke to the dusty board in front of her.

CHAPTER 19

Same week

Stephanie glided toward the table in her usual lighter-than-air gait, plastic fork held aloft in one hand and a collection of salad greens on a thin, fluted paper plate in the other. She had rummaged in the large stainless steel bowl of lettuce until she had found a satisfactory mix of romaine and iceberg. She sat down on the hard plastic seat with a mere murmur of fabric sliding across the surface.

Jeffrey John gulped hard as a chicken nugget got caught in his throat and hampered his already unsteady breathing. There was something almost spiritual about Stephanie that made his heart thump to a quicker beat. The palpitating in his chest was difficult to control until Stephanie began to stab at the leaves on the plate, and the nugget finally slipped down to wherever half-chewed chicken chunks go.

He was a man. He had experienced feelings for the opposite sex before, but he felt quite adolescent whenever he snatched a whiff of Stephanie's fragrance. He believed it was shower gel. He felt that even motor oil would smell wonderful on the young woman opposite him.

Stephanie looked up from her lunch and smiled at him. He felt sunshine and heather and cool river breezes, at least until she used the nail of her index finger to remove a small bit of green from between two side teeth. He didn't care. He knew he would successfully delete that awkward moment from his memory by this evening. Too bad he was involved in this teaching gig. Teaching was hard work and he had to keep focused on the classroom.

*   *   *

Christie knew her approach to the table was unnoticed until she dropped her tray a little too abruptly next to Stephanie's. The two who were already seated looked up briefly from their seemingly intense concentration on their meals. Christie had opted for the thirty-five cent cup of soup that came with two crackers. They were probably stale she had come to learn, even though they were wrapped in cellophane and sported a blurry blue expiration date. She sat down and began to stir the greasy broth to cool it down. The plastic spoon began to bend with the heat from the soup. She had anticipated the meltdown and had brought extra spoons to the table. She put her fist to the side of her cheek and leaned heavily, imprinting her knuckles on her pale skin.

She noticed that Jeffrey swallowed a whole nugget without chewing.

"How's it going?" he asked seriously of both women.

Christie sighed. She knew his question was more than polite inquiry. The three of them had come to rely on their eighteen minute meal break to support each other in these trying weeks.

"I think maybe I pushed a kid too far in class today. Nothing seems to add up anymore." She stirred her soup again.

Jeffrey John perused her fatigued features and nodded sympathetically.

"I sometimes wonder why I even thought I could do this. Of course, I don't get to teach completely. Mr. Polep is always sitting or standing in full view of the students, smiling or frowning. Sometimes he even tells me what to do when I am fully engaged in my own lesson plan."

Jeffrey put down his fork, and one tine snapped off and settled in the yellowish rice on the left side of his plate.

"We're supposed to be interns, and we are treated like classroom aids and clerks." He ran his hand through the scrap of hair at his temple, knocking his glasses askew. He righted them and gazed into the student cafeteria through the open double doors that separated it from the teachers' area.

"Now there's a contented school employee." Directly in front of the a la carte line sat a hefty woman in a full armor pink apron. A large net covered her close cropped gray curls. The coils appeared in bunches under the webbed cap, with flat valleys of scalp in between. Her straight skirted cotton dress stretched over her ample thighs, her sleeveless arms ending in plump fingers that clutched a silver cash box.

Jeffrey waved an arm in her direction.

"She comes into school in the morning, makes the peanut butter and jelly sandwiches, and then sits through four lunches, collecting tokens. There are no great expectations from her. As long as there are tokens in the till at the end of the day, she has done her job. We want nothing more from her, and she demands no more from herself. Yes, there sits a very successful woman." The lunch lady stared into space.

"Why can't things be that simple for us? Must we aspire to great things and then feel frustrated when we don't achieve them, or when no one lets us achieve them?"

Christie watched him intently as he seemed to refocus, pick up his mangled fork, and pop the last nugget into his mouth.

Stephanie was the first to break the ensuing silence.

"Actually, things are going quite well for me. I had the most wonderful composition session in Period B. The students wrote on a piece of artwork I showed them. They were so responsive, even if Miss Harvey did object to the prompt. I had a nice talk with Dr. Bradford, and he was very supportive and encouraging after we came to an understanding about what I can use and what I can't for a stimulus," she enthused.

"Good. Good for you," Christie said blandly. "I am so happy for your progress."

She laid a proprietary hand on Christie's sleeve. "You'll get there, I'm sure. Just give it your all and all will come to you."

Christie tugged her arm from under Stephanie's hand.

A sharp buzz shot through the conversation.

"Well, I guess lunch is over. Back to class," Jeffrey muttered. He picked up his tray, pushed the debris on it into a nearby receptacle, and then placed it on the waiting stack by the soda machine. Before he left the room, he took one more look over his shoulder at Stephanie, who was gazing dreamily out the plexi-glass window.

Christie watched his retreat and speculated on his attraction to the delicately featured woman beside her. She could not help but think that she didn't even get the attention of her peers easily. How could she capture the interest of her students?

*　　*　　*

Penelope was at the head of the lunch line when Jonathan approached her. "I'm so glad I bumped into you, Jonathan. The meeting is Monday afternoon. Do you think you could get set up by then?"

He liked the way she said his name. "That won't be a problem. I'll double check with Claire to make sure I have everything."

Penelope grabbed a sandwich. "Sorry, I've got to go to finish book inventory."

He had been hoping that he would be able to have a few words with Nell. She seemed to be a bit more relaxed in his company of late. When they had gone out for coffee the other day, they had talked a lot about trivial matters.

The subject of her students was always near the surface, and her concern for a couple of them made its way into the conversation. He didn't mind, however. He was beginning to match names with faces as he was called to different classrooms because of computer malfunctions. The new system he had installed was top of the line, but there were power problems at times, and the individual computers occasionally had issues. He had rather enjoyed the time here. He especially enjoyed any time with Nell. If he were the kind who could actually be serious about a woman, he would choose her. He wondered why no one else had as yet.

CHAPTER 20

Monday of the next week

Claire ruffled the papers in front of her. She had made copies of everything, and she was as prepared as she was going to be. She breathed in and out slowly. It felt like the old days, before she became the consummate conservative, before she decided that to be an English teacher meant that you had to be the ultimate role model, before she had turned all her enthusiasm toward classroom presentations. Not everyone compromised their lives for their careers, but that was the way she had operated all these years. When she undertook a major project all of her energies were dedicated to it. She realized now that she should have taken stock of her activities and career much sooner. She should have made time for other things in her life beyond her schoolwork and writing. Well, that was the proverbial water under the bridge, so she would concentrate on the matter at hand.

The other teachers began to file in. She had gone the correct course and asked permission from Bradford to hold this meeting. She had also gone to both Nesbit, the English department chairperson, and Harry Feinstein, the math department chair, so that the proper channels had been approached. Everyone she talked to had agreed that the time had come for the two branches of the faculty to coordinate their efforts.

Claire didn't mind running the meeting. It felt good to be a mover and a shaker again, but she had to be careful not to move too fast or shake the wrong people because that would defeat her purpose. Any new strategy for student success had to be well thought out, and as many administrators and teachers as possible had to be in agreement. It also had to be something that was student friendly.

She was glad she had asked Penelope to help coordinate the meeting, and the younger woman had done a great job of researching methods used in other schools that had proven useful. After all, it was part of her doctoral dissertation material. Together they had reproduced the various plans and had added other ideas that the two of them had brainstormed.

She looked over at Penelope, who gave her a reassuring smile as the last members of the two departments took seats near the front rows of the auditorium. The lighting was dim, and there were a few teachers who chose to convene in the shadows in the back of the room. She motioned them forward with a wave of the papers in her hand.

"Please come sit down here with us. This isn't a faculty meeting; it's a discussion, and it will be a lot easier to talk if we're all together."

Reluctantly, they hauled their bodies out of the back seats and strolled toward the front rows. One of them stifled a yawn as he squeezed his bulky body into the steel and fabric seat.

Taking that as a sign that she had better begin before anyone fell asleep or hedged away after a long school day, she started, "Thank you all for coming today. I want to especially thank Matt and Harry for spreading the word and making it easier to get everyone together."

She coughed and swallowed to clear her throat. "As you all are aware, we have a problem here at Skinner. We have been labeled as underperforming, and the state is threatening to come in and do something about it. We may not like what they will choose to do, so we should execute a success plan on our own. We know our students better than anyone else, and we have a much better chance of boosting their performance than someone from the outside. Penelope and I have some tactics that have been used effectively in other school systems. Perhaps we could take a look at them."

At this point, she signaled Jonathan to start the presentation she had prepared with his help. Everyone remained silent until the final frame faded on the screen behind her.

"What if these new ways don't work?" someone asked from the second row.

Claire was a little taken aback by the question, and Penelope drew to her side and retorted, "We know that our present methods are not enough. If these don't work, then we try something else and something else until we do hit what brings about the results we want. We can talk about the test being unfair, but this is our reality at the moment, and we have to deal with it. At the same time, the district is appealing to the state to take another look at what they are asking these kids to do in order to graduate."

"I don't think the state cares. They're looking for a scapegoat, and we're it. They aren't going to be satisfied with anything we do," complained a veteran teacher as he sipped at a half empty water bottle.

"Who knows? Maybe you're right, but that doesn't excuse us from trying to make things better for our students," Penelope countered.

Claire stepped a few feet closer to the seats where the restless crowd sat. "She's right. Are we going to go about our business and let the state keep pointing its finger our way or are we going to be proactive about this? Math and English are their prime targets for now. We are the ones who can make the biggest impact."

She was almost shuddering in a fit of indignation. She watched as math and English teachers stared ahead and then began to fidget in indecision. Claire knew it was more from past frustration than current defeatism.

Matt Nesbit rose slowly and stepped into the aisle. "Personally, I want to thank you for doing all the background work and for calling us together today. I'm in."

There was a formidable stillness that settled over the gathering until one by one, they rose to join Nesbit, murmuring, "Me, too" and "Let's do it."

Claire had not noticed how rigid with apprehension she had become until her body began to relax bit by bit as more and more teachers came up to claim a copy of the material. She became infused with an exhilaration she had not experienced outside the classroom in many years.

CHAPTER 21

First week of November

Jonathan knew he was making excuses to enter Nell's room. Her computers were fine, but he could not help going to Room 208 to check wires and software, test programs, and provide an opportunity to see the woman who seemed to have insinuated herself into his thoughts. For the last four years he had liked the idea that he did not have to think about anything but mainframes, processors, and software. He had at first resisted the idea that he could be more than just attracted to the striking math teacher.

When he came to the doorway to her room, he saw her bent over a student desk. Her impossibly long legs were shapely under the straight black skirt that also emphasized her tight, rounded bottom. The stiletto pumps completed the sensual picture. His mind hummed, and he felt the ache of desire that had not been this intense with any of the other women in his life. There had been a number of them, but for the life of him, he couldn't remember the name of a single one right now.

She looked up, seemingly startled to see him. It was then that he noticed the student she had been helping was Hector Cortez. He couldn't help but recall the look of pain he saw in his face after the fight the first day of school. He looked a lot better today. In fact, there was something about the teenager that reminded him of his own troubled teen years. The Marines had saved him, had strengthened him, had educated him, but in the end had almost broken him. He shook off the memories and concentrated on the scene before him.

"We're almost finished here. Then the computers are all yours," Penelope said in an unconsciously alluring voice.

"That's all right. I'm in no rush. How are you doing, Hector?"

The young man nodded an acknowledgement.

A shuffling behind Jonathan brought everyone's attention to the doorway. Sammy Johnson appeared as if by fairy dust at the edge of the first row front

102

desk and stood in a posture of casual concentration at the scene before him. Both boys began to bristle simultaneously as they spotted each other. Although they didn't make a move, Jonathan sensed the tension in the air.

Penelope seemed to pick up on it as well.

"What can I do for you, Sammy?" she asked, watching Hector from her peripheral vision as she focused on the dark skinned newcomer.

"I got a major math problem with that homework you gave. I tried to do it in detention, but I got stuck."

Jonathan noticed that Hector's eyes remained riveted on Sammy.

"You know, Hector, I consider math one of my strong suits. Since Miss Parsons, here, has already started you, why don't we go into Mrs. Treadwell's room where you won't be distracted from your work?"

Hector snatched up the papers in front of him, glared at Sammy, and headed to the connecting door to the next classroom.

There was a silence as Jonathan and Hector disappeared.

*   *   *

"What seems to be the problem?" Penelope began after they left.

"It's the one about the hat boxes and deliveries, and it asks how they got to who and how many went to where," he informed her as he advanced toward the gray metal desk.

"Penelope looked at the numbers and illustration on the young man's paper. "Oh, here we are. You went a bit off track right here." She used the fine point of her pen to indicate the trouble spot.

"Are you sure? I went over it a hundred times and didn't see where I went wrong. It's really a stupid problem anyway. I ain't never going to deliver ladies' hats, so I can't relate."

"A hundred times, huh? In a forty-five minute detention? Come on, Sammy, that's a bit of an exaggeration. Besides, what if they're very expensive hats and you make a lot of money? Wouldn't you consider doing it then?"

"I ain't never going to deliver no women's hats because they don't wear them anymore anyway. Hats are stupid. Almost as stupid as this problem."

Penelope smiled involuntarily.

"They're old books. Some of the examples come from situations in the past, but they are good just to exercise your math skills. Lots of women wore hats not too long ago, you know. You wear a hat, even in warm weather, I've noticed."

"That's not a hat. It's a statement."

*   *   *

After they entered Samantha Treadwell's empty room, Jonathan carefully shut the door behind them.

"Take a seat, Hector. We're going to put math on hold for a while."

"You sure can shoot the orders. Did you used to be a cop or something?"

"No, what you're hearing is pure Marine talking, and you better pay attention. We need to talk, Hector. I think we have more in common than you think. The Corps saved me and I think your music can save you."

"You don't know nothin' about me. You don't know what it's like for me."

"You're right. I don't know anything about you, but you also don't know anything about me, either. Don't be so quick to judge whether or not I can understand. I'd like to know you better, and in good faith, I'll even tell you a few things I've learned along the way."

Jonathan leaned his six foot frame against the teacher's desk, close to Hector and right in his face. The stand-off could only be defused by Jonathan since the boy sat silently in the chair. He was shocked by his own proposal. He needed a little time to think this over, but he could only buy it by slowing the pace of the conversation.

"Well, let's get started. First, some ground rules. Listen to the whole story, no interruptions and no nodding off. I'll do the same when it's your turn. This is going to be a no holds barred, no lies told conversation. At the end we'll either hate each other or respect each other. I *had* anger and you've *got* anger. Let's see what we can do to get to the same place."

Hector held the stare, nodded, and muttered, "Fine."

Jonathan took a deep breath and slowly mentally recounted the low and high points of his youth. He had never looked back with anyone before, but he instinctively knew that this was a way to set this kid straight. Maybe he had to do it in order to face some of his own demons, too, so that he could move on. He needed to find the key to this boy's soul. He cared, and that surprised him. Maybe this would give him a chance to right some of his own wrongs.

He would have to carefully choose his words to sincerely tell his own story. It wouldn't be easy. He was a private man and for him opening up to someone involved a risk he was hesitant to take. He didn't want Hector antagonized any further than he already was, and he certainly didn't want to alienate him. Somehow, he had to convince the boy that his story was real and that he actually understood most of Hector's anger.

Penelope was beginning to play a role in his desire to move beyond the past. It had happened before he could do anything about it, but that situation would have to be pondered at another time. What could he say that would convince this teen that there was hope and that he could rise above the doubts, suspicion, hostility, and lack of trust?

Hector interrupted his thought process, "Well, what's the problem? Start already."

Taking a deep breath and mustering the guts to reveal part of himself, he began.

"I was born in Spanish Harlem in New York City. My Irish mom was fifteen when I came along, and she wanted the good life so she ran off with my father, a Latino from her high school, never to be heard of again. My mother's mother wanted nothing to do with me because I was half Latino, and so my father's mother raised me and the streets educated me. I was one tough kid; school didn't matter, and my grades showed it. I was angry, but my grandmother did the best she could. Later on, I realized that the values she gave me would come back to me. We were very poor, living on Welfare, but her home was my safe place."

Hector sneered, "Yeah, like my brother Emilio, but not like me."

"Because of all the rage bottled up inside of me and because I didn't think much of myself," Jonathan continued, "I needed to prove that I was the man. I fought with anyone who challenged me, and as a result missed a lot of school. My time on the streets wised me up to a different world. I had a reputation of being tough, but inside I shook every time I fought. My notoriety got me an invitation to join my local chapter of the Latin Kings. Running with the gang was exciting and dangerous."

Hector shifted in his seat and leaned nearer as the narrative hit closer to home.

"It was like being on drugs. Never did get involved with them or booze, though. I had enough issues, and my grandmother would have picked up on it, and she would have been destroyed. I couldn't do that to her. I wasn't going to bring street life home. I was clean and my pals knew it. It was okay with them as long as I held to the rules. I was the wheelman. I became an expert driver who eluded the cops on several occasions. One night, three of the gang members decided to hit a convenience store."

Hector's dark and penetrating eyes widened with the familiarity of the circumstances.

"They needed cash and this was a quick way of getting some. Of course, I had the wheel. They covered their heads and most of their faces with their hoods and walked into the store. I stayed with the car. I could see them casing the place, and then Jose approached the counter and placed his hand in his pocket. The clerk reacted quickly, reached beneath the register and pointed a forty-five at Jose. The others ran to help their friend when the clerk opened fire as Jose pulled his own weapon out of his pocket. He never got the chance to retaliate.

"The clerk, fearing for his life, continued to shoot, hitting the other two. Hoping to escape detection, I gunned the car and sped into the night without any lights. I never looked back. I got away, parked the car, and ran to my grandmother's apartment. I knew I would be branded a coward by the Kings and that was not good. The next day I read the carnage had been complete. The only ones who knew I was there were dead. The paper reported that the police believed there might have been a getaway car. I had to move quickly. I left my grandmother's house without saying good-bye. I couldn't involve her. I had just graduated, barely, and so I took a taxi to the Marine recruiting office and signed up. I took advantage of the courses they offered. I didn't have a life outside the corps, but I was free and out of trouble." He took a deep breath. This had been a big step for himself. He hoped that it was not for nothing.

"Hector, it's your turn," he prompted.

Hector just sat there with a sullen look on his face, rounded shoulders, slouched in the desk chair.

Jonathan waited for what seemed like five minutes before he sternly uttered,

"Well?"

*   *   *

Hector grunted and came to the conclusion that he had to respond even though he had not thoroughly swallowed the story. He looked directly into Jonathan's eyes waiting to see tell-tale signs of deceit or manipulation. He wasn't going to buy the pitch just yet.

"He'll have to prove himself," Hector murmured in an almost inaudible voice.

"Did you say something?"

Hector shook his head "no".

He slouched even further with eyes solely focused on the "techie", clenched his teeth and snarled, "You're not as fucked up as I am. You're half white. You had an in."

"Hector, I know we made a deal, but I also detect your reluctance to talk now. I'm letting you off the hook. In fact, I don't want this conversation with you until you're ready. No pushing, no more pressure. Now, if it's okay with you, we can talk about chorus for a moment unless you want to go over some math before tomorrow's test."

"What's up with chorus? They're not going to take me out of it again?"

"No, no, don't worry. Mr. Tottman would never let you go, especially with districts and states coming up. He also told me that you like to work with melodies and sometimes come out with your own. I found a program for his computer lab that simplifies the current song writing program. Now you can sing the songs rolling around in your head into a microphone and the tune and lyrics become sheet music."

"You gotta be shit'n me! I got music and lyrics in my head all the time, but I don't how to get them out."

"Well, it just happens that I'm setting up the program after school tomorrow. Mr. Tottman has another commitment, so I'll need someone to test it. Lord knows there are no songs in my head. I'm tone deaf. So if you can make it, I'll see you in the choral room at three."

Hector quickly bounded from the chair. "See you at three tomorrow, in the choral room." Jonathan knew he had lost the proverbial battle, but there was more than one way to connect to the kid. Music would help him win the war. He may have exposed some of his ghosts, but in the long run he felt he and Hector would become closer. Maybe then he could save the kid from himself. He wished someone had saved him sooner.

CHAPTER 22

Penelope was exhausted after her session with Sammy. She sat at her desk and tried to finish grading the last paper in the large stack she had started before Hector's arrival. She put down her purple pen. She hadn't used red since one of her students had remarked that his corrected paper looked rather bloody with all the scarlet x's and lines. She never could shake that gory image afterward and now chose from an array of colors when she had to mark student work. She rubbed the bridge of her nose where the small plastic grips on her reading glasses had make pink depressions.

She had opened the door between the two rooms after Sammy's departure, but Jonathan and Hector were in deep discussion about something, so she had quietly closed the door and waited. She wondered what was taking them so long.

Hector trooped by and waved as he walked by her door, heading toward the stairwell. She reasoned that he must have used the main door leading to the hall to leave Samantha's room. He made no effort to revisit hers, so she assumed that he was done for the day.

Jonathan re-entered her room by the connecting door and smiled smugly.

"Alone at last," he asserted.

"Is that a good thing?" Penelope inquired as she began to clear her desk.

"Alone with you is always a good thing," he said.

She began to quicken the pace of her task. He was coming closer, too close. He sat on the top of the student desk in front of her, extending his long legs and folding his arms. He regarded her as if he were studying a piece of forensic evidence with extreme attentiveness.

The temperature seemed to have elevated in the room.

"How did it go with Hector? Any problems? Did he learn what he needed?"

He regarded her a moment more.

"Everything went well, I think." His almost back eyes were serious with recollection of what had just transpired. "Did he learn anything? I hope so."

Penelope retuned his watchful gaze. "Something tells me your conversation was not limited to math."

"True, but I think we made progress, important progress. We also learned a little something about each other."

"Good. He's a very angry kid. I think I know what started it. I've often wondered what fuels that fire and wished that he would channel it into something positive. He seems to have found a niche in the choir." She stood up and pulled her bag from the desktop.

"Why are you in such a hurry to leave now that we're alone?"

Penelope cleared her throat. "I want to give you your time with the computers without a distraction," she answered uneasily.

"Well, you are right in that you are a distraction. Then again, I didn't come to look at your computers. I came to be with you."

Penelope's bag dropped to the floor. Jonathan came around the desk and picked it up by the leather handles and handed it back to her.

He was so near, she thought. She saw just how breathtakingly appealing he was. He was not classically handsome because the planes of his face were too solid and sharp, but there was no denying the intense, dark eyes, the strong mouth, determined lips. The scar that arced over his left eyebrow served to heighten the sense of danger that radiated from his features. He was dangerous in so many ways that she did not want to contemplate.

"I've got to go. Office hours were over about an hour ago. There will be no one here but the custodians."

"Actually, I saw them on leaf raking duty when I came in. They probably won't make their rounds of classroom cleanups for a while. I spend a lot of time after school. You get to know these things."

He gently grasped her forearm and hauled her a bit closer still. His lips loomed above hers, enticing, inviting. She felt herself falling forward, responding to the unspoken summons.

The first touch echoed throughout her body. She even felt her toes tingle in response. She felt the heat intensify in parts of her body she had not known existed. There was a tightening, a buzz that transmitted to every extremity.

What was she doing?

"Not here," she pleaded at the first break in the kiss. "We can't."

He seemed to surface from some deep place within him.

"We can, but we won't. Not if you're uncomfortable. This isn't the end. I won't let it be."

"No," she agreed through the lifting fog of sensation. "It isn't the end."

"Let's go."

"Where?" she asked.

"Where do you want to go?"

"Home. I have to go home. The dog needs to be let out."

"Can I assist you . . . with your dog, of course?"

When he let her go, Penelope's reason rose to war with her passion.

"Not this time. It wouldn't be a good idea."

"When will it be a good idea?" Jonathan countered.

She turned to face the door, took inventory of the conflicts of emotions that threatened to immobilize her. She took a few steps forward, away from the cause of her confusion.

"I don't know," she finally answered and walked out the door.

*   *   *

Jonathan lingered in the empty classroom. He could still feel her warmth on his lips. He was only half Latino, but he cursed in Spanish now, fluently and intensely.

Of all the war zones he had occupied, this high school was proving infinitely more hazardous. He had let his guard down twice today. He wondered if he was moving forward or self destructing.

CHAPTER 23

The next day

Hector rounded the corner of the ground level classroom that had been made into the music lab. He could hear musical notes intermittently coming from the partially opened doorway. He stopped to listen, but it didn't sound like anything that he had ever heard before. The notes were random and diverse, not a song or melody. He advanced slowly toward the door, and the noises became louder although not more pleasant. When he finally was close enough to peek into the room, he saw Mr. Perez leaning over a computer monitor. Each time he touched a key, another note played plaintively.

"What you trying to do? You aren't making music."

"I don't expect I am. That's not my field of expertise. That, son, is your job," Mr. Perez told him.

Hector wasn't sure he liked the way this guy called him "son". When his father used the term, he was merely acknowledging the blood relation between them. He knew what to expect, or not expect from his Papa. What did this guy want from him? He didn't want to think about that right now. He wanted to find out about the program Mr. Perez had talked about.

He watched, fascinated, as Perez surfed through various options and called onto the screen a music bar with a G-cleft at the beginning.

"All you do is sing or hum into this microphone and the corresponding notes will appear." Perez explained. "Try it."

Hector's throat felt paralyzed. How could he just sing into the machine? It felt awkward, to sing with no one around except the two of them. It was different when he was working with Mr. Tottman on a specific musical piece, but to just bluster forth in song was uncomfortable, to put it mildly. He was not one to sing in the shower or break out tunefully when he found himself alone. Most of the music he created was born and buried in his head.

"Don't be afraid of the equipment. It's really quite safe," Mr. Perez said softly, never taking his eyes off the screen, as if waiting to see something pop up on the glowing monitor.

"I ain't afraid," Hector blurted emphatically. "I'm thinkin' is all. I don't know what to sing."

"How about one of the tunes from the play that's coming up? I overheard you auditioning. Anything will do, actually."

Hector thought about it. He tried to push away the sight of wires and keyboard and conjure a mental image of the stage in the auditorium. He could sing there. Maybe if he pretended a bit.

He began to hum and then sing a slice of a song from the middle of *West Side Story*. It wasn't coming out quite the way he would have liked, but he saw the miracle notes appearing on the screen just as he had sung them. He stopped abruptly and so did the progress of the notes.

"Holy shit!" He jumped away from the microphone.

"You might want to amend your vocabulary on school property, but it is quite amazing, isn't it?" Mr. Perez laughed a little, so Hector knew he wasn't going to write him up for his language.

"Did you see what this can do?" Hector pointed to the apparatus on the desk.

"The real question is 'Do you see what you can do with it?'"

Hector's mind was exploding with the possibilities.

CHAPTER 24

November, 2009

The thud of clashing bodies punctuated the conversation along with the howls, catcalls, and whistles. Skinner High was playing high and mighty in the pre-season exhibition basketball game, and Penelope sensed the vigor of the players and the resolve of the coaches as they paced the sidelines of the court. The head coach of the opposing team was surreptitiously nibbling his fingernails and spitting them out as he strode back and forth. Penelope guessed that was a good sign for her school, but she also noticed that the home team's coach, Frank Putzen, had a face as scarlet as a Macintosh in October. Skinner High was ahead by a mere three points, and so the blue and gold pom-poms of the mini-skirted cheerleaders shook and waved in encouragement.

Penelope's eyes shifted from one side of the court to the other as the action jostled and jammed across the center line, and so she barely noticed the man who sat down beside her on the hard wood of the bleachers. She felt his presence before she actually caught a glimpse of him.

"I suppose that I should ask, 'Do you mind if I join you?' but that sounds so trite. We did talk about going to the game, after all."

Penelope's concentration on the game came to a hasty halt, and she looked to her left to see Jonathan Perez parked next to her. His appearance startled her momentarily before she blurted out, "How did you find me?"

"I was looking for you, and I always find what I'm looking for."

"It's still a surprise that you found me in this crowd. It is a public event, and you are free to sit wherever you wish." She added a partial smile so that he did not interpret her remark as a rebuff.

He was still dressed in the same gray suit and darker gray topcoat that she had seen him wearing when he departed at the end of the school day. She had been surprised to see him leaving at that time because he often lingered long after school hours to complete a system setup or troubleshoot when a computer became particularly ornery. She was also taken aback that she even noticed.

"That looks like a favorable scoreboard to me. Is it rigged or are we really ahead?" he asked, never taking his gaze from the game.

"We are for now," she replied, startled to realize that he had used the pronoun "we" in referring to the team. He wasn't permanent faculty, so his loyalty was surprising.

The action continued to the opposing basket. The other team scored, and so they tied the Flyers for an unnerving long period. Finally, an intense campaign on the part of the blue and gold brought the ball to the basket for a two pointer, giving them the lead at last.

"The price of admission here is a lot better than the last professional game I attended," Jonathan relayed to the woman at his side.

Penelope tried to ignore the heat that had smoldered within her at his words. His voice had kindled the flame. Her life was quite tidy right now, and she did not want to be experiencing any complications. Heat was not good, she warned herself, memories of their encounter in her classroom rising to the surface.

"I would guess so," she responded noncommittally.

Jonathan turned toward her and stared intently.

"You seem distracted tonight," he commented quietly.

A faint flush of crimson dappled her cheekbones.

"I . . . I'm sorry," Penelope stammered. "I guess I was just caught up in the game." Trying to suppress the unfamiliar fluttering, she continued to make small talk. "Do you attend professional games often?"

Her bearing straightened and became much like an interviewer addressing a bystander at a celebrity match.

Jonathan chuckled with amusement, and the straight white teeth were prominent. "Why are you still in teacher mode?"

The red deepened in Penelope's cheeks. She wasn't sure what had made her so socially inept around this man lately. She had been asked by the principal on several occasions to represent the school at various conferences because she had a reputation for being articulate and sophisticated. She reflected on the absurdity of her becoming verbally flummoxed by a mere man when she had even remained calm during some vicious student brawls. Finally, her guard collapsed, and she tried to assume a more casual attitude. She slumped her shoulders slightly and grinned. "It's a reflex, I guess. As soon as I set foot anywhere on campus, something clicks on the professional veneer. I just can't help myself, I guess, especially in front of students."

He leaned to the right so that their shoulders abutted.

"Of course, you can," he assured her.

A collective howl rose up from the horde of spectators. Sonny Suarez had lost the ball with less than a minute left to the game. Luckily, the Flyers recovered and called a quick time out. The remaining seconds of the game became an intense crusade to pull ahead to ensure victory.

No words were exchanged for the rest of the game in deference to the dramatic commotion produced by the nerve wracking maneuvering of both teams. With seconds left, Tommy Fletcher executed an overhead throw that sailed into the outstretched arms of the Sonny, who had two feet firmly planted under the basket. The Skinner High fans went wild, yelling and screaming and some even chanting Sonny's name over and over. He made a successful dunk, with no time on the clock, which gave the Blue and Gold the victory by four. As the team left the court, the fans continued their applause, shouts, hoots and foot stomping. The players managed to tousle each other's hair, slap backs, and punch arms as they headed to the back doors of the gym. This preview game seemed to promise the season would be successful.

Penelope and Jonathan rose in unison, joining a standing ovation to the conquering heroes, and as if by habit of long standing, Jonathan took Penelope's hand in his and led her down the eight steps to the ground floor of the bleachers. Sonny sprinted by them, giving his math teacher an enthusiastic high five with his moist hand. She didn't mind, nor did she mind the sweaty embrace that Tommy Fletcher gave her in his dash to catch up to the rest.

Samantha pushed through the crowd to meet Penelope. She had been sitting with the cheerleaders. Their coach had been sidelined with the flu the previous two days, and the assistant had quickly followed suit with symptoms manifesting themselves that very afternoon. Samantha had graciously volunteered to be the faculty advisor du jour, so that the cheerleaders themselves would not be scratched by default.

"There you are. Are you ready to go? I'm exhausted after this event. I kept imagining one of the girls would lose a mini-skirt or one of the guys would drop someone while . . . ."

Samantha's eyes abruptly took in the pair before her.

"Mr. Perez." She greeted him amiably, extending her right hand. "I don't see too much of you because my computers are running quite smoothly."

Jonathan enclosed her hand for a friendly tug and released it. "It's good to see you on such a triumphant night."

"It certainly is exciting," Samantha replied. "Of course, we'll have to hear the last few plays repeated and analyzed over and over in class on Monday, but it will be worth it."

"Could I interest you two ladies in something to eat? I had only a brief break at the end of school to get a part I needed. Then I was busy supervising the set-up in your library. I haven't had anything since those fish sticks at ten–thirty this morning during that period you insist on calling first lunch. It's a wonder you have digestive systems left upon retirement."

"You get used to it," claimed Penelope.

"Actually, I have to get home," Samantha hastened to inform them, "because I promised Jake—that's my husband—that I would take in a late movie with him at the multiplex. We've been trying to see this film for a month. You two go ahead, though.

I'm Penelope's ride, so this works out perfectly. You don't mind taking her home after, do you? It isn't often that the kids are at my mother's on a Friday night."

Penelope was mortified. She felt as if she were being bartered and battered.

"Do I have a say in this? You go ahead, Samantha. I can find my own ride.

Wally has to go by my house to get home, and I know he's here somewhere. He told me he would be, so it's not a problem," she declared.

"I'm disappointed that you can't come, Samantha, but I understand. You haven't mentioned a pressing engagement, Nell. You can't turn me down this time." He clutched his hand to his chest in mock dismay.

"Have pity, *Nell*. The man is on the verge of apoplexy. Of course, she'll go with you," Samantha asserted. "Trust me, you don't want Wally escorting you," she whispered quietly to her friend. "He's been looking for an excuse to park his Chevy in your driveway." She gave Penelope a push toward Jonathan.

"How about Chinese?" he offered.

Penelope countered, "I can't. I have to get home to feed the dog and let him out."

"I won't let you use that excuse again," he affirmed. "We'll order take out and get to your place in time to save your pet from starvation and bladder inflation."

Penelope had not been ready when he had counteracted her protest with his swift solution, so she had no reasonable objection. They walked out of the gym with his hand at the small of her back. She could not explain the shudder of anticipation as they moved with the crowd toward the parking lot.

CHAPTER 25

The same night after the game

They sat companionably on the woven carpet in the den, several opened food cartons in front of them on the low coffee table. Both of them used conventional flatware to dig into the boxes and place pork fried rice and sesame chicken on paper plates.

Since Jonathan had insisted on paying for the meal, Penelope had provided a bottle of Merlot to accompany the Chinese fare. Unfortunately, it was a large bottle, which she had purchased for her uncle's birthday bash and had left it behind at her house when she attended the event. She opened it and figured she could always save what was left for the next time she had Jake and Samantha over to dinner.

She sipped at the edge of the blue crystal, bowl-shaped glass into which she had poured her share of the dark liquid. Jonathan raised his own glass in a silent salute before taking a swallow. Sitting with him seemed like such an easy thing to do. She had temporarily overlooked the fact that she was dining with a virtual stranger in her own house. As she took another sip, it bothered her even less.

She abandoned all pretense of eating. Her stomach bothered her. Actually, something bothered her. It had reawakened deep within her the moment he had removed his sport coat and loosened his tie. When she had first joined him on the carpet, she sat with her back rigidly supported by the sofa.

Jonathan asked her about how she had started in education, and she slowly began with a brief shrug of her shoulders and then told of her desire to work with young people. For some reason, Penelope began to talk about her childhood, how she had been born in neighboring Benson, Massachusetts, how she had gone to college in Boston, and finally how she had entered teaching ten years ago.

He leaned forward, his elbows on his knees and listened with interest. When she paused, he encouraged her to continue, as if he could not get enough information about her. She tried several times to reverse the conversation to his past, but he deftly avoided turning the tide in that direction.

"So, how was my cooking?" he asked over the rim of his glass.

Penelope smiled. She felt so comfortable at that moment. She removed her shoes and tucked her legs beneath her.

"I would never have guessed that you prepare Chinese."

"Are you kidding? Didn't you ever notice my almond eyes? Actually, my ancestors might come from the mountains of Puerto Rico and the hills of Ireland, but I have rather exotic tastes in food. I have Yen Su's and Antonio's Pizza on speed dial."

Penelope could not prevent a small chuckle from escaping. He was so close, too close. She took another gulp of wine. When she lifted her eyes to his, she saw him staring back at her as if he were examining a museum exhibit. He poured another half glass for both of them.

"The more I get to know you, the more you're as I always thought you would be," he ultimately said.

Penelope swigged another portion of Merlot.

"How is that?" she almost choked.

"Well," he started, "I knew that you had one of those 'tough, but fair' reputations among the students." Penelope quirked an eyebrow.

"Don't look so surprised. Students talk quite freely in front of me since I am not on the faculty roster. Anyway, I had a feeling that the 'tough' part was merely just a component of your classroom persona." He shifted a little closer. "You are actually very soft once you get out of that classroom." He ran the back of his index finger along the lines of her cheekbone.

Penelope stiffened at the touch.

"I thought this might be that 'right' time we talked about in your classroom. It's just that I've wanted be closer to you. You are just so . . . . intriguing." His finger skimmed her throat, and his hand traveled to the back of her neck.

Penelope elevated her glass to her lips and sipped again. She had meant for the drink to serve as a wedge, but Jonathan removed the glass with his free hand and set it on the coffee table.

"Stop putting things between us," he commanded as his face drew nearer, so near that she began to pull her head away, but his hand clasped her firmly beneath the hairline at the base of her neck. "Just what are you afraid of? Not me, I hope."

His kiss was very gentle at first, but intensified within seconds. Penelope had the sensation of being propelled at high speed toward an unknown destination.

Their lips parted briefly, and he sipped in her lower lip as they withdrew ever so slightly. She heard Jonathan's difficult breathing, saw his dark eyes shadow, and felt him being drawn back to her before their lips fused once more in a heady union. As if in slow motion, the perfectly manicured fingernails of Penelope's right hand speared through the thick mass of Jonathan's inky hair, surprisingly soft in spite of its thickness.

Somewhere she heard a glass softly thump to the carpet. She thought absently that she should retrieve it, but the thought never became action, so engrossed was she in the sensation of their contact. She became aware of his hand slipping beneath her shirt and the feel of his palm massaging her spine.

That heat she had felt earlier became a furnace within her as her mind buzzed with the effects of the wine. It was then that she knew their destination, and she had never before had such a smoldering desire to get there.

CHAPTER 26

Early Saturday morning

Penelope shuffled in the sheets, trying to defend herself against the onslaught of light that struggled through the gap between the shade and the windowsill. She pulled the violet sprigged sateen sheet over her aching eyes and attempted to loll to the left and take comfort in facing the dark side of the room. Her foot thudded against another presence on the queen-sized mattress.

"Damned dog," she mumbled. Spartacus was always climbing into bed after she had fallen asleep, knowing he was not supposed to be atop the lavender comforter. He shed shamelessly on the tufted material while she was at school, but he quickly vacated her bedroom when he heard her key in the lock. She knew, however, that the immense warm and fuzzy section she always found at the foot of her bed had been left behind by none other than the mixed breed monster with whom she shared a home.

"Get off, get off right now," Penelope commanded as she pushed at the massive bulk on the other side of the bed.

"Don't you think it's a bit early," the mass replied as a human head sluggishly lifted from beneath the pile of pillows. "But I'm game if you are."

The obsidian eyes of Jonathan Perez paralyzed her with their early morning playfulness. He rose on his elbows and an indolent smile widened the line of his lips. His body rose like a slick sea creature from the depths of the bed covers. The flowered material slinked off the bronze of his shoulders.

Penelope tried to bury herself in the bed. The higher he rose, the lower she sank. This could not be happening. She never woke up to anyone but Spartacus or her six-year-old niece when she made her overnight visits every couple of months.

A scream, a shout, a denial, some form of verbal entity rose in her throat and was on the verge of erupting while her mind scrambled to recall the circumstances that led to this man being in her bed, her house, her life.

Her quandary seemed to amuse him. He laid long fingers on her pallid cheek and trailed them lightly as a sigh down to her jaw before sliding them over the edge to her throat. As his fingers lowered, so did the sheet that had been held rigidly over her face. Penelope's head bored more deeply into the down pillow.

"What's the matter? Regrets already? None here." His voice was hypnotic, soothing, dangerous, she thought.

She shot to an upright position.

"Oh my, the game!" she spat out as the first glimmer of memory began to fill in the blanks from her fuzzy, after sleep thoughts.

"Yes, lots and lots of games," he rumbled, laughing lazily.

"No, the basketball game. What were we thinking?" she cried.

"With all the playing around last night, the only scoring you remember was on the basketball court? I must be losing my touch." He did not appear offended despite his complaint.

"You don't understand. I don't do this," Penelope sputtered and slid off the bed, realizing too late that her clothing had somehow been discarded during their nocturnal activities. She snatched her pillow and covered what she could. Thank heaven she had purchased the queen-sized pillows to match the bed, she thought. The heat from her humiliation crept upward, turning her features crimson. She thought about the ludicrous image she made hiding behind a large rectangular bag of goose feathers. She hastily slithered back into bed and covered her eyes with her trembling hands.

"This can't be real," she wailed.

"Well, I would hate to be thought of as someone's worst nightmare," Jonathan snapped.

"No, you don't understand. This is just not me," she tried to explain.

"Well, whoever it was last night, she and I had very good time. Don't spoil it," he scolded.

*　　*　　*

Penelope made the coffee in a daze, recalling how she had been caught in the moment last night. She'd like to blame the wine, but the truth was that she had willingly entered into what followed dinner. The mystery of it was that she didn't really know why, and the horror of it was that she had never been so swept away by her emotions that she surrendered her control. It had simply caught her off guard, perhaps because she didn't want to remember how easily she had succumbed the night before.

Jonathan strode into the kitchen as comfortably as if he had lived in the house for years.

"I've got coffee brewing, and some eggs and bacon on the way," she told him, trying to act as natural as possible after her outburst this morning.

He walked over to the counter where she was working on pulling apart strips of bacon, Spartacus looking up longingly at the meat. "I'll put the toast in."

He extracted four slices of the wheat bread from the bag near the toaster and placed them in the slots, pushing the lever down.

They worked without further conversation until they were seated at the small table in the breakfast nook. "I just want you to know," Penelope began, "last night was . . . well, unusual, for me."

His black eyes breached the barriers she was trying to resurrect. "It wasn't run of the mill for me either," he finally said, "but it was inevitable. We both knew it would happen." He then picked up his fork and dug into the scrambled eggs.

*   *   *

Shortly after breakfast Penelope peered between the two lace panels that hung from the white metal curtain rod. The long, frilly scalloped valence that was layered over them scraped gently against the top of her head.

"Look, just make a run for it, will you? Maybe she won't notice."

Jonathan folded the blue silk tie and pushed the wad into the pocket of his gray jacket.

"Who won't notice?" he inquired off handedly as he advanced toward the window to catch a glimpse at whatever seemed to be the cause of such apprehension.

"It's Filomena Whipplewhite. She's the neighborhood morality police. I just don't want her to know you spent the night."

Jonathan looked through the gap between the long lace columns. He noticed an elderly woman hovering at a height of about five feet. She was perusing the potted mums that bordered the wooden front porch of her Victorian home. She stepped primly around the rows of shrubs in her cotton terry mules and muted plaid housecoat. Her short and sparse silver hair was set in smooth waves that were elevated to a shape that closely resembled a metallic space helmet.

"You're afraid of that?" Jonathan smirked.

"Look, I have a solid reputation, and I don't want it sullied by letting the neighborhood gossip queen see someone leaving my house at eight o'clock in the morning."

"You are aware," countered Jonathan, "that this is the twenty-first century? No one has a reputation. You also should know that no one uses the word 'sullied' anymore."

"All right, maybe I am being a little obsessive here, but I really do have to be concerned about what people think. I'm a teacher. They expect more from someone who makes a living working with children, even if some of them are bigger than I am."

"I understand, sort of." Jonathan nuzzled her neck behind her right ear before she shook him off and left her position by the window. "Look, I saw you face down a two hundred pound offender in the hall two days ago. How can you be afraid of a little old lady?"

"She's no little old lady. She's a vicious viper with a tongue that cuts you to the quick if you cross the morality line."

"The effectiveness might depend on where that line is drawn and by whom," he mused.

"What's that supposed to mean?" Penelope snipped.

"Well, one man's morality is another man's mortality. What could be the death of one man's soul could be the salvation for someone else," he stated cryptically.

She watched the finely etched lips quirk slightly.

"That makes no sense whatsoever. Look, you've got to leave. Wait till she goes in the house and just drive away."

"You don't think she noticed the big black vehicle in the driveway yet?"

Penelope's fingers began to massage her throbbing temples, and she closed her eyes.

Jonathan watched her briefly with his arms folded casually across his chest.

"I've got an appointment at nine. I can't wait until the Wipplewhite threat is over, but don't worry, I'll do my best not to embarrass you. Try to forget you have a neighbor, or, if you prefer, try to forget I was here."

She heard the door open and then scrape across the nap of the hallway carpet. She raced to the window to see if his departure would be noticed by the woman next door. To her horror she watched as he approached the dreaded Mrs. Wipplewhite and started to speak. She saw Filomena's face change from suspicious to friendly, to almost flirtatious as the conversation continued. After a five minute interlude, Jonathan crossed the grassy divider to his car, donned his sunglasses, and slid behind the steering wheel of his SUV. He was gone in a short puff of exhaust and a flash of ebony.

Mrs. Wipplewhite was watching the departing vehicle as Penelope moved out onto her own shadowed porch. The elderly woman waved.

"It was thoughtful of you to put up that nice young man when he got sick last night. He said your couch is a little lumpy, though."

Her voice was loud enough for the entire neighborhood to have heard the statement. Georgia Frotham's head popped out of the second story window of her brown colonial across the street. Penelope went inside, pulled her shades down and closed her eyes. This could never happen again, she vowed.

CHAPTER 27

Later Saturday

Penelope tore lettuce leaves with a vengeance, dropping them, almost pitching them into a large, yellow ceramic bowl. She intended to make enough salad for dinner tonight with some left over for tomorrow's lunch. She peeled the waxy green skin of a cucumber and began to chop it with the same ferocity that she used to mince the green pepper and Vidalia onion. Each time the image of Jonathan in her bed seeped into her consciousness, she came down hard on the vegetables lying on the durable plastic cutting board.

She never went to bed with just anyone until she really got to know them. Only once had there been an instance that she had broken that hard and fast rule. She had met Mark when they were both in their last year of undergraduate school. She fell easily under the spell of his athletic body, handsome features, and glib demeanor. She had been drawn to him with all the ardor of first love. They were together constantly for a month. She had pictured a future with him as she had finally succumbed to his sweet entreaties to make their relationship physical. Not a week after their first and only encounter, she had gone to his dorm room and found a raven haired freshman stretched out on his bed, looking into his eyes with the same devotion she had imagined she felt the week before. She had not listened to his explanations or excuses, had not listened to her heart since that time. With Walter she had listened to her head, and that hadn't worked either.

She had always mentally disapproved of women who considered sliding between the sheets with a man as mere payment for a pizza and a bottle of mediocre wine. She had fancied herself in love the first time, but what about now? Had she become the same kind of woman that she had censured?

A plump, gray mushroom was about to fall victim to the butcher blade and her own self-admonishment when the kitchen phone shuddered to life with a plaintive ring. She read the words "private caller" in the ID window, and she knew, of course, who it was. She considered not answering, but she snatched the phone from its base against her better judgment.

"Yes," she snapped as soon as the phone was in position at her ear.

"Well now, that's just what I wanted to hear," declared Jonathan's deep masculine voice on the line. "I was hoping we could go out for dinner tonight."

"I can't," she answered a tad too quickly, too defensively. She began to poke with her free fingers at the lettuce leaves that were haphazardly layered at the bottom of the bowl. Why was she jittery anyway? "I've already started dinner."

"Nell, I hope you still aren't having second thoughts about last night. Personally, I wouldn't give back a minute of it."

She expelled a long, labored breath and felt some of the tension bleed from her body. She really didn't regret last night. She may not think the timing was good; it was too soon, but she knew, as he had stated that morning, that it would have happened sometime. She knew it would happen when she first rounded the corner and saw his sturdy body poised against the bricks. She accepted this now as her mind replayed the languid lovemaking of the previous evening.

"Are you still there? I know it was unusual for you to move that quickly, and I respect that, but I still want to see you," he continued in a low, steady tone. "I can assure you that you will be the navigator in this relationship, and I am a man of my word. There can be a relationship, can't there?"

Penelope pushed with her knife at the still whole, solitary mushroom.

"Last night was different for me, too" he resumed. "This phone call is different for me. Hell, I haven't used the word 'relationship' in . . . well, maybe I've never used it. Whatever a relationship means, you can define it here, decide if it begins, continues, or ends." He paused, then concluded in a lighter manner. "I'm risking my masculinity just doing this."

His attempt to lighten the subject did little to ease the strain between them.

Penelope pinched her thumb and forefinger at the bridge of her nose. "Let me think about it," she retorted before hanging up the phone, even though she realized already what her answer would be.

CHAPTER 28

Two days later

Hector was pissed. All the hours talking to Emilio about keeping his chin up and his life straight had done no good. He had heard from his grandmother, who had called him in a panic, that his kid brother was going to be "jumped" into the Monks today. The Monks were actually a feeder group to the big time Apostles. They were a rough collection of humanity. Drugs and heavy artillery were their stock and trade. The smaller, more inexperienced Monks were usually used as their "shorties" or leg men.

He knew their routine. First they would gather courage by drinking beer and puffing weed. They would siphon the smoke as long as possible and then make their new recruit take a few hits from a joint while they questioned him gruffly about his loyalty and commitment to the gang. Of course, a new recruit also had to be tough. Emilio would be surrounded by the members and each would have his turn beating the kid with fists and booted feet. Hector still shuddered remembering how he had passed the test.

"Oh Shit!" He couldn't imagine, didn't want to imagine his brother going through it, "I hope I get there in time," he muttered to himself as he quickened his speed. One whimper from Emilio, and they would pound him again and dump him in a ditch. *Oh God, he's only twelve.* Another thought crept into his brain. *The test—the damned test.* He had to take it today and pass it. His diploma was on the line, and math was the enemy. He couldn't be late or they would lock him out.

He put on his street face. He narrowed his eyes, set his jaw, and sneered. Hector demanded respect on the streets, and he knew how to get it. He clenched his fists, pounded one into another, and stomped heavily and quickly to the abandoned railroad yard, the Monks' favorite spot, a safe place for these hoods.

It had long been abandoned, and since it was out of sight behind the stone edifice that was once a terminal, people paid it little mind. The city had other priorities than to make the rusty rails and empty boxcars look socially acceptable.

Hector made his way to the abandoned railway yard where Emilio's launch into "ganghood" would supposedly take place. He could still rescue Emilio and get to school in time for that stupid math retake exam. This would have to be fast.

He wished his grandma had called before this morning with her concerns, but apparently she had just found out from Emilio's girlfriend when Nina had called the apartment to plead with him not to go. A girlfriend at twelve! His own mother had been fourteen when she had given birth to him, and look where it all had led. Having a girlfriend was another mistake Emilio's brother was making even though it was not uncommon in his neighborhood for middle school kids to hook up and pop out the babies.

The Monks were not that difficult to spot with their orange and black jackets in the still bleak atmosphere of the morning. They were huddled near a corroded coal car, looking like extras from a local production of *Grease*. The leader of the gang was a twenty-three-year-old nicknamed, "Teach", signifying his role as recruiter and trainer for the Apostles. Teach also took pleasure in drumming out the weaklings with another ceremonial thumping. He loved playing the part. He wore a dirty triangle of fabric on his large shaved head. His stubbly chin sported a jagged scar, probably etched by a blade during a gang fight.

Hector had long ago broken his affiliation with the Monks, but not without repercussions. He had been "V'd", or "violenced," out of the gang when he refused to participate in an armed robbery of a local liquor mart. After the job he was to be moved up to the Apostles. He had earned a reputation as a hothead and a street name that had fit his persona at the time, El Toro, but there was compassion in his soul, however, that he kept hidden from others, knowing they would see it as a weakness. After all, he had to maintain the street image in order to survive.

The old man who was on duty at the store that night of the scheduled robbery lived in the same block he did; he didn't want to do anything that would endanger him. The old man had always been kind to Hector, giving him candy and soda when he was younger, and when he was older the old man, Reynaldo, still never hesitated to say, "Hello." He hadn't wanted be a part of anything that would hurt Reynaldo in any way.

That night had been the awakening, when he realized that the Monks weren't the family he had craved, but just a bunch of felons in the making. He had conveniently overlooked that in his need to be a part of something, but now being a part of them meant turning his back on someone who had treated him like a son. He had been keenly aware of his allegiance to the brothers, however, and didn't go so far as to report the impending crime to the police, but he did tip off Reynaldo, who closed his store early for the night. The gang did break into the dark store, but there had been no money in the register. Someone had guessed Hector's treachery, and for this he had been gang jumped and beaten. That was the end of El Toro, but because he had kept his mouth shut and had taken the "V'ing" without a murmur, they had cut him loose.

On that auspicious night, his mother had been still alive, and he had not dared go home until he cleaned himself up and could walk a straight line. He still vividly recalled coming to in the early evening rain and wondering if he was actually alive or if his soul would rise from out of his body like he had once seen on *Unexplained Mysteries*. He did survive, but the jumping signaled his exit from the gang and the entrance into a world he never really knew existed until high school and music. He shook off the past to deal with the present.

As Hector entered the railroad yard, he slowed to regain his composure and to re-establish his game face and gang stance. Hector glanced at the time on his cell phone. He could afford no more than fifteen minutes of confrontation time so that he could return Emilio to school and still be admitted to the test room.

He stepped out of the dimness and into the morning light in the dingy yard. He lit a cigarette and approached the gathering with attitude.

He spotted Teach and was surprised that he still was at the helm in the three years since his brutal ousting from the gang.

"Hey Teach, you got my baby brother there?"

Emilio blanched at his brother's voice. Hector knew what he was thinking. He was here to be a man, not to be rescued by big brother. He desired initiation and admiration, not dishonor and humiliation, and the appearance of Hector would insure the last two. He backed away toward the rear of the group from his original position in the center. Emilio was small in stature, but not diminutive enough to escape Hector's notice.

As Hector walked toward the gathering, he saw the light of recognition in the gang leader's face. Teach stood up straighter and narrowed his dark eyes, his unshaven chin jutting forward in defiance.

"What you doing here? You got kicked out a long time ago. You come crawlin' back now, we don't take you." Teach studied the cigarette stub between his thumb and forefinger in a dismissive gesture.

"You know what I want. Emilio, here, ain't ready for you guys. Besides, he got to come back with me. Our Grandma is real sick and needs him," Hector stated with no sense of urgency, but with decisiveness. If there was one thing that the gang appreciated, it was family loyalty, which is why Hector had chosen that approach. The families of most of the gang members probably consisted of odd assortments of single parents, step parents, grandparents and various sisters and brothers, both half and whole, as well as a multitude of cousins. They were also most likely scattered and detached in some cases, but when it came to a family crisis, they would always stick together until the catastrophe had passed. They understood the importance of "familia" and especially the role of the grandmother.

"Well, it seems real convenient that your grandma goes down just when this little piece of shit is getting ready to become one of us. What you gonna do to take him?"

Hector took an extended drag of his cigarette and snatched a quick look at his cell phone again. "I got no time to mess with you, and neither does Emilio."

He turned to Emilio and addressed the boy directly.

"How you gonna feel if Grandma dies, and you're not there 'cause you was being jumped into the Monks? Where's your head at?"

Emilio's head was down, his left foot kicking the rail-side gravel. He probably doubted his grandmother was sick, but could he take the chance? Hector knew that Abuela was all Emilio had, and he loved her.

"Well, little bro, whatcha gonna do?" As Teach's fist grasped the lapel of the fake leather jacket that hung too large on Emilio's slender frame, he withdrew a metal blade that glinted in the morning light as he held the tip to the boy's throat. The Apostle tattoo was visible on his wrist, and Hector was aware that anyone who had proven himself sported the emblem on the lower arm. Right now that pitchfork with a set of sharp horns forming the outside two tines reminded Hector that he had to think clearly and fast. Teach was big league and had cut before.

Emilio began to cry, climaxing in muffled sobs, begging to live. Teach grunted with disgust, let Emilio go and pushed him to the ground. The edge of the blade made a slight nick in Emilio's neck, and a thin rivulet of red began its descent to the ribbed edge of the young man's shirt. Hector stepped forward and grabbed him by the front of his shirt to pick him up. He pulled a bandana, used to style his outfit, out of his back pocket and held it to his brother's neck.

"Take him," Teach commanded with a sneer surrounding the smoking butt drooping from the center of his lips. "He ain't worth much anyway. It's like throwing back a fish too small to fry. Just remember, you shut your mouth about us. If it gets back that you ratted, the Apostles will make sure your grandma goes to *your* funeral."

Hector never released his brother until they had rounded the terminal's wall, well out of sight of the Monks. He pushed his brother in front of him.

"Move. I'm taking you back where you belong so I'm sure you don't run back there. Are you stupid or something? What happens if you get yourself busted by the cops or busted up by those hoods? You think our mamma wouldn't whip your ass if she was still here? Stupido! Stupido! I'll whip your ass myself if I catch you with them again."

"Easy for you to say. You got your own place. I need family, somebody to count on. I got stuck with an old woman, and she won't be around forever," Emilio finally spewed.

"Emilio, whatcha want, you already got. That old woman took you in. She loves you. Nobody wanted me. I was a loser when I was with the Monks. Now I'm bust'n ass try'in to get it together. Want to trade places?" Hector clouted his brother on the back of his head, causing the younger boy to stumble forward.

Emilio turned and walked back to his apartment silently, Hector dogging each footstep. He knew he couldn't watch Emilio every minute, but he would make it a point to be with him as much as possible, watching his back. He still had his blade from when he was a Monk.

Abuela was sitting at the kitchen table when they entered the four room flat. Her eyes were wet and red. She ran to Emilio and embraced him with her plump arms.

"Dios mios," she kept murmuring as she held him in her grip. Emilio gently eased her away and assured her he was all right.

Hector waited impatiently as his brother cleaned his cut, changed his shirt and grabbed his backpack. "I ain't no baby and you ain't my father," Emilio spat at Hector as the older boy walked him toward his school.

"Then grow up so I don' have to go pulling you outta stuff like that again." He gave Emilio one last stern look. "We may not be living together, but I'm watching you," he warned gruffly as Emilio entered the middle school just up the hill from the high school. "I'll see you after school and walk you home, like it or not," Hector called out to him as he dashed down the pavement toward the high school.

Hector took another glimpse at the time. He had only five minutes to get to the high school. He started running. He hoped they still provided pencils for the test because he couldn't afford the two minutes it would take to retrieve one from his locker.

*　　*　　*

Hector pulled frantically on the locked front door of Skinner High. They always locked it after the tardy bell. He pushed the buzzer at the entrance and after apparently checking the monitor someone in the main office electronically opened the door. He would waste precious time if he went into the office for a tardy slip, but he had little choice if he wanted to get to take the test. He sped into the office and grabbed a tardy slip, shoving it across the counter to be signed by a clerk. He went directly up to the room where he would be taking the test.

He arrived at the designated room just as Miss Parsons finished distributing the test copies. Technically, since he wasn't present at the appointed time, he knew that she had the option of barring him from the room. She looked up as he entered, and he wondered for a second if she was going to send him out. She went to the her desk in the front of the room and opened the right top drawer. He pictured the disciplinary form that she was no doubt extracting and groaned that he might have to take a trip to the vice principal's office, missing the test. He exhaled with relief as he realized she had actually lifted a sharpened pencil out of the drawer and offered it to him. He went to her and took it gently from her hand, realizing that she was doing him a favor. She then picked up a copy of the test, handed it to him, and whispered, "Find a seat."

He held the pencil tightly in his sweaty hand. He hoped he didn't stain the test and throw off the electronic reading system when it was scored.

"Oh, and Hector," Miss Parsons said. His name sounded so nice when she said it, but he was afraid she had changed her mind about letting him take the test. "Good luck."

He let out a deep breath and turned to the first page.

CHAPTER 29

Wednesday morning before Thanksgiving

S tephanie turned her car into the parking lot of the school an hour earlier than her usual arrival time. She swung into her designated space reserved for non-tenured teachers, substitutes and practice teachers. She thought that maybe her place assignment was a good thing as younger personnel could perhaps withstand the longer trek to the building better than the older, less agile group of veterans. The thought that she may someday by among them didn't bear contemplating.

This Wednesday before Thanksgiving was a special day for her. She had been trying to redeem herself since the writing lesson fiasco. Stephanie had to cope with Claire who had been adamant about keeping her reined in and under her tutelage. She had not been allowed any freedom to follow her own instincts lately. She felt smothered, but there was no way she could get a new mentor in a different school at this late date. She was forced to deal with whatever her fate was here. Much to her surprise Claire's inflexible stance bent ever so slightly when the students had asked Stephanie to oversee the skit for the Thanksgiving rally the day before the Flyers battled their archenemy, the Cougars, on the football field for the last game of the season. This was to be the day that she would prove she could handle things well. She had worked with the students effectively, she had been sterner, and her mentor had been impressed. Claire had cautioned her that the seniors usually crossed the line of good taste and that Dr. Bradford always blamed the person in charge.

"Remember, they just might try to take advantage of your liberal nature in order to slip some impropriety past you," she had warned.

"Just wait," Stephanie had assured her. "This is my chance to prove to you that I can handle twelfth graders as well as anyone else on the staff." She just knew this would vindicate her and that Claire would finally give her more responsibility in the classroom. She had always been blessed with confidence in herself, whether or not others shared it.

She opened the door of her pristine 1966, restored red "Bug" and stepped from the ribbed vinyl covered running board and into the sunshine of an unusually warm November morning. This was a good omen, she thought, as she gently closed the door of the little four seater that her mother had received as a college graduation present from her own father. Her mother had driven it for a few years until she married and started life with her new husband in a second hand van. Mom and Dad had followed the Woodstock ways and had loved their nomadic, communal life. Before they left for the open road, her mother had entrusted her precious vehicle back to her father. He had babied the old girl, keeping her garaged, covered, and in tip top running condition.

Stephanie sighed as she recalled the story she had heard so often. The vagabonds returned when the babies came along, first the twin boys, Robert and Rodney, and then the girls two years later Stephanie and Delia, ten months apart. It was time to grow up, and they did - to a certain degree. They joined the mainstream, got good jobs, settled in a white garrison with, of all things, a picket fence. They also reclaimed the "Bug".

Stephanie was raised as a liberated individual, and just before her practice teaching began, Mom and Dad had presented her with the little gem. She circled to the front of the car. Her eyes ran admiringly along the chrome strip that continued from back to front, starting under the side vent rear window. The strip ran further past the large roll-down window and under the small side pane. She found herself appreciating the chrome moon hubcaps. The fog lights sat on each fender above the oval shaped headlights. The split rail bumper guarded the perpendicular chrome handle that looked like it belonged on a kitchen cabinet. She unlocked the front end trunk with a small key, no fancy gadgets for this piece of family history. She sighed as she removed the two boxes of props and costumes she needed for the skit, placing them on the ground before she re-latched the hood. She stood back, cherishing this gift, picked up the boxes, and headed for the front door and redemption.

*   *   *

Stephanie checked into the office. "Could you tell Dr. Bradford that I will be in the small gym?" she asked one of the office clerks who was manning the phones. "Could you also tell the students in the skit to meet me there if they come in looking for me?" The woman nodded silently, acknowledging her request.

The small gym was adjacent to the large gym where the rally would take place. As she patiently waited for her cast to appear for their final rehearsal, Stephanie reveled in the thought of her successful endeavor. The kids had written the skit with her guidance and Claire had read and approved it.

"But we always have some slightly offensive stuff," they had whined.

"Not this time. This isn't Saturday Night Live, and I'm just a practice teacher. We'll stick to the script," she had insisted.

It had been a struggle to keep the seniors focused and consistent. Reluctantly, they had accepted her terms.

Her self-satisfaction soon turned to suspicion. As the students started to drift in, she noticed a lot of whispering and giggling.

"What's going on?" she asked.

"Nothing. We're just excited," explained Annie Tristam, a blond and petite senior.

Stephanie dismissed this behavior as pre-performance jitters. The main participants had not arrived yet, but she called the group together to begin rehearsal without them. The supporting players were very well prepared, and she only wanted to calm her nerves by running through the dialogue.

The basic concept for the sketch was based on a gym class being schooled on the rules of football. One classroom was to be orderly and attentive; the students would know all the answers to the cool, hip instructor's questions. They would be wearing Skinner High's Flying Aces sweatshirts. The other gym class, representing the Cougars, was to be taught by a character with broken, horn rimmed glasses, a pocket protector and pants held up by suspenders. The so-called students would be dressed in garish colors, hair and clothes in total disarray. The feeble voiced teacher, supposedly from their rival school, would be totally ignored at first and then, after trying to explain the football rules, he was to be bombarded by erroneous and farfetched information about the game.

After the classroom scene, the action would shift to the traditional mock football game between the two schools. Naturally, the Flyers would prevail and the Cougars would be soundly defeated. Stephanie would have liked to leave the spoof of the game out because it was hard to control the actions with a bunch of students wanting to ham it up, but, alas, she wasn't about to break with custom.

The rehearsal limped along with five of the key players still absent. The top of Stephanie's lip was beading with perspiration as her nervousness increased. She really needed these kids to show up now. Just as she was going to leave to call their homes, the door banged open and Principal Bradford and Vice-principal Colon herded in the tardy actors.

"Everyone, to your feet. *Now!* Line up against the wall. Miss Lewis stand with me," bellowed the principal.

The students jumped up with startled looks on their faces, and they instantly responded to his command. The five latecomers joined their classmates.

Stephanie thought that this couldn't be standard procedure. It looked as if it were a raid in some army barrack.

Principal Bradford continued in a less threatening but sarcastic tone. "It has come to my attention that there was a pre-rally bash this morning. I believe the locale of this celebration was off of Jones Road. The fire pit flames could be seen from the highway and when the fire department investigated the so-called blaze, they found a cozy little area scattered with empty bags of chips and beer cans."

Vice Principal Colon added, "Circumstantial evidence suggests, at least to me and Dr. Bradford, that maybe some of you have acted imprudently. If I can prove that any of you, even one of you, imbibed this morning, we will call off the skit. Do you all understand?"

Bradford demanded that suspected offenders, plus the other students, stand in a circle, facing center. He motioned for the student teacher and vice-principal to join him in the middle. Puzzled looks were passed from one student to another. Stephanie's own mind raced to figure out where all of this was leading.

Bradford ordered, "Eyes straight ahead and no giggling or talking. The three of us are about to determine if any of you have been drinking. Lacking a breathalyzer, we will ask each of you to blow in our faces. Two of the three of us must agree before we single out anyone for imbibing. Is that clear?"

The sound of stifled mirth made Stephanie very nervous. She had little chance to reflect on how she would handle the situation. She wanted to protest, but she remembered that it was redemption day for her, and she felt the best thing to do right now would be to cooperate. The three educators started with a shy girl dressed in pink. On the count of three, she was told to blow her breath in their faces, starting with the principal and ending with Stephanie. The girl managed two breaths and choked on her tears for the third. Showing some sympathy, the two administrators mouthed, "Okay," to each other and told the shaking girl to sit at the other end of the gym. Stephanie had been spared being breathed upon that time, but not for long.

The trio remained on sniffing duty as they leaned in to catch the lingering odor of beer. The longer this test continued, the more ludicrous it seemed to Stephanie. Students who had choked back their laughter so far, began to cough and sneeze in order to disguise their giggles. Bradford turned to the remaining students and sent them a glare that quieted them immediately, but not for long.

Stephanie was in agony. Every time she asked someone to blow in her face, she had to hold back her own impulse to protest, but yet she felt a chuckle lurking ready to be expelled.

She stole a glance at the remaining ten students, including the late arrivals. She saw a small plastic container of breath mints that was covertly being passed to the prime suspects. She decided to ignore all and follow her leader as instructed.

The administrators and Stephanie finished their rounds, and Principal Bradford looked as if he had been defeated. He turned to the now sitting group and threatened them all with suspension if there was any unacceptable behavior during the course of the skit. He abruptly headed out the door with Mr. Colon following behind him.

Stephanie addressed her charges. "I'm glad you all passed the test." Several students snickered, a few laughed audibly, and one senior even fell to the floor, pounding on the polished boards while hysterically laughing. The group let go of all their repressed laughter and roared uncontrollably until they were spent.

She knew when to let go and dismissed them from rehearsal. "Why don't you all get some water and decompress for awhile."

CHAPTER 30

Two hours later

The rally began with the gym vibrating to the sounds of the band playing the school song. The principal introduced the Spirit Queen, nicknamed the "Turkey Queen" by the students who were not in her court. The football team followed, speeches were given, and it was time for the skit.

Stage hands, dressed in dark jeans and black tee shirts, set the scene. There were two classrooms, one pristine and one disheveled. The "teachers" took their respective places, and the audience hooted and hollered in anticipation. First, the very neat and appropriately dressed Flyers filed in, and then the unkempt, sloppy Cougars stumbled in, looking clueless in their disarray. The students clapped and cheered their counterparts and booed and hissed the actors portraying their rivals.

Penelope, Jonathan, Claire and Christie sat in the front row of the senior section of the bleachers, Sidney and Jeffrey right behind them. Claire had been a bit surprised to see Sidney sitting. He usually stood by the far wall with his arms crossed, looking bored and distracted.

Claire had her fingers crossed. She was beginning to like her free spirited student teacher after she promised to be more careful with the visual aids she used, but Claire knew she still had the responsibility of curbing some of her exuberance. After thirty-five years of coming to these rallies, she knew how devious the seniors could be. She had supervised them herself a number of times. There had been shocking, irreverent skits slipped in at the last moment in the past. She had helped Stephanie take every precaution so that this would not happen today. She had approved the script and observed yesterday's dress rehearsal. She was confident that her protégé had gained the students' respect, but there was always a chance they would do something unexpected.

She noticed Penelope glancing at Jonathan who sat one seat away. She had discreetly placed Christie between them, probably hoping to divert the gossip that had already started to circulate about the fair Miss Parsons and the suave Mr. Perez. Maybe her next romance novel could gain inspiration from this turn of events.

*   *   *

In a far corner of the gym Stephanie clutched the script in one fist and silently went over the scenario and the lines. They weren't the same as the ones being spoken. The "teacher" was introducing a lesson on sex education, not on football. Students participating in the mock football game, which occurred after this scene, crowded in front of her, blocking her view and trying to drown out the dialogue. Face red, heart pounding and fear creeping through her, she ran to a better vantage point.

She found a gap in the crowd the moment the quiet, shy little girl dressed in pink screamed the line, "Cougars should not be allowed to procreate."

The rivals yelled, "What's procreate?"

A boy representing the Flyers screamed, "Give them condoms!"

The response, "What's a condom?"

Stephanie bolted forward just as the principal jumped heavily from the platform, almost falling. Both were heading for the group in the middle of the basketball court when a blur ran past them. It was a skinny young man dressed in beige with a real condom stretched tightly over the top of his head. He was yelling, "Here I am, Condom Man, and I've come to save us all from the Cougars."

"Hey, look. It's a dickhead," someone from the bleachers screeched.

The crowd was out of control. Stephanie and the principal seemed to move in slow motion. The vice-principal finally managed to shout into the microphone, "The rally is over. Teachers, escort your classes back to homeroom and wait for further instructions." Not all heard the announcement, so he kept repeating the command until the crowd started to move along in a loud, but somewhat orderly fashion.

Stephanie saw Claire stand up, eyes wide, lips parted. They made their way toward each other as Bradford corralled the offenders and commandeered several male teachers for backup.

When they were on their way and the gym had cleared, Bradford turned his angry visage toward Stephanie. His eyes flashed with ire.

Before he could utter a word, Claire spoke loudly and clearly. "Don't you dare berate this girl for what just happened. I personally vouch for her integrity. I approved the premise and the dialogue. I was present at dress rehearsal, and let me assure you, this was not planned or even anticipated. Stephanie worked diligently with this group, perhaps putting in more time than necessary trying to ensure that this would not happen, but guess what? It did. Put the responsibility where it belongs, on these kids. They need to be put in their place, and you need to call their parents."

Claire grabbed the stunned Stephanie by the wrist, and led her out the door, leaving the principal standing alone in the now empty gymnasium. Claire yelled from the doorway, "Don't just stand there. It's time for action."

Stephanie let out a deep breath once they were in the hall and noticed that Claire had done the same. Stephanie, drained from the events of the day, managed a whispered "thank you" as Claire put her hand to her own head.

"I'm not sure from where that scolding came," she gasped.

"Neither do I, but I appreciate it." Stephanie stared at Claire as if she were an Amazon goddess she had just met. She looked more closely to make sure it was indeed Claire who had just rebuked the principal.

Droplets of sweat swelled on Claire's brow. She fanned her face. "I think it's getting awfully hot in here." Her cheeks reddened.

"Are you all right, Miss Harvey?" Stephanie asked.

Claire looked about as if she had just awakened from a prolonged coma. "Of course. We'd best get back to the classroom before we're missed. Who am I kidding? I'm sure they would prefer that we never arrived."

She hustled to the stairwell and waved at Stephanie to follow her.

*   *   *

"Well, that was interesting," Jonathan drawled as he joined Penelope on the first floor landing. "Never a dull moment. I take it this wasn't a first? Everyone seemed poised, waiting for something to happen."

"It's always a challenge to keep the students on track around the holidays. Wait until Christmas approaches."

Jonathan was encouraged by the breezy exchange. The edginess he usually sensed was gone. Had she come to accept what had happened between them? *What could happen?* He wasn't going to analyze it.

"Where are you going tomorrow?" she asked casually.

"Tomorrow?"

"You know, Thanksgiving? What are your plans?"

He mentally scrolled through what he needed to accomplish before school reopened on Monday. "I think I'll come in here and do a set up for the new computer lab. My employees all have the day off, so I can get a few things done by myself."

"Don't you have family expecting you for dinner?"

"Not anymore."

Penelope's gaze flew to his. She seemed startled by his succinct reply.

"I'm used to it," he assured her. "There's a certain peacefulness to working while everyone else is occupied."

She continued to focus on his face. "It's not necessary to be alone. There must be some place you want to be on such a holiday."

"There is - here. I've been alone on holidays for years. Trust me; it doesn't bother me."

"It bothers me. Why don't you come to my place? My sister and her husband are coming with my niece, and Samantha and Jake will come with their daughters. You know them."

"I really appreciate the offer, but it would seem out of the ordinary."

"This would be out of the ordinary for me, too. I really want you to come, though."

"I don't accept pity invitations, but thank you anyway."

She rounded on his words. "Pity? Is that how you took it? I asked you because . . . ."

"Why? Tell me what the reason was if it wasn't charity."

She began to tremble and looked away. "It's because I want to see you tomorrow."

"Why?" he asked quietly.

She blinked to keep the tears at bay. "I want you to be a part of my life, I guess. Why are you making me do this?" She looked around to make sure there were no students to witness her embarrassment.

He reached out and captured her hand, squeezed it lightly. "I want you to be sure. Are you?"

She felt the heat from his hand begin to settle her quavering nerves. She started to talk several times before the words finally came. "I am sure. I want you to be with me tomorrow," she admitted.

He cupped her cheek with his free hand. "All right, then. I'll be there."

CHAPTER 31

Penelope hustled toward the cafeteria for duty. She had promised Samantha that she would cover for her since her friend had a doctor's appointment. Bradford had said Samantha could leave school as long as she had someone to take her place. The doctor's office was only a half mile down the road, and Penelope was more than glad to fill in on the third lunch supervision.

Lunch duty wasn't bad as long as one realized that no schoolwork would get done, and there was always the undercurrent possibility that a grilled cheese sandwich might be tossed at any random time. This didn't happen too often since the police department had kept someone patrolling the lunchroom. Actually, the uniformed officers had been recently replaced with plain clothes cops, who wore teen friendly clothing of jeans and plain shirts. They were now called "mediation and intervention specialists" who smiled instead of snarled, schmoosed instead of patrolled and discussed disruptive issues instead of arresting the disrupters. The results were pretty much the same as when the men in blue were present. Actually, the uniforms were still on duty before school and after dismissal.

Penelope gave a short salute to the first cop she saw and took a position near the large front windows where she could survey the activities in most sections of the cafeteria. She knew the drill. She would take periodic strolls among the tables where the students conversed in animated fashion. Sometimes the conversation took on a momentary combative air, but usually de-escalated quickly enough. She noticed that the food choice of the day was limp brown burger on a bun with a macaroni side. The students didn't even seem to notice what was on their plates as they shoveled pasta into their mouths and nipped at the meat and bun. The voices were usually kept to a continuous, low buzz.

As she watched the crowd, her mind still meandered to the Thanksgiving break. It was a mere two days off from the regular classroom schedule, but it had revitalized her physically and mentally. She was ready to tackle the difficult period that started now and ended at the Christmas holiday. She had spent days agonizing over asking Jonathan to dinner for last Thursday, but the end result had been worth the anxiety.

He had shown up in casual tan slacks and a black polo, and he had brought a bottle of wine, the same brand and variety they had sipped on that night after the game. He had a quiet, authoritative air about him as he mingled with her other guests, but he seemed to fit into the gathering easily. He had even listened attentively to her uncle's stories about his time in Korea while serving in the army. Samantha's children had stayed a distance from him for the first half hour, but when Theresa had hesitantly given him a drawing she had made of him before dinner, he had praised it profusely and gained her and her sister's approval. Penelope hadn't meant the invitation to be a test, but she had to admit that she now felt as if there was a next step, a moving toward something. Well, she thought to herself, she had better get her attention away from Thanksgiving and back to the meal in front of her and to those consuming it.

Penelope noticed that Sammy Johnson was at a corner table scribbling something into a large notebook. She doubted he was practicing math, but she was curious to see what commanded such concentration from a young man who claimed to be interested in nothing this school had to offer. His participation in math ran hot and cold, as did his attitude. She had to admit she was encouraged that he had attended office hours recently. She approached his table and angled her head over his shoulder to view the markings on the paper in front of him. There were horrific reproductions of skulls, faces with ravaged features, creatures of which nightmares were made. They were difficult to behold, but she could not help but admire the workmanship. The lines were definitive, and the images so startling that it appeared that they would leap from the notebook, causing mass mayhem.

"What you looking at?" Sammy asked without glancing back. He seemed to sense her presence behind him.

"Those are very impressive pictures, Sammy. Do you take art?"

"I take art class, but it's a waste of my time. You can't teach somebody something that comes natural," he grumbled.

"But art class can help a talented person become even better."

Sammy snapped the notebook shut. "I don't need to get better. I just do stuff because I feel like it. Right now I feel like leaving." He rose and headed toward the large doors that led to the corridor.

Penelope had learned long ago not to take such things to heart. If she had, she would have quit the profession long ago. Something was devouring this kid from the inside, where no one could see, where no one was allowed to see. She had glimpsed at the pictures, though, and perhaps that was a way in.

She was aware that Jonathan had made an impact on Hector when he introduced him to the music writing program. One of the pieces was to be sung by the choir at the Christmas assembly. Hector had also written a special composition for a baritone, and he planned on performing it at the auditions for acceptance to a prestigious music program at Mr. Tottman's alma mater, Harris Conservatory.

She'd noticed the change in Hector's academic demeanor soon after he had become comfortable with the software. Hector not only had stayed after school for the mandatory math tutoring sessions, but he also spent hours in the music studio.

She decided to approach Jonathan about helping Sammy. If the computers had helped Hector, perhaps a good graphic arts program would give Sammy a direction for his art and a start at a future career. She had to ask Jonathan about the prospects. He was to drive her home this afternoon while her car was being repaired, so she would have an opportunity then.

CHAPTER 32

Same day

Penelope saw that Jonathan was waiting. The bustle of the office faded to a distant hum as he lingered, and she tended to last minute business. At Thanksgiving dinner she had told him her car needed work on the following Tuesday, and he had offered to drive her to and from the shop. She had told him that morning her car was supposed to have been ready after school. The mechanic called her cell phone, however, and said he was behind schedule, and he might not even be able to open the hood until almost closing time. She could pick up her car after school tomorrow.

Penelope marched into the office like Gunga Din on his way to a water-deprived soldier. She headed straight to her mailbox, pulled out a variety of envelopes, memos, and odd slips of paper. She turned toward the door and Jonathan leaning lazily against a tall file cabinet.

"I'm sorry I kept you waiting. I wish I didn't have to inconvenience you," Penelope teased as she admired the man standing so casually with his coat hung over his forearm.

"I could take that as an insult. After all, I was hoping that you would be looking forward to my company all day, even if it is only for a ride back to your car," he replied in mock offense.

Penelope's lips curved. "My car won't be ready until tomorrow afternoon. Can I impose upon you again tomorrow and have you just take me home now?"

"I'll take you anywhere you want you want to go."

"I owe you one."

"Just remember that."

He raised his arm and touched his fingers to her shoulder, nudging her toward the door. "Let's go before they find some new crisis for me to deal with."

The sun beat on the parking lot pavement with less intensity than it had last month. There was a fluttering of the remaining dry leaves as they skittered along the paved path to the lot. One curled, brown leaf whipped up and caught in Penelope's now tousled hair. Jonathan picked it out of the locks and returned it to the circling breeze.

When they arrived at the SUV, he unlocked the doors with a click of the remote attached to his key ring. They both settled their heavy black bags in the backseat and slid into position for the drive to her house. Seat belts in place, they drove out of the lot and onto the road, heading north.

*   *   *

Penelope shifted her body in his direction.

"Why are you so secretive?" she asked softly.

"What?" Her question had been more than casual. He couldn't help but wonder where this was going.

She spoke again. "You seem to know a lot about regret, for instance, but you don't mention why that is. What is it that you regret?"

The rather bold statement from Penelope surprised him. He was silent for a moment, and he was not certain if he should respond, even in a general way.

He did manage to say, "I'm not sure what you mean."

She pushed a little further. "Yes, you are. I always get the feeling that there is something more, something that you don't outwardly acknowledge. Under all that confidence you present to everyone, there's something vulnerable about you."

"Vulnerable? That's a new one. I don't think anyone has ever suggested before that I was vulnerable, and believe me, there have been those who implied plenty." They rode in silence for a while, the soft rock from the radio filling in the void.

"Where do you call home? Where do you come from?" Penelope finally asked.

"Why all the questions now?"

"Maybe it finally occurred to me that I have actually slept with you, and I still don't know much about you. I want to know if you still have parents. What did you do before you started your company? Do you like seafood? Are you into commitment?" She abruptly halted the inquisition. "I'm sorry."

"Ah, the truth comes out." He reached across the console and put his hand on her thigh, lightly, comfortingly. "I told you that you were safe with me."

"How safe?" she shot back. "I don't fear that you would ever hurt me physically, but I do feel that there's a mystery about you. It's as if you sprang fully grown from a hard drive. You never talk about your past or even your present or future. I want to know who you really are."

"Maybe there's not much to tell."

"If there weren't, then you would give me the whole history in a quick, boring flashback, but you don't. You never even allude to a sibling, a mother, school, nothing."

Silence once more filled the space between them.

"What are you really asking? Sometimes filling in the past can jeopardize your present. You might discover things you didn't really want to know."

"I think I can handle it. Please, what is it that makes you want to forget you have a past?"

Jonathan let out a sigh, as if resigning himself to the difficult task ahead. It was easier to talk to Hector.

"Let's just say that I was in a position to have people's lives in my hands once. I was considered pretty good at what I did. Then one time I blew it, and I decided I just wasn't going that route anymore."

The SUV made a tight turn onto Penelope's street. The two passengers stared through the front windshield as the images of trees, houses and neighbors whizzed by the side windows. Jonathan nosed the black vehicle onto Penelope's driveway and came to an easy stop. He stared straight ahead, avoiding any further communication.

Penelope pressed her hand slightly on top of the hand that still clung to the steering wheel. "What happened?"

Minutes passed. "I was in Iraq. My crew and I were highly trained for rescue and undercover missions. We would go beyond the lines, locate key people in enemy operations and bring them in. Sometimes we would be sent in to retrieve our own men who had been captured or left behind. It was all rather intense, but we were prepared, and we knew what to expect. Usually. There was always the possibility of things going terribly wrong."

Penelope's quiet presence urged him to go on, breaking the years of avoidance, of pretending that last mission never happened. He knew, however, it would be always imbedded in his mind and soul. "One time everything disintegrated. Somehow, our arrival was anticipated and there were armed men waiting for us. The guy we were sent to bring back wasn't there, but those who had captured him were ready with a full supply of ammunition. What only took seconds, seemed like a lifetime. I pulled out my men and made it back to our rendezvous spot. I went in with seven men and brought back five. How's that for bad math, teacher?"

Penelope's hold on his hand became taut, but her voice was muted with emotion. "How long ago was that?"

"Not nearly long enough." He paused. "I demanded a desk job after fallout from the incident cleared. I had re-upped for another two years just before all of this happened, so they retrained me in computers and technology. I threw myself into it. If something bad happens, wires and disk drives don't have families that have to carry on without them. They don't have faces that will insinuate into your dreams and leave you in a cold sweat when you wake." He closed his eyes to erase the images that had resurfaced. "I guess, I became very good at technology, too," he stated with a smile. His good humor returned, his tranquil facade back in place. "I got out, did some consulting, started my own company, and here I am."

He lifted his hand from the steering wheel, Penelope's coming with it. He turned his palm upward to capture hers and hold it. He then raised his eyes to meet hers and judge her reaction to what he had revealed.

Her eyes were soft with some emotion, sympathy or understanding; he couldn't quite discern which. He certainly didn't want her sympathy, but wasn't sure he could expect her understanding.

She gently released her hand from his grip with a softly uttered suggestion, "Would you like to take Spartacus for a long, leisurely walk? We could fix some dinner afterward."

He nodded a mute "yes." He could feel that she still wanted him, and heaven help him, he needed her right now.

CHAPTER 33

It had been a rough day, and Penelope was relieved that it had ended. The few weeks between Thanksgiving and Christmas were always fraught with chaos. First, there had been a fire alarm that had gone off during her first period test. She later discovered, not surprisingly, that it had happened with a little help from a student. The fact that her class had to evacuate the classroom fifteen minutes into a test invalidated the whole exam. She would just reschedule with a different test and use this one as practice, she had decided. She had then led the twenty-five members of the class back into the building after they had spent ten minutes probably discussing the answers while they waited for the re-entry signal.

By the third period, she had also been asked to substitute for Vice Principal Colon while he attended a hearing for a case involving a chronic offender he was attempting to expel for the rest of the school year.

"It's Winslow's turn to sub, but he's out today. Could you just cover for a few periods? After all, you have a student teacher, so you're free to do it. Thanks," he had said hurriedly as he donned his winter coat and left before she could protest that this wasn't a good day for her to be out of the classroom. She had promised Christie she would observe and comment at length on her student teacher's methods and lesson plans.

She had approached Christie with the news immediately after Colon had left her with no alternative but to act as his proxy for a while.

"Don't worry, Miss Parsons. We can do my oral evaluation another time."

"I'll be right down the hall if you need me," Penelope had assured her. "When are you going to start to call me by my first name? We've been together for three and a half months now. That's longer than some marriages."

Christie had given her a partial smile. "All right, Miss Penelope. I mean Penelope. This is still kind of hard for me. I always called my teachers by their formal names."

"Well, at this point, I'm not so much your teacher. We're a team in the classroom now." She gave her a reassuring hug and left for the vice principal's office. This sense of team spirit was new to Penelope as well. She had always felt teaching somewhat isolating during a class. She loved being with the students, but she had always remembered that whatever happened in those forty-five minute sessions was all on her. Her triumphs, her failures. Yes, it was nice to be part of a team.

When she arrived at the pale green room with the sport figures plastered on the newly painted walls, she gave a sigh and sat in the imposing leather bound chair. Charity Bloomberg, the student aid for that period, handed her a list of AWOL slips that needed to be addressed. These papers were submitted by teachers when students were absent from a class, but were not on the daily absent report. She counted seven. Not too bad, she considered, but just as she had made a list of the order in which the parents would be called about these missing persons, the line up had started at the door. Three students needed to be excused for various reasons. One had a dentist appointment, one had a funeral to attend for a third cousin, and the other needed to accompany his mother to the doctor's because she didn't speak English.

Colon never did return for the remainder of the day, and she was forced to skip lunch in order to catch up with the paper work, so when Jonathan came by during the last period and suggested dinner out that night, she accepted immediately.

"Yes, yes, YES." She fanned herself with the remainder of the AWOL slips.

Jonathan's lips twisted in amusement. "Well, if you're uncertain, we can make it another night." At her thunderous look, he stopped the teasing. "I see you have a lot to do. Christie told me where I could find you, and I figured you would be busy, so that's why I waited till now to track you down. I'll pick you up at six?"

Penelope nodded her head in the affirmative and blew out a breath of irritation as she scanned the pile of reports she had to file before she left. She pulled open the top drawer of the file cabinet next to the desk.

*   *   *

Penelope sat across from Jonathan at an oval, linen-draped table at the Trade Winds restaurant. She had been there a few times before, and the meals had always been pricey, but well presented and plentiful. She extracted a slice of the still warm bread from the basket on the table and began to butter it absently.

"You're rather quiet tonight. Did being in administration today wear you out?" Jonathan asked.

She lifted the bread to her mouth and paused. "I wish it were that simple." She bit off a small section of the bread and chewed daintily.

"Few things are that simple, I guess," Jonathan mused. "What's the problem?"

She swallowed. "This whole thing with the state has me upset. There was a memo on Jorge's desk today about possible visitations from education experts. Do you know that the person who is heading the state committee on improving our school has taught a total of three years? This guy, who is the 'expert' will be telling veteran teachers how to do their jobs. The superintendent hasn't said a word about it officially." She stabbed at Jonathan with the buttered bread in her hand.

"Be careful there," he warned. "French bread is especially dangerous when used as a weapon. It's second only to the Swiss army knife."

She put the bread down and curved her lips in a mild smile. "Sorry. I just get so agitated when I talk about it. Everything we do is not good enough. Did I tell you that the strategies that the math and English departments worked on for the last month and a half were rejected by the state committee on recommendation of that upstart? We had a good combination of traditional and innovative tactics that we wrote up and combined in bound copies. I think I need a glass of wine." She snatched the wine list from the middle of the table.

"I think I know what you need," Jonathan said as he playfully commandeered the leather bound list from her shaking hand and called a waiter to take his order.

She continued. "We started implementing these plans with some really good progress as a result," she continued. "The committee didn't want to hear about it. They wanted us to use the books they suggested instead. You know what those were? They were practically study guides to the state test. Page after page of examples that they wanted the kids to do for that test."

"Boring, I would guess."

"That's not the half of it. It is such a narrow minded approach. We're supposed to be preparing these kids for life after high school, not just for a single test. The superintendent is scrutinizing the art and music programs to determine if they are necessary, so they can add more academic courses. If they do that, then there will be a lot of kids who won't bother to come to school. Tottman alone has rescued a lot of kids. Look at Hector." She stopped abruptly. "I'm so sorry. I didn't accept your invitation to regale you with all my frustrations."

Jonathan took a sip of water from the goblet near his bread plate. "I don't mind. I've worked with Hector, and I know he's really making progress. I understand what music means to him. It keeps him focused."

"I really find this whole situation disturbing."

"It's pretty much what I was feeling before I quit the military," Jonathan reflected.

"It must have been pretty intense for you to walk away from something that you believe saved you from a life on the streets." Jonathan had told a very brief account of the reasons he became a Marine.

"It was, but you can't completely walk away from something that was a fundamental part of you."

"I guess not," Penelope admitted. "There are times I feel as if I should resign because I am heartbroken about what they're doing to education. You did manage to leave, though, and not look back, didn't you?"

He stared directly into her crystalline eyes for a long moment. "Yes and no. When you do something that requires you to invest your soul to save others, it will always be a part of you." His gaze remained steady. "Sometimes, though, you need to save yourself."

Penelope considered his last statement. She shrugged almost imperceptibly before raising the glass the waiter had just delivered. "Merry Christmas, Jonathan. I wish we could spend that day together. You could still come with me to my cousin's in Pennsylvania." She delivered a soft smile with the invitation.

"I wish I could, but I usually make visits to my employees on Christmas to give them their bonuses personally. Maybe next time."

Warmth grew within her. He was talking about a future with her in it.

Their glasses touched, and Jonathan's free hand sought hers.

CHAPTER 34

Second week in December

When Tottman had produced a musical for the first time in twenty-five years, the faculty and staff rose to the challenge and volunteers were many. This year's production was *West Side Story*. The announcement of this choice had caused a stir in some of the other surrounding communities because some very socially conscious people had deemed it racist. Stonefield was different. There had been a large Latino community established in the city for years, and the high school had been dealing with the related issues for a long time.

Tottman had ignored type casting and everything was running smoothly. The show had garnered a great deal of publicity and now, with a couple of days to go, everyone involved was working feverishly toward perfection.

Penelope had volunteered for costume mistress, a job she had done previously. Jonathan had been drafted to oversee the technical demands with the newly purchased computerized audio and lighting system.

It was a Tuesday night as Jonathan and Penelope pulled into the parking lot for the six o'clock rehearsal. As they strolled across the asphalt, Penelope turned to Jonathan.

"I enjoyed the weekend. I'm glad you stayed. There's still a great deal more I want to learn about you." Penelope smiled and she felt her face go warm when he didn't respond immediately.

Finally, he spoke. "I could spend more weekends like that." He drew her closer and kissed her gently. "Working on this play is a whole new world for me, and I'm sure I wouldn't be involved if you weren't. I'm not sure I'll be thanking you for that. The kids are very talented, though. This school is always surprising me."

"Tonight is the first complete run-through with costumes and tech. If you were impressed before, you'll definitely be surprised when you see it all together. The scenery is built, and Sammy has done a great job on the graffiti backdrop that they are using in the rumble scene."

"It's interesting to see that kid interested in something. I've been working with him, and he's caught on quickly to the new drawing program I brought in for the art department. In fact, he used it to plan the mural, and he learned how to keep the proportions correct when he enlarged it so he could paint to scale."

"I hope Sammy's art can help carry him away from where he was headed. Hector's music has helped him find his way, so there's hope."

Jonathan held the door for Penelope as they entered the empty lobby of the school.

"I'll see you after the rehearsal," Penelope said as she headed to the dressing room.

"If it's not too late when we get out of here, maybe we could get a drink somewhere," he suggested, his voice low in the deserted hallway.

"That sounds good. We may need it by that time. These things can get pretty intense."

He leaned in to touch his lips to her cheek when a loud laugh came from around the concrete corner.

Penelope quickly pulled away and ran a hand over her hair to straighten it.

"Hey, Miss Parsons, I'm glad you're here. The ruffle on my skirt is hanging down. Can you fix it?" pleaded an enthusiastic girl in a bright red and blue dappled loose skirt. She was in the chorus as one of the Sharks' girlfriends. She was accompanied by several other members of the cast.

"Well, we certainly don't want any material dragging when you do your dance numbers, do we? I'll get to your skirt as soon as I find a place for my coat." she told her pleasantly. "Where is everyone?"

"They're all in the teachers' lounge. Mr. Tottman said we could use it for costume changes."

"I guess I'll head that way, then. I know you have to set up all the technology, Mr. Perez, so I will see you later." She followed the kids to the double doors that eventually led to the teachers' lounge.

*   *   *

Jonathan had made note of all the settings that would be needed on the equipment and had angled the lights for the best effect for opening night on Friday. He had always been able to put everything out of his mind but the task at hand, but when the last switch had been turned off and all the cords were properly placed, he began to think once more about that last moment before the kids arrived on the scene.

He remained in the entrance hall and craved a cigarette. He had only been there a few minutes when Penelope arrived, pulling her coat on and talking with Ted Tottman.

Tottman stopped near Jonathan. "Thank you both for coming tonight. I think Hector and the rest of the cast finally know all the lines and the music. We had a few missed cues, but I'll be praying to the muses that everything will be perfect Friday. Well, as close to perfect as possible with teenagers. I've got front row seats for you two for opening night. See you then."

He gave a wave and followed the last of the student actors into the parking lot.

"So what the hell was that all about before?"

"What are you talking about?" Penelope asked, seemingly baffled by his words.

"The frigid treatment. Even cold fronts give fair warning. You turned off the warmth as quickly as a miser at an overactive thermostat."

She looked away. "I just never show emotion in front of the kids. It's an inclination from way back. I told you; I go into teacher mode when there are students around."

"I can understand not being too emotional, but you don't have to morph into some robo-teacher at the sight of anyone under eighteen."

"I'm sorry. It's a habit hard to break. I didn't even think about it," she explained.

"It's like being with two different people. I liked the first one better."

"I didn't mean to hurt you," she said softly.

"You didn't. You just surprised me. I guess I'll have to watch for hidden hazards, like pop up pupils, when we go anywhere."

Penelope looked toward the door. "How about that drink?"

"Okay," he said simply and put his hand behind her to guide her through the door.

CHAPTER 35

Sunday night

It was the last performance of the play. The auditorium was animated with the whoops of students showing their enthusiasm, with proud parents clapping wholeheartedly, and with well-wishers waving congratulatory bouquets. Hector took his last bow with the rest of the cast, joining hands in the line of actors, singers, and dancers. They all bent at the waist to the volcanic eruptions of appreciation from the crammed audience.

He tried to spot his father or Emilio in the throng, but it was difficult to identify anyone with the lights flaring in his line of vision. He did manage to see Miss Parsons and Mr. Perez in the front row and Ruckmeyer in the right third row, but there was no one who resembled his father or grandmother, for that matter. The ecstasy of the evening began to fade and familiar disappointment diffused through his perspiring body. His math teacher and the computer guy had been there all three nights.

Sprays of roses were handed to the choreographer, the dance coach, the head student technician. A humble Mr. Tottman accepted a wrapped assortment of daisies and carnations as he, too, took a final bow to acknowledge the adulation that seemed so abundant in tonight's crowd. He felt the joy, but a twinge of pain went through him as he glanced down the long line of actors in the first row on stage. Hector was the only one without a token of appreciation in his hands. He shrugged off the hurtful feeling and told himself it was just a bunch of stupid stuff. *I don't need no daisies*, he thought.

The music ceased, the crowd began to move sluggishly toward the exits, and the curtain closed on the budding thespians. Hector felt as if he had just won the Olympics, and there was no one there to admire his gold medal. It would shine and glitter with no one from his family to care or notice. Emilio was supposed to come. Hector hoped that his brother had not taken him seriously when he told him that it wasn't necessary, but hadn't Emilio sworn that nothing could keep him away?

Tottman gave him a clap on the back as he walked off the stage. The band started a medley from the play as the mothers, fathers, cousins, siblings, and friends dispersed. Hector remained in front of the cardboard New York skyline a few seconds beyond the rest of the cast members. He blinked vigorously to rid himself of the moisture that had begun to accumulate in the corners of his eyes. He didn't need his supposed family anyway, he reasoned. To hell with them. He had managed quite well without them for a while now.

He saw Miss Parsons coming out from stage left, heading right toward him. "Hector, I haven't seen a better performance on Broadway. You were wonderful!" she enthused.

"You did do a fantastic job, son," Jonathan stated as he held out his hand for a manly shake. Then Miss Parsons reached in back of her and presented him with a bouquet of roses.

"Jonathan and I want you to have these to remind you of your triumph. We didn't give them to you earlier because we had to work backstage right after the last scene."

"Uh, thanks." Maybe flowers weren't stupid after all.

He also realized that he liked it when Jonathan called him "son". He only wished that it were true, even if it were just for tonight. His father was who he was and wishing didn't change that. He didn't even like the bastard. Maybe he didn't want him around when he did something he was proud of. He had to wonder, though, if his grandmother would have shown up if it had been Emilio on stage tonight instead of him.

As if the thought had conjured him, Emilio came running up to Hector and threw himself against his older brother in an all-consuming embrace that had Hector rearing back in surprise. He steadied himself as Emilio pulled away.

"I lost my ticket, but I listened from the hall. I had to tell the snotty girl with the programs to shut up talking because I wanted to hear it all. You did real good," he prattled admiringly.

He thumped his brother on the back and fled as quickly as he had come, yelling over his shoulder, "Gotta go. I promised I'd be back home a half hour ago."

"That's quite a fan club you've got there," Jonathan observed.

"Yeah, the kid's all right. Too bad he couldn't get in," Hector said regretfully.

"Yes, it is, but he tried," Miss Parsons reminded him. Emilio was the only member of his family that had tried. She looked up at Mr. Perez in a silent signal that he immediately seemed to understand.

"We came to invite you to come out with us for a little something to eat. A performance like that deserves a reward," he proffered.

Hector stared at Mr. Perez and his math teacher for a few seconds in astonishment. He was touched on some level that he didn't totally understand, but he feared he would feel a bit awkward if he went. "There's a cast party in the cafeteria. All the kids will be there."

"Of course, we should have considered that. Maybe next week we can do something," Mr. Perez countered.

"Yeah, that'd be great. Uh, thanks, though."

"You bet. Have a great time tonight. You earned it," the math teacher said as she leaned toward and gave him a friendly hug. "You really gave the audience something they won't forget for a while. Be proud of that."

She and Mr. Perez gave him parting smiles and left the stage.

Hector felt his skin where her cheek had brushed his. He contemplated that maybe there was something that went beyond blood family. He was almost as satisfied with these teachers telling him he meant something as he would have been had his father or grandmother made the effort. It wasn't the same, but it was getting to be just as good.

Hector had previously no intention of going to the cast party. That had been just an excuse to Mr. Perez to avoid an uncomfortable situation. He had been going to head home and bask in the approval he had received from the masses of clapping hands, but now he was thinking that maybe he would go to that dumb get-together. After all, the other kids had treated him okay after they had worked with him. He had played Bernardo, the leader of the Sharks, and even though it wasn't the lead, everyone had told him that his performance stood out.

The music ended abruptly, and Tottman came from behind the curtains to where Hector was removing the leather jacket that was part of his costume. The teacher waved a thick white envelope in his hand. "The night's not over for you yet. They sent me the results of the competition before it's officially announced. You do remember the competition, don't you? We sent recordings, and you had to give a private live performance. They told us they'd need a week to do all the judging."

Hector nodded, still frozen in the moment of his biggest achievement, still fresh from shaking off the displeasure at finding yet again that his family did not consider him a priority. "What about it?"

"First place, Hector, first place." Tottman thrust the envelope into Hector's reluctant hand. "Read it and rejoice."

Hector pulled out the sheaf of papers that had swollen the envelope and opened the tri-fold. The words were a blur of ink and paper, but his name screamed from the page in bold type. Next to his name was the word "scholarship".

"What's this mean?" he quizzed his teacher.

"It means, young star, that you get to go to the Harris Conservatory free of charge once you graduate. This play was only the beginning. They'll teach you things about music there that I can only scratch the surface of here. This means that you are on your way. Guess it's a bigger night for you than anyone could have imagined."

Hector wasn't sure what to say next. The thoughts of having a career in music went beyond anything that he had ever hoped, ever dreamed, ever dared to contemplate. He was going to be somebody people listened to, someone people came to see. His father and grandmother would be very sorry they had cast him aside.

"Speechless, I see. I don't blame you. I'm so very proud of you, Hector. Come on, there's a pepperoni pizza coming with our names on it in the cafeteria. Get the garb off and the goop off your face and let's celebrate. There's an awful lot to be thankful for." He took back the papers and the envelope and winked at his student. They left the stage together.

Hector couldn't believe it. He was an award-winning singer with a college scholarship. Not only would he be the first in his family to graduate from high school, but he would also be a college man.

As he hung his costume on the rack inside the boy's bathroom, his mind raced through a future of record deals, big money, and hot babes. He also dreamed of helping Emilio. He would be a local hero who never forgot where he came from. He would also make sure that Mr. Tottman would have the latest and best equipment for his classes. The reverie was interrupted when Mike Bender, another boy from the play, came in.

"Hey man, good job tonight. I also hear you knocked them dead at states."

"Thanks man. You had a good night yourself. Guess we all kicked ass."

"You got that right," Mike said as he began to wash the heavy makeup from his face.

Hector joined him at the sink, and as he grabbed for the paper towels, he glanced at himself in the mirror. Reality stared back. *Nice dreamin' Hector. You better have passed that damned test. None of this happens without a diploma.*

He crumpled the coarse towel, wiped the last of vestiges of the play off his face, tossed the paper in the trash, and headed for the door muttering, "I know I passed. I had to. Mr. Perez told me that I knew my stuff. Everything's falling in line."

Hector's longtime friend, Gracia Diaz, was waiting for him in the hallway. "You made me so proud, seeing you like that in front of everybody. I always knew you were special."

He had known Gracia for a long time, and what she said touched him. "Thanks."

She stood on her toes and kissed him on the temple before disappearing around the corner that led to the exit.

As Hector set foot in the cafeteria, a cheer rose from his classmates. They shouted congratulations. Hector's face flushed with embarrassment.

Hector grabbed a can of soda and a couple pieces of pizza. He was famished and happy to chow down the free food. Was this what it was like to feel appreciated? He couldn't wait to tell Miss Parsons and Mr. Perez about his scholarship. First, he wanted to tell his brother, even if it meant going to his grandmother's apartment. She was old and really didn't understand what was happening to Hector at school. He would forgive her.

*   *   *

The star of the night devoured his last piece of pizza, washed it down with the remainder of his Coke, and then found Mr. Tottman.

"Hey, Teacher, I gotta go. Can't wait to tell my brother. Thanks for everything." He lowered his voice. "This has been the best day of my life."

Tottman gave him a friendly hug of his shoulders. "You're a good man, Hector, and you deserve the chances that have been given to you. Go, celebrate before it's too late."

Hector glanced at his watch, a Rolex imitation that his father had bought off the streets of New York. His father was always going into the big city on "business", he claimed, when Hector was younger, and his mother had still been with them. He had always brought home gifts, and this watch was one of them. They had been a family then, hadn't they? *No use thinking about things that were gone.* He had something just ahead he could think about.

It was just after eleven, but he knew that on the weekend his grandmother and brother stayed up to watch the news on the Spanish channel.

He hurriedly left the school, crossed the street, and took a short cut through the housing project, into the area known as the "Bottom". He was out of breath as he climbed the stairs to his abuela's place, taking two steps at a time. He knew that Emilio should be home.

He knocked on the door and his grandmother unlocked it. "Oh, Hector, I was hoping it was Emilio."

Hector hesitated for a moment, "Why isn't he home? The play was over at nine-thirty." He turned to kiss his grandmother, hoping she didn't detect the worry on his face. "Abuela, I've got some great news."

"Good, good, but I worry about Emilio."

"Why? He's been late before."

"He no come home yet. I don' see him all day. I'm afraid. I think he with Teach and his boys. Oh, mios Dios. What to do?"

"He'll be home soon. He went to the musical at the school. I saw him. I'll talk to him, find out what's going on. Can I tell you what happened now?"

"Hector, I ready to hear now."

"Well, I did a good job in the play. Everybody said so." He handed her the bouquet that Miss Parsons had given to him. "Look, I even got flowers. They clapped and yelled a long time when I took my bow. I wish you were there. Why didn't you come? I gave you a ticket." Abuelo hugged the flowers to her.

"I know, I know. I don' feel well and now I worry about Emilio. I stay and wait. I can't take it no more. It makin' me more sick. You have to fix, or Emilio have to go, maybe live with you."

"I said I'll talk to him. You know he'll listen to me, especially when I tell him my news. Now listen to the best part."

"Oh, Hector, I hope and pray Emilio not in trouble. *Sentirse mal.* Oh Hector, please help."

Hector had hoped his grandmother would listen, but no chance. His grandmother was only focused on his brother and there was no way he could sway her to listen. He sat down and waited for Emilio. His news would have to wait. He was on another mission, now. He'd straighten out that brother of his, again.

*   *   *

Hector took his grandmother's indifference to his news with an understanding only a life of rejections and disappointments could grasp.

He leaned over to give this aging gentle soul a kiss on her cheek. It wasn't her fault. She was of a different time and from a different place. Since his mother had died, it had been rough on his grandmother. He knew she loved him, but when he was running with the Monks, she had refused to take him in so she could protect Emilio.

"It's late. Tell Emilio to call my cell phone. I'll talk to him. Don't worry. He'll be home soon."

"Bye Hector. That's nice about the music thing."

She waved a weak goodbye. Hector knew that his brother was her fulltime job.

He left the peeling, shabby porch of the run-down apartment building and headed for home. As he approached his own apartment, he hesitated and suddenly turned and faced the block where his father lived.

After all, he thought, Papa used to play in a band in Puerto Rico. Music had been his ticket to the States. He'd understand. Hector ran to the door and bounded up to his father's third floor apartment. He knocked, his heart pounding, waiting for a response.

"Yeah, Yeah, I'm comin'. Who's there?"

"It's me, Hector."

"What'you want? I'm busy."

"I gotta talk to you." He waited for the door to open.

"Say what you gotta say. I don't need to open the door to hear."

Hector wondered about his father's life behind those walls. Sometimes he was allowed in without even a hesitation and then at other times, like tonight, he felt his father was hiding something. After the death of his mother, his father quit the band he was in and also his day job at the bodega. Papa went on a drunken spree that ended when he crashed his car into a tree. The demise of the Cortez family took only a month.

His father was on disability, but he managed to live a pretty good life, especially since he had taken up with Margarita. She was twenty-three years younger and had a five year old daughter. When she moved in, Hector and his brother were asked to move out.

There still must have been some emotional connection because his father found him a room across the street. There was no rent as long as Hector swept the halls and did light repair work around the place.

"Come on, Papa, it's important. Let me in."

"Just a minute, kid. Hold on."

Hector heard furniture scraping on the floor, the rustling of papers, and slamming of a door.

"What's goin' on?"

"None of your business. If you want to see me, you'll have to wait."

Hector was sure that he heard male voices, but they subsided as quickly as they had started.

Suddenly, the door jerked open and Hector almost fell into his father.

"What you been doin'? Listening at the door."

"No, Papa. I was leaning on the door."

The anger in his father's face vanished. "Come in, kid. What's so damned important that it can't wait 'til mornin'?"

"Who's here, Papa? It's after midnight, and I thought Margarita and Maria would be asleep by now."

"They are. What you heard was the TV. I turned it off. Now spill it, it's late."

Hector would have to buy the excuses for now, but he always suspected that his father was earning cash on the side. He really didn't want to know how.

The excitement of his success and of his scholarship to college dwarfed any negative feelings. He couldn't hold the news back any longer.

"Papa, you should've come to the show. We got a standing ovation and the audience kept calling my name. Mr. Tottman had me sing an encore. That's never happened before."

"That's great, but I was busy. Maybe I'll catch the next one."

"Papa, there is no next one. But I guess I understand now how you loved your music and how you loved to perform. I'm really hooked. It's my way outta here."

His father looked around his apartment, and then his gaze fell on his son. "Hector, get a hold of yourself. It didn't happen for me, and it ain't goin' to happen for you."

"But Papa, Mr. Tottman got me into a real good music school and on a full scholarship. All I got to do is pass the state test and graduate."

"Don't let that guy fill your head with bull. You ain't gonna make no money singing. I know about this. And you ain't gonna make it in college. You'll be lucky enough to graduate high school. I know about you not passing those tests. The school told me last year. They called here lookin' for you. Now, Emilio, that's a different story. That kid's gonna be okay. He's got your grandmother to set him straight. Sorry kid, it's a little too late for you. Maybe I shoulda done more for you, but don't worry, your Papa's goin' to set you up in the family business after you get out of school."

Hector watched as his father reached for a cigarette out of his pocket before speaking again. "Good job though, kid. I know what it's like to want it, the big money, people knowin' who you are. I'm just trying to save you from the drop when you find out it's all smoke. I had to find out myself."

"Yeah." Hector turned and left, his pace picking up when he crossed the threshold of the apartment.

When he got to the street, he breathed in the cold air and watched his breath frost over when he exhaled. A figure passed under the light across the street, and he recognized Emilio's profile.

"Hey, wait up," he called.

His brother stopped and lingered as Hector jogged toward him.

"Where you been? Why aren't you home? Are you hanging out with the Monks again?"

"Are you kidding? You made sure the Monks will never take me. I been hanging with my friends," Emilio grumbled.

"Well, get home, and don't give Abuelo a hard time anymore." He decided now was not the time to share his good fortune.

CHAPTER 36

First week of January

In contrast to the high energy of the holiday season, the first week of January found the students apathetic and dreary in spirit, Claire noticed. Her class filed into the library on the second floor, scanning their ID's into the security system. The mechanism beeped once for each ID that passed the red beam. Claire was at the beginning of the line and directed the sluggish students over to a cluster of wooden tables that allowed a maximum of six students.

Stephanie herded in the stragglers, making certain that all twenty-eight bodies went into the room without detours. Claire waited for all the students to find seats, then took a few minutes to untangle two amorous couples and relocate them apart from each other. For the most part the class had managed to assemble in groups according to gender.

"All right," Claire began, "I have outlined your research assignment on this handout. You may work alone, with a partner, or in a group no larger than three. I have listed the available topics. When you have made your selections, write them on the signup sheet and begin collecting the data on your topic. Are there any questions?"

She paused for responses, and Stephanie smiled benignly in support. The blond highlights of her loosely coiled hair glittered gold under the fluorescent tube lights.

There were no questions. There were no remarks. There was no enthusiasm. Still, Claire took this as a good sign since there were no objections.

She looked at Martha Hemlock who had been the librarian for fifteen years. Martha kept the large main room of the library in tidy condition and seemed to fret when anyone came to do research because it upset the natural order of things. There were those who speculated that Martha would be quite content to lock the library doors and just dust and catalogue the contents of the room. She had been known to hide recently arrived acquisitions for a few months because she didn't want the students to abuse them while they still smelled new. If she had been allowed her way, the entire cast of books would be on reserve, but the school system dictated that students be allowed to actually take the books home. Claire hoped that Martha was up to today's visitation.

Only three students chose to work alone, and they were the first to write their topics on the empty signup sheet while the partnerships and groups were delayed as they haggled about which poet or author to address. Two groups stared silently at the topic list with disgust as if nothing on the list were palatable or possible.

*   *   *

Stephanie exuded an "I'm here to help you" attitude toward the activity, or at least she hoped she did. Fiona Flores came up to her, extended a freshly polished fingernail, and tapped the paper.

"Who's this?" she demanded, pointing to a name in bold black print.

"Richard Lovelace," Stephanie read. "He wrote some truly romantic poetry in his day."

"He sounds weird," Fiona remarked, her lip curling at the sound of his name.

"If you don't like him, how about William Blake? He's three topics down."

"Isn't he that actor?" Fiona inquired.

"No, that's Robert Blake. Maybe you can choose someone more modern. Let's see." She perused the list of names, all of which seemed to have been wrenched from centuries gone by. She set the paper on one of the tables.

"Look, why don't you choose a poet or author you know? I'm certain Miss Harvey won't mind." She wasn't completely positive of that, but surely Claire could see the merit in letting a student come into the twentieth century with a topic.

"Really?" Fiona's left brow lifted.

"Really. After all, literature in any time period is worth investigating," Stephanie assured her.

Sean Finster shuffled from one shelf to another.

"How do you find the frickin' books you need?" he posed to Martha as Stephanie watched from a distance two tables over.

Martha pointed to a row of small drawers along the back of the room.

"You can use the card catalogue over there or you can access the online catalogue." Her hand switched direction and indicated a line of ten computers that stood humming behind the tables on the left side of the room.

"Haven't you ever used the library before?"

Sean snorted and rubbed a finger beneath his moist nose. "Uh, no. I must have been absent on library days."

Without comment, Martha held out a box of generic tissues, one sheet peeking through the open oval on the top of the box. It seemed to take a few seconds for the boy to realize what she wanted him to do. He scuffed nearer to her, extracted a tissue and touched it to his leaking nostrils. Martha put down the box and picked up a plastic bottle of disinfectant gel, proffering the bottle to Sean.

"I don't use stuff like that. You wind up smelling like a petunia." He placed his used tissue on her desk and slouched away.

When she saw that Sean seemed to be on track, Stephanie moved to lean over Donald Haberman's shoulder as he entered the name of Edgar Allen Poe into the computer's database. Her flowing fragrance mingled with the musty smell from a nearby set of ancient encyclopedias. She heard Donald inhale deeply, and he turned to look at her as the drive whirred and beeped, searching for references. She felt invigorated as the boy returned her warm smile, but she noticed that his expression came closer to a smirk.

"I'm going to need a lot of help," she heard him murmur.

*   *   *

Claire watched as Stephanie bent over a student and knew that she had never been able to capture a student's attention by her mere presence the way Stephanie did. She had relied on powerhouse lesson plans, plotting unusual activities, and the enthusiasm she had for her subject matter. She didn't resent Stephanie as much as regret that life just wasn't fair. It took Claire hours of preparation to get as much interest from the students as Stephanie did from a casual glance. She felt a constriction in her chest that made concentration difficult. She wasn't sure if the tightness was brought on by the American chop suey the cafeteria had served that day or the realization that she was getting older and possibly losing her connection with the students.

At least she still had her writing. She was half finished with her latest project, her fourth unpublished romance novel, and she was at a crucial point in the plot. Her last book had not been accepted because it didn't have enough sex, one of the notes accompanying a rejection had implied. Where could she do research about that, she wondered.

CHAPTER 37

Same day

With an inner sigh Penelope watched Sammy saunter into the room, a solitary book dangling between the thumb and forefinger of his right hand; the other hand was fisted and shoved into the pocket of his voluminous gray sweatshirt. The earplugs of an iPod were planted firmly in his ears, but whatever music flowed from the device could not be heard by anyone else. Who knew what tunes Sammy used to get through his day? There was no movement of his body that suggested a rhythm, no look of pleasure on his face to indicate enjoyment. There were some stories circulated by his rival "toughs" that he actually listened to nothing. The earplugs, they claimed, were just used to prevent anyone from talking to him if he didn't want them to. Penelope was not sure she believed that.

He was not a tall teen, maybe five foot six, possibly seven. It was hard to tell because of his habitual slouch. He was over the threshold two seconds before the tardy bell sounded. He always made it on time, just barely. Penelope pointed to her own head to signal him to remove his headgear. He waited until he reached his desk before complying, stuffing the wires and plugs into the pocket that his hand had just vacated.

He sat, sullenly silent. His body slumped into the curved cradle of the desk's seat. He looked straight ahead, his book unopened on the flat surface in front of him.

Penelope lifted the shade-like movie screen that was fastened to the front wall over the backboard, revealing the review problems on the board beneath. With a satisfied exhalation, she noticed that most of the students immediately retrieved pencils from their book bags and started to scribble on the papers that had already been placed on their desks. Penelope had asked Christie to distribute the paper between the classes so that the students would have them on arrival.

Sammy made no attempt to produce a pencil. His eyes appeared focused on the numbers that were scrawled across the board, but at the same time those same eyes were dim and distant. Penelope knew that he did not think of the numbers, the problems they posed, or the solutions he might find. Maybe his mind was still on the music he was not allowed to hear right now. Perhaps it was something darker that drew him away from his classmates into his own quiet world.

Several of the students raised their hands for help or clarification. Christie was seated in the back row observing, and Penelope motioned for her to assist in attending to the quandaries and complications that arose as other twelfth graders struggled with the work.

After most of the students had finished the assignment, Penelope reviewed the answers and the process.

"Who needs to review again?"

Over half of the class shot hands into the air.

"All right, those of you who managed to work your way through without a glitch, open to page fifty-eight and look over the next concept. Read the first four paragraphs that explain it and do the sample problems."

She proceeded to call the other students to the board and asked them to put up their partial solutions. "Even if you don't think it's correct, write up the process and put it next to your work. Maybe others did it the same way. We can help each other here." Penelope continued to encourage their efforts.

Christie visited the desks of the others who had not even neared a solution.

Penelope approached Sammy's desk. His closed book remained where he had dropped it, and both hands were now pocketed.

"Are you having a problem today, Sammy?" She spoke quietly so none of the others could hear. He shook his head.

"Do you want some help?"

Again, a soundless reply in the form of a head jerk to the side was the only hint that he had heard her.

Penelope knew better than to confront him, but she still battled with her own philosophy that no student should have to fail. After all was said and done, she inwardly debated, didn't a student have a right to choose his own academic destiny? "Not if I can help it," she thought.

Just then class ended with the bell, and within seconds the room was cleared except for the two teachers and Sammy, who seemed in no rush to leave.

"Sammy, is everything all right?" Even to her own ears it seemed a trite question.

He looked up at her as if defying her to ask it again. He slid his body out of the seat, not breaking eye contact.

"You forgot your book," she reminded him.

He looked over at the text, and then at Penelope.

"No I didn't." He ambled toward the door.

Christie collected the papers that were left behind in the rush and made her way to where Penelope was standing, her eyes still fixed on the doorway.

"I heard he just got suspended for two weeks for drawing some rather profane figures on the play's scenery."

"What?" asked Penelope incredulously "I saw the play. I didn't see anything inappropriate on the canvas background."

"I know. Neither did anyone else. The vice principal found several drawings near the bottom when he was helping to dismantle the boards, and Principal Bradford suspended him immediately. Technically, he shouldn't have been in class just now."

Penelope shook her head, as if by doing so, she could make the news go away. She worried about this young man almost as much as she did about Hector. She wished she could earn more of his trust. She knew Hector's situation, but no one seemed to know Sammy's. He would probably laugh if he knew how deeply she was concerned, but it didn't stop her from caring.

CHAPTER 38

Second week in January

At precisely nine o'clock Claire could feel the tightening in her chest, the constrictions in her throat, the dryness in her mouth. She rose from the plastic cushioned chair in the faculty lounge and staggered toward the built-in sink in the narrow niche near the microwave. She reached up and took a mug from the wooden peg rack, not bothering to check whose mug it was. Each cup was labeled with masking tape along the bottom, the name of the owner written in black magic marker. The one she had carelessly plucked from its place on the wall was the thick, white generic variety. "Probably belongs to a man," she thought as she filled it with water from the tap. The water was never hot or cold, just warm. She drank the tepid fluid in quiet gulps, and it lubricated her mouth, soothed her throat, but it did nothing to ease the tightness in her chest. *I'm having a heart attack.* The idea flashed like the light on a neon sign.

Matt Nesbitt came into the room, a newspaper under his arm and a set of vocabulary quizzes in his hand. One look at Clare's red visage, panicked eyes and the cup clasped tightly in her fist, and he went into emergency mode. Dropping the papers, he leapt behind her, clutched her body with his lean but surprisingly strong arms and began pumping inward.

Claire recognized the Heimlich maneuver on the fourth jab of his clenched hand into her diaphragm.

"I'm not choking," she gasped. Will stopped the piston-like motion and dropped his arms.

"What's wrong?" he shouted into her left ear.

"I'm also not deaf. I'm having a heart attack!" she sobbed.

Matt led her to the plastic couch that matched the texture and color of the surrounding chairs.

Stephanie, her hair in tightly coiled tendrils, floated through the door. She noted her mentor reclining on the couch, Matt massaging her hands.

"Oops, I'm sorry," she whispered, attempting to leave the questionable scene before her, without disturbing the participants.

"Get back here," Matt bellowed. "Claire's heart! Call the office. Send the nurse."

Stephanie immediately ran to Claire's side, muttering, "You'll be fine, Miss Harvey."

"She will be if you get on the phone. I'm trying to keep her circulation going," he spoke with authority for a five foot three inch English department head.

"Of course," Stephanie replied, reaching for the beige phone dangling from its cradle on the wall.

Claire watched as Stephanie made the call. Stephanie stood tall in her woodsy hued peasant skirt and almost off the shoulder white cotton blouse. After a thirty second interval, one of the clerks evidently picked up because Stephanie stated to speak.

"I think Miss Harvey is dying. Could you please send the nurse to the first floor faculty room? You might want to call an ambulance, too."

Claire's pain seemed to intensify at Stephanie's words.

"Help is on the way, but they said that the nurse and the police officer on duty would be here immediately to assess the situation," she called across the room and then went back to be with her mentor after she replaced the receiver.

Claire thought this might be fitting. She would die right here, her dreams, still dreams. She had always thought someone would come to rescue her from a life of other people's poetry and tangled composition. But her own verses and stories had never became famous, and she had to correct the papers to get paid. She never minded working with the children, though. She still loved being the one who introduced them to new literature, until Stephanie came along. The twenty-something, quirky personality was slowly stealing the attention of her students, but she still had her two classes. She would keep those. What was she thinking? She was dying. She didn't know if she would see any of them ever again.

Freida exploded into the room, pushing a wide brown wheel chair in front of her. She parked it next to Claire and put her frigid, metallic stethoscope to Claire's chest.

"What's up?"

"Heart attack," Matt fired back.

"Maybe, maybe not." She listened thoughtfully. "What's happening old girl?"

Claire bristled but related her symptoms.

"Maybe an anxiety attack," Freida ventured. "But we'll take you to the ER anyway."

Stephanie sidled up to the indignant Claire who had the look of someone who defied anyone to say she wasn't dying.

Stephanie put her hand on the veteran teacher's shoulder. "Don't worry, Miss Harvey. I'll take care of all your classes, even those honors courses. Leave everything to me."

Claire thought of the racy bulletin board, the nude writing prompt, the salivating male teens, and thought she could not die now.

CHAPTER 39

Next night

The meal had been a delectable combination of pasta and seafood at the Grist Mill Inn. The large portions of lobster in a thick sauce had clung to the perfectly presented penne, and the wine was a full bodied pinot noir that complemented the meal well. Penelope sighed as she tried to fend off the guilt of eating such a sumptuous meal so soon after the holidays, but then decided that she deserved to be pampered after having to deal with all the issues at school. She and Jonathan sat back, sipping the wine and talking about the school and how Bradford seemed to be on the verge of a nervous breakdown for the last month.

"Do you think that vein in his head will keep from exploding if things don't start looking up?" Jonathan had wondered.

"I'm not sure, but if it does, Marci will put a bandage on it, prop him up, and write his memos like she usually does. No one would know the difference."

Jonathan had smiled at the image. "Is he married or is there something going on between him and the formidable Ms. Wickers?"

Penelope laughed lightly at the very suggestion. "Both of them are or were married. Principal Bradford has a lovely wife who is extremely active in community affairs—oh dear, maybe I shouldn't have said that."

"Nell, please don't turn into a Claire Harvey." He rolled his eyes for emphasis.

"There are worse things I could be. She's was . . . *is* a great teacher," she retorted irritably.

Jonathan put both his palms up as if to ward off a blow. "Hold it. I never claimed that she wasn't good, just a little, shall we say a bit of a stickler about proprieties?"

She thought about that a moment. "Well, maybe just a little," she conceded. "When I was in her class, she would avoid pages in Shakespeare that had any sexual references. She would always claim that those passages were too 'complicated' for high school reading." She winced a little at the memory, wondering if Claire was still censoring the authors she taught.

Jonathan relaxed a bit, emptied his wine glass, and grinned perceptively at his companion. "Are you trying to picture the old girl teaching *Catcher in the Rye* to today's savvy students? I'll bet she's had to change her MO."

"From what I hear, she's mellowed considerably."

Jonathan's smile fell. "Have you heard anything about her condition? I know you went to see her at the hospital today. I was very sorry to hear of her heart attack."

"I do feel a lot better after seeing her. She was pale and mad as heck that she wasn't at the high school, but they expect she'll be fine. She'll be home soon but will be out of commission for a while. No surgery was required. I brought her a plant and some reading material."

"Good. She is a strong personality, so she'll probably recover more quickly than they anticipate."

Jonathan leaned forward, forearms resting on the table's edge, and toyed with the butter knife. "I was with Hector today. He's pretty excited about working with that software program. He's done some remarkable compositions with it. I knew the kid was sharp, but I would never have guessed the depth of his talent. I don't know too much about music, but I do know that what he produces, I like. Of course, Tottman is having a ball working with him, too. He told me he thinks Hector's a real prodigy."

"You and Ted have done a tremendous job keeping him occupied. I've noticed a terrific difference in his attitude. He's already setting goals for himself and achieving them, one by one," Penelope mused.

"He was telling me that his brother Emilio is also into music, and he's trying to talk him into joining the choir next year when he comes to the high school."

"Hector has mentioned Emilio a few times. I guess the music bug runs in the family." She looked at her watch out of custom. During the day she constantly checked it since the wall clock in her classroom lost several minutes a day, and so was not a reliable timepiece.

"What's the matter, Nell. Are you bored or does your coach turn into a pumpkin at midnight?" he teased.

"No, it's just become a habit, I guess, but it is almost eleven."

"Yes, it is. It's also Friday. You don't have to get up too early, but I'll take you home so that you can let out that bulldozer you call a dog."

"He speaks very well of you, you know," she replied, not offended.

"I like the mutt. After all, I was in the military; I'm used to heavy equipment."

*   *   *

Jonathan's SUV crunched onto her driveway twenty minutes later. He turned to face Penelope as soon as he came to a complete halt. "Is there an invitation to come in?"

"You're probably tired," she shot back automatically.

He waited a moment before he breathed out a sigh. "Are you still afraid? What we had last time was magnificent. You said you didn't regret it."

"I don't, but I'm not sure we're ready for a repeat performance."

"Why not? Repetition breeds perfection."

"You can come in for coffee if you'd like. I think we can handle coffee."

"All right," he allowed. "It's your call. Coffee sounds great."

They were welcomed with open paws by Spartacus who danced around their legs and leaned into Jonathan for attention. Penelope held the door open, and the wall of fur blasted across the threshold into the fenced back yard.

"How fickle," Jonathan complained. "I got thrown over for a potty break and a jaunt in the dark."

"It's nothing personal. He'll be back in about ten minutes even more affectionate than he was before, unfortunately."

She removed her coat and held her hand out for Jonathan's. His hand grazed across her arm as he relinquished it, and he felt the heat of her skin, surprised that it was warm after just coming in from the January bitterness. The touch brought a heat to his body that lingered even as Penelope left to put their coats in the next room.

Damn it! He would not let his need for her overcome his promise to allow her to set the pace. He crossed his arms, something he'd been doing a lot lately to avoid reaching for her, touching her, ravishing her. He was a man accustomed to making decisions and acting on them quickly. He couldn't do that with her. He didn't want to alarm her. What he wanted from her wasn't a quick encounter. He wanted . . . he didn't know what he wanted here.

He heard a whine at the door and moved to let in the panting hound. "A little too cold for you out there, boy?"

The dog's tail thudded on the linoleum floor as he came to a sitting position in front of his sizeable monogrammed bowl and lapped water as if he had spent a week in the desert instead of five minutes in the back yard.

"I'll put the coffee on. I hope you don't mind decaf since it's so late," Penelope said in a rush of words as she reentered the room.

"No, decaf's fine."

She ran water into the carafe as she flipped the switch of the coffeepot to "on" position. He watched as she measured the dark granules and spread them into the filter of the pot. He was mesmerized by her movements and noticed the way her elegant fingers tended to the task before her.

*   *   *

When the pot started to hiss and pop as it brewed, she turned, leaning her trim hips against the counter. The rich aroma filled the kitchen and brought back memories of her recent holiday at her mother's.

What would she do without her family? Her mother, sister, aunts, and uncles were always huddled near a tree of titanic proportions at Christmas. She always took their presence at holiday celebrations for granted. She admitted to herself that sometimes she considered it a nuisance to have to be part of the Christmas chaos, but what must it be like to have no one? She thought of how Jonathan had spent this last holiday. A few brief visits to employees did not make up for the fact that most of the day he was alone by choice.

She reached out and feathered a touch along his sharp jaw line. Slowly, she spread her fingers and caressed the beginning growth of his beard. The abrasive sensation rippled though her body.

She felt his hand come up to cover her own. "Don't do this unless you want what comes next. I seem to lose a lot of restraint where you're concerned. If you want to keep this casual for now, you'll have to help by keeping your distance."

*   *   *

She lifted her other hand to trace the scar that curved near his eye. The contact was like a delicate breath hovering over him. He closed his eyes to concentrate on the sensual urgency that had surged at their connection.

He felt her lips join his, igniting something in him that he had suppressed for too long. This was even more intense than their passion driven first encounter. He deepened the kiss and moved his hands around her in a gentle embrace, pulling her inexorably closer, feeling the exhilaration diffuse throughout his body.

He lifted her lightly so that she sat on the counter, repositioning himself directly in front of her slightly parted knees. His lips broke from hers and traveled to her neck, breathing in the subtle scent she wore. He pushed back her long hair with one hand and kneaded the muscles just below her hairline.

He heard her swallow as if she were drowning, and he let his mouth journey to her left ear. "If you want to stop this, do it now. It's my final warning."

"No," she gasped. "No, I can't let you stop now."

His body went rigid with need. He made a conscious effort to allow her time to adjust, time to feel, to take what she wanted. And she did.

* * *

Penelope had slept soundly for several hours before she was awakened by a stream of invectives that startled her into consciousness. She rose onto her elbow in the queen sized bed and felt Jonathan thrashing in the tangled sheet. As she touched him, he bolted to a sitting position.

"Bastards!" he bellowed. He was slick with sweat and breathing as if he were the last gladiator standing. He sucked in several labored breaths before he seemed to become aware of Penelope's presence.

"Sorry," he said, scrubbing his face with the palm of his hand.

"Don't be. Are you all right?"

"Yes," he ground out as he rose from the bed and made his way to the bathroom.

She heard the faucet running and envisioned him dashing water onto his face. Now that her heart was no longer trying to escape from her chest, she grabbed her silk robe as Jonathan exited the bathroom with a bath sheet secured at his waist.

"I hope I didn't scare you."

"No, of course not," she lied. "Has that happened before?"

He hesitated. "Too often. I'll go."

He began a search for the clothing that he had so untidily dropped somewhere.

Penelope stretched out her hand and caught his arm before he could leave the room. "Please, stay. Let's talk."

He stopped his search and stood immobile, silhouetted by the fragile moonlight that seeped beneath the half drawn shades. Slowly, he sat back down on the edge of the tufted mattress.

He turned to face her. "I'm sorry," he said again.

"Don't be sorry. Do you think a little thing like a nightmare would scare me off?"

"It's not really a nightmare. It's history, mine, and I didn't want to expose you to it."

"I already have been exposed, as you put it. I'm a good listener; you can tell me anything. After all, you started to tell me part of the story," she entreated as she massaged his shoulders gently.

She could feel his tension ease as his muscles relaxed under her soothing touch. He was silent for a long time.

"I already told you about my last assignment. It went bad, and I keep reliving it. I never know when it's going blast its way into the early morning hours. When I first came back, I didn't sleep for five days to avoid letting this happen. Now it's better, but it's still there. It may always be there."

Her hands ceased their circular motion and gripped his powerful shoulders from behind. She rose to her knees and laid her head on the raven hair now damp from the water he had splashed to revive himself. It seemed to encourage him to go on.

"I was the one giving the orders. I should have been able to sense the trap. I caused the deaths of those men, and there's nothing I can do from here on that makes up for that."

"You're right that there's nothing you can do now. There was probably nothing you could have done then either. The past should stay where we left it."

He turned and placed her face between his large hands. "I don't know if the past will ever leave. These episodes may always be with me."

"I could be, too, if you let me," Penelope ventured.

The room started to blaze with the faint hint of dawn.

CHAPTER 40

Third week in January

Stephanie was on a curriculum high after her last class of the day. She had just consulted her lesson plan, and she noted that she had reached all of her goals and objectives and even managed to get in a personal story of her first trip to Paris. She had stood on the banks of the Seine and had written a free verse poem that ran thirty-seven lines. It was as deep as the Seine itself and probably as muddy, but she read it to the class anyway, and they had seemed enraptured. She had never realized how poetic teenagers could be, especially the boys. For some reason their eyes had almost protruded from their sockets as she had read her poem "Rivers of My Heart" with her right hand resting on her bosom and her light voice carrying the heavy words throughout the classroom. Now she knew she could get the male members of the class engrossed in verse if she only made the effort.

She put a green check at the top of the word processed sheet, indicating that this lesson was a victory and began planning for the next week. She sat by the window in the teachers' lounge and sorted through the pile of notes she had made for the upcoming units. Now that Claire was out on leave, she had to be especially astute in doing the paperwork that needed to be submitted on a monthly basis to Principal Bradford. The department head, Matthew Nesbit, had volunteered to mentor while she substituted for Claire.

Stephanie heard a subtle clearing of the throat. She looked up and a hesitant Claire, clasping a puffy brown envelope to her midriff, entered into the modest space of the square room, stopping in front of a hefty sized poster of Nathaniel Hawthorne on the side wall.

Stephanie immediately went to her, placing a solicitous arm around her shoulders.

"Miss Harvey, what are you doing here? You're supposed to be home relaxing. A school is no place to be when you're not feeling well."

"I'm all right. The classes are my responsibility," Claire responded, her face resolute.

"I understand your feelings. After all, I've heard so much from the students about how they always felt you knew everything about literature. They've been really concerned about you."

She led her advisor to a blue vinyl straight chair that was mismatched to a green topped computer desk where she had been working. They both sat down soundlessly and scrutinized one another, Stephanie searching for a reason for the visit.

"I brought the lesson plans for next week. The principal requires everyone to send in plans during absences. I know you have already done them for Period B, but these are for the rest of the classes."

"Why thank you, but it really wasn't necessary. I made all new plans for the other classes already. Mr. Nesbit approved them. In fact, I made copies and was going to mail them to you tomorrow," Stephanie related with fervor. "I'm already excited about implementing them."

"Well, that's all well and good, but I am the teacher, and these are the assignments for the next few weeks. The doctor suggested that I take several months off, and I want to be certain everything goes well in my absence. I'll send more plans for the long term substitute."

Stephanie patted the older woman's shoulder, somewhat surprised at the woman's brown tweed blazer and dark, slightly flared skirt. Claire was dressed as if she had come in to teach. Her thick soled shoes were side by side, her feet set firmly, as if she were sitting at the old desk in her room.

"I'm sure they're really fine lessons, and I will certainly use them as a guide, but don't you worry about those classes. I have everything under control," Stephanie assured her mentor.

The hand clutching the envelope began to quake noticeably, and Claire put her other hand to her lips.

They sat in a nonverbal face-off, like two contestants in a debate who had not yet been able to form a strategy. The buzzing of the office phone shot through the silence. Stephanie hesitated to answer it, but she noted that Claire made no move to respond.

"I'll get it," Stephanie offered, her long crepe skirt swishing as she rose and tread buoyantly toward the wall phone. She lifted the plastic receiver and huskily greeted the caller with a soft, "Yes?"

She listened attentively to the speaker on the other side of the line. A few times she bobbed her head in response to the voice on the other end. "Hmm, of course. Why, naturally, I'd love to." Her face beamed with intent and exhilaration, and she released the receiver into its matching plastic cradle.

"Oh, Miss Harvey. Guess what?"

Claire seemed in no mood for amusement. "What?"

"The principal said that you have an official doctor's note to be out for quite a while and . . ." She paused to foster a bit of anticipation. "He asked me to stay on as a permanent sub until you get back. Isn't that simply fantastic? This is going to be great! I'll have all of your classes, and you will know exactly who will be with them, and that should help with those health problems you've been having." Stephanie reduced her volume considerably in uttering the last sentence, so that no-one would overhear, disregarding the fact that the room was empty.

Claire blanched and began sinking toward the tiled floor just as Wally Winslow pushed the door and entered the lounge.

"Oh no, not again," he whispered.

CHAPTER 41

Jonathan inhaled the scent of lilacs that seemed so refreshingly out of place in December. There was no more than an intimation of the delightful fragrance that caressed the air around Penelope. He ran his hand through her hair, feeling the lightness of it as it slid between his fingers. The flames that snapped and sputtered around the logs in the fireplace highlighted the red streaks in her long locks.

They both stared into the blaze, mesmerized by the shadows that rose, tangled and retreated as the wood was reduced to smoldering stumps on the floor of the hearth. Their lovemaking had been languid and lingering, and they both were physically exhausted, but emotionally exhilarated.

"Comfortable?" he asked as Penelope lay with her head on his chest, her body nestled by his side.

"Umm."

He ran his hand down her bare arm and felt her shiver. They had dragged a blanket from the downstairs closet, and it served to stave off the chill of the winter wind that rattled the shutters and battered at the windows.

"It feels like a storm brewing out there. I wonder if there will be a snow day tomorrow. You people still have snow days, don't you?"

She lifted her head and looked into his eyes. "The kids consider them the best part of the winter session."

She pulled herself up onto her elbows next to him and ran a finger down the side of his face. "What are you doing during the February winter break?"

He pulled back to look into her eyes. She seemed so soft, and yet she had tensed slightly when she asked the question.

"Why?"

She breathed in and her finger stopped its progress at his chin. "Well," she began, "I'd really like you to come with me to my mom's. I usually spend a

couple of days with her over the vacation. It only takes a few hours to get there."
She seemed to stop all movement as she waited for his response.

He rose to a sitting position, the edge of the blanket falling to his lap.
When he saw that it had also uncovered her upper torso, he pulled it back up
to her shoulders. "Look, I don't need to be brought home like some orphan. I
am quite used to my own company."

She held onto the blanket as she, too, sat up. "You think this is charity? It
isn't," she stated emphatically. Her voice softened. "It's just that I want you to
meet her." She cast her eyes to the curls of smoke that rose from the glowing
embers.

He pushed his hand through his hair. He didn't know what to say. He
wasn't prepared for this. They had spent a lot of time together, but he had not
allowed himself to think beyond each day. If he were honest with himself, he
had to admit that the thought of her being hours away made him miss her
already. He needed to know she was near.

He said in barely audible tones, "All right. Let's make the trip."

She reached up to encircle his neck with her arms and haul him back down
to lie beside her. She kissed him feverishly, and he caught the passion, savoring
the taste of her.

He withdrew to let his lips hover a few inches above hers. "I wanted to
tell you earlier, but we got, shall we say 'busy'? I think I might be taking a full
time job at the high school."

Her eyes opened wide. "What do you mean?"

He tried to kiss her, but she put her hands on his chest and kept him at
bay. He sighed. "Bradford called me into his office today. Some guy named
Stanley Hayden just handed in his retirement papers, effective the third quarter.
Bradford asked if I would take over, and I'm seriously considering it since it's
the computer classes."

"When were you going to tell me this?"

"I just did. I only found out today."

She opened her mouth to reply when the doorbell rang. Penelope jumped
and grabbed at the robe she had shed so eagerly an hour ago. She glanced at
the clock above the mantle. It was nine on a week night.

"Who could that be at this hour," she wondered aloud.

*   *   *

Penelope peered through the small window of the front door and saw a
shivering Mrs. Wipplewhite smiling back at her. Penelope quickly unlocked
and opened the door for her neighbor.

"Come in, come in. Is everything all right?" She could not imagine what would have lured the eighty-year-old out on such a night.

"Everything is fine. I baked some of my cranberry bread and brought you over a loaf. So you could enjoy it for breakfast."

Her small, faded blue eyes darted from one place to the other as if she were gathering information for the CIA. It then occurred to Penelope that even in the midst of a storm Philomena's curiosity was not to be denied.

"I saw that big black car in the driveway again. If you have company, you'd best warn them that the roads are getting bad."

Jonathan came to stand in the arch that separated the hall from the living room. He loomed high and dark above the two women.

"Good evening, Mrs. Wipplewhite. It's a pleasure to see you again." He smiled charmingly in her direction.

The older woman seemed mesmerized by the sight of him in his jeans and tee shirt. Penelope thought that he must have pulled them on quickly when she had gone to answer the door.

"I was just saying to Penelope here that the roads are getting bad. I was listening to the police scanner, and they were warning people to stay off the roads." A pair of wire rimmed spectacles stood guard over her small nose.

"And so we shall," he said lightly.

Penelope felt the lump of embarrassment rise in her throat, but swallowed it as rapidly as it had formed. "Yes, I'll make sure Jonathan spends the night. We wouldn't want him in any danger."

Jonathan's eyebrow arched in surprise when she glanced his way.

"Thank you so much for the cranberry bread. We'll enjoy it tomorrow morning. Would you like one of us to see you back to your house?" asked Penelope.

Mrs. Wipplewhite seemed speechless for three or four seconds before she stammered, "No, I'll be fine. It's just a few yards."

"Nevertheless, I insist," Jonathan commanded before going back into the living room and retrieving his shoes. He jammed them onto his feet and opened the door for their unexpected visitor to exit. As Mrs. Wipplewhite passed through the doorway, he bent and whispered to Penelope. "Congratulations. It's Independence Day."

CHAPTER 42

The cafeteria was enveloped in a pall as Stephanie bounded into the green walled room. She pulled a chair out at the table where Christie and Jeffrey were quietly sipping soup from Styrofoam cups. She plopped down uncharacteristically and glared at her two fellow interns. Her entry had been so aberrant that Jeffrey swallowed quickly and cleared his throat.

"What's going on, Steph?" he asked urgently.

"A lot. First Claire showed up yesterday with a stack of lesson plans. Then Principal Bradford informed me that I was the permanent sub for Miss Harvey. I'm not sure if that was the reason she became dizzy and nearly collapsed. Thank God it wasn't another heart attack, but she could have had one if she had known who would appear in her class this morning." She paused to catch her breath. "Have you ever heard such a thing? There was a representative from the state in my classroom when I was doing a writing lesson. All the kids were engaged, and I thought that everything was going extremely well. I was thrilled, but this guy came up to me after class and said that I'll have to get more practical in my lessons since the state test fiasco. He said that he is recommending that the principal adapt the WISE program for the English Department. What's that?"

"I heard about it in one of my education classes," Jeffrey said. "It means 'Writing Improvement for State Evaluation.' The teachers give weekly writing assignments, and they are holistically scored. Then samples of the assignments must be submitted to an independent company, which evaluates the teachers' ability to give a good prompt and the students' ability to follow it. It allows a lot of feedback for both the educator and the student." He scraped the last of the noodles from the side of his cup and devoured them.

"My education teacher said it was a lot of crap," he continued. "They found out that some of the evaluators from the company hadn't been in the classroom all that long or not at all. There's also a great deal of paperwork involved, and they haven't proven yet that the scores improved because of all this flurry of activity, but they did prove that some of the existing curriculum had to be cut because there was no time to present the material in the new guidelines."

Stephanie continued to fume. "That kind of sounds like the fun is taken out of teaching and learning. Didn't our education teachers also say that you have to get their attention first?"

"Well, yes, but there is now a new god in education, and that is the state test. We must worship at its feet if we're going to keep our jobs, and if the kids are going to get out of here with their self esteem still alive." He dumped the spoon into the empty cup and sat back.

Christie, who had remained silent during the exchange, spoke up. "We're having the same problem in math. We received a memo that they want us to have the kids write out the answers to the problems in paragraph form. Penelope says that it's difficult enough to get them to put the solutions down in numbers without adding a new layer of difficulty. Usually the kids are so thrilled when they actually 'get it' that they don't really want to take the time to go through it again and find the right words to clarify and explain what they've discovered. Has anyone actually seen a sample of this test?"

"I have," Jeffrey assured them, "and it's not mere understanding they're looking for; it appears to be mastery. They seem to forget that not every kid is college bound even if the government insists that they should be."

"But shouldn't we treat them as if they are? You never know, and we should be fair," interjected Christie.

"Not everyone's strong suit is math or English," added Stephanie.

"Well," stated Jeffrey, "they better be now. Polep was just gloating upstairs that the history department doesn't have to be concerned with such things yet."

"Isn't there a history section of the test?" inquired Stephanie.

"Yes, but it doesn't count for graduation requirements just yet. Who knows what will happen in the near future, but for now, we're safe."

"I don't feel very safe," Stephanie complained. "I feel invaded."

"For once," Christie commiserated, "I know just how you feel."

The trio sat quietly, each lost in thought. Slowly, Jeffrey rose to his feet, dragged his tray from the table, and left.

"I've got to get back. The stairs are usually clogged now, and I've got to get to class."

"Me, too," moaned Christie. "If it's any consolation, Penelope is still trying to formulate a plan to get the state off our backs."

"I never saw this coming. This is not how I envisioned teaching would be," lamented Stephanie.

"Maybe you just were looking somewhere else when it was on its way, but it's here now, and we have to deal with it if we want to pursue our teaching careers."

"Well, I'm really glad that you and Jeffrey are staying until the final exams. You didn't have to, but it's good to have someone to talk to now that Claire isn't here anymore," Stephanie admitted.

Christie hesitated before scooping her tray. "I'm glad, too."

CHAPTER 43

J onathan and Penelope walked across the icy parking lot to the front entrance. Jonathan looked at Nell and whispered, "I can't believe it, but I'm actually a bit nervous."

Penelope patted him on the arm and said, "Don't be ridiculous. We talked this through. You have your lessons, and your goals and objectives are very clear. The kids love computers and they respect you. In fact, you know more of them than I do. Just be your wonderful self."

Christie ran toward the two of them and called, "Hey, Miss Parsons, I hope you already know my extension has been officially granted, up until winter break. I really appreciate you letting me stay after exams."

"Yes, your professor called. I think it's a great idea since you have no class work left to complete. You are truly becoming a teacher, and a little more practice never hurt anyone. We'll use the extra time to help you spread your wings a little further, and you'll be a great teacher."

"Hi, Mr. Perez. You're here early."

"Oh, I'll be early from now on. I'm on the staff full time until the end of the year. The regular computer teacher retired right after the holidays."

They entered the building together, checked in at the office, and then Jonathan left for his room. Penelope and Christie sauntered to the second floor as was their usual routine.

Christie turned and called back to Jonathan, "You'll be magnificent. The kids already love you."

*   *   *

Christie felt drained of energy when the last class ended. The sweat beaded on her upper lip, and her knees bent a bit in relief that the class was over.

Penelope was right. It was a hard job, and it took a lot out of you, but her mentor had also insisted that it was all worth it. Christie wasn't so sure at the moment. The paper airplane on her desk was an aerodynamically advanced model compared to the ones that she had seen in her own high school years. She had managed to grab it in mid-air as it had sailed toward the front of the room. She had also almost tripped over a book bag in the aisle as she did so. It was a wonder she was still standing, she thought.

As usual, Sammy had also made a big show of yawning as she went over the formulas for solving today's problems. She always felt that she was boring, but Sammy's actions today seemed to confirm it. Of course, she knew that he was doing it partly just to annoy her. She saw the gleam in his eye when the red rash of irritation rose on her cheeks. Sammy had just come back from another three day suspension, and it looked as if he was working on his next.

She sat down on the chair behind the teacher's desk and wondered if she would ever be able to teach like Penelope. She definitely had moments that made her wonder if she would ever be able to teach effectively at all. Hadn't some of her experiences been proof enough? She had run out of time for several lessons since she had started teaching. She had also made a mistake in calculation when she was demonstrating a procedure on the board, and the students barely acknowledged her presence in the hallways. Even though she realized she had improved, her head sank to the blotter that covered the middle of the desk. She could feel the imprint of a pencil in the middle of her forehead and didn't bother to lift her head to remove it. She had agreed to the extra practicum when they told her she had promise. She hoped not to disappoint them.

"Hey, Teach, what you doin'? Taking a nap?"

Christie bolted to an upright position. It was Marisol. The tall, young woman with attitude stood next to the desk looking down at her.

"No, no, I was just taking a moment to meditate," she stammered.

"Better not let Bradford catch you. You'll get fired or else get yelled at. I'm pretty sure it's against the teacher contract or something." She put down a spiral notebook that dripped papers onto the floor. "I got a question about that homework assignment."

Christie was still wallowing a bit in her sense of failure, but she quickly caught herself and concentrated on the crinkled sheets that the girl set down in front of her.

"I got this far." She pointed to a set of numbers with an extraordinarily long, scarlet fingernail. "I forgot how you said to go from there."

Christie looked at the series of numbers on the paper and studied the work. She picked up the pencil that had creased her forehead a moment ago and began to explain the process of getting to the next level of the problem. Christie bent down, and she could smell the berry scent of the girl's shampoo. In reflection, she could not help but recall several of the students in the last class who emanated a scent a bit stronger and not quite so pleasant. Jeffrey had told her that Sidney had put a couple such students by the open window, and neither one of them seemed to have ascertained the reason their seats were changed.

The sharp snapping of the gum Marisol was chewing as well as the soft "hmm" of understanding brought her back to the task.

"Okay, I got it," Marisol declared after ten minutes had passed. "You made it real clear now." She grabbed the papers and stuffed them once more inside the unkempt notebook.

Marisol's open-backed shoes slapped gently against her heels as she headed back out the door. She turned to look at Christie just before she exited. "You know, you're a pretty good teacher. Don't let those jerks in class bother you. They're just babies, but they think they're such big men." She rolled her eyes as if to indicate there wasn't much a person could do in such situations.

Finally, Christie smiled.

CHAPTER 44

Later that day

The man was relatively short and seemed to have a habit of rocking onto his toes as he watched from the side of the classroom. He took copious notes as he alternately observed the classroom décor and the students addressing the problems of the day. Penelope had asked, "How can I help you?" when he had first entered the room along with the students at the beginning of the third period. He hadn't answered.

"Excuse me." She had directed her voice again to the older man with the thinning hair and creased brow. "Have you authorization to come in? We have strict policies about people other than faculty or administration dropping in during instruction periods."

The man had wheezed and looked at her with a barely disguised attitude of entitlement. "I have the highest authorization. I'm from the state Department of Education. As you know, we have been sent to look at the ways you people are approaching the problem of under-performing scores by scrutinizing your pedagogy and curriculum. It is our hope that we can help you by offering some suggestions. First, however, we observe."

He had then continued to the back of the room. He varied his observation stations several times during class. Penelope was startled at one point to find him situated behind her desk, glancing down at the lesson objectives she had listed in the pebbled black plan book. She had gone to the front of her desk and delivered a glare so intense that the intruder swaggered toward the side of the room where he continued his note taking. She was very aware of each time he shifted his location, and she had speculated the students also felt the weight of being sized up and judged.

Christie was at the back of the room during the majority of the lesson, but when it was time for the students to undertake several practice problems themselves, she rose and assisted Penelope with the individual help.

After what seemed like hours, the class ended, and the room was cleared within seconds. The interloper made a note of that as well.

"Thank you, ladies," he said in what was probably an unintentionally patronizing manner, Penelope thought. He appeared in no hurry to get to his next destination, but she hoped that whoever was next on his list would have more warning than she did.

"What was that all about?" Christie inquired as she collected the homework assignments that had been left on the front desks of each row.

"Gathering evidence, I think," Penelope responded thoughtfully, "but I'm going to find out why we weren't told about it."

Penelope left the next class to Christie and marched to Bradford's office. With each step her anger grew and her patience waned. The closer she got to the office, the more her head pounded in agitation, the more her mouth went dry with rage.

Marci was in her usual sentinel watch mode as Penelope approached.

"He's busy right now. I don't think he can talk to anyone."

"Then I'll wait until he is ready." She sat down heavily on the ancient wooden chair that served as a repository for those with urgent issues or proposals that the principal had to address. She crossed her arms and then her legs as she sat arrow straight in the chair, determined to speak to B. B. the King.

It was only a matter of minutes before Bradford peeked out the door and looked to his left and right like an inmate preparing for an escape. He saw Penelope and almost managed to pull his head in like an alarmed turtle.

"Dr. Bradford," Penelope managed before the door could completely shut. "I really must speak to you. Now, please."

Bradford looked at her resignedly, opened the door a bit wider, and gestured her into his office.

"Do sit down," he suggested.

"I don't think so. This should not be lengthy. Why was there a strange person in my room without even a heads-up from anyone? If we are going to be put under the microscope, we should at least be told when, why, and who will be doing it."

"It wasn't my idea to spring this stuff on you. It was theirs. They said they wanted to see teachers in their natural state."

"In our natural state? That sounds like we're zoo exhibitions. The way that guy was acting, I think he may actually think of us as specimens. Our kids deserve better than this. You've always been a champion for us before, so what's so different now?"

"For one thing, even my job is on the line. Look, I only want what's best for this school. Our students are going out into that world with a label. It says they come from an under-performing school, and I'm cooperating as much as I can so that they don't go out thinking they're losers. We've got some truly great kids, and I want the state to see that."

"Ben," she hissed, dropping all formality, "they're going to see what they want to see. That person in my classroom didn't get his job because he's a half full kind of guy. If you look long and hard enough at a solid brick wall, you'll find some chinks. I'm afraid that if he doesn't find enough of them to fill his quota, he'll make some of his own. We can't do everything perfectly and they'll capitalize on that. You know it's not going to be a few ideas and a 'good luck in the future' wish."

Bradford sat back in his leather office chair that his wife had presented to him upon his appointment to his present position. He rubbed the furrows in his forehead as if he thought the motion would relax them.

"I'll be honest with you. For the first time, I don't know what to do."

"Well, do something, before it goes too far," she demanded. Her body vibrated with tension and intent. "We teachers have always stood behind the kind of education we have offered these kids, behind the kids themselves, behind the school, and most of all, we have stood behind you. You know why? Because we were convinced that ultimately, you always made decisions with the students in mind. Don't disappoint us this time."

She pivoted so sharply she almost lost her balance and strode out of his office as swiftly and decisively as she had sailed into it.

* * *

Bradford called Marci into his sanctum. "Make a memo, will you?"

"Concerning what, exactly? Where do we start?" Marci had brought a yellow legal pad with her in anticipation of just such a circumstance. Bradford knew that the door had not been tightly closed when Penelope had delivered her tirade and did not doubt that his administrative assistant had heard every word.

"I wish I knew," he sighed.

CHAPTER 45

One week later

J onathan looked over at the huge round clock that seemed to always run about fifteen minutes slow. He had to take into account that the time was really later than the time piece would indicate. At the moment, it was supposedly ten o'clock. That meant that it was really a quarter past, so he had better give the word to start closing down the programs.

This was his third class of the day. He would have two more after the lunch period, but he was constantly surprised at how quickly the time flew when he was engaged in the classes. He now understood why Nell loved her profession.

"All right, let's wind down what you're doing. We only have ten minutes left."

Two young women began to type furiously to finish a project, and a number of other students started to shuffle papers and click their way through the programs they were using. This course was called Applied Technology for the Modern World 101, and Jonathan had taken the title and used it extremely broadly, so that each of the students could use the computers for individual academic endeavors. They were partnered, in small groups, or working alone to complete some assignment that was of interest to them.

Hector was working on a book of his own musical compositions, several others were using statistics to build up a list of probabilities for sports plays, and several of the girls were working on fashion design. The approach seemed to be working because almost all of the students would get right to work as soon as the starting bell rang, and they usually didn't stop until Jonathan gave the signal. He worked the room, monitoring their progress, making suggestions, and fixing any technological problems that came up. He usually introduced several new technical and programming concepts a week that they could incorporate into their individual work.

Sammy was in the far corner of the classroom, working alone on an isolated computer that no one else wanted because it was situated away from the rest of the class. The remoteness seemed to appeal to Sammy, however. Jonathan checked on him periodically, and saw that he had transferred some of his original drawings to computerized versions and worked to give them a unique, almost eerie look. Other artistic interpretations were created right to the program, and Jonathan noticed that Sammy also had a good eye for graphic art.

Sammy pulled his chair back and readjusted his ear buds. Jonathan never said anything to students who preferred to work with headphones or other such equipment. Some of the head pieces were actually part of the program set-up, but others were used to listen to music while they worked. As long as they finished their work without disturbing others, he figured that it really didn't matter.

"You know, these pages you have here could be the start of a career in advertising. There are a number of high profile companies that would love to have someone like you on the payroll. These images are quite dramatic." Jonathan leaned in a bit closer to the screen to scrutinize Sammy's latest techno illustration.

"Whatever."

"You don't believe me?"

Sammy yawned. "Sure, why not. Ya gotta go to school for that, though."

"True, it would certainly help greatly. You've got a flair for this kind of work, but advanced classes in the subject will help you to fine tune your talent."

"I've heard stuff like that before. They told me I'm goin' to graduate from this hell hole, so why would I ever want to go to another school?"

"Because it would make you an even better artist."

"Who cares?"

"I do, for one."

Sammy pulled one of his ear pieces out by tugging on the cord. "Then I guess that makes you all alone in that." A smirk rode low on his lips.

Jonathan saw Hector's hand in the air several yards to the left. It was very unusual for Hector to ask for help, so Jonathan reluctantly straightened and left Sammy to his arrogant grandstanding.

When he reached Hector's table, he pulled up a chair and looked at what Hector was doing. Music notes flowed across the screen like little clouds dotting a spring sky. "What's the problem?"

"Listen! Listen to this," Hector commanded enthusiastically. He had never seen the boy so excited since he had first been introduced to the computerized music program.

Jonathan picked up a pair of ear pieces and plugged them into the computer's port. A melody drifted through, leaving a mellow, tuneful trail. The music was far different from what he had heard Hector compose in the last week and a half. All of his previous pieces had been hard hitting strains that almost assaulted the ears with their intensity, the harsh notes striking and powerful. This was like an oasis in the midst of his other forceful work. It was just as impressive, but different, more peaceful. Was Hector actually finding some peace?

"That's great, Hector. You've really got something unique here."

Hector's eyes were closed, and his face was serene as if he were no longer in a classroom, but in some paradise of his own conception. He suddenly broke from his reverie.

"I got this idea. There's pictures in my brain that go with this. I can see this music."

Jonathan nodded. "It certainly conjures some beautiful scenes in my mind."

"I bet one of the girls could make some pictures to go with this," Hector suggested.

"Well, none of the young ladies in the class are currently working on anything like that, but you could certainly ask some of your classmates if they'd be willing to help."

Hector tapped a couple of keys and stared at the changes he had made.

Jonathan's thoughts returned to what he had just examined at Sammy's work station. He had no doubt that Sammy could very easily come up with something that would match the music Hector was creating.

He remembered the day when Sammy and Hector both realized they had signed up for the new class that Jonathan had added to the schedule. It was placed on the spring schedule as a half year course, something that would give the students every opportunity to work independently. The former teacher of the computer classes had usually dropped one for the spring and assisted in the library for his fifth class obligation, something that Jonathan had no interest in doing, so King had told him he could either take the period off or create a class of his own. He had taken the second option, and this was his favorite time of the day.

The first day of class, Hector was the third student to arrive. The course was offered in the slot where students had taken the required gym in the fall. Students were given the choice of taking it again or changing to one of the several other half year courses that were offered. When Hector learned Jonathan was teaching this course, he had hurriedly signed up. Apparently, it was definitely no sacrifice since he hated gym and had quite often skipped it. Jonathan had warned him that he would not tolerate unnecessary absences in the new class.

Hector had strutted to a computer table that first day and settled in, but when Sammy had appeared, slouching and slinking behind one of the other tables, the room practically crackled. Sammy had seen Hector and turned to grin snidely in his direction before turning his attention to the front of the room.

Jonathan had explained the premise of the course to the students on the first day and then got everyone started thinking about what they had hoped to accomplish. He had stated also that each project would have a presentation at the end of the year that would count as their final exam.

"Ya mean we don't have to take a written test?" one of the sophomores had asked hopefully.

"No," Jonathan had assured her. "There will be no written test. It's all application."

A cheer had erupted at the information. The only two students who did not immediately start exploring the possibilities for their projects were Hector and Sammy. Jonathan had made a point to visit both to suggest several proposals for them, based on what he knew about them. Hector had immediately jumped on the idea of putting together several original compositions. Sammy, however, had given no indication that he was interested in what his teacher had said, but later Jonathan saw him pick up the art program and upload it into the machine he had chosen for the day.

For the most part, the two boys had avoided each other since that day. It was time that ended, Jonathan thought.

"Sammy, come here," Jonathan called.

Sammy seemed startled, something that almost never happened as far as Jonathan had observed.

"Why?"

"I want you to see something."

Hector looked up at his teacher as if he had just invited the devil to the table. Jonathan ignored him for the moment.

Sammy eased himself off his chair and rambled unhurriedly to where Hector and Jonathan were seated.

"What?" He looked at the screen, appearing both bored and distracted.

"Do you think you could get some pictures into a program that could match what Hector has done here?"

Hector looked incensed. "You kiddin'? He couldn't do nothing like that. Besides, I don't want him to touch my stuff."

Sammy growled, "I don't want him messing with what's mine either."

Jonathan straightened and looked at boys, his eyes and mouth hardening. "You don't have to speak to one another. You can be as far away as you like.

Your computers will do the talking while still protecting your work. We'll start next time. No arguments."

Hector and Sammy continued to glare at each other.

CHAPTER 46

Jeffrey had begun to deep-breathe before each class in order to calm the tension he felt before a performance. And it was a performance. Five shows a day, five days a week. And they better be good or he would lose his audience. He felt he had it now. Except for the unfortunate incident when Sidney had openly challenged him in class, he had been able to work with little interference from his mentor. The older man still sat in the back of the class each period. He still sneered, snickered, and scowled according to his mood or attitude toward what was happening, but at least he was relatively quiet. He was surprised that Sidney had agreed to his extra time, and he wasn't going to question his motives.

Jeffrey was having a great time teaching and was operating near the top of his game. The students were responding positively, and he was totally invested in their progress, especially Hector. All of his own class work had been completed, and he had just received his degree although the actual ceremony wasn't until May.

The class, including the Cortez kid, began to file in, and he glanced down at his notes. He hoped he remembered the points he intended to touch in today's lesson. He was so concentrating on the sense of internal composure that he almost missed the man who had entered and moved smoothly to the back of the room. At first he had thought it was Sidney making his usual ostentatious entry, but the man was nowhere near Sidney's six feet two inches. He glanced up at the dark suited, semi-balding figure who panned the class and classroom with a seemingly judgmental eye. Probably an observer from the state, he thought, remembering the conversation with Christie and Stephanie about the visitor in math. *What was one more watcher in the crowd?* he reasoned. He was too focused on his lesson to worry about an extra body.

Sidney entered a half minute after the bell and walked to his usual spot in the back row, smiling and nodding at the students he still considered his. *Don't worry, you can have them back in a few weeks*, Jeffrey thought.

Jeffrey scanned the room for absentees and wrote down two names on the absent report in a speedy scrawl that took only seconds. He checked his notes, sent up a silent entreaty for success, and nose-dived into the issues of the day.

"All right, who knows what capital punishment is?" he began. There was at least one arm per young body that thrust into the air.

"Excellent, excellent," he commented. "Now how many of you believe that capital punishment is warranted in some cases?"

Some of the students looked at each other. Others shrugged their shoulders in ambivalence. About half the class raised their hands, some leaving their arms at half-mast, implying uncertainty.

"Well, it looks as if we have a bit of a difference of opinion here. Let's discuss it. Put yourself in the place of a victim's family. Do you think the death penalty would make you feel better?"

Marisol, shifting her neck in attitude, declared, "It sure would make me feel better. Somebody offs one of mine, I want to see him fry." She pointed an index finger in the air for emphasis.

"Right, an eye for an eye and a nose for a nose. That's the way it should be," piped up a voice to her right.

Several other students came to her support.

"What good is catching the guy if he goes to some prison where he watches television and has his nails done if he killed somebody?"

"Yeah, a killer deserves to die. That's poetic justice."

"Nice going. Miss Harvey would be proud of you for that one."

"Well now," Jeffrey interrupted, "we have to recall that there are two sides to every story. What if these people could reform, regret what happened, and turn their lives around?"

"But what about the guy he whacked? He don't get to turn himself around," protested a sophomore with major make-up and Hollywood hair.

"You're absolutely right," admitted Jeffrey, "but there is nothing anyone can do to bring that person back. If we believe that the killer did not have a right to kill in the first place, how can we say we have a right to kill the killer?"

There was a ponderous hush on the class, and Jeffrey thought that maybe he had just destroyed their arguments and enthusiasm. It was only a few seconds, though, before Hector added, "Yeah, I guess then we'd have to execute politicians for allowing it. I guess that's one way to control the population." Jeffrey was surprised, but gratified, that Hector had responded.

"How can we hold other people to a standard that we fail to apply to ourselves?" Jeffrey was feeling the adrenalin begin to bubble.

"What are you trying to say?" Jeffrey immediately recognized the voice that exploded into the conversation.

Sidney crumpled the newspaper that he brought in with him and tossed it onto the desktop in a puckered pile. "It seems to me that you're confusing the victim with the perpetrator here. Don't you realize that we have to be strong in enforcing the law because an un-enforced law is no law at all?"

At least ten cheers of encouragement followed the question.

Jeffrey fiddled with the frames of his glasses. "I don't disagree with you there, sir, but it is the nature of the enforcement where we seem to diverge."

"We need a deterrent to our most violent crimes," Sidney countered, moving to the side of the room where a mere turn of the head would make him plainly visible to all in the classroom.

"Capital punishment has not really proven to be enough of a preventative tool to justify its existence," Jeffrey rejoined.

"I'm not exactly sure what you said, but that sure sounds right," reinforced Hector, his eyes riveted on Jeffrey.

"Well, it's not right," Sidney roared. "We are very lax in our punishment in this country." Sidney spouted statistics to prove his point.

Several students exchanged seats with those who were seated next to where Sidney was standing. "We're with him," they proclaimed, pointing to the mentor teacher.

"Perhaps we are," Jeffrey confessed, "but there is a difference between penalty and oppression. Did you notice how many people have immigrated to our country to escape such stringent laws?"

More students began to change seats to be nearer to the person they were championing. Some began to shift back and forth depending, in their opinions, on how strong the last statement was. They began to add their own arguments for and against the death penalty as the debate raged on. Jeffrey noticed that Hector stayed seated in the middle. It seemed only a short period of time before the bell rang, and the room cleared. Hector flashed Jeffrey a "thumbs up" as he walked out the door.

The forgotten, anonymous guest sauntered forward, the too long laces of his shoes clicking against the floor as he moved. His hands were clasped behind his back, and his head was slightly bowed. Sidney and Jeffrey lay aside their battle as he made his progress toward the front of the room.

"Who are you?" Sidney asked bluntly, one eye squinting at the approaching individual.

"Stanley Nederland, DOE," he announced as he extended a hand to the veteran teacher and then to Jeffrey. "You two put on quite a performance. I was just observing the English and math classes, and I must have misread the schedule they gave me. Once class started, however, I didn't want to leave."

Sidney and Jeffrey side-glanced each other and turned back to the visitor.

"That was the best example of team teaching I ever saw. They all got really into it. Did you flip a coin and choose sides before class? How did you plan that?" Nederland looked from one to the other, waiting for a response.

Sidney recovered sooner than his intern. "You could say we just see how it goes."

Nederland pulled a thin wallet from his back pocket and extracted a card. "This is an agency that gives demonstrations on effective teaching. They offer grants from the state. I'm going to recommend that the two of you take this on the road," he said excitedly. "I just love to discover talent like this. It's so gratifying."

He shook both of their hands again and left as abruptly as he had arrived. Sidney turned the card over and read the front. "Well, I'll be damned!"

Jeffrey slowly wagged his head from side to side. "I think we are."

*　　*　　*

Jonathan unwrapped a chicken salad sandwich from its cellophane casing. The mayonnaise dripped over the side of the crust and the chicken meat looked dark. He had eaten meals that were unrecognizable in his military days, but he had rather expected that a school would have food that was appetizing and tasteful. Another myth gone, he mused.

Stephanie and Christie slid their trays onto Jonathan's table. Stephanie noiselessly moved her sandwich to the table alongside her apple juice and pushed the tray aside.

"How are your classes going, Mr. Perez?" She canted her head to the side beguilingly.

"Jonathan, please. Everything is going well, thank you." He put down his own sandwich, eyed it suspiciously again, and folded the cellophane over the remainder.

He saw Christie watching him. "That does look a little lethal. What do they claim is between the bread?" she asked.

"Chicken salad. I wasn't really hungry, and I'm not a chicken salad kind of person anyway. There's not much left at the last lunch."

Stephanie looked over at him, her eyes becoming unfocused and dreamy. "You do seem like the type who would probably prefer steak . . . raw or something."

Jonathan was about to respond when Jeffrey banged his tray down next to Stephanie's greenery.

"I can't believe it. Of all the rotten turns of events. Some guy from the state comes into the class and says he wants Sidney and me to go around into different school systems and demonstrate our teaching methods together. I love being with those classes, but not with Sidney. I thought I would be free from that bombastic blowhard and now we're going to be a team." He quickly looked around to see if anyone at the other tables had overheard what he had just spouted. He sat down and lowered his voice. "I'm sorry." He shoved a forkful of limp green beans into his mouth.

"I don't understand," said Christie. "Someone came into our classroom, too, but Penelope went down to complain to Dr. Bradford. I guess they're just randomly stopping in rooms. What happened that made him suggest that you and Sidney stay together?"

Jeffrey did a whole body shrug. "He caught us in one of our big debates and misunderstood what was going on. He wants us to take six months to do this, maybe longer. We'd get paid and everything, and the school will receive more grant money to initiate new teaching methods."

"What does Sidney think of all this?" Jonathan inquired.

"He's all for it, surprisingly. He says it's a good opportunity for both of us. We can make a name for ourselves and get good publicity for the school. I don't know if I'm willing to be a sacrificial lamb."

Jonathan let Jeffrey blow out a frustrated sigh. "This actually could be a good thing. You would be surprised at what you can learn from the experience. Don't turn down a prospect unless you think it might kill you."

Jeffrey thought about it for a moment. "It might not kill me, but I can't guarantee I can bring Sidney back alive. I won't be responsible for my actions if I have to pal around with him for another half year. The company we'd work for even wants us to do something in the summer for potential teachers."

Jonathan clapped him on the back. "We have complete faith in you."

"I guess it will be really hard to find a job in the middle of the year, anyway. It will look really good on my resume, too." Jeffrey sighed again, accepting the inevitable.

Penelope joined the group, carrying only a Styrofoam cup of tea to the table. "Mind if I sit with you?"

"Jeffrey's going to be a traveling teacher and Jonathan . . ." Stephanie let his name roll out in a soft sigh. ". . . was just telling us how well everything is going for him as a teacher."

Penelope took a sip of tea. "Sounds exciting for both of them."

A shrill buzz announced the end of the lunch period, and the three interns automatically lifted their trays and stood up to leave.

"You don't have to come to class, Penelope," said Christie. "I really enjoy this class, and there are no problems in this one I can't handle."

"Actually, I hadn't intended to go with you. They're all yours, and you're doing a remarkable job with them."

Christie beamed her thanks and followed her companions out of the teachers' cafeteria.

Penelope turned to Jonathan. "So, is it really going that well?"

"It's going well." He nodded to confirm the sentiment. "Once I decided that it was no different than instructing young recruits in the art of combat, I felt better. There were times during a couple of classes that reminded me of when I was back in a hostile environment, but the kids kind of grew on me quickly. I see why their future is so important to you. Sometimes they look up at me as if they expected I had all the answers to everything, and I get disappointed in myself that I don't. You want to help them find what they need."

Penelope nodded. "I guess that makes you a real teacher."

CHAPTER 47

Principal Bradford looked at the wall outside the cafeteria with a great deal of consternation in his dark eyes. He let those eyes roam across the massive drawing on the plaster space halfway up the wall. The colors were startling and caught the immediate attention of anyone passing that way. The vivid reds and yellows of chalk swirled and blended to form an image of an older man with a sleek, hairless head and a severe visage that looked down on the observer as if passing down a sentence on Judgment Day. The long nose, full lips, and bushy eyebrows on the figure made it a foregone conclusion that this was indeed a parody of Bradford. Each facial feature was exaggerated to almost cartoonish proportions. There was also a pointing finger in the foreground as if the figure were singling out a passerby for punishment.

"I don't care what it takes! Get rid of it," Bradford thundered to George Fenwick, the head custodian, who stared at the wall as he slid a toothpick back and forth along his wide lips. The principal gestured a hand in disgust at the image and turned to leave.

"First take a picture of it for evidence," he added as he pounded his way down the hall.

He headed straight for the art rooms that were tucked into a corner near the science wing. They had strategically kept all of the classes that might produce an aroma, odor, or stench in the same section of the building. There were two classes currently in progress in two different studio rooms as he approached. He knocked on both doors as he passed them, and within a minute two female heads poked from behind the hefty, partially opened doors.

"I want you both to come with me," he commanded and commenced to march back toward the cafeteria.

"We can't," protested Phyllis Hemmingway, the older of the two middle-aged art instructors. "We have classes. You know we can't leave them unattended."

Mary Reinhardt nodded in concurrence.

Bradford scanned the corridor and spotted Wally Winslow correcting papers in a student desk by the "up" staircase. It was his job this period to make sure everyone out of the classroom had a pass and that no one attempted to go down those "up" stairs.

"Wally," Bradford barked at the startled faculty member. "Come over here and guard these two classes. No one in and no one out while we're gone. Is that clear?"

The math teacher hastily gathered papers, pencils and briefcase and rushed to comply. He practically saluted as he arrived at the appointed place of his new assignment and stood guard halfway between the two art doors.

Mary and Phyllis followed Bradford's speedy pace as the trio traveled to the scene of the crime. When they arrived at the artwork, which George was now photographing with a cardboard disposable camera, Bradford indicated the imposing drawing by pointing at the wall.

"Can either one of you help me here?" he challenged.

Both of the art teachers squinted and stared at the lines and shades of chalk used to create the piece.

"Oh my," exclaimed Phyllis.

"Do you recognize this?" Bradford seized on the comment.

"Why, of course," she stated. "That's you."

"I don't mean the likeness, I mean the artist. Who could have done this?"

The two teachers continued to gawk at the image.

"Well," Mary ventured, "it does look like the style of one of my students."

Bradford's outrage was only surpassed by his desire to nail the culprit who had compromised his dignity. "Who?"

"I don't know him as well I might if he were in school more. He's been suspended three times already this year, and he was out for undisclosed reasons here and there. I have seen some sketches similar to this style in his notebook, though."

"Who are you talking about?"

"Look, I'd hate to get the kid in more trouble. I'm really not sure it's him. After all, we should be careful of where we lay blame. There is that whole thing about a person being innocent until he is proven guilty. Besides, I'm kind of afraid of him. What if he does something to retaliate for my telling on him?"

"Just tell me who you have in mind. I'll take care of the guilty or innocent part, and if you're worried, I'll get the policeman on duty to keep an eye on you and your classroom. I'll get you a SWAT squad if it will make you feel better. Give me a name," Bradford insisted.

Mary still seemed a bit hesitant even after the rather dubious assurances of her safety.

"It certainly seems like the work of Sammy Johnson," she finally proffered apprehensively.

"I should have known." Bradford's voice almost cracked with the force of the statement. "Is he in your class now?"

"As a matter of fact, he is," Mary muttered, almost inaudibly. "I don't know if it would be a good idea to call him out and accuse him now. After all, we wouldn't want to disturb the other students. They're working on their still life projects."

"I'm already disturbed, and when I get finished, Sammy will be the one who's disturbed. You go back to that class and tell him to come out. I'll wait right outside the rooms so he doesn't have a chance to skip out."

They returned to the art sector with the same velocity as they had departed. Bradford dismissed Wally, and Mary tentatively entered her room, feathering her fingers through her short, fluffy brown hair as if she were just coming in from a windy walk in the park.

Bradford waited impatiently outside of Mary's room and watched distractedly as Phyllis, too, reentered her classroom and started to speak. She was directing the students to begin putting away the art supplies in preparation for the end of class. It seemed to take forever for Sammy to come out of the room. He did so languidly, making every step a choreographed movement. Bradford moved toward the teen.

"My office, now," he growled and strode toward the first floor front office, fully expecting Sammy to follow. He did, but in such a slow swagger that the principal had to stop and wait for him several times.

"Marci, call the officer on duty, or that mediation person, or whatever it is they are calling him today and apprise him of the situation." He didn't even consider that Marci didn't know what the situation was.

Bradford and Sammy crossed the threshold of the principal's office as Marci called for the officer, who appeared within minutes. When he arrived, the administrative assistant absented herself.

He was motioned to where Sammy and Bradford awaited him. He stood by the door as Bradford was still composing himself.

"So, Mr. Johnson, it seems that you have chosen to share your talent with the population of the school." Bradford sat behind the barrier of his desk, fingers clenched together on his blotter, eyes narrowed in accusation.

Sammy, seated in a leisurely sprawl on the fake leather chair, fixed his stare on the principal. "Don't know what you're talking 'bout'," he declared.

Penelope materialized at the door with a requisition in hand, apparently unaware of the battle of wills that was in progress. "Hi, Sammy," she said in greeting. "I'll just leave these papers for you to sign later, Dr. Bradford. Marci wasn't at her desk, and I didn't want them to get lost in the shuffle. Sorry, I've obviously interrupted something."

She began to take her leave.

"You can wait in Marci's office. This won't take long, Miss Parsons. You obviously know our visual arts expert here."

Sammy smiled slyly and looked up at his math teacher with a feigned look of innocence before she retreated from the room.

"Sammy, you are quite a talented and speedy artist. I want to know how you got in here to deface our wall so quickly. It wasn't there yesterday," Bradford stated.

"Nope, it wasn't," Sammy said, not fazed by the inquisition. "I guess someone with a free breakfast pass musta done it. They 'probly got here very early to do it. I bet the janitor let him in 'cause he's a regular. That might be how it went down."

Bradford fumed. He finally erupted in a deafening proclamation, "You are suspended for five days, and you are going to help the custodian clean that wall."

"I'm not saying I did it, but I got no objection to helping out the janitors," Sammy replied after a moment of silence. "As for the suspension, I could use some rest." He pulled a headset from his voluminous sweatshirt pocket and began to bob his head to a beat. He rose and left the office with no protests or complaints, and as he passed Penelope, he flashed her a devilish smile and a wink.

Bradford was even more infuriated and felt a need to get in the last word. He moved to the doorway. "If you keep this act up, Sammy, you'll probably be out of here before June."

Still looking back at Penelope, Sammy said, just loud enough so Bradford could hear, "I hope so."

CHAPTER 48

M arisol was sad. Penelope could tell. Her against-the-rules, off the shoulder pink sweater hugged her bare brown upper arms and drooped into the valley of her considerable bosom. She stared beyond the numbers scrawled on the board to a place only she inhabited.

Penelope did not call attention to Marisol's preoccupation, but continued to saunter from desk to desk, checking the other students' progress on the word problems they had started for their homework. They had dutifully ducked their heads over their papers and scratched their pencils across the expanse of eight and a half by eleven stock. She noticed that some had doodled abstract configurations along the sides as they thought about the dilemma of two men riding different trains, going at different speeds and on different routes, estimating where they would eventually meet and at what time. According to Jordan's calculations, they would remain strangers for life.

Marcia Pikette had written her name on the paper eight times, each time with the last name of a different boy in her class. She had put a heart next to the "Marcia Mastrianni". Poor Mario had unwittingly won the prize, and there he worked over his math, oblivious to Marcia's romantic intentions.

Penelope had a vested interest in Marisol. The tall and pretty girl, with an attitude that matched her height, was going to be one of Penelope's success stories. The senior had been floundering in math and had failed the state test, but with guidance, tutoring, and Penelope's expressing an interest in her future, she had succeeded on the last state exam, was passing all her classes, and was on track for graduation. She had seemed happy.

Today was different, however. Penelope walked toward the front of the room as she told the class to put their work into their folders and leave them on the front desk.

The bell sounded as the first manila folder was dropped onto the designated desk. Marisol rose slowly as if her morning alarm had just wakened her from a deep sleep. Penelope closed the space between them.

"Marisol, do you have a minute?"

"I'll make up the test, Miss," she responded. "I got suspended two days ago, so I couldn't make it to the class."

"You got suspended? What on earth for? You didn't mouth off to your VP again, I hope. We talked about that," Penelope reproved.

"Me? No. I don't do that no more. I want to graduate." She handed her teacher her thin folder. "I was in a fight."

The thought of Marisol in a physical battle was ludicrous. Her vocabulary was colorful, to say the least, and she had given more than her fair share of verbal abuse to those who crossed her, but she was very careful with her appearance. Her hair was always neatly pulled back in a smooth ponytail, and her makeup was always applied with the precision of a portrait artist. Penelope could not imagine that she would put all her painstaking work at risk.

As if sensing her teacher's disappointment and disapproval, Marisol explained. "It was a matter of honor. Vanessa was moving in on my man, Bernardo. I had to protect myself."

Penelope knew that most fights among students had a boyfriend or girlfriend as tinder for the flare-up. Even still, Marisol fought her battles with her tongue, not her fist.

"It' usually not worth it. Boys and girls both shop around for a while before settling down, especially at your age. I wouldn't let it get to me if I were you. You'll find someone else. So will she, probably," Penelope reasoned.

"Not me. And better not him, either. I'll get in more than a few slaps and punches if it happens again. Of course, I did get her ear."

"Her ear?"

"Yeah, she had those big bangle hoops on. You can get a good grip on those."

"Marisol, you didn't!"

"Yeah, but I didn't pull too hard. Did you notice, teacher? I always wear studs. It was her own fault."

"Marisol, you're lucky they let you back in school already. You can't afford any more days out. Besides, as I said, in the long run most relationships aren't worth that much trouble."

"Well," she sputtered and straightened up in her spiky boots that made her look like an Amazon, "I'm not going to have this baby by myself. He's going to be there if he likes it or not."

Penelope let the information penetrate, then looked at the young woman in front of her who was toying with her ponytail.

"You're going to have a baby and you got into a fight?"

"Oh, Miss. I'm pregnant, not stupid, but sometimes you gotta take care of business. That's what I'm teaching this kid."

Penelope could not help but glance at her flat, pierced navel that peaked between her low rise jeans and her high rise sweater."

"Don't worry, Miss. I'll be a good mother, and Bernardo will be a good father - or I'll beat the crap out of him."

Penelope thought she saw the sadness descend again as Marisol walked out of the room.

What would happen to Marisol? Fortunately, she would graduate, Penelope thought. Then what? She would have a baby with Bernardo, who probably would disappear after the baby's cute and cuddly stage was over. Bottom line, Marisol and Bernardo were two ill prepared children having a baby.

She shook her head not in judgment, but in concern. Marisol would need to mature very quickly to deal with the issues at hand. In this case, passing the state test did not solve the problem.

Penelope started to collect the folders and shuffle them in to a quasi-neat pile. She went to her desk and sat down heavily on the vinyl padded chair. The cool material felt foreign to her as she gazed around the classroom. She looked at posters, the crack in the ceiling near the back window, the scuffed tiles of the floor as if she were seeing them for the first time. Maybe this was not where she could make the most impact on these young men and women. She was comfortable in the classroom, as much as she was in her own home. She couldn't imagine leaving this place, but maybe that was exactly what she had to do. There was only so much she could do by offering her students skill with numbers. She had fed their minds, but maybe she was still missing the mark.

She pushed the palms of her hands against her closed eyes. She was preparing them for the test, but what was she doing to prepare them for the life they would encounter outside these walls. She had to show them that destiny didn't just wait for a person someplace. If things are going to get better, sometimes you just had to make sure that happened. Destiny was, she thought, not an end, but a work in progress.

She took hold of the folders she had just laid on the corner of her desk and flung them up toward the broken fluorescent light above her. The folders and the papers in them rained and fluttered toward the floor, one paper landing on her shoulder and another glancing off the side of her head.

Maybe there was no solution, she thought.

CHAPTER 49

Hector muttered viciously "This is the worst. What am I gonna do now? What am I gonna say to Miss Parsons and Mr. Perez? This stuff they been feedin' me about you get whatcha want if you work hard is a bunch a bull."

Just as he was about to scream out loud and punch his fist into the nearest wall, he spied Sammy, grinning ear to ear and bursting into a hearty laugh. Mrs. Ruckmeyer, Hector's guidance counselor, stuck her head out the door and began to shush the two of them. She gave Hector a woeful glance and then a sympathetic nod. He was about to utter an obscenity when he realized that she was smiling at Sammy.

"Congratulations on passing the test, Sammy. Well done." She gave an awkward "okay" sign in approval before ducking back into her office.

Hector's mouth opened slightly, revealing gritted teeth. His hands curled into fists as he heard a half-audible response from Sammy. "Thanks." And then he continued in a softer utterance, aimed directly at Hector, "I don't know how I did it, but I'll take it. I guessed at all the questions that I couldn't get from Louis, the kid sitting next to me. Cheatin' ain't all that bad."

Hector kicked the door open at the end of the hall and headed down the corridor towards choir, which was his last class of the day. He stopped short of entering the room where so many achievements had been reached and where he had felt at home for four years. Then he heard it, the refrain they had been working on for graduation. He was to sing a solo, with the choir backing him up. Tottman had chosen an old tune, "What a Difference a Day Makes", and the teacher had changed the lyrics to fit the message of seniors starting a new adventure after graduation. Concluding the performance, the choir director was to announce publicly that Hector was the recipient of a full scholarship to the prestigious Harris Conservatory of Music.

I screwed up, Hector thought. *I still missed the passing score by two lousy points again after working my ass off this year. Five times, and I failed. Now I'm done. I can't face Tottman.*

He dropped his hand from the door handle, turned, and walked back to the first floor and out the door.

*   *   *

Hector bolted down the street and headed for his shabby one room apartment.

"Man, I ain't goin' nowhere. Papa won't be givin' me my allowance after July. I'm in deep shit," he griped to himself as tears welled in his eyes. The Harris Conservatory wasn't going to take someone who didn't graduate.

His body stiffened with anger and fear. He pounded the chain link fence aligning the sidewalk, one brutal punch after another in rapid succession until the anguish in his soul was overshadowed by the physical pain of his bleeding and swollen knuckles.

He reached his building, pushed at the main entry and took the stairs two at a time until he was standing in front of his apartment. He kicked at his door until the lock gave way.

Gracia huddled in the corner, arms covering her head and face. At seeing the girl, Hector stopped his tirade.

"Gracia! What're doin' here? How'd you get in?"

"Your Papa was doing his thing on the corner and he let me in. I was crying, and he couldn't do nothing, so he let me crash in here for a while. Hector, I got no place to go. My mom kicked me out."

"Why? You don't cause trouble and you're graduating in less than three months. You can get a decent job and help out."

"Yeah, that was the plan until my fourteen—year-old sister got pregnant. She just brought the baby home, and she needs her own room. I'm the oldest and can work, so out I go. But Hector, I'm so close to graduating. What can I do?"

"Look Gracia, I ain't graduating. I flunked that test for the last time. You can stay here. We've known each other since kindergarten, and we've been neighbors even before that. So, no strings attached."

"I don't know, Hector. I don't want to end up like my sister."

"It's okay, Gracia. I don't plan on doing anything to make my life more wrecked than it already is. We're friends, and friends can help each other out."

He walked over to the sniveling Gracia and gave her a hug. It felt good to have a friend, almost too good.

CHAPTER 50

The students started to file into the auditorium one class at a time. They strut, sauntered, marched, and shuffled as they scouted for seats next to their friends. Penelope watched from stage left as the teachers attempted to corral their charges into a section where they would sit together as a group.

The annual Spring Variety Show was one of the few assemblies that Bradford allowed all students to attend. Two other shows would take place on Friday and Saturday nights for the general public. Since it was the week that directly preceded spring vacation, attendees and performers were all in high spirits.

Penelope sighed. She used to look forward to this event, volunteering each year to help coordinate the acts and recruit other faculty to execute the little tasks that came together to make the event a resounding success each time. She waited for the exhilaration that usually overtook her as the show was about to start. Ted Tottman had already given her a gift certificate to The Red Pony Grille as a thank you for her efforts this year. She had assured him that it was not necessary.

"You've gone above and beyond this time, Nell, and I really appreciate it. It was as if you had demons propelling you through all the long hours of rehearsals. Are there?" It seemed strange to have even Ted call her by the nickname that Jonathan had christened her with. It seemed all of her friends on the faculty had picked it up. It was as if she became a different person with the name change. For just a little while she felt a little stronger, a little more connected. The more casual version of her name seemed to soften her, make her more vulnerable and more accessible.

She had looked up at Ted curiously from her crouched position as she pinned a hem into place on the long skirt of the soloist who would sing the national anthem at the start of the extravaganza. "Are there what?"

"Are there demons hounding you?"

The young singer swished the skirt to see if the safety pins would hold, murmured a "thanks", and left to join two other performers.

Penelope straightened and brushed nonexistent lint from her sleeve. "Don't we all have them?"

"Yes, but there is always someone to help a person fight them off. Is there anything that I can do?"

Penelope shook her head. "Thanks anyway, Ted. I have to work this out myself. You'd better do something about that young man who is trying to help Linda Frank with the bodice of her costume."

Tottman turned. "All right, everyone back in the classroom behind the stage and wait. You!" He pointed to Linda's helpful male friend. "Tend to your own attire." He moved toward the costumed crowd behind the curtain, and they began to troop into the adjoining room.

Penelope peeked back out at the audience once more. The freshmen were relegated to the back of the auditorium. They slouched into the seats, chattered with those behind and in front of them. This year they had enrolled five hundred and twenty-three ninth graders. Her gaze switched to the first rows where the seniors sat, smug and restless, all three hundred of them. She wondered not for the first time what had happened to the present twelfth grade which had also started as a much larger class. Somewhere between the first and fourth year, students disappeared. Some moved, some dropped out, and others simply evaporated. Since the advent of all the testing, the school's vanishing rate had increased.

There in row two sat Sammy Johnson, his left leg hooked over the seat in front of him, his ever-present ear buds plugged into the sides of his head, transporting him to some other place. He had passed the test, but by his own admission, it had been a fluke. Penelope knew Hector was still depressed over his last math test failure. According to the standards of the state, Sammy was the success, Hector another statistic.

The school band began the opening medley and the students quieted with the urging of the teachers. Vice Principal Colon stationed himself halfway down the middle aisle, arms folded in front of him, face implacable.

The enthusiastic strains of the melodies warred with Penelope's despondent state. She breathed in. There was the faint fragrance of flowers that a number of significant others had brought for their special students, the combined scents of shampoo, body lotion and cologne that still lingered from performers who rehearsed on the stage earlier. There was also the faint smell of sweat from the overworked stage hands who had just finished hauling the backdrops and setting up the props a half hour before show time.

She looked in front of the elevated stage to see Jonathan untangling wiring for the sound system. He looked more content than when he first came. He had the same intense concentration and attention to detail that he had brought with him, but she had noticed lately that some of the hardness was gone. At first even his outward smiles were tinged with something deeper, darker. She could almost see the shadows that threatened to strangle his soul. He would never be at ease, even when he seemed relaxed to the casual observer, she thought. Now there was some light. She could not help but wonder if she could live with the ghosts that would always be a part of him.

Maybe she didn't have ghosts, but she certainly had some mental and emotional obstacles to combat. They seemed to become more ominous every day.

The lively music stopped abruptly. The curtain began to pull back, and the young soloist stepped into the spotlight. Penelope pulled back further into the back stage area as the young woman cleared her throat and sang the "Star Spangled Banner" in almost perfect pitch.

The solo was followed immediately by three sophomores who had formed a break dance routine that had the crowd hooting and clapping as the trio took turns spinning on elbows, knees and heads. The audience roared as they did a series of somersaults that ended the act.

Their last tumble segued into a chorus of ten that sang Broadway show tunes from recent years. This was met with hearty appreciation from a small segment of eclectic music lovers and halfhearted claps and yawns from the majority of the young spectators.

Penelope was uncertain how Ted did it, but he was usually able to persuade several faculty members to perform each year, and so Valerie Steinberg, the Spanish teacher, stepped out onto the stage with her bagpipe as she pumped out a haunting Irish ballad. There was something soulful in the notes that filled the auditorium. Penelope heard nothing from the multitude until several seconds after the last note resounded. To her surprise, the students broke out in a thunderous round of applause as Miss Steinberg left the stage.

Through all the acts that followed, Penelope recaptured a bit of the excitement, the zeal, the pride that she remembered from past years. She applauded as a slapstick comedy duo did their shtick, Ralf Kramer, the football coach, read a poem by Edgar Allan Poe, four Latina girls sang "Old San Juan" in Spanish, and a contingent from the Drama Club recreated a scene from *Twelve Angry Men*.

Penelope did have demons, and they would return when the stage lights dimmed and the music ceased, but just for now, she wouldn't let them bother her.

CHAPTER 51

Early May

Penelope felt replete and complete. She burrowed the back of her head into the queen sized down pillow and turned to look at Jonathan. He was magnificent in the folds of darkness that surrounded his half-exposed body. His hands were stacked behind his head, and he stared at the ceiling almost motionlessly. As if he felt her scrutiny, he shifted toward her.

"What are you thinking about? If it's not about me, then I'll have to try to distract you again." He brushed her forehead with the back of his hand, smoothing the damp strands of hair back from her face.

"I am thinking about you, but that doesn't mean I couldn't use a little positive reinforcement." She smiled and put her hand to his cheek, unable to see his features clearly in the shadows, but knowing them so well it wasn't necessary. She kissed him delicately, daintily, then deeply. He responded as if he needed the kiss for survival.

"It's never enough," he whispered huskily.

"I know," she agreed, barely audibly before their lips touched again.

They broke the kiss, but Penelope dropped her head to his chest and pulled herself closer to his warmth.

"What would you say if I told you I've decided to leave?"

Jonathan's body stiffened. "Leave what or whom?"

She lifted her head and looked into eyes that were fastened on hers even in the eclipse of the blackness around them.

"I mean the school. I can't deal with the frustration of always seeing defeat in the eyes of some of the students, especially when it just isn't necessary."

He seemed to weigh her question with a great deal of gravity. "You love those kids, and you love that school. Are you sure?"

"No, I'm not sure. I don't think I'll ever be sure, but I can't go on like this. I know I've threatened and hinted before. I feel I have to do something other than give in to what we are being forced to do. I would feel as if my career would be built on a lie. I don't believe in what they are doing, and if I stay, I'll have to do it or they'll ask me to leave. Either way, I'll be out. I'd rather it was my decision. It's not just the testing. Those kids have insurmountable problems that seem to be ignored, and yet they are the main obstacles to success."

He massaged her naked arm soothingly, then bent his head and kissed it.

"You'll always have to live with whatever choice you make so be sure it's the right one. Go with your heart and your head working together."

He tilted his head back as if waiting for a reply, then added, "What would you do if you quit?"

"I was thinking that I could complete my dissertation. I'm almost finished, and my advisor has been urging me to speed up the process. One of the reasons I've been stalling is that I've done a lot of research and writing, but the focus was a bit off. I know now exactly the point I want to make."

He pulled her closer still. "What's that?"

"I want to write about the children left behind."

Jonathan was silent as he continued to move his hand up and down her arm. His gaze was directed at some spot in the dark, but she could almost feel him withdrawing. It was difficult to know what Jonathan was thinking, but Penelope was hoping he would support her. She didn't know what she would do if he didn't.

*   *   *

Penelope held the envelope tightly in her right hand as she marched resolutely toward the office. There was a slight tremor in her fingers. She wanted to deliver the letter before she lost her nerve and surrendered to her desire to stay in the environment that had given her as much pleasure as it had pressure, as much enjoyment as frustration. This was something she had to do, she kept reminding herself.

Marci was not at her desk, a rare occurrence, and Bradford's door was shut tightly. She could hear a slight murmur from behind the barricade, however, and knew that he was probably on the phone because there did not appear to be more than one voice. She knocked sharply at eye level. There was a scrape of a chair and shuffling before Bradford opened the door.

"Penelope?" He seemed surprised to see her. After all, it was a Friday afternoon, last period of the day. She had wanted to hand in her resignation at a time that did not provide too much opportunity for discussion. She figured that on the last day of the school week, everyone wanted to leave, and there was the weekend for things to calm down.

"What can I do for you?" he asked when she merely stared at him for a few seconds.

"I just wanted to give this to you." She handed him the slender business envelope addressed to him. "I'm sending a copy to the superintendent, but I wanted to let you know first."

Bradford opened the envelope and extracted the paper. He read only the first few lines before he lifted his eyes to her. "Why don't you come in and we can talk."

"I don't want to talk about it. I assume there is plenty of time to find a replacement for next year."

"That's not the issue here." He gestured to the nearest chair. "Why do you want to leave?" he asked, moving to sit behind his desk.

Reluctantly, she moved to the chair and perched on the edge, her back straight and her hands folded. She felt if she relaxed just a little, she might break.

"I've come to the conclusion that perhaps I can better serve the students in another capacity. I'm going to work full time to complete my doctoral degree. I just have to finish up my dissertation."

"If you want to finish up your degree, why don't you just take a leave of absence? You know you're one of the best we have. I'd hate to lose you, Penelope." He tapped the empty envelope on the desk as he spoke.

"After I finish, I want to educate the public about what's going on in the school systems. I want them to know that we are slowly smothering the people we are supposed to be helping. I think my degree and experience will give me the credibility to do that."

"Can't you do that from the classroom as well as in the public forum?"

A long silence separated them for a few minutes. Finally, Bradford stood and leaned toward Penelope. "I'll tell you what. I can't in all conscience take this right now. I want you to use this weekend to craft another letter, one for a leave of absence for the year. Give yourself some options, and give me some hope."

"I don't think I can come back and be a part of what I'm protesting," she said with finality.

CHAPTER 52

Late May

Hector opened the new door with the key and entered the still chilly apartment. The dampness still permeated the floorboards and the windowsills. The only two windows in the apartment were facing a wall of the next building, and the shadows created a false coolness that did not reflect the true warm spring weather. It was actually ten degrees warmer outside than it was in the apartment. He knew that once the heat settled in the summer, things would be different. There was no escaping the muggy temperatures of July and August.

He flopped down on the tattered recliner that was in a permanent recline position. Some of the stuffing had worked its way out, but there was enough of the filling left to be comfortable. He just wanted a brief respite from the hours he spent at the warehouse. He worked at a fresh flower distribution center, and he had hauled carnations and roses all day until he smelled like a frickin' funeral director. He rested his head on the back of the chair.

"Hey, Gracia," he said as he closed his eyes in exhaustion.

"You want a glass of water or something?" Gracia asked from the minute kitchenette that was little more than an indentation off the main room.

"No, I'm okay," he answered wearily.

She emerged from the area near the old stove and came to stand near his chair. He was glad that they had a chance to be together. He had never felt more at home since she had moved in with him. He liked to think it was some kind of destiny that had brought the two together. Maybe they weren't in love like couples in the movies, but they provided something for one another that had been lacking before. He may not be content, but he was comfortable.

He looked up when she continued to stare at him. "What's the matter?"

Please let it not be anything major, he thought. He was still adjusting to the fact that his dreams had been splintered and his life was in the toilet. He wondered now if that other Hector ever existed. Did he really have one of the leads in the school play? Had he really been given a scholarship? Did Tottman, Parsons, and Perez really care about what happened to him? He felt as if all of that was some book he had read somewhere, and he couldn't recall the details. Maybe someday he'd get that life back, one dream at a time.

"I gotta tell you something," she started nervously.

"Go ahead," he urged, staring at her tearing eyes. "It can't be that bad. You're graduating in a few days. That's a good thing."

"Yeah," she said, "That's a good thing. There's something else, though."

"Come on, Gracia. You know I don't like head games. Just tell me."

She knelt by the side of the chair until they were eye to eye, her large round ones gazing into his sharp, narrow ones.

"I don't want you to be mad or anything. I can handle this, but I think you should know. You and me, we made a baby."

Hector's breath stopped and his tapered eyes widened. "Are you sure?"

"Yeah, I'm sure. I wouldn't say anything otherwise. If you let me stay here, I'll get a better job right after graduation and help out with the stuff. My job at the convenience store's only part time, but somebody told me they're hiring at one of the factories in Groverton. That's only a few miles away, and my friend Tanisha already works there, so I can ride in with her."

He barely heard what she was saying. "Are you sure it was me?"

Gracia seemed stunned by the question. "You know I ain't been with nobody since I moved in here. I got no time to fool around."

Tears began to leak from beneath her thick lashes, and he felt like a bastard for having asked. He didn't hold many females in high regard, but he did Gracia. In spite of her circumstances, she had stayed in school and was going to get a diploma, and that was more than he could say.

"Don't cry. I didn't mean it. I know it's me. When is this going to happen? I mean when is the kid coming out? You know what I mean."

"I can't tell yet. I guess in about eight months or so. I took a home test this morning. I'm really sorry." She started to sniffle a bit.

"Look, we'll think of something."

"I'm not getting rid of it. I can tell you that. I can't. My momma will be mad if I do anything to the baby."

"Your momma kicked you out to make room when your sister had her new baby. I don't think she can say much to you about anything."

"It's the way I was raised. I couldn't do it," she wept.

He scoured his face with his rough hands. He felt as if a huge boulder had been added to his burden. He remembered that he was a man now, and a man took responsibility for what he did.

"It's not just your baby. I wouldn't make you get rid of it." He pulled Gracia down onto his lap and enfolded her into his arms. He patted her hair and concentrated on the problem. One thing he knew was that he had to have more money. He and Gracia might not get married, but he would take care of his kid. He would provide for it and Gracia, too.

He knew only one way to get the money he needed, and it was not pushing petals. His Papa always provided for him and Emilio in one way or another although he didn't figure out his primary source of income until recently. He had just not wanted to know. Now, maybe it was time to grow up and make some real money helping his father.

CHAPTER 53

Class Day, First Friday in June

Penelope could not believe that she had been snagged for a final committee duty. There was something comforting, however, about keeping occupied in these last days at Skinner High. She had asked for a leave of absence, but she already knew that she probably would not be returning. Several of the parents had already expressed disappointment that she would not be there in the fall to teach their younger offspring. She had smiled with genuine regret and thanked them, but she knew that she had other things just as important to do.

She hurried toward the cafeteria where the staff was to have already prepared the feast for the pre-ceremony parent gathering. It was a tradition at Skinner to host a reception for the seniors and their parents before the soon-to-be graduates collected their robes and mortarboards and left for the Class Day activities. The kitchen staff had only been in for the couple of hours that it supposedly took to prepare the platters, arrange the tables, and decorate the room. The glass paned metal doors were slightly ajar, and she stepped across the threshold.

"Hi," greeted the enthusiastic voice behind the door.

"Christie!" Penelope gave her former student teacher an eager hug that left little doubt of their fondness for one another.

As they parted, Penelope put her hands on Christie's shoulders.

"What brings you here? Class day?"

The younger woman gave a slight shrug. "Yes and no, I guess."

She hesitated a bit before she continued. "Dr. Bradford called me and asked if I would take your classes for next year. He told me you decided to take a leave of absence. I hope you don't mind. I promise to do my best. I know I once said I didn't want to teach, but I missed the classroom so much after I left, and when I went back home, I couldn't stop thinking about the students. It's just for a year."

Penelope looked at her fresh face and the apprehension in her eyes. "Christie, this just might turn into something permanent. You should know this before taking the position."

"What do you mean? I can't imagine you not working with the kids. What happened?"

"A lot, but we can go into that later, after the ceremony. I won't be working so much with the kids now as much as for the kids. First, I have to make sure everything is in place for the parents' reception."

She patted Christie's shoulder and proceeded past her to where the tables were supposed to be set and laden with fruit, cheese, crackers and other nibbles to go with the soda cans and bottled water. There was nothing but the stacked tables and glistening metal counter tops that usually held a variety of food offerings on school days. Confused, Penelope consulted the instructions on the committee paper she had folded into the pocket of her jacket. There on the paper it read, "Check cafeteria set-up and food for parents." She was in the right place. She checked the time, and that was right as well. *Was this one of those Twilight Zone moments?*

"What's the matter?" Christie asked.

"There should be grapes." Penelope gestured widely with her hands, "and cheese, lots and lots of cheese."

Stephanie flowed into the large, quiet room. A smile sliced into her unruffled expression. "Christie, how wonderful to see you. We haven't emailed in a while. Did you decide to take up Bradford's offer?"

"I did."

"That's great. I just found out that Claire is definitely not returning. Her health is fine right now, but she said it was time to 'pursue other options' or something like that. Even with all our history, Dr. Bradford gave me a good evaluation. I'll be teaching here, too. I guess he figured that I can really do the job now that I've settled in. I learned a lot from Claire, and I'm even beginning to sound like her."

Christie giggled. "You're right about that and also about how we have developed from naïve interns to real teachers. Everything's going to be great."

"It would also be great to see some cheese," Penelope complained.

As the two younger women hugged, she dashed to the industrial sized refrigerator beyond the bank of gleaming counters and pulled open the seven foot stainless steel door. On the center rack of the massive fridge sat a single tray of triangled American cheese, government issue, she was certain from the color. Sliced, browning apples edged with canned pineapple chunks cozied up next to it.

"I think we have a problem, ladies," Penelope stated.

Christie and Stephanie came to look over her shoulder at the two forlorn platters.

"I assume we aren't expecting many parents," intoned Stephanie.

"Let's put it this way, there are three hundred graduating seniors and let's assume that they all have at least one parent and extended family members, who often show up uninvited. That makes approximately nine hundred snackers, and we can't even afford to offer them a half nibble of cheese and a small bite of apple. There must have been some miscommunication with food services because they're usually on top of things. I believe we had better go into rescue mode, here."

"Maybe they have food in other places," suggested Christie, biting her thumbnail.

"Like where?" inquired Stephanie.

"I don't know. The teachers' room maybe?"

"You know they don't trust teachers around food. There wouldn't be anything in the lounge," Stephanie countered.

"You're probably right. Let's see what we can do," Penelope interjected. "Christie, go to the custodian's room and ask Jim to bring out the green and gold tablecloths we use for special occasions. Stephanie, go to the grocery store down the street and get supplies - any kind of snack that seems appropriate. Keep the number nine hundred in mind. There are always groups of parents who don't show, but let's be liberal in our estimate. Use your credit card. You'll be reimbursed later."

Footsteps resonated in the near empty room. All three turned to see Claire Harvey come toward them. She was actually wearing dress slacks, a silk blouse, and two-inch high black pumps. `

"Claire?" Stephanie and Christie gasped together.

Penelope's eyes rounded at the sight of her friend, and she smiled at the transformation. She had never seen her look so calm and carefree, so tranquil in spite of the fact that she wobbled a bit on the high heels. They had visited several times in the last few months, but this was a revelation.

"What's the matter?" Claire inquired as she scanned the looks on the faces of the other women.

"Nothing, nothing at all. You look terrific," Penelope responded after a brief pause. "As a matter of fact, you could not have come at a better time. We have an emergency here, and we need your help. Could you go with Stephanie and assist her in getting some food for the parents' reception? You can tell her what we usually serve for these affairs."

Stephanie recovered from her astonishment about Claire's appearance, grabbed her by the sleeve of her silk blouse, and began to tug her toward the door. "Come on, we have a mission, and I don't know how to go about it. I really need you."

"You do?" Claire questioned in amazement.

"You have no idea." The two exited together.

"I'll go get the tablecloths," Christie avowed and left with a determined air.

Penelope began to pull the tables out and arrange them in a line at the front of the cafeteria. She hauled one table toward the forefront where she would put the copies of the latest school newspaper which contained the names and plans of all the graduates. She scurried into the attached teachers' cafeteria and snatched the small vases of fake flowers that the staff had set out for their spring decorations and brought them out to the main room.

Jonathan strode in as she was struggling to haul a large table from the corner to the center of the room. He immediately went to her and took hold of the edge of the table. "Let me do that. Where do you want it?"

She indicated a spot and quickly filled him in on the situation.

An hour later, as Penelope had positioned the last cluster of grapes on the new and improved fruit plates, the first group of parents wended their way into the cafeteria. The room was festive with the blue and gold linen covering the extensive line of tables, the yellow and pink plastic flowers blooming from milk glass vases at the ends and in between the food offerings. Green napkins were artfully displayed next to each presentation. Large serving dishes were mounded with cheese chunks, crackers, and slender slices of pepperoni. A veritable garden of fruit and vegetables was assembled around a bowl of white, speckled dip. Penelope didn't know what kind it was, and she really didn't care. It looked good.

After she placed several more bottles of water into the large pan of crushed ice, she moved to Jonathan's side. It had been interesting to see him struggle to make some kind of artistic statement with the celery and carrot sticks. He had finally just stacked them randomly.

"It's a guy thing," he had explained.

Claire, Stephanie, and Christie gathered next to the couple.

"Another crisis averted," Claire affirmed.

"It seems to be a daily event around here," added Jonathan.

CHAPTER 54

Graduation Day

T he sun struggled to make its presence known in the early afternoon warmth. The clouds coasted by the playing field in large clumps that occasionally hid the light and sent shadows skittering across the makeshift stage. The custodial staff had spent the day before erecting the scaffolding and arranging the folding chairs so that the administration could sit in a semi-circle on the dais, facing the crowds. They had also set up over three hundred seats for the graduating class and faculty.

The bleachers, rows of wooden benches that climbed upward to dizzying heights, were now dry after the storm of the night before. The audience would be spared damp seats, but any latecomers would have to scale the steep steps and sit where the graduates' identities would be indiscernible.

It was Penelope's duty to see that the graduate line was in the correct order from the "A"s to "H"s. The last person about whom she had to be concerned was Barnett Huntington. Barney was in place, talking animatedly to the girl behind him, his golden graduation tassel leaping from side to side as he did so. The young woman was smiling as she listened and toyed with a silver charm bracelet that hung loosely from her wrist. Penelope guessed that it was probably a graduation gift.

*   *   *

Jonathan made his way across the field from the stage where he had helped to repair a malfunctioning microphone. He watched as Penelope counted her charges, making a comment or two as she prodded them into their proper places in the line. Her chestnut hair rustled around her shoulders, and he could almost feel the energy she radiated as she went about her task. She loved this. It was going to be a terrible wrench to leave the school and her students behind. He knew that the decision was born out of more than frustration; it had also been created from a genuine concern for these same students. She said she could not be a part of the system and work against it at the same time. She claimed it was the old "two masters" philosophy. She could only serve one, and she had chosen the students.

Still, Jonathan could not help feeling that she was making a mistake. He supposed that it was hers to make, but the thought that she was running away kept resurfacing. One of the things he had admired about her was her commitment to her profession, and now he was wondering if she was making excuses to turn tail and immerse herself in research and high concepts that would sound great, but do nothing to improve things for the students.

Jonathan realized that the students and some of the teachers here had made quite an impression on him. Even he had become caught up in the problems of these young people, and of those who taught them. True, he had first become involved because of Nell, but he was drawn in further by the students themselves. He saw the raw need in their eyes, the desperation, and the elation when they had found something they could be proud of.

It wasn't long before the band began their warm-up. Some of the band members were graduating, and they wore their blue and gold robes instead of the formal band uniform the rest of the musicians wore. The choir was dressed in their formal black attire, the graduates in their robes. Tottman was speaking in the ear of a freshman who tugged at his tie and wiped his hands on the serge of the black suit. Jonathan thought that he must be giving last minute instructions to the rookie.

The crowd finally settled down to a manageable muttering mass when the band struck out the first strains of "Pomp and Circumstance." He hadn't realized that they still used that old piece at graduations. The long blue and gold line began to advance toward the folding chairs in front of the stage. It wasn't as orderly as it could have been since the ground was uneven, and some of the girls were tottering on high heels that they had just slipped on for the first time that day. Several of the boys swaggered confidently, indicating the pride they took in having made it this far.

As he watched with some degree of satisfaction, Jonathan noticed the flutter of a red shirt contrasting with the silver of the chain link fence that surrounded the field. He knew before looking directly at him that it was Hector. The young man's forehead was pressed tightly against the criss-cross of the fencing, and his fingers dug though the diamond shaped gaps. He stared at the proceedings as if he were mesmerized by the grand ceremony of it all.

Jonathan watched Hector cautiously. He wanted to invite him to come to the other side of the fence, to persuade him to continue what he started, to not give up on himself. Penelope had taken Hector's disappearance very personally, he knew. She had wept when he failed to come to school after the state scores were announced. She knew what his absence meant. Not only had he given up, but he was on his own and had to make some money. She worried about where he was, what he was doing.

Jonathan looked to where Nell was standing and saw the veil of sadness come over her face as she, too, spotted Hector outside the parameters of the field. Jonathan's instinct told him what she was probably thinking.

"I'm sure you've run across this situation before," he had consoled her right after Hector's disappearance.

"Yes, and it bothers me every time. Maybe it's a good thing I'm leaving. What use am I like this? Sometimes I wonder if I'm trying to be good or trying to be God. I wish I had the power to influence them all enough so that they stayed, they learned, they went on to be the someone they always hoped to be."

"Things don't always happen because that's the way it should be. Trust me. That doesn't mean we give up," he had advised.

He had liked the way she had fallen into his arms in response.

Jonathan cleared his thoughts and headed in Hector's direction. Hector's gaze never wavered from the field as Jonathan approached. With each step forward, Jonathan noticed the boy's defeated stance.

"Hector," he ventured when he was near enough so that the young man might hear his quiet tones and not be startled.

Wordlessly, the boy lifted his intense stare to that of his past teacher and friend. Hopelessness was reflected in his mocha colored eyes.

"We've been worried about you. Why don't you join us here? You're still a part of all this, you know."

"Not any more. They won't let me," Hector choked out.

"Of course, they will. We'll try again. I'll help you. The school will help you. You just have to keep trying."

"Yeah, trying really got me someplace, didn't it? It's never enough. I just can't do it no more."

"You *can* do it. You've always known that. You've got a scholarship. Mr. Tottman talked to the people at the conservatory, and they said they'll wait another semester for you. You were so close this last time, maybe we can file an appeal, and if we win, you won't have to take the retest. It's a real possibility since you only failed by two points. There are options. Don't turn your back on them," encouraged Jonathan.

"Don't do that! Don't tell me what I can do. I did all the stuff they said. I got an award. I even got a fuckin' scholarship, but because of two lousy points on some stupid test, it don't mean shit. Besides, I quit and I don't have the credits. None of this makes any sense. I'm tired of trying. Anyway, I got responsibilities now."

He pushed himself away from the fence and began to walk from the field, from the friends he had made, from everything that had made him believe that things would turn out all right after all.

"Hector!" Jonathan shouted above the percussion section's staccato that pumped out the school song in preparation for the guest speakers. He scaled the fence without considering how long it had been since he had done so in the line of duty. He snagged the hem of his sport coat on the pointed top of the chain link. He removed it in one deft movement, left it dangling on the fence, and dashed after Hector.

Hector seemed to sense that the chase was on and picked up his pace, darting toward the nearest building where he ducked behind a wall of chipped brick and crumbling mortar. The wall had been scheduled for demolition by the first of June, but the city council had decided to delay destruction until after school ended for the summer to avoid the student traffic on the street.

There were many shallow chambers and cavernous hallways that could hide a person in the structure. Jonathan saw Hector slip down the side passage. He was sure that Hector hadn't gone through the entry where an old metal door hung droopily from its hinges, but he heard echoing footfalls in the alleyway where the damp concrete was unyielding and anyone passing could be heard.

"Hector, come on. Please! Damn it, Hector, where are you?" Jonathan thrust his hand through his thick, dark hair. He looked skyward as if seeking some sign of where to go next. If he had to wait in this alley all day, he would do it. The kid had to come out sometime, and he knew he was there. His old instincts were perking back to life. He could almost feel the boy breathing somewhere nearby.

He slammed his fist into the uncompromising wall, and the pain that shot through his hand reminded him that losing his restraint wouldn't make Hector appear any sooner. He shook his hand as if the throbbing could be cast out by the action, then slowly put his back to the wall. He listened warily to the silence that threaded through the steady dripping remnants of last night's rain. If he concentrated hard enough, maybe he could pick up on some unintentional movement. Here he was, alone again with someone's life at stake. He had to be here, but it didn't have to make him remember. He thought he could hear distant gunfire, the distinct click of weapons engaging, the moans of men who wouldn't live beyond the next encounter.

*   *   *

Moisture clouded Penelope's vision as the students walked across the stage to collect the certificates that would officially declare them graduates. Barney Huntington crossed the platform and gave an arrogant wave and smug smirk to his parents as he accepted the diploma from Principal Bradford. She huffed out a slight sigh of relief that at least her section of the line had trundled through the ceremony without incident. She scanned the field for Jonathan. She had last seen him when they had both spied Hector by the fence.

She squinted her eyes to further concentrate on locating him on the sun spattered field. Using her hands as a visor, she began to search the mass of cheering onlookers in the bleacher area to see if perhaps he had found a seat among them. It seemed as if he had evaporated since she had last caught sight of him. Where could he have gone? Tiny bristles of alarm began to suffuse her body.

Don't be ridiculous, she chided herself. What could possible happen to him at a high school graduation? She just felt as if something was very wrong.

As she moved closer to the area where Hector had leaned against the fence, she saw a grey jacket move listlessly in a gust of June breeze. Penelope's heart thumped thunderously in her tightening chest. The jacket suspended from the top of the chain link fence was Jonathan's.

*   *   *

Jonathan braked his breathing and listened with experienced attentiveness. A creature he couldn't identify leaped from a tipped trashcan onto the hard surface of the passageway and scurried out of sight. A breeze caught at the cragged corners of the building's surface and hissed toward the street. A scrape - then a soft, guarded footstep. Someone was just around the edge of the building, moving furtively toward the alley. He could hear the movement, as light as it was. The hair bristled on the back of his neck. His head jerked in the direction of the shuffle. Jonathan transformed into combat mentality as he reached into his pocket for the Swiss army knife he always had with him, appropriate or not. He opened the blade and waited.

He remembered that Hector had been wearing his battered black sneakers as he leaned against the fence before the chase as a large dirty white shoe appeared from around the corner. Who was this interloper? He peered intently into the shadows.

The shoe was followed by a familiar, slouching body.

"Sammy," breathed Jonathan.

Sammy Johnson's black headband was bound tightly over his broad eyebrows. A cigarette was gripped loosely between his left thumb and forefinger as he glanced at Jonathan's hand. "What's up with the blade, man. You plannin' on cutting somebody?"

Jonathan relaxed, folded the knife, pocketed it and uttered a sigh of relief.

Sammy continued, "I'd a thought you would be out there with all them grads today." He took a long, leisurely pull on the cigarette, closing his eyes and concentrating on the mouthful of smoke, which he appeared to swallow before exhaling into the gloom of the alley.

"What are *you* doing here? I would have thought *you* would be with all those graduates," Jonathan retorted.

"I graduated, sort of. I passed all that piss they throw at you. I ain't going to no chicken shit noisy show. I got my pictures and my music. That's all I need. In fact, I can hear the music now," he declared while he looked up as if in rapture. Jonathan noticed the earplug and wire that snaked down his side and ended at the rim of his pants pocket.

"Yeah, you've got them, but what are you going to do with them?"

Sammy seemed to deliberate the issue for a moment. "I don't have to do anything with them."

"I've told you before. You could develop your talents, so other people can enjoy your work, too."

"I don't need no one to enjoy my stuff. I don't need no one, period." He pitched his cigarette to the ground and flattened it with the heel of his shoe. "If you're looking for that asshole Hector, he's probably long gone. I saw him head out the back just before you got here."

Mockingly, he whispered, "Hey, you think he's dealin' for his old man? He looked as if he had big business. Maybe you trying to save him." He laughed.

Jonathan wasn't sure he believed him. He did believe, though, that Hector didn't want to be found right now. In his present state, he doubted that the object of his pursuit would listen to anyone at the moment. He would try again later. He turned and walked back toward the pomp and away from the circumstances in the alley.

*   *   *

Sammy stood legs apart in warrior fashion and watched Jonathan leave. "You can come out now, you miserable wimp. I covered your ass."

Hector emerged from the room where the peeled paint had stuck to his clothing when he had brushed against the wall. He had heard the exchange when he had put his ear to the gaping crack near him.

"Why'd you try to make me look bad?" he asked angrily.

"Just havin' some fun. Does it matter?"

"Guess not, anymore," Hector admitted.

"Maybe I just don't want you to be saved by some do-gooder," Sammy suggested as he, too, exited the alley.

CHAPTER 55

Same day

Graduation had been a long, tiresome project, but Penelope was always pleased to see her students walk across the stage. It was their moment, the culmination of four years, sometimes one or two more, of hard work and resolve. She was pleasantly exhausted, as usual, by the end of the ceremony. She could not help but notice the ones who were not there, the ones that slipped through the cracks or fell through the gaps in the educational system. They stood out as much by their absence as the others did by their presence. Hector was very much on her mind as she thought of the ones absent. The brief glimpse of him before he had vanished had seemed like a mirage. He had been there one moment, and after one of the graduates walked by and obscured her vision for a few seconds, he was gone.

Jonathan had miraculously reappeared on the field as the students had broken formation to join their families.

"Let's go," he had commanded before she had a chance to ask what had happened. She decided to wait and question him when they returned to her house.

The car ride home was strained as she drove home more quickly than her usual moderate pace. She filled the quietude with the details of the day. Jonathan didn't respond.

She tossed her car keys on the marble counter and collapsed onto one of the kitchen chairs. Jonathan followed her although he seemed as intense as she was tired. His dark features were clouded with some indiscernible quandary.

"Is there something the matter?" she ventured. "I lost track of you for a while today and when I noticed your jacket hanging on the fence, I was worried. I can't explain it, but I felt something was very wrong."

He leaned against the counter and folded his arms across his broad chest. She remembered the night they had made love against that very surface, and her

234

cheeks suffused with color. He didn't say anything for a long moment, something she was becoming accustomed to. There were often lengthy minutes of silence before he spoke, as if he were in some other world that she could never enter.

"I saw Hector at the ceremony today."

"I did, too." A glimmer of hope infused her spirit.

"He ran away, and I chased him. I lost him."

"Did you get a chance to talk to him at all, even for a second or two?"

"He ran off."

She just stared at him, waiting for something else, some information he had been holding back.

"Then we know he's still in town. Maybe we can contact him, persuade him he should come back to school."

"That would be a little hypocritical on your part wouldn't it? You're not going back."

The words sliced through her and cut deeply. "How can you say that? You know I'm going to write about what's happening, maybe do some good that way. I explained it all to you."

"Yeah, you explained it all. I saw you with those kids today. You love what you do, and there are a number of them in that line that wouldn't be there if it hadn't been for you. And you're going to walk away? What about those kids you're not there to save next year, or the next? What about them?"

"What about them? If I stay, it's like putting the proverbial bandage on a hemorrhage. I can do more by getting the word out about these kids who are being left in the dust of political policies."

Jonathan tipped his head back and let out an extended sigh. "I guess that I've always thought that actions speak louder than words. How is some dissertation going to get these kids out of the hole?"

Penelope seethed so deeply that the words came with great difficulty. "I will still be trying to get them out. Research leads to action on a different plane. I want to cover that hole too, so that others won't fall in. Words can sometimes accomplish what actions can't, and they can lead others to action. I've been fighting this battle lately one kid at a time, and I haven't been that successful. I'm not used to failure. I want to reach more people, the ones that can make change. I see this as the most effective way to do it."

"Then I guess I see it differently. Kids like Hector need you so they have a fighting chance. He may be gone for good."

Penelope knew that the loss he had suffered in his last reconnaissance mission loomed large in his head. He saw this as one more failure to add to his list.

She took a chance and approached him even though the space between them seemed extremely wide and treacherous because of his mood. "You, of all people, should know that there is more than one strategy to get something done. I tried one, and now I'm moving on to another. The goal is the same. It's just a different route to get there."

She reached toward him, and he grabbed her hand, kissed the palm lightly, and then let it drop. "I'm sorry. I just can't do this. I can't stand and watch you leave behind so much. It just seems to be against everything you've been talking about, and working toward."

Penelope felt the salty sting in the corners of her eyes. How could she make him understand? "Didn't you walk away after that last assignment? Didn't you feel that you had to do something different, get away from the carnage?"

"Maybe I shouldn't have," he said with finality. "It's a different kind of carnage now."

*   *   *

Jonathan had left without telling Penelope where he was going. She had sat on the chair near the window, only getting up to feed Spartacus or to take him for a break in the yard. The time crept by as if there were no end to the hours and minutes that marked the afternoon and evening. It gnawed at her that he was out and she didn't know his whereabouts. She had called his cell phone so many times that she had lost count. He never returned her calls. Maybe Hector wasn't the only one who might be gone for good.

When the darkness came, she flipped the switch for the outside lights. They flared to life and illuminated the dreary driveway. She stared at the gravel pathway through the lacey patterns of the curtains, and the effect was hypnotic as a spring breeze made them billow and sway.

She dozed periodically until she felt powerful arms scoop her up and carry her to the second floor bedroom. She heard the gentle thud of paw steps as the dog followed in their wake. She felt herself eased onto the comforter.

The darkness was still blanketing the room when she awoke enough to view Jonathan as he rose and turned from her. He had caressed her throughout the night, but they had not made love. She was well aware that he was not happy with her plan, but she also hoped that in his own way he would support her endeavors as always, but she knew that Hector was part of the equation as well as part of the solution.

Penelope had made her decision after much mental agony. The doctorate had always been part of the plan, but now it had even more purpose and direction. She hoped that Jonathan would see that someday, and she wished that it would be sooner than later. She hoped to schedule her orals for the fall and to have her degree so she could launch her campaign for real reform during the next school year. Claire had volunteered to edit her work and check all formatting. The older woman had been more than happy to be involved with a revolution she had started.

As Jonathan pulled on his pants, she could not help but think of the barriers she had allowed him to deconstruct, all of the dreams she had of finally trusting a man enough to build a future with him, all of the internal warnings she had ignored in order to allow him into her life, and now she would have to be patient. It had taken a whole school year to fall in love, and now that love was being tested. She felt her mind go numb, her body ache for his warmth, her heart fracture within her. She had chosen a new course, but Jonathan himself would have to come to the conclusion that she really needed him now more than ever. "He'll come around," she muttered to herself. "I hope." She fell back into a dreamless sleep.

CHAPTER 56

The next morning

Penelope sank deeper into the oversized down pillow, her face buried in the softness of it. She inhaled deeply and felt the balmy breath at her neck. She reached over to the body beside her and felt the hair beneath her hand. She moved her fingers, massaging the mane. Her eyes flew open and she twisted to get a better look at her bedmate.

"Spartacus! You're not supposed to be up here." She reproached the massive hound that had crawled onto the bedspread. She was almost ashamed that she had lapsed back into slumber although it had been a good way to escape the hurt of Jonathan's leaving.

The dog stood up and lapped at her cheek, then lazily jumped from his elevated position, the thump to the floor sounding as if a giant rock had just rolled off the bed.

Penelope snatched the robe that was lying on the trunk under the side window of the bedroom and slipped it on to ward off the early morning nippiness. Still, she shuddered a bit as she headed for the staircase. Where was Jonathan?

Her question was answered when she caught the bouquet of fresh coffee wafting up from the kitchen. She followed the revitalizing aroma to the Mr. Coffee machine on the kitchen counter. The dark liquid gurgled invitingly, and she reached for the carafe and then snagged a cup from the cabinet above it. After she poured the brew into the ceramic cup, she glanced around to locate the one who had put the pot to work.

She heard a faint rustling of paper from the dining room, and she headed in that direction. Jonathan was perched on the window seat, newspaper dangling loosely from his hand, looking out into the morning as if he were expecting some extraordinary event to occur.

"You look like you're waiting for something," she said as she moved to stand next to him, peering over his shoulder to see if she could discern the focus of his attention.

"I am," he said, not removing his gaze from the view beyond the window.

Penelope took a sip of the coffee as she put her hand on his bare shoulder. He was wearing plain blue jeans, but his broad upper torso was exposed to the chill that had settled into the house during the night.

"I'm waiting for you," he finished and stroked her hand that had moved to a spot near the edge of his throat. He then gently nudged her hand, dismissing her touch of tenderness.

She tried to ignore the rejection. "How long have you been up? Did you have another dream?" Concern creased her brow as she searched his face for signs of distress.

"I've been up a while. Today the nightmare is in the waking hours."

"What do you mean?" Penelope asked, anxiety pricking at her senses.

He reached behind her and picked up the front section of the morning paper that he had placed on the window seat when she had walked in. She took it from him and scanned page one.

Youth stabbed, in critical condition was the headline above the fold.

Penelope gasped involuntarily as she read the lead that announced that one Hector Cortez had been rushed to the hospital and a spokesman stated that his condition was critical. Police hoped they could speak to him, but they would have to wait because Cortez was in surgery.

Apparently the police had been summoned to the location several times in the last month when irate neighbors reported suspicious activity in the alleyway where drug deals and the accompanying violence had commonly taken place. Police were investigating and were asking potential witnesses to come forward. Their identities would be protected. The "code of silence" in neighborhoods where gangs ruled was almost impossible to break, but once in a while someone stepped up. The article went on to give more details, but the lines began to blur as Penelope attempted to read further.

She now tasted the tears as they rolled from her lower lashes to spill down the side of her face to her mouth. Jonathan folded her into his arms.

"Now he's swallowed up in the violence. He's truly lost," she murmured, almost breaking into a sob.

"I'll see to it he isn't," he stated.

"You mean 'we' don't you?"

"No, I mean 'I'. I'm not going to lose another one. I have to do this alone."

"This isn't the war, and you are not a Marine any longer."

"Well, according to you it is a war. You've chosen your plan of attack and I'll choose mine," Jonathan snapped.

Penelope's heart sank as she realized he was cutting her out. "Won't you let me help, Jonathan?"

Curtly he replied, "I've told you, 'No'. You get on with your thesis and when it saves a kid, let me know."

The words strangled her heart as she acquiesced. "Okay, you do it your way and I'll do it mine. I care about Hector, and I care about you. There is also no way you can stop me from becoming involved."

"Fine, just stay out of my way."

He went upstairs to finish dressing and quickly left for the hospital.

Penelope stood alone at the door, calling after him in an almost inaudible voice, "I love you." She knew that the fight to save Hector would be a fight for his own life. If he failed, she was afraid he would not be able to get close to anyone again, especially her. She also knew there was nothing she could do. As soon as Hector could have visitors, she would be there. She was certain of that. Right now, though, she couldn't be certain of anything when it came to the other man in her life.

CHAPTER 57

Wfile driving to the hospital, Jonathan thought of his encounter with Emilio in front of Skinner High the last week before graduation. He had asked about Hector, and Emilio told him that he had talked to his brother only once since he had stormed out of school for the last time.

"Hector found out in May that he was going to be a father. Gracia moved in with him cuz she had nowhere else to go, and things kinda got out of hand. But you know my brother. He wanted to do right by her."

"That's another tough break, but you're right. He's a decent kid."

"Yeah," Emilio muttered. "In some ways he's lucky too? Funny, eh?"

"What do you mean?"

"Gracia left to be with her grandmother in New York. The last time I talked to Hector, he hadn't heard from her, and he didn't know how to reach her. Anyway, Gracia said she didn't want him involved anyway. Her grandmother was going to become the baby's guardian so Gracia could go to college."

"How did Hector take it?"

"She told Hector that he wasn't the father and that she was already a month pregnant when they hooked up. He didn't know if he believed her, but he still offered to help her. She said no."

"What's he doing for money?"

"He got a job at some flower warehouse."

"How'd he look?"

"Kinda sad, no smile, just a beaten kind of look. He told me to stay clean, study hard and not screw up like he did. He said I should think like he's dead, then left."

"Have you seen him since?"

"Nope and don't 'spect to. He can be a hard ass."

That, Jonathan knew was true. It had been reinforced yesterday when he left school and refused to even listen to reason.

Jonathan pulled into the parking lot of the hospital, confidence and apprehension warring in his mind. He felt the prickles of sweat beginning to form on his forehead. He was responsible for another human being, again. That was something he had been trying to avoid for the last several years. He had to get it right this time. Maybe this was the way to end the nightmares.

*   *   *

He approached the nurse at the information desk. She was round faced and freckled, with short, artificially reddened hair. She looked up as Jonathan approached and gave him a "what do you want?" look that would be intimidating to the ordinary visitor. He had been hoping an elderly volunteer would be on duty, but he knew he could handle this as well.

"I'm here to see Hector Cortez," he stated bluntly, laying on a bit of a Latino accent.

She consulted her computer over her half glasses. "Family only. Are you related?"

"Would I be here if I weren't?" He smiled to offset her frown.

She looked a bit doubtful, but finally she pointed down the hall to a row of elevators. "Third floor, intensive care." She returned to the papers on the desk.

It was relatively simple to gain access to the intensive care space. The voice on the call phone never questioned his claim that he was the boy's uncle.

Once he was inside, the young nurse, her hair pulled back in a ponytail that made her look about seventeen, introduced herself as Mandy, a name which only emphasized her youth. She told Jonathan that Hector had lost a lot of blood, but the several stab wounds had miraculously missed any organ that would have been immediately fatal.

"He's had surgery to remove his spleen and to stitch the nicks to the veins and an artery, which caused internal bleeding." She shook her head as she looked down at her unconscious patient. "He's very lucky that someone came along and found him so soon."

Jonathan's eyebrow rose in surprise. "Who found him?"

"Some teenager, they told me. He stayed with him until the ambulance came and then disappeared. The police never got his name before he took off."

Sammy, Jonathan thought.

Mandy checked the numbers on the machine that beeped at Hector's bedside and made a notation on his chart.

Jonathan recalled his medical training in the Corps. He was well versed in the rudimentary medical aid on the field, but that did him little good now.

"How do things look for him right now?" Jonathan scrutinized the youth's face to check for color.

"He's still asleep in a light induced coma to help the healing process. It would be too much of a risk to have him move and start the bleeding again. It will be a long several days. He's young and strong, though. You'd have to speak to the doctor for anything further." She smiled sympathetically and patted Jonathan's arm.

Hesitantly, Jonathan asked, "Were there any drugs in his system?"

"No," Mandy responded, checking an IV line. "We were actually surprised at that. So many kids come in here strung out on one thing or another, and when we heard this might be a gang hit, we automatically checked."

Jonathan let out a long sigh of relief. *Thank God*, he thought.

* * *

Jonathan's car slowed to a stop as he arrived at the front of the large, dilapidated brick building sitting alone in the midst of empty lots, which were overgrown with weeds and littered with papers, cups, and beer bottles. Hector had mentioned where his brother lived during one of their long conversations while they had worked together with the computerized music program.

Jonathan left the car, double-checking the locks and alarm system, and slowly walked to the graffiti decorated stoop and doorway. "Someone should shoot these landlords."

He opened the front door and slowly made his way through the debris in the hallway to the back apartment on the second floor. Jonathan knocked and he heard Emilio's voice behind the door.

"Who's there?"

Jonathan was relieved. He didn't want to have to explain his proposal to the grandmother alone. Emilio's presence would make things easier.

"It's Jonathan Perez, Emilio."

"Why are you here?"

"It's about Hector."

"Yeah, we know what happened. Word on the street's he's in pretty bad shape."

"Yes he is, but wouldn't it be easier if we could talk face to face?"

"Why? He don't want nothin' to do with me or Abuela."

"I know. I want to talk to you about helping Hector, and I'll honor his wishes for keeping you and your grandmother safe and away from any trouble. Please, Emilio."

The door creaked open and Jonathan entered. He was temporarily blinded by the ray of dusty light coming through the window. The room was small, but cozy. There were chairs with homemade afghans neatly arranged on the backs, a couch, a side table with a small clock and several pictures, and an old television that was running, but muted. The grandmother sat in her rocking chair and nodded in his direction as he crossed the threshold. Emilio motioned Jonathan to sit on the sofa. After a strained minute of silence, Jonathan began.

"Look, Emilio, your brother's in trouble both physically and maybe legally. He needs someone to speak for him, to be his advocate. You know, a friend who knows the ropes. By the way, you can translate if your grandmother doesn't understand or I can speak in Spanish, even if I am a little rusty."

"Nah, it's okay. She understands most everything, just can't talk English good."

Jonathan pressed to the point. "If Hector makes it, I would like to support him until he's able to take care of himself. I'm guessing he may have to stay out of sight, especially if all of this is somehow connected to gang activity as the police suspect."

Emilio stared. "He tried to work for Papa, but just couldn't do it in the end. Teach still thought that he was dealin', though, and on the Monk turf. I guess that's what got him stuck. Why do you want to do this, anyway? Hector knows what he's doing. He cut the two of us loose 'cause he wanted to keep us out of trouble. He wants no ties, you know?"

"It's my business because I want it to be. Hector and I have a connection, an understanding of sorts. I need to be involved, and no, I won't explain further. I know you two still are worried about him, and I just want you to know I'll take care of things. I'm not asking permission, just making sure you understand that you'll all be safe."

"What about Ms. Parsons? Is she helping you?"

"She's not involved with this. She cares, but this is about Hector and me."

Emilio got out of his chair and began to pace in circles. The kid obviously didn't fully understand what Jonathan was telling him.

"What you going to get out of it?"

His Grandmother glared at Emilio and shook her arthritic finger in his direction. "Listen."

Jonathan continued, "I knew when I went to the hospital that I wouldn't be able to get any information or even be allowed to visit your brother because only immediate family can inquire about his condition. As of now, I am his uncle. Neither of you can really help him, but I can. I'm also hoping your father and his business can lay low for a while. Do you think he'll cooperate?"

"No problem. Papa left in a hurry. It was getting too hot around town. The gangs were fighting for his action. It was going to be a full out turf war with him in the middle. I don't know where he is, and it doesn't matter to me."

Jonathan nodded in understanding and then said, "I promise to keep you uninvolved but informed."

Abuela nodded, and Emilio followed suit. "I hope you know what you're doin'."

So do I, Jonathan thought.

CHAPTER 58

Two days later

T he next days passed slowly as Jonathan kept watch over this boy who had reminded him so much of himself, a good kid, lost in a world that only wanted to forget him.

On the third day Hector was well enough to be placed on the regular surgical floor. He would still be hospitalized until his body responded positively to the surgery and the medication. Mandy had told him that a Penelope Parsons had called several times a day when Hector was in intensive care.

Jonathan contacted Penelope and informed her that Hector was going to live. The conversation was friendly but cool. It was the first time they had spoken since the morning Jonathan left.

"What's going to happen when they discharge him?" Penelope asked.

"I'm hoping to convince him to live with me until he figures out the next step. I have my own business, so I'll take some time off to help him get back on his feet."

"I see. I heard he's out of intensive care, so I'll be over there tomorrow."

He interrupted, "I don't think that's good idea. He's still pretty weak."

"I respect your concern for him, but I don't care if you think it's a good idea or not. I'm coming, and if that bothers you, you don't have to be there when I arrive."

Jonathan let out a long breath. "You're right. Come when you want, but just remember that I've taken responsibility for him, and I'm just trying to do what's best."

"I know. You don't have to be his sole savior, though. Keep in mind what's best for you isn't necessarily what's best for Hector." Her voice was strong, but gentle.

"Goodbye, Nell."

Jonathan stood in the busy stairwell where he had gone to make the call. He could not move forward until he had made reparation for the past. Hector had to be saved. Jonathan had to prove that he could make the right calls this time.

Mandy was climbing the stairs toward the intensive care unit. "I'm sorry. I didn't mean to interrupt your call."

"That's all right. I'm done." He pressed the end key and pocketed his cell. He couldn't help but wonder where this commitment to Hector would lead. He just hoped it would not destroy either one of them.

*   *   *

When the phone disconnected, Penelope felt disconnected, too. She was going to have to be patient until things were resolved.

Hector was eighteen, a man now, no longer her student. He had his whole life ahead of him, and she intended to assist him in any way she could. She had a general idea of how she could do that. She could help him get back into school or get his GED. She could give some suggestions about employment or college.

But what would she do about Jonathan? He had slipped into her life despite her initial resistance. Walter had merely been unfaithful to her, and had made her angry, but Jonathan had wounded her much deeper and much more thoroughly. She had begun to hope, begun to think that she would have a future with him. She had mistakenly believed that he had the same vision for the years ahead, the same beliefs she did. She admonished herself for her foolishness. She thought she could wipe away his nightmares. Apparently, she couldn't.

"I don't need him," she chided herself out loud. "I was fine before he came along. In fact, things were a lot less complicated. To hell with you, Jonathan Perez."

She strode determinedly to the kitchen and opened the refrigerator to look for lunch. She stared at the items on the shelves and realized that she had no appetite. The tears started to roll over her bottom lids, and she made no attempt to keep them in check.

She slumped to the floor and gave in to her tears. The cool air from the refrigerator enveloped her as she sobbed and one dream began to evaporate. She would not let the other one disappear as well.

CHAPTER 59

The next day

J onathan looked out of the fifth floor window of Hector's new hospital room. The post op floor was not filled with all the machine noises and bustling of personnel as the ICU, and Hector had periods of semi-consciousness. The prognosis of full recovery was very encouraging, but Jonathan was still concerned about the youth's future. Thankfully, the police had not stopped their search for the assailant, but the intensity of their investigation was currently shared with another problem. A murder on the east side of town now took up quite a bit of their manpower. The gangs were getting more active. While he wished that the person who had done this would be brought to justice, he knew that it might not happen. The "no snitching" code was alive and well and hindered the best of cops in the performance of their duties. He was also grateful that the focus was off Hector in case there was something going on in that alley where Hector was found that would put Hector in a suspicious light. He didn't think so, but he couldn't be certain.

Jonathan heard a movement coming from the bed, and he noticed Hector turning his head restlessly on the pillow. Jonathan moved to the bedside and placed a sturdy hand on the boy's shoulder.

"Take it easy. Things are looking up for you," he reassured him.

Hector opened his eyes and seemed startled to see Jonathan standing over him.

"What happened?"

Jonathan explained as succinctly as possible.

Hector stared almost uncomprehendingly for a moment. Then he started to nod as the memory of the dark alley and the pain came back. "I heard music. I remember falling into the music in my mind." He swallowed. "Could - could I have some water? I'm so thirsty."

"Sure." Jonathan tipped the nearby pitcher so that a splash of water fell into the plastic cup on the side table. A straw had already rested on the side of the cup, and he aimed it toward Hector's dry lips.

Hector sipped at the end of the straw and then wiped his mouth with the back of his hand. He seemed to just notice the tubes attached to his arm as he lowered it back down to the mattress.

"We were worried about you. It's good to see you awake." Jonathan let a smile slide into place.

Hector looked around the room as if searching for someone else.

"Miss Parsons and I have been taking turns watching over you. She had to go home to get some rest." Jonathan and Penelope had barely spoken, just nodding to one another as they changed shifts.

He hated those brief encounters where Penelope's pained expression matched his own dark mood. He had longed to reach out to her, to touch her once again, to feel her next to him, to love her.

That can't happen. Not until this is over.

"Anybody else been here?"

Jonathan decided that Hector would want the truth. "No, son, I'm afraid not, just Miss Parsons and me. Some don't want to disturb you while you're trying to recover. Mrs. Ruckmeyer and the rest of the guidance staff sent you some flowers, though."

Jonathan pointed to a lush basket of carnations and baby's breath.

Hector glanced at the floral display. "She's still a bitch," he said weakly and closed his eyes again.

Jonathan ignored that.

"Mr. Tottman has been calling constantly. He said he'll come tonight to check in on you." He paused a moment. "I also spoke with Emilio. He said that you told him to stay away." Jonathan extracted the folded piece of paper from his jacket pocket. "He sent you this. You can read it later."

He placed the paper near Hector's hand where it rested on the neat white sheet. The boy opened his eyes once more and reached for the note. He fingered the paper carefully as if it were a precious historical document and then crumpled it into a compact ball in his fist.

Jonathan broke the quietude. "Emilio told me about you and Gracia."

"Yeah. I thought I had something and again I lost it."

"What happened?" Jonathan asked, almost at whisper level.

Hector stared at the light green wall in front of him. It was blank except for a large, round clock and a small whiteboard that announced the names of the nurse and aid who were on duty that shift.

Jonathan had heard the story about Gracia before, but he listened intently. Perhaps if Hector talked about it, he could deal with it

"She told me it wasn't mine even though she swore it was at first. She went to the doctor for a check-up and found out she was already pregnant when she came to me. She said she didn't know. She was sorry."

Jonathan suspected the roughness in his voice was to counteract the sense of loss he felt.

"She said she couldn't use me like that. She thought she could, but she just couldn't do it. I wish she had. Then at least I would have somebody."

"You do have somebody. I will make sure you get back on your feet. When you're feeling a bit better, we'll make plans."

"What plans?"

"You've got to decide where to go from here."

"Gracia went to New York to her grandmother's. She says she's going to go to college."

"That's something you could do if you wanted," Jonathan said quietly. "Just think things over right now. Don't look behind you. Look ahead."

"I am looking ahead. It looks just as dark as behind me." Hector threw the wad of paper against the green wall.

*   *   *

Penelope massaged her forehead. The dull ache was threatening to grow into a full blown migraine. She had not slept well since the day they had received the news about the assault. She could perhaps have managed things better if Jonathan had not walked out on her. He had walked out and slammed the door behind him. Maybe someday the hollow feeling in her stomach would go away, that sense that something was missing and would never be replaced.

She heard the whoosh of a door opening. She turned from the window where she had been gazing down at the parking lot and looked up to find Ted Tottman stepping quietly into the hospital room.

She walked to meet him at the foot of Hector's bed and gave him a half smile.

"The patient is still sleeping. He does that a lot, but it's the best thing for him right now."

Ted narrowed his gaze as he examined her face, zeroing in on her eyes. She looked away, afraid he might see her distress.

He took both of her hands in his own and said nothing as he turned to watch Hector's even breathing. "I really miss him; so does the rest of the choir."

He was quiet for a few seconds. "I'm not going to say anything to him now, but I received a letter from the Harris Conservatory. They had originally told me that they would wait for him until he passed the state test, but they needed for Hector to sign the commitment papers to verify that he was coming. No one seemed to know exactly where he was, though, since he left school. There was no one home when I went to where his apartment was supposed to be, and there was no listed phone number. I'm sorry, but the deadline passed May thirtieth, and they gave the scholarship to someone else. How and when should I give the news to Hector?"

"Don't worry about it. I'll tell Jonathan. He'll take care of breaking it to Hector at the right time. Jonathan's closer to him right now."

"Okay, I'll leave it up to him."

His voice stirred something in Hector, and he opened his eyes, "Mr. Tottman?"

The music teacher stayed where he was, but fixed his former student with a comforting smile. "It's good to see you awake and getting well. Rumor has it that they are going to spring you soon."

Hector did not seem either upset or consoled by the idea. "I guess."

Penelope could feel the tension in Ted's voice as he addressed Hector again. He cleared his throat, his concern evident in every syllable. "We're all wishing you a fast recovery."

"I heard what you said," Hector stated flatly.

Penelope watched Hector closely. The boy stared down at the sheets and cream colored blanket. He said nothing more. He didn't move.

"I wish there was something more I could do, son," Tottman said, "but I'm afraid that we'll have to find you another way to get into a program somewhere."

"I don't need no program," Hector finally murmured, so muffled Penelope wasn't sure she actually heard him.

She moved closer to the side of the bed. "There are alternatives, Hector. We'll find something for you. You'll be all right."

The boy's lips pulled back in a sneer. "Yeah, everything will be just great. This was just a bad dream. The Monks really aren't after me, and my test scores were the best in the district. Now I can go to Harvard and sing in their fuckin' chorus." The words poured forth in a venomous spew. He slapped at a vase on the side table that contained a jaunty arrangement of daisies. The flowers flew to the floor and the glass exploded on the tiles.

"I'm really sorry," Ted reiterated. When he attempted to approach the bed, Hector pitched a glare at him that was so full of fury that he went no further. Wordlessly, Ted left the room.

"Please don't you tell me how sorry you are. It ain't you who's got no place to go. I don't know why I survived if this is the reward. They shoulda left me in that alley."

Penelope put her arm around his shoulders, pulling him loosely to her. "Mr. Perez said you could stay with him until you get back on your feet. You do have somewhere to go, and you'll go further still when you're ready."

To her surprise, Hector did not pull away, only sat rigid in her relaxed embrace. Then his sobs erupted.

*   *   *

Jonathan sat outside Hector's room as he waited for the nurses to remove the boy's IV tubes. Why had he quit smoking? He could really use a cigarette. He remembered that those things had helped him through more than a few aftershocks. When he had completed a particularly difficult job in some godless desert or jungle, he would light up and let the smoldering cloud rise and circle around him. The pain between his shoulders would dull to a distant throb, and his head would cease to pound as he inhaled the smoke. He hadn't cared if his lungs were blackening or that his life might be shortened. What had he ever done that would make him want to live longer? He once struck a match to the tip of a fresh smoke within ten minutes after gunning down a swarthy, lean extremist in some hot, dirty place. The guy had terrorized an unarmed family with four children. The bastard had looked him in the eye and raised his rifle. It had occurred to Jonathan at the time that he might just let the other guy finish the job. He hadn't though. His instinct was to make sure what was left of that family would be safe, and if he had to save himself in the process, then so be it. That last mission had destroyed that instinct. He had shut down so much inside for so long that he hadn't even realized how hollow he had become. Now the impulse to save, to protect, was back, and he had to follow through to become a man again.

A middle aged woman with dark hair threaded through with gray hurried to his side. She put out her hand as if she were going to touch his shoulder, but then pulled back. "You're Hector Cortez's uncle, and you teach at the high school, right? Mr. Perez?" Her forehead was ridged in worry, and her upper teeth gnawed on her lower lip.

Jonathan rose. "What's the matter?" His instincts were again buzzing through his body.

"We just got a young man in the ER. He won't give us any family information even though I pleaded with him to do so. The doctors seem to think he might not survive his injuries. We were wondering if maybe you could help us get some information. We figured you might know him. He doesn't look to be eighteen yet, but it's hard to tell."

"Let's go." Jonathan followed the hurried stride of the woman. She led him through a long, polished corridor and down a flight of stairs.

The emergency room came into sight with nurses and doctors tending to a multitude of patients in cubicles separated by canvas curtain dividers. A uniformed police officer stood nearby.

The dark haired woman hurried to the third compartment on the left and gestured toward a young man lying on stark white sheets. Jonathan gripped the bars of the gurney as he looked down at a glassy-eyed Sammy Johnson.

The boy looked up at him with a gaze that was devoid of his usual arrogance. The cockiness was replaced by terror filled tears.

Jonathan rounded the bottom of the gurney and lowered his head toward Sammy's face, placing his hand on the youth's arm

"What happened? No, don't talk unless you have to. They need to know who to contact, Sammy. Can't you tell them that?"

Sammy just stared at him, jerkily moving his head from side to side, wincing.

A doctor pulled the curtain back further, clipboard in hand. He had on green scrubs that fit a little too snugly over his expanding abdomen. "We're getting ready to move him up to surgery. We were hoping to locate a family member, but . . . Do you know how we can get a hold of them?"

Jonathan shook his head. "No, I'm afraid not."

"Well, we'll just have to take him up anyway. I'll get an orderly over here." He left as abruptly as he came.

"Sammy, please. Tell them what they need to know."

"Don't matter . . ."

"It does matter. It matters to more people than you know. It matters to me." He was saying that a lot lately.

Sammy continued to stare at Jonathan, his breathing becoming more labored by the second. Electronic boxes beeped in the background; a crowd of voices barked and murmured around them.

"People were going to know who I am . . . my art." Sammy coughed and red fluid bubbled between his lips. "I never had nobody, really. They don't care. Never did." He closed his eyes and swallowed.

"Sammy, Sammy, listen to me. Stay with us. Come on. I really do care." His voice came out almost as a shout. His grip on Sammy's shoulder tightened.

Sammy's eyes slitted. "Yeah, I know."

His breath hitched as two orderlies pulled the bed out of the cubicle and pushed it toward the hall that held the elevators.

Jonathan watched the gurney disappear as the automatic doors whooshed open and Sammy was gone. The police officer came up behind him, pad open and pencil at the ready.

"You know that kid?"

Jonathan nodded. "How did this happen?"

The officer scribbled something on the pad. "Gunshot wound, stomach. According to a witness, he yelled at a couple of Monks who were tagging a mural on one of the buildings downtown. They got into it; this kid was shot."

"It was probably his mural."

"Well, whatever the reason, this is the third gang related incident this week. Just tell me what you know about this one." He pointed his pencil toward the door."

"Sure." Jonathan's head raised. "His name is Sammy Johnson . . ." he started as they walked toward the lounge.

CHAPTER 60

The day after

Jonathan was barely aware of the unusually cool June temperature even though his senses were resonating with everything around him. He wore black jeans and a fitted shirt that matched the pants in color. This was a city where he had worked in a very civilized profession, but it had the feel of an enemy territory today. There was dampness to the air, and the old brick wall near the train station was dark and unyielding.

He walked carefully, each step a tentative advance into the unknown. The environment was familiar, but there was a tinge of danger today. He thought taking care of Hector would put away the hunger to make things right, to save those who sometimes didn't want to be saved. Well, here he was again, crawling through shadows to attack an enemy he knew he should leave to the police. This really wasn't his mission.

He put his back to the wall and listened. He detected the faint voices that seemed to be grumbling close by. He eased to the edge of the wall and the sounds became more distinct. He peered around the jagged brick and saw a lean, dark man puffing a cigarette and wearing a leather jacket. Jonathan could smell the smoke as it curled toward him with the slight breeze that fluttered through the open space.

Several other boys, most looking as if they were mid and late teens, pushed at each other and laughed. The majority were wearing white tee shirts or too long colored shirts that hung loosely from their hunched frames. Some of the visages seemed familiar, but he had no names for the faces.

"Teach, what we gonna do now?" a short, stocky Latino asked the leather clad man who appeared to be the leader.

Teach didn't answer right away, but continued to take a long pull on what was left of his cigarette. Finally, he looked at the lad who had asked the question.

"You got your work. I told everyone what they had to do today."

"You didn't tell *me*," the stocky kid persisted.

"Well, maybe you wasn't listening," Teach taunted.

The thickset one just stared at his leader. Jonathan could almost hear the kid gulp as he backed away and stood next to a set of three other members of the group.

"You know what you gotta do," Teach said in a low voice. "Now, get out of here."

The cluster of kids began to disperse. They were quiet in their exit, some of them stamping out their cigarette stubs before leaving. They made a pretense of not rushing, but it was clear that they would not consider lingering.

When the last of the gang had gone, Teach remained. He stood looking over the discarded rail equipment and rusty metal as a sovereign would survey his kingdom.

Jonathan stepped out of the shadows and moved closer to the gang leader.

"I was wonderin' when you were going to show yourself," Teach said as he looked up and tossed his cigarette stub toward a rusty pipe on the side of the track. "What the hell do you want?"

Jonathan stopped several feet from Teach, never taking his gaze away from the other man's squinting eyes. He kept his arms loosely at his sides, ready for any sudden movement.

"I think we both know what I want. I want you to stay away from the Cortez family, including Hector, permanently."

Teach smiled, a baring of the teeth with no warmth. "Who elected you guardian angel?" He spit in Jonathan's direction, and the action left a sliver of saliva glistening at the corner of his mouth.

"Who elected you the terminator in this town? I won't ask if you and your thugs were responsible for what happened to Sammy Johnson because you probably won't tell me, but I have a strong hunch you were the one wielding the knife in that alley when Hector went down."

Teach spread his legs and put his arms by his hips in gunfighter fashion. "Maybe. I ain't saying I was, but that prick had been a problem since he jumped out of our little family here."

"Really? How's that?"

"I'm just talking, ya know." He leaned his head forward as if to impart some secret. "He sticks his nose in when his wimpy brother wants to become a man with us. He turns his back on his friends here." He spread his arm wide as if to point out the boys who had just departed.

"Rumor has it you thought he was moving in on your drug trade."

Teach sneered. "Us? We don't do that shit. We're just a bunch a guys hanging out. It's a nice neighborhood, ya know?"

He had barely spoken the last word when Jonathan pulled him forward by the right wrist, twisted it up and back, and had him on his knees, Jonathan's own knee in the small of his back.

"Listen. I will say this one time." Jonathan snarled as Teach grunted. "I am very aware of what you can do. You, however, have no idea what I'm capable of. If I find you or your 'little family' anywhere near those people or anywhere near the high school, for that matter, you'll know firsthand what I can do."

He could hear Teach on the verge of a whimper. The guy was breathing in very heavily and seemed to be unable to speak.

Jonathan put his mouth within a few inches of Teach's ear. "The police are working on some evidence that just may put you at the scene for Sammy. If I were you, I'd lay low for a while, maybe for the rest of your life, for however long that may be." He pushed the twisted arm a bit further up toward the thug's shoulder blade and kept it there until Teach grunted.

Jonathan let go, and Teach slowly rose, swaying slightly as he got to his feet. He shook his right hand and wrist to ease the pain.

He looked up at Jonathan, who was several inches taller. "You'll see me again."

Jonathan straightened. "I hope not, because if I do, I will be forced to tell everyone what a sniveling coward you really are."

"I could kill you first."

Jonathan smiled. "I doubt it. My combat skills are much more advanced than yours, and if you don't succeed, it's over for you." He paused. "Think about it."

He turned away and walked toward the street.

CHAPTER 61

One week later

Hector still looked a little thin after three days out of the hospital. His recuperation was going well according to the physician whom he had seen for a follow-up visit. The surrounding dark, shadowy circles still made his eyes seem enormous, Jonathan noted.

He watched the boy staring at the television screen. He knew Hector was not paying attention from the faraway look and limp posture. The TV was on mute and several animated characters performed harebrained antics in silence.

Hector seemed to rouse himself from his reverie as Jonathan approached.

"I made us some sandwiches for lunch."

"Sounds great. Thanks." Hector replied as he took his sandwich from Jonathan, who sat in the chair that matched the couch in color and style. Both were dark brown leather with burnished rivets attaching the material to the frame.

"How are you feeling? Are you in pain?"

"I'm all right. I got those pills the doctor gave me."

"Have you been using them?"

Hector shrugged. "Sometimes I think maybe I deserve the pain."

Jonathan studied the younger man, then nodded slightly. "I know what you mean."

"You don't think I'm crazy?"

"No, but I do think you are being very tough on yourself."

Hector sat quietly munching on his sandwich, and Jonathan remained silent as he watched the young man. It was time to have a talk about the future. Hanging around too long only made one lazier. Hector couldn't be allowed to vegetate. He had to make decisions and the sooner the better.

Hector finished his lunch and placed the plate on the table next to him.

"Hector." Jonathan spoke softly.

Hector spun his head and moaned, "What?"

"I think you are well enough to put your dish in the dishwasher where it belongs."

"I was goin' to, but it's just I'm hurtin' right now."

"I know you are, but you can't use the pain for an excuse to be lazy. Life does go on even though you've made mistakes and gotten yourself hurt. It's time for you to do some serious thinking about your future."

"What future? I blew it. No diploma, no scholarship, no music, and no second chances. When I get on my feet, I'm leavin'. I can take care of myself."

"Oh is that so? You've done just a great job of it so far." Jonathan stopped, gentled his voice. "I think I can help you sort things out. Give you choices and a good start."

"You don't owe me nothin' and I expect nothin' else from you. You got me this far and now I'm on my own. You're in the clear."

"You don't understand. I had trained men who thought they knew it all because they were tough, smart and well prepared. They didn't think they had to depend on me for the success of the mission. I wasn't forceful enough in making them follow my plan. I compromised and gave in to a couple of men who truly believed their way was better and they went against my orders. They ended up in a body bag. I should have trusted my instincts and my rank and stopped them. I'm not making that error again. I still live with the guilt. I have knowledge you don't, and believe it or not, I outrank you in this situation. Understand?"

Hector did not immediately respond and then acquiesced. "Yes, Sir."

"Okay. Let's look at the big picture and then we can discuss the options."

"That's easy. I got nothin' and I got nowhere to go."

"Enough self pity, I told you. Right now, you have no diploma, no job, and no opportunity for an honest way to make a living. You do have your life, very soon your health, your brain, your talent, a roof over your head, food, clothing, Miss Parsons, and me. The plusses far outnumber the negatives."

"I'm not sure about the brain. I didn't graduate and I flunked that damn test."

"That's done, Hector, and you know you're smart. All that stopped you was the test, and some very smart educators know that the test alone does not determine who is smart or not. Let's talk options. If that test means so much to you, you can enroll for a couple of high school math classes in the fall. Take the test in October. You'll probably pass it this time and if you don't, then as an enrolled student you have another chance to file an appeal."

"I know I screwed up when I left school. Mrs. Ruckmeyer had talked about the appeal process, but I was so fuckin' mad I stormed out. I'd feel like a fool going back"

"Just think about it," Jonathan continued. "Another option is going for your GED. Having it is almost as good as a diploma. You will be able to enroll in a community college and get a job or go into the armed forces. Without it you'll lose your option for college, the military, and even decent employment."

"Yeah, I just got to pass another stupid test."

"Don't rush your decision, but don't take too long, either. I'll expect an answer in a couple of days, and then we'll get to work on your future."

"Well, one thing that will help me decide is somethin' you don't know. Remember, Emilio gave you a note for me. The nurse got it out of the trash. He told me that Abuela was scared that he could be the next target. She's going back to relatives in Puerto Rico and taking Emilio with her. I don't have to worry about him anymore. I just got to hope the Monks go after someone else and forget about me. My plans have to do with avoidin' them and the streets."

Jonathan nodded slightly and then offered, "Well, I don't exactly live in gang territory, so if you stay here while you do your thing, you should be safe enough. Also, I have a hunch they just might leave you alone for good."

*   *   *

The next morning while having breakfast, Hector suddenly spoke up, "I know what I gotta do now. I'm gonna be a Marine . . . like you were."

Jonathan did not react, just scrutinized Hector's face for a long moment. "When did you decide this?"

Hector looked away. "Today. You said that I should be a part of something, do something with my life, be somebody. I decided I want to be you." Seconds that seemed like epochs ticked by. Jonathan shook his head slowly.

"Trust me. You don't want to be me. The Marines gave me skills I couldn't get anywhere else, but they also gave me my darkest nightmares. You've just come close to losing your life. Are you sure you want to put it in jeopardy again? Especially with the Marines putting out fires all over the globe these days."

Hector glared at him intently. "For the first time, I'm really sure what I want to do. I think I really need to do this. I gotta' get out of here. I gotta' protect myself and others from my mistakes.

"Like who? Emilio is safe, your father is gone."

"Like you, Miss Parsons and . . . . Sammy." He looked away.

"What do you mean, Sammy?"

"The Monks will be after him. I know he was with me after the attack. It wasn't a dream. He tried to help me and that's a big 'no'. Nobody helps an enemy of the Monks and gets away with it."

"Okay, Hector. One, Miss Parsons and I are safe. I can take care of the both of us, and even the Monks tend to leave the school and the teachers out of their fights. They at least have some limits. Now, about Sammy. He was always on the outside, doing his own thing." He cleared his throat as Hector stared at him.

"What's the matter? You havin' a heart attack or somethin'?"

"Hector, I have something to tell you, and I can't hold back any longer. I can't lie to you."

"What you got to say? I can take it. You really want me outta' here? Cuz I can take care of myself. Always have." He started to get up.

"No, of course not. It's bad news, Hector. You don't have to worry about Sammy anymore."

"Why? Did he leave?"

"No, Hector, he's dead."

Hector's face contorted in anger, eyebrows furrowed and lips firmly closed. Then the words tumbled out. "See, I told you! It's all my fault!"

"Don't put that on yourself. I spoke to him in the ER before he died. He was protecting his art, not you."

"You just sayin' that to make me feel better?"

"No, you have to make your decisions based on the truth. Whatever you do, don't join the Marines because you want to run away."

Jonathan saw the determination in the boy's face as Hector clenched his teeth. "It's what I want."

"First, I want you to think a little bit longer about all the choices you have. If you still want to join the Marines, I'll assist you in any way I can. You'll have to get a GED and then attend at least a year of community college before they'll take you. It can be a difficult road to even get to step one."

CHAPTER 62

Penelope walked three steps down into the restaurant and shook the moisture from her coat. Her hair had suffered no ill effects from the weather, but she patted it down out of habit. The eatery was small and had a Tuscan touch of spices in the air, wall murals of the Italian countryside, and muted music in the background. She saw Hector wave from a table near a pillar as the host approached to ask if she would like to be seated.

"I see my party already, thanks," she explained and headed toward her former student and the darkly handsome man with him. She was always taken aback when she saw Jonathan, even though she knew he would be there. Her stomach and heart clenched when he stood out of courtesy as she approached. He looked healthy, strong, and a little dangerous, as always. Well, he was dangerous. He had dealt a powerful blow to her trust in their future. *Stop whining*, she told herself and affixed a warm smile on her face as she nodded to Jonathan and laid a hand on Hector's shoulder as he, too, started to rise. She knew the boy would never have thought to do such a thing nine months ago.

"Please, don't get up." She sat in the empty chair on a third side of the table that Jonathan had pulled out for her. "So, how is everyone?"

She could see the excitement in Hector's eyes. "Great. That science test that you helped me with? I got an eighty-eight on it. I'm on the dean's list at the community college. Jonathan says I should have no problem getting into the military now when I complete my first year. He helped me write all those frickin' papers for the English courses I had to take. He's been really great." Penelope smiled at his use of the modified expletive. It seemed Jonathan was making progress with his charge in a few other areas as well.

Penelope turned to Jonathan. He took another swallow of his scotch and water and looked away, as if he were embarrassed by Hector's praise. She still had to consciously hold back from touching his slightly unshaved cheek or staring into those dark eyes. She gave a sigh of frustration.

"I'm glad to hear things are only going up for you." She saluted Hector with the diamond cut water glass, tapped Hector's, and then Jonathan's. She felt the familiar jolt of longing.

The three of them had been meeting every last Saturday of the month since Hector recovered. She also saw Hector at the town library where she tutored him after he finished part-time work at the gas station. Jonathan had thought that it was a good idea to keep the boy busy so he could stay focused.

It was Hector who had initiated the monthly get-togethers. He had treated his two mentors with his first paycheck from his new job and insisted that they all meet at a time when they were not driving him someplace or assisting him academically. Ordinarily, Penelope and Jonathan did not see each other in the course of their commitment to Hector, and she preferred it that way, but how could she refuse Hector's simple request once a month?

"How are you doing with your dissertation?" Jonathan inquired politely, too politely.

"My defense is scheduled for two weeks from now. I'm extremely nervous, but Samantha says she has confidence in me and is planning some sort of celebration. I'm sure she'll be in touch with both of you. Personally, I'd like to just go home and go to bed after it's done and get back all that sleep I missed."

She could see Jonathan's jaw working, and she knew he still was angry that she had given up her position at the high school, still believed she had turned her back on those who needed her. She drank more deeply from her water glass. She had asked for an extension on her leave of absence to allow more options, knowing that Christie was doing a fine job in her stead.

"You know you'll ace that thing," Hector said. "You can do anything. That's what you always keep tellin' me. Don't you think so?" He turned to Jonathan for affirmation.

Jonathan nodded in agreement. "Of course. She can definitely do whatever she wants."

The subtle change in wording and meaning was not lost on Penelope. "Thanks for the vote of confidence, gentlemen." She opened her napkin and placed it across her knees even though there was no food on the table. "How is everything at the high school?"

She always asked and Jonathan usually gave her a terse "fine" as if to imply that she would know the answer if she were still there. Jonathan was teaching several classes and consulting on the technology systems even though his major income was still from his business, which was thriving.

This time he at first said nothing, but then turned toward her. His gaze was intense, but not hostile or accusatory. He seemed to be studying her as if he was taking inventory and discovering some new facet of her. "Things are pretty much the same. Everyone misses you, of course."

She glanced down at the linen napkin on her lap. "I miss them, too," she said and then looked back up to him. "Everyone."

CHAPTER 63

Two months later

Penelope had just picked up the mail after taking Spartacus for a walk. She stuffed the one letter in her pocket as she led the dog into the fenced back yard. It was a beautiful day, and he would enjoy chasing the squirrels around the grassy half acre lot. Entering the house, she touched the letter that crackled in her side pocket. It was not the call she had hoped for, but it was better than nothing. She knew it was from Hector. She could not mistake the cramped scrawl that she had seen so many times on the tops of the papers that he had submitted for her class.

She had not seen Hector or Jonathan for over a month when they had last met for pizza. It was the beginning of the third week in May, and Hector had completed his mandatory year at the community college before he was to report to basic training. She had missed the two of them in that month, but she had immersed herself in a marathon to finish her dissertation requirements. She was informed immediately that she had passed the orals and she had her doctorate. She started promoting her ideas at speaking engagements and at meetings with those in charge of education for the state and with legislators. Her plan was set in motion, but surprisingly it did not have the level of satisfaction she thought it would. Things still didn't seem complete. She needed to be with Jonathan again. It had been too long. She hadn't seen Hector either, but she knew he was now a Marine recruit and wondered when he would be leaving for basic duty.

She slowly extracted the envelope from her pocket and stared at the front. There was no return address. She tore at the flap of the envelope with her index finger, creating a ragged edged opening. She pulled the letter from its wrapping and unfolded the lined paper. It looked as if it had been torn from a notebook. She scanned the first few lines before going back to the initial salutation and reading more carefully.

Dear Miss Parsons,

I owe you a lot, almost as much as Jonathan. It still feels funny to call him that, but since I've been living with him, he told me it was okay. I made it through my year at college, but as you know, I want to be a Marine like Jonathan. It'll make me a man. He says it'll be tough, but he knows I can make it. I'm not the school type. I'll be leavin' in a couple of days.

Get this. They got a choir and my recruiter says I can try out for it. If I make it, I can travel to help sell the Marines to other kids like me. I'm going to be all right. I can't face saying good-bye, but I'll write from boot camp when I get a chance.

Thanks for everything. You are the greatest teacher ever.

Hector

Penelope refolded the letter and forced it back into the envelope. She wiped her eyes and straightened her jacket.

"Wish I could say good-bye in person, but this letter will have to do. Good for you, Hector. You rose above the test," she said softly. She put the letter back into her pocket. "What about those who can't?"

Her thoughts turned to Jonathan. His protégé was gone. Maybe his nightmares were, too. "So what now, Jonathan?" she asked to the emptiness in the room.

CHAPTER 64

Last week of June

Penelope had received a long, official looking envelope at her house. The return address was the university where she finished her dissertation and her PhD. The chair of her committee had been very impressed with her work and had passed it on to several contacts in education and the political arena.

As a result, John Ruggleby, the Department Head, who had shared her findings with a member of a state congressional committee that was investigating the needs of students and the efficacy of state testing. Penelope had been asked to testify at one of the meetings, drawing from both research and experience. This had led to still other appearance requests. Tonight it was the Concerned Parents of Secondary Students who had asked her to come and share her findings not only with them, but also with the members of the State Board of Education who had also been invited as guests. The parents were determined to make an impact on the state controlled system, and Penelope was to be their weapon of choice. She was more than willing to cooperate.

These appearances made her nervous. She had to keep reminding herself that her message was more important than her comfort zone. It was an uncomfortable topic, but it had to be addressed from the teachers' and students' sides, not just from the political viewpoint, and if she had to sweat herself into a puddle to do it, she would.

Penelope arrived at the brand new Crestwell Hotel in downtown Boston. As she entered the lobby, she spied the large event board announcing the meeting in The Grand Ballroom and beneath that, "Penelope Parsons, PhD" and underneath that "No Child Left Behind: The Fantasy, the Myth and the Tragedy." She paused. *Maybe the title is a bit too dramatic.*

Mrs. Hackleson, the organization's president, approached her as she stood there. "Are we ready, Dr. Parsons?" The title still seemed unfamiliar to her.

"Yes, thank you."

They headed to the double doors across the foyer and when they opened, Penelope gasped as she saw the standing room only crowd. The members of the state board were sitting at a table below the raised dais. The speaker's space was a sizeable stage with a podium in the center and curtained panels on either side where a speaker could enter without coming from where the attendees were seated in long rows of straight backed chairs. There were two spotlights that illuminated the podium area. This was going to be the challenge of her life, and for a fleeting moment she thought about how much easier this would have been if Jonathan had been here with her. She had received a short message from him telling her that Hector had left for training, confirming what Hector had said in his letter.

Feeling very much alone in her mission, she bravely glanced around the auditorium in hope of finding just one familiar face. Then she spotted them in the fifth row center, her own personal cheering squad, Claire, Stephanie, Samantha, Christie, Dr. Bradford, Mrs. Ruckmeyer, Ted Tottman, several other faculty members and even some of her former students. *They understood. Why couldn't Jonathan?* She was sure there were just as many detractors as supporters out there, but she couldn't think about that now.

When she was introduced, the crowd responded with a hearty round of applause. The entire fifth row stood. When she stepped behind the microphone, the lights blurred her vision.

The words on the paper seemed to fade. They appeared as a jumble of letters before her as she felt moisture form at her hairline and in the palms of her hands. How was she going to present her ideas if the words were shifting and her thoughts were an untidy heap in her brain? Her voice began to work in almost raspy tones before it became more clear and assertive.

Imagine a baseball game in which two teams are contending to garner enough points to win the game. One team runs out onto the field with fresh, new uniforms, the most expensive equipment, and with training by exclusive coaches who center all their efforts on making these players the best at what they do. The parents of these players are in the grandstand cheering their offspring to victory.

The other team enters onto the diamond with dirty and ill-fitting outfits, nicked and pitted bats and worn gloves. Their coach can't spend the time he would like with them because he has other important duties to perform. Their section of the bleachers is almost empty. A few of the parents are present, but there are not enough to give the team the confidence and support they need. The players themselves are tired, and some cannot understand the coach's directions.

Who is going to win this game?"

She paused for a few seconds before continuing.

This scenario is much like watching the differences between the more privileged school systems and the poorer ones as they step up to the plate to take the state test. Until we address the issues that prevent the students from working at peak performance, we will not see progress.

What is progress? How should it be defined as we look at student accomplishment?

There are many students in our so-called underperforming schools who struggle with life problems so overwhelming that coming to school every day is a monumental feat. We should be encouraging their efforts with all the energy that education allows so that they can taste some measure of success.

Instead we test them. If they do not measure up, they are not allowed to graduate. Yes, they are given more chances to pass, but how many times can the numbers tell them they are failures before they give up trying? Before they give up on themselves?

Schools are being judged by state test scores, and they keep upping the stakes. English and math tests are now not enough. We are venturing toward making tests in other subject areas mandatory. The appeal process has loosened, but the score requirement has tightened.

We are testing students whose first language is not English. We are ignoring the fact that some students move through numerous school systems before they take this test. We are not taking into consideration that many schools do not have budgets large enough to adequately staff their schools, that students come from fractured families or homes in which education is not a priority, and so they do not receive the assistance and cooperation to supplement that which they receive in the school. We cannot always undo in six hours what an indifferent home life or a violent street life does in their time outside of the school building.

Students are being left behind every day when they are being discarded by their families, lured by gangs and drugs, infected by health issues from the unwholesome environments in which they live. A written test alone cannot determine if they are being successful. With some of these students, coming to class with a completed homework assignment in their hands is not just an achievement. It might be a minor miracle.

Decisions about what to do to remedy the situation are not being made by those most impacted by them.

Her voice grew stronger with each point she made. Her fervor sustained her to her last sentences.

As parents, educators, concerned citizens, and politicians who have an investment in our youth, we must come together as a force that will even the playing field across the educational spectrum. There is an expansive gap between the school systems that have, in terms of funding, social economic status, parent involvement, and student motivation and those districts in which poverty smothers students, parents, educators and resources.

As my research proves, the solution to rid the educational experience of gross inequalities is complicated, but doable if all who are vested in gaining equality are willing to agree on the causes and solutions. Prejudice and bigotry must be eliminated from the formula. Poor districts need public support and more funds. Poor districts need the best teachers, and more has to be done to attract them to the systems which need them most. Poor districts need adequate numbers of psychologists and counselors, not just a token team. Poor districts need programs, in addition to school sponsored activities, to keep our youth off the streets. Poor districts need positive recognition for what is going right. The students of these communities can and should be saved. The failure rate is high in these communities, and it isn't just because the kids don't care. We can right the wrong. It can be done and will be done with your efforts, your caring, and your support.

Penelope dipped her head as she finished the last sentence. Her hands shook as she folded the sheets of paper that contained her notes, and she prepared to leave the podium. The silence in the auditorium was palpable. Where was her pep squad? Had they left before she finished? Hadn't the warm reception meant anything? What had she said to turn so many off? She didn't care if they didn't agree with her. It had to be said. Even if only a few grasped the importance of her words, it would all be worth it. In light of her obvious failure to communicate, surely some of her friends and a few others could have managed some polite response.

It seemed forever before she thought she heard a slight cough before the first clap sounded. It was followed by other hands coming together for a resounding applause that reverberated throughout the room. With the lights shining into her eyes, she saw only shadows until she stepped to the side of the podium with its protruding microphone. Out of the brightness that had partially blinded her, she noticed that those seated in the fifth row, followed by the first, second and subsequent rows were rising to their feet.

She trembled from the clamor that she heard, and moisture began to build a well behind her lower lids. She stepped back to the microphone and huskily gave a "thank you" before departing the center of the dais. Her chest constricted and her entire body felt flooded with warmth. *This is what triumph feels like,* she thought.

Through her watery eyes she recognized a familiar figure waiting in the wings. Jonathan was standing just beyond where the curtain marked the end of the performance space. He stood as if everything between them had never happened. His face was expressionless until she drew near him. Waves of contrasting feelings flooded her. She found she could not speak.

"I'd say you got your point across," he stated dryly.

She listened a moment more as the applause died down, and she heard the sounds of people exiting the room. "I hope so." was all she could manage.

Several people were attempting to push toward her at the off stage door that led to the front hall of the building.

"Your public awaits." He gestured toward the technician who was attempting to prevent the intruders from coming into his territory of wires and sound equipment. He was pushing the air in front of him, signaling them to back away.

Jonathan put his arm around her. She wanted to pull away, but couldn't bring herself to do it. She wanted him and needed him. How could she even have thought she could fall out of love with him? He had hurt her, and in some ways deserted her, but he was here now, and she knew in some deep place within her that after they had talked, she would forgive him and welcome him back if that was what he wanted.

They pressed past those who waited for her after she shook hands with several middle-aged couples. She also spoke briefly with two school principals whom she had never met and with an average height woman with blond hair that straggled just below her shoulders.

"I'm so glad someone has finally said what you did. My child is in special education. He went to school in tears the days the test was being given. Please, let me help. Call me." She pressed a piece of paper into Penelope's hand, turned quickly away, and headed down the hall.

Before Jonathan had managed to navigate Penelope down the marble walkway that led to the lobby, there had been several requests from school administrators of neighboring towns that she speak in their communities. She had written her number on papers from a small pad that Jonathan had provided. She knew he had always carried one in his inside pocket for notes on the various computers and equipment he set up or repaired.

Finally, they made it to the parking lot where more people called out that they appreciated what she had said. Not surprisingly, there were a few who approached them with barely controlled contempt.

"Just because you can't handle the classroom, don't blame the state for your problems. Teachers better learn how to teach," one had taunted.

"It's because of you, kids can't perform. You're making excuses for them," another had spat out. Penelope was unnerved by the time they had reached her car.

Many of her friends and colleagues were waiting there. Claire was the first to speak. "Thank you, Penelope. You have completed what we started. Now you have a support system that will take over the movement with your help. Maybe you'll be back teaching in very little time."

"Perhaps you're right," Penelope said. She noticed a smile play on Jonathan's lips.

In turn and one by one, each of her colleagues shook her hand or gave her a quick hug.

"Great job, Penelope," said Christie and Stephanie almost simultaneously. *When had these two begun to think alike?* Penelope wondered.

"We all appreciate what you're trying to do," Ben Bradford assured her, "but I still have hopes that I will see you back at Skinner."

"Thank you, all of you. You don't know what it meant to me to see you in the audience tonight. It gave me that last bit of strength I needed to stand up there." Her throat seemed to close, making it difficult to continue.

"Well, of course we'd be here. How could you think we wouldn't? You were saying what all of us have been thinking for a long time. We should be thanking you for doing what we didn't." It was Mrs. Ruckmeyer who had spoken, looking to her companions as she did so. They were all nodding their heads in agreement.

Ted Tottman merely gave Penelope a wink and headed to his own car, and soon the rest of the group dispersed to their vehicles.

It had been a trying and exhausting day. Jonathan, never having left her side, ushered her to the passenger side of her own vehicle. He had taken the keys from her without asking. "I'll drive. You shouldn't be behind the wheel after your big night." *The old Jonathan was back.*

She put her face in her hands after she settled into the passenger seat. Jonathan slipped behind the steering wheel after walking around to the driver's side.

"What about your car?" asked Penelope.

"We'll pick it up after dinner. I think you made a lot more friends than enemies. You knew it wasn't going to be a day in Disneyland. It's only the beginning, but I'd say it was a damn good start."

She massaged her temples as if trying to erase the negative thoughts. "I know," she sighed. "I've made up my mind about something, though."

"You've been doing a lot of that lately." He smiled at her in the darkness of the car's interior. He reached for her hand. His thumb rubbed along her knuckles.

"What is it?" he urged.

"Someday, when I think I've made an impact, when things start turning around, I'm going back to teaching."

He laughed heartily, something she hadn't seen him do in a long time.

"I knew you would. So, let's start the turn around, but first, dinner." He put the key in the ignition, but he didn't turn it immediately.

"Dinner? Aren't you assuming a bit much? We haven't had a date for a long time, and you show up starting where we left off."

"Look, Nell." She couldn't help but melt a little. She had not heard that nickname in so long. "You and I both know that when I left that morning I had thought I had lost another kid. I had failed to save one of my men. The nightmare I had after seeing Hector in the hospital was worse than any that came before, and just when I thought loving you would be all I needed to stop those night terrors. When you left teaching, I thought you were letting your students down just as I had let down my men. I felt we both had failed. I knew we wouldn't work as a couple as long as we both had things that still haunted us. It's taken me time, but helping Hector and watching you interact with him made me realize that you had not let anyone down. You were finding another way to fight for them, just as I did for Hector. He showed me the way by putting his trust in the man I had once been. If you can, I'd like to start again. I need you and . . . I love you."

Where were these words in the past months? It didn't matter. She whispered, "I love you, too."

He reached across the console and gently pulled her closer to him. He searched her eyes for permission before touching her lips with his. The familiar feel and taste of Jonathan filled Nell. She felt him tremble slightly and immediately knew what would follow dinner.

Edwards Brothers,Inc!
Thorofare, NJ 08086
02 September, 2010
BA2010245